UNDER
the
BRIDGE

UNDER
the
BRIDGE

ANNE BISHOP

Roseway Publishing
an imprint of Fernwood Publishing
Halifax & Winnipeg

This is a work of fiction.
Any resemblance to actual persons or events is coincidental.

Editing: Linda Little & Fazeela Jiwa
Cover image: *Bridge in Wet Fog* by Paul Hannon, used with permission
Design: Tania Craan
Printed and bound in Canada

Published by Roseway Publishing
an imprint of Fernwood Publishing
32 Oceanvista Lane, Black Point, Nova Scotia, B0J 1B0
and 748 Broadway Avenue, Winnipeg, Manitoba, R3G 0X3
www.fernwoodpublishing.ca/roseway

Fernwood Publishing Company Limited gratefully acknowledges the
financial support of the Government of Canada through the Canada Book Fund,
the Canada Council for the Arts, the Province of Nova Scotia
and the Province of Manitoba for our publishing program.

Library and Archives Canada Cataloguing in Publication

Title: Under the bridge / Anne Bishop.
Names: Bishop, Anne, 1950- author.
Identifiers: Canadiana (print) 20190046414 | Canadiana (ebook) 20190046473
| ISBN 9781773630434
(softcover) | ISBN 9781773631622 (EPUB) | ISBN 9781773631639
(Kindle)
Classification: LCC PS8603.I837 U53 2019 | DDC C813/.6—dc23

This book is dedicated to those who give years of their lives, and sometimes their lives, to the struggle for a world where life and health for all mean more than wealth for a few, especially Nova Scotia's anti-poverty, anti-racism and Indigenous rights activists and the Mayan people of Guatemala. I am inspired by your courage, insight and wisdom.

CHAPTER ONE

"You. Yeah, you." Young man turns to look at me, mouth open. I point. "Those roses in your hand. Why do you think they're red? Blood."

He actually looks down at the flowers in his hands, steps back like I've cursed him.

"Where do you think flowers come from in winter? Who grows them, on whose land?"

Where am I? A flower shop. Don't remember coming in.

"Multinational corporations, that's who, on land stolen from peasants. Where they grew food for their families."

The man clutches his paper cone of roses to his chest as he makes for the door.

"Now they work in the flower fields, twelve, fourteen hours a day, for a couple of dollars."

Metallic thump as the door shuts behind him. I yell at the blank glass. "And the pesticides. Workers get sick. No income. Starving. Drift off to a massive city slum to live in a cardboard box. Die in a cardboard box."

People are staring. Woman behind the counter slides her hand toward the phone. Damn. What have I done? I turn so quickly I have to grab a display to steady myself a moment before I stagger toward the door. People scuttle out of my way.

Crowded sidewalk. No cop weaving toward me through the people. No flashing lights. But I'm not waiting around. In my mind, I run. Heavy old body can only manage a shuffle, though.

All I want is to hide. Go to ground. Broke my conditions. Again. Just left the probation office, too. John with his Newfie accent. "How many times did I warn you, m'dear? 'Keep the peace and maintain good behaviour.' After a few breaches, the judge had no choice but to give you thirty days. But now you've served it. Chance for a fresh start."

John, John, why won't you write me that letter? I need the hope to hang onto. "Let's wait and see," he says.

Why do they need a letter in the first place? They know me. All my years of Latin American solidarity work, teaching refugees English, helping them organize housing and income co-ops. And now they want reference letters? Not just from John, but from Doctor "Tell-me-about-it" too?

I'm puffing less, though my chest hurts. Below the ramp to the Angus L. MacDonald Bridge, just down the slope, there's a bit of scrubby woods where the homeless guys go. I pause, listen. They drink down here.

There are remnants of parties, scatter of bottles, couple of fallen trees pulled up to a sodden black bonfire pit, but no one's here now. I find an old blanket, scrunched into the roots of a tree so long ago it's crusty. Holds its shape as I pull it out. By the chain-link fence at the bottom of the slope, the bushes are thicker. I drop to my knees. They're sore, but I crawl in, pull the dirty blanket behind me. There's a bit of log I can lean against. I squirm the blanket around my legs. Comfortable enough, for now. And hidden.

That flower shop. Have the brake pads on my tongue worn right through? But my head was full of flowers, fields of them, brilliant in the sun. Emilia, only fourteen. Big dark eyes flooding with tears, telling me she wanted to die. And then she did. Her blood, a scab in the dust.

I lie down, curl up so my shoulders are under the blanket too. Carpet of chocolate bar wrappers, coffee cups, mostly Tim Hortons, rims rolled. Traffic rumbles over my head. The Beast, roaring. Chain-link fence beside me, a view down into the parking lot of the dockyard. Hulking grey buildings fade into a greyer evening. I read sideways: *Canada's East Coast Navy/Marine Canadienne.* Above, the bridge soars out into space, bridge to the sky.

Actually, to Dartmouth, to Burnside. Excuse me, I mean the "Central Nova Scotia Correctional Facility." I'm never, ever going back there. Before that happens, I swear, I'll jump off the Angus L. MacDonald bridge-to-the-sky.

I follow it with my eyes, arching up. The lights come on, a trail of stars leading out into the darkening night. What would it feel like to climb over the railing and let go? Fall, down, down, toward the icy water under the bridge? When you hit, would it knock you out? How long does it take to drown? Would you feel the cold? Would there be time for terror? Relief?

I should just do it. Get it over with. Last time in court, Judith argued I'm harmless. Judge agreed, then gave me thirty days anyway.

Harmless. Powerless. God knows, I've tried. And the rich are richer, and the poor are poorer than when I started. "You want to help us? Then go home," Rosa said. "Our poverty and suffering come from *el Norte.*" The North. So much more than just a direction.

Dear Rosa. Where are you now? Alive? *Quiché* women don't get old. And Nicolás? Against all odds, they're negotiating Peace Accords. Hard to believe there might actually be peace in dear, tormented Guatemala. I always comb the papers for little bits of information in the back pages. That's where I saw it. The refugees camped in Mexico and hidden in the northern jungles will be allowed to go back home. The solidarity networks want volunteers to walk with them. Witnesses, for protection.

Rosa said that too. Some of them thought I would bring trouble to the village, but Rosa said no, a foreign witness keeps us safe, especially a Canadian. And maybe I would have, if I'd been there that morning.

I want to go. Witness. Accompany. Protect those I failed before. Find Nicolás.

All I need is a letter from John. Oh yes, and one from Doctor "I-can't-help-you-if-you-won't-talk-about-it."

I root in the pockets of my old wool coat, close my hand around the plastic bottle. Did I take my pill this morning? Can't remember. Stopped taking them in jail and did better. Or maybe it was the routine, or the chance to feel just a little bit useful again, teaching, after all these months. Not that they stopped giving me the pills. Got good at it, didn't I? Tucking them into my cheek, swallowing the water, popping them out later. Drug company's happy anyway. They got paid.

Sky's suddenly full of fat snowflakes, twirling around the lights of the bridge. Fall's moving along toward winter. I'm cold. And hungry. Food wrappers, food wrappers everywhere and not a bite to eat.

I pull the bottle out of my pocket. Hard to open with frozen fingers. Evening pill, supposed to calm my mind, help me forget, sleep. Not enough to kill me, says Doctor "I-don't-believe-you're-delusional." But maybe knock me out long enough to freeze to death? If I take them all? Wish it was midwinter so it'd happen fast. Wish it *were* midwinter.

No. I haven't the nerve for that. Just forget, sleep. I take two, swallow them dry and push the bottle back into my pocket. Touch something else. A key. My apartment. Gone now.

CHAPTER TWO

Cold. Curled up tight, half buried in the earth-smelling mould of the jungle floor. Cold. Frightened. Listening. Chirps and croaks of night creatures. Was that a footfall? Are they coming back? Do they know there is a scattering of people left alive, burrowed into the hillside, hidden? Freezing. Cold. Cold. Listening. Roaring. Vehicles. Coming back.

I start awake, roll over, brace my hands on the ground to get up and run, breathing hard. Fingers gripping not leaf mould but gum wrappers, chip bags. The roaring, it's overhead. Just traffic approaching the bridge. I sag back to the ground, puffing, joints complaining. I can't believe I actually fell asleep. I don't sleep much at the best of times, but under the bushes, below the bridge ramp, in the snow?

I'm freezing. Crusty old blanket drenched, bits of snow in the creases. Melting down the back of my neck. And I have to pee, badly. I push myself up and over onto my knees. God that hurt. Grab the trunk of a small tree, shift my feet under me. Can't even feel them. Use my free hand to work my pants down, just far enough, I think. Too late for the underwear.

Yanking my pants off over my soaked sneakers, I abandon the underwear, tuck it modestly under a piece of bark. Modesty? Here? Why? Somehow, I get my pants back on, use the tree to pull myself up.

Bits of snow drift through the air. I'm hungry. St. Marks drop-in? Wait. Out-of-control rant in a florist shop. I'm hiding. From John. Not going back to jail. Ignore the hunger. Too fat anyway. Damn meds. Ignore the cold. Well, maybe not the cold. Got to find some place warmer.

Force my wooden feet, one ahead, then the other. Drag the blanket behind me. Up the slope, under the bridge ramp. At least it's sheltered here. Concrete bare of snow. Traffic deafening. The Beast. I slump against wet graffiti, crawl under my rag of a blanket, curl up as tight as I can. Teeth clattering.

A bundle of rags further along moves, turns. Thin, dark face, young, toque pulled down. Two figures come around the concrete corner, silhouettes against the lightening sky, walking loose-limbed. Hoodies, baggy jeans, baseball caps. "Hey, Casey. What you doin' here?"

"Hey."

"Come on, man." One of the young men holds a hand out, pulls Casey to his feet.

I can see them now, one Black, one white. Black one looks at me. "Who's this? You know her?"

"Nope." Casey is brushing off his pants, trying to straighten up all the way.

"Hey, Gran'ma." White one comes over, looks down at me. "Too much booze last night?"

Black one joins him, Casey tagging reluctantly behind, not looking at me. "This is our place, eh? Maybe you'd better clear out."

Exactly what I have in mind, but my feet are dead under me.

"Hey, Germaine," says the white one. "She never makes it out of here, who'd care?" Nasty laugh.

Fear curls through me. Can I get up?

"Hey, what's going on?" A woman's voice, and I know it.

Kids step back, straighten up.

Click, click, click. A pair of brown legs comes into my line of vision, fishnet stockings, unbelievably high heels. "What are you kids thinking? Germaine? Lewis? Casey?"

Lewis, leader of the nastiness a moment ago, scuffs his toe on the pavement. "Nothing, Miz Beals."

Cindy Beals. Thank God.

"Doesn't look much like nothing. I've a mind to tell your mothers about this." She leaves a cold pause for them to squirm in. "Unless you get home first."

They waste no time.

Cindy bends over me. "Lucy? My God, Lucy, what's happened to you? Are you hurt?"

She kneels in front of me. Pretty oval face full of concern, heavy makeup, the worse for wear. She's got on a satiny thing, bright blue, neckline so low it nearly meets the shortest skirt I've ever seen. Four or five silver chains and long dangly earrings brush her coffee-and-cream skin. She looks exhausted. My heart sinks down toward my stomach. "You okay, Cindy?"

She laughs. "About as okay as you."

"You're …"

"Yeah, back on the stroll. Money's too good."

I look at her eyes. Big, black pupils. "The boys?"

"Back in care." My heart sinks even further.

"I'm sorry."

"Me too. But hey, let's get you … God Lucy, tell me you're not living on the street."

Living on the street. Is that what I'm doing?

"Let's get you to Althea. She'll get you dried off and fed."

"No …"

"No?"

I'm cold and hungry and so tired. Maybe Althea will understand about the hiding. Cindy's smaller than I am, but she knows how to lever a body, gets me to my feet, her arm around my waist. After a moment, we start out. I have to lean on her.

What a pair we make in the cold light of morning, me hobbling along on swollen feet, her click, click, clicking on her skinny heels.

The noise of the place hits us, feet echoing on wooden floors, children shrieking. Talk, laughter. Dark, panelled rooms that once held choirs and Sunday school classes now house a child care, a single parent support centre, classrooms and agency offices, with a drop-in, soup kitchen and used clothing depot in the basement. I've spent hours here, days. My second home for years. As a worker, teacher, community organizer. Now look at me, a client.

Althea's office faces the door. Now that she's Community Services Director she likes to keep an eye on everything. We're just a few feet inside when she spots us. "Cindy? Oh my God, Lucy. What's happened to you?" Between them, she and Cindy help me in, lower me into Althea's chair.

"She'll take care of you." Cindy smiles at me, pats my hand and disappears.

There's a plate on Althea's desk, a sandwich from the drop-in downstairs. She sees me looking, passes it over. I wolf the sandwich then find myself studying the scattering of crumbs left behind.

"I'll get you another one, but first …" Althea goes down on her knees in front of me, unlacing my soggy sneakers.

"Althea, don't." Embarrassed by her bottomless Earth-Mother cleavage, I flick my eyes away.

"You can't walk like this." The worried lines between her eyes fold deeper into the dark skin of her broad, open face. Althea's not even coffee-and-cream, just coffee. "Hold still."

I can't help flinching as she eases off the wreck of my shoes. "Sorry," she says. She holds my dripping, filthy socks in the very tips of her fingers while she uses the arm of the chair to get to her feet. Drops them into the wastebasket. The sneakers she sets on the clanky old radiator to dry.

"Stay there." As if I'm going anywhere. My feet look like old rotten tomatoes, purplish. She returns with a basin, towel, soap. She goes down on her knees again and carefully lifts one of my feet into the warm water.

"Oh for God's sake, Althea." I try to pull it away, but she gives me that fierce look she perfected on her own kids. She's gentle, but I still have to hold my breath from the pain. Were the Apostles this embarrassed? Or is it because this is a servant thing, me white, her Black?

"Lucy, Lucy." It's her scolding voice, and my hackles start to rise. She leans back and holds up my foot, pointing between my toes. Even clean, they smell bad. "You're starting to get thrush. Can I get you to go to emerg?"

I glower at her.

She lets out a big, gusty sigh and begins dabbing my foot dry with the towel. It hurts and itches at the same time. "Will you go to the Community Clinic?"

I sigh. "Sure." Do I mean it?

She finishes, throws the towel into a heap beside the basin of filthy water and sits back on her heels. She levers herself to her feet again, more effort this time, stretches her back a minute and sits down in the other chair. "I got a call from Magdalen House this morning, wondering where you were. Obviously you slept outside, but why, Lucy?"

I shrug.

"What did you do?"

"What do you mean, what did I do?"

That look again. "Okay, doesn't matter. Did you talk to John?"

I can hear the big clock on the wall. One tick. Two.

"You have to, you know. It'll just be worse if you don't."

Tick. Tick.

"And I think you should talk to Judith. She's coming ..." Althea looks at the big calendar on the wall above her desk. "Two thirty. Meeting with a group of moms at the Single Parent Centre. She's going to try and set a precedent, so the power company can't cut people off if they fall behind on their bill."

She studies me. "Are you taking your pills?"

I dig into my pocket, pull out the little plastic bottle.

She reaches out, and I let her take it. "Seroquel. What's that?"

"Supposed to calm me down, but sometimes I think it just makes me fly off the handle easier."

"Lucy, don't be thinking that way. Just do what they tell you and get off probation. Then you can take back charge of your life." She hands the bottle back. "And then come back here. I miss working with you, girl. There's only me and Judith left."

"Althea?" A young woman's voice.

Althea steps out into the hall. I can't hear what they're saying, but a minute later she leans through the door. "Something I got to deal with. Back in a minute." I hear her steps going into the Single Parent Centre.

My chance. Socks gone and sneakers still pretty wet, but I work at it, wiggle them onto my sore old feet somehow. They throb when I stand on them.

I use the heavy old wooden bannister to get down the stairs to the basement. Quick trip into the clothing depot. Pair of wool socks. Coming out, I pause, look longingly at the drop-in door. One of the old guys comes out, weather-beaten face framed in scraggly white beard, equally white hair hanging from under a battered wool toque. Nods at me, heads for the back door. He's been homeless for years. There's a bunch of them. They talk about places to sleep under bridges, over warm-air vents, diving dumpsters for food. Big on which restaurants throw out the best stuff. But all restaurants have them, right?

I use the bannister to pull myself back up to the main floor, the cupboard where Althea keeps donated stuff. I gave her lots for that cupboard myself, back when I was on the giving side of life. Not locked. Couple of plump new sleeping bags on the bottom shelf.

CHAPTER THREE

How can anybody eat this? Smelly muck and maggots. Do they pretend it's white rice? At least it's killed my appetite.

Someone's coming. I look up and down the cracked concrete lane behind the buildings. It's backed by a high wooden fence lined with garbage cans and bins. There's a skinny alley between the restaurant and the building next door. I slip into it. Hey, it's dry here. I glance up: building next door has an overhanging roof.

"They'll be dumping the first supper plates any minute." It's a male voice out in the lane. Young. "Think about that whole tray of cupcakes we found two nights ago. Just a touch burned." Laughter.

I peek out. Who are these guys? Serious rain gear, jackets with reflecting strips, nylon pants, hiking boots. One, his back to me, hasn't even bothered to put his hood up. Mass of wet, dark curls. The other one, facing me, is a tall guy, hood up, bit of blondish hair showing, glasses.

Door hinges creak; footsteps, coming from the restaurant. The young guys disappear around the end of the fence. A stocky young man, back to me, carries a plastic bucket to one of the bins, lifts the lid and dumps it in, lets the lid clatter shut. He turns. I catch sight of his stained apron as I step back out of sight. Silence, then a cough. Whiff of cigarette smoke.

The door creaks again. "Put that out and get the hell back in here. Now." Female voice. Rough. Probably a smoker herself. Susan, maybe. The restaurant's called "Susan's Place."

Footsteps across the lane. Door bangs again.

A pause, then soft thumping sounds. "Hey Gord. Look at this. A whole piece of breaded fish." Even coming out of that wretched

bin, the thought of breaded fish clenches my stomach. I lean forward, peek again.

"What else did he dump?" says Not-Gord. He's holding the lid
of the dumpster while Gord rummages.

Gord's head pops up. He lets out his breath, holds something
out to Not-Gord.

"Hey, pasta. Whole plate of it."

Can't stand it. Lever myself away from the brick wall, step into
the alley. "You're not taking this *seriously*." They jump a foot off
the ground.

"Shit, you scared us," says Not-Gord.

"What are you guys doing, digging your supper out of a bin?"
I nod at their rain gear.

"We're freegans," says Not-Gord. "We've challenged ourselves
to consume less, use what others throw away."

"Yeah, well. There's people have no choice. They come along
and you've got it all ahead of them."

He looks at my sopping jacket and pants, turns to Gord and
says, "Let's see what we can find her." He bends back into the bin
beside him. Gord pulls something out of a big pocket in his rain
jacket. Paper plate. Within a few minutes they've come up with
enough to make a little arrangement — some kind of meat, gristle
mostly, canned vegetables with bits of black stuff stuck all over
them, the pasta. Not-Gord pulls an old fork with a slightly bent
tine out of his pocket, stands it up in the pasta and passes me the
plate. "Enjoy."

I pick a black speck out of the vegetables, examine it on my
finger. Coffee grounds. They're already headed down the lane. I
fork the food into my mouth right where I'm standing, beside a
smelly green bin in the rain.

As soon as my belly is full, I feel like a bag of rags. I crawl
back into the narrow, slightly dry space between the buildings. My
nice new sleeping bag waits against the brick wall. The streetlights

come on, sending a sliver of light the length of the alley. I can see some stuff piled part way down. Might be something to lie on. I work my way along, one hand on the cold bricks of the wall, poke at the pile with my toe. Nothing but newspapers, pretty soggy. It's going to be a long night.

I pull the sleeping bag out of its sack, wiggle and squirm until it's wrapped around me, settle in as best I can to wait for morning. After a while, my nest starts to soak up the damp. Cold seeps into my bones. Only warm part is my hands, pushed deep in my pockets. The bottle. Did I take my evening pill? Too tired to bother.

The key. I turn it in my fingers, feel its jagged teeth and … wait … a piece of string? This isn't mine. I pull it out. It's got a cardboard disk tied to it: "Basement." Of course. Judith's house, the cellarway door. My stuff is there. I'm supposed to give it back after I pick up a few things for my room at Magdalen House. I can see her face as she made the decision to give it to me. Wasn't easy.

Flash of headlights in the end of the alley, car passing, sloshing water with its tires. Concrete gritty under me, on me, *in* me, joints full of grit. My teeth are chattering, on and off. What if I get pneumonia?

Think warm. What's the hottest I've ever been? No question. That day we fetched the rabbits and their hutches. The young women, Emilia, Mía, Adela, came back from their winter job in the flower fields. The farm was expanding, they said. Owner bought land from a neighbour who'd given up raising rabbits. The rabbits were released, cages pushed aside. He would pay someone to take them away. They found a man with a truck and half the village of San Marcos climbed in for the trip to the lowlands.

The highlands of Guatemala are cool. Not the coastal plain. It was like driving into a steam bath. We ran with sweat as we salvaged and loaded lumber and wire. The men fixed a cage to hold the rabbits the children caught. The truck left with a load so tall and wobbly I wondered if everything would make it. We walked home, through the night and well into the next day, eating the cold tortillas we'd stashed in our pockets.

The women in my literacy class spent days mending wooden frames, straightening wire. I walked to San Piedro and found books, our new literacy texts: a battered manual on raising rabbits and a book on co-operatives.

What a gift those gentle creatures were. More protein than San Marcos had known since they lost their good farmland. Plus, income for building materials, school fees, thread for weaving. They bought casings and dug a new well. And that expression, "breed like rabbits"? It's true. In a few months, the women had dozens and were building more cages from bamboo and twine.

I don't feel so cold now, but my heart feels like it's breaking. I can't think of the rabbits, or the women, without remembering what happened to them.

After forever, the sky starts to lighten. Rain stops. Leaves the broken pavement all shiny. A motor hums somewhere, soft, like a cat purring. I feel a warm patch on my leg, reach down, touch something as wet as I am but, after a minute, warm. It *is* a cat purring. I stroke soggy fur.

Time to move. I shrug off the wet sleeping bag, try to get my feet under me. Holy cow — *pain*. The cat leaps away. I lean on the wall, bricks biting into my hand, waiting to feel better. The cat has settled a few feet away, squinting his eyes at me. Brown and black spots on white? He's so wet and dirty it's hard to tell. No ears.

"Hey there," my voice so rusty it creaks. "Freeze your ears off?" I put my free hand to my own ear, wondering if it's frozen off, along with my toes and fingers.

Cat disappears like smoke. "Hey Raggedy, where you going?"

I'm tempted to slump back into the only dry spot. The one I made by soaking up the rain through the night. But I can't just lie here and die in an alley.

Back door of the restaurant creaks, then slaps shut, footsteps and off-tune humming. Green bin lid squeaks a bit, bangs. Hummer returns to the kitchen.

What a tumbled-together mess. If it smells like this in November, what's it like in summer? Imagine the flies and maggots then. No, don't. Yellow chunks, scrambled egg, some bread, mushy with, what? Ketchup. Something's wrapped in newspaper. I tear a piece off, use it to hold my eggs and bread while I sidle in between the two buildings again, lean against the wall. I spot the old cat, sneaking up all cautious. I drop a piece of egg. He takes his time sniffing it before he chews it down, purring the whole time. "Hey Raggedy, how can you have such a tough life and not lose your purr?" Am I actually talking to an alley cat?

Exhausted beyond thinking, but have to think about where to go. I shove my freezing hands into my pockets, feel for the bottle of pills, the key. I hesitate, rubbing it between my fingers. Sweaters, socks, warm, dry.

Pushing the sleeping bag back into its sack, I take a deep breath and set off, hobbling on my wooden feet. She'll be at work. I'll just slip in, get something warm and dry on, leave.

CHAPTER FOUR

Somehow, I expected Judith's basement to be clean. She's so orderly. I've never seen more than one file on her desk. But this is a cave: dirt on the concrete floor, bare lightbulbs with dangling strings, dirty cobwebs festooned from the joists making haunted-house curtains in front of dingy, high-up little windows. Packed full of stuff. Furniture, smaller things balanced on larger ones. A bookcase overflowing with old books. Boxes piled on boxes. A rail hung with garment bags, newer plastic ones and older cloth ones. Everything covered in a thick layer of dust. Is the upstairs a mess too? Is that why Judith never invites anyone here?

This was Judith's parents' house, and her dad's parents' before that. The generation before lived on this lot too but in a house the Halifax Explosion smashed to pieces. The Halifax Relief Commission built this one. It looks like no one, in all those generations, ever threw anything out.

I spot a pipe running along the side wall. Mostly it is hidden by piled things, but a section is exposed. There's even a sort of path to get to it. I pull the string to click on a second light, pick up my sleeping bag and make my way there. Thick layer of dust on the pipe, but who cares? I pull the sleeping bag from its sack, turn it inside out and hang it. My wet coat too.

How am I supposed to find my things? At least they won't be buried under other stuff yet. It's only been a month since Judith and Althea packed up my apartment. Landlord, the creep, started an eviction procedure as soon as the judge sent me to Burnside. He could, Judith said, since I hadn't paid rent in three months, and she gave me a rare exasperated look. She was always after me to save some money when I had it, but I hated the thought of a bank investing it in corporations, and besides, there was always someone with a need greater than mine, more urgent than "someday" when I would need it. Except, "someday" came.

So, my furniture's gone, sold to pay the back rent. All from thrift stores anyway. I look for boxes, out front, a little cleaner than most. I spot them. Make my way over, shifting a wooden ironing board along the way, a bucket with a string mop dried inside, click on another light. Yes, boxes from a grocery store — "Ritz Crackers," "King Cole Tea." Beneath the product labels, in Judith's neat lettering: "Lucy — Bedding, Towels," "Lucy — Tapes and CDs." It's a pretty small pile. Not much of a coffin for a whole life. "Lucy — Kitchen Drawers" hurts. Memories of cooking for friends, discussing politics over dessert and tea.

"Lucy — Nightgowns, etc." includes underwear and another painful memory, a worn cotton shawl, handwoven, its once-bright colours faded. A quick root through "Lucy — Sweaters" produces a blue turtleneck and a big, soft, old brown thing I used to wear at home in winter to avoid turning up the heat. I strip off everything I'm wearing, drop them in a sopping pile on the dirty floor. I pull on the turtleneck and the sweater over top. My skin is icy, but the minute the sweater is on, there's the beginning of warmth.

I've gotten so big since I started taking the pills, can't imagine any of my pants will fit. My eye falls on "Lucy — Skirts." I pop the flaps, a long, tweedy brown one on top. Don't remember it, but it looks warm. Doesn't quite fit around my middle. Lucky the zipper has a catch. I can leave the button undone. I rescue the pills and key from my wet pants, stuff them into the skirt pocket.

I go digging again, this time in a box marked "Lucy — Winter Jackets, Gloves and Hats." Wool coat isn't the best for rain. Soaks it all up. I look at a nylon winter jacket, but it's too small now. Socks, hat and mitts will help. A box marked "Lucy — Winter Footwear" provides boots.

Warmth brings sleepiness. Beside my boxes, there's a big, comfy chair, fabric worn bare on the insides of the arms and along the top where a head would rest. A small cabinet, maybe a bedside table, sits upside down on the seat. I bend to move it and spot something even better leaning against the wall behind the chair. A small, thin mattress, wrapped in plastic. I slide it to the floor where it lands with a puff of flying dust. I cough. Behind the mattress, against the wall, is a taken-apart crib. Yellowed decals, grinning white rabbits with big bows around their necks. Looks nineteen forty-ish. Judith's? Hard to imagine Judith as a child.

That mattress, so tempting. I drop myself down onto it and stretch out my sore legs. My eyes won't stay open. I'll just doze a bit, an hour or so. Out of here long before Judith comes home.

What a racket. Furnace coming on. Feet throbbing. Have to roll over on my hands and knees to haul myself up. What a disaster if Judith found me invading her precious space. Is the light fading? Can't tell. Time to go, anyway. I lean the crib mattress back up against the wall. My wet clothes have made a muddy spot on the floor. I gather them up and make my slow way to the pipe against the wall. The sleeping bag is much drier than when I came. I stuff it back into its sack, leaving the wet clothing on the pipe in its place. Several pieces of old rope hang from a nail. I choose one and tie it around the sleeping bag, a strap of sorts. The wool coat is pretty damp, but I put it on anyway, with a knitted hat, and stuff a pair of mitts into the pockets. I click the lights off by their dangling strings and leave, locking the basement door behind me. I feel a moment's guilt but then slip the key back into my pocket. Before leaving the cover of the garage next to the house, I check the street. Anyone coming? Judith, for instance? Thank God it's stopped raining. Cooler, though. Clouds scudding through the sky.

⟁

I find a row of bins behind the restaurants in the Hydrostone. It's dark, but one is full enough to see what's on top. I luck out. A whole hamburger, bun, mustard, ketchup, scattered about but easy to put back together. I eat it standing right there, slopping ketchup on the lid of the bin.

Full, warm, dry, I poke south along Gottingen, my sleeping bag slung over my shoulder by its rope strap. North Street is almost stopped, traffic heading for the bridge. Normal people. Going home from work.

I'm almost as far as St. Marks. They'll be serving supper at the drop-in. For a moment I think about dessert and tea. Stop it, Lucy. You're hiding, remember? Someone will spot you, tell John. I slip in under the wooden stairs that connect the sidewalk to the back door of the church, out of sight, to wait for the light to fade.

Even out here, huddled against the blackened red brick of the church wall, I can hear the bustle going on inside — talk and laughter, children's shrill voices, footsteps rattling up and down the wooden staircases. St. Marks is a dignified, overweight Victorian lady, her skirts spread over half the block, shocked by the raw, rowdy life roiling around inside her. When most of her former congregation departed for better neighbourhoods, a few stayed, looked around and thought, blessed are the poor. But what do you do with a towering gothic sanctuary, a wing of Sunday school rooms and a cavernous basement?

Evening school. Classes in rows, teachers at blackboards delivering English grammar, math. There were teachers at blackboards for the GED students, the ones who missed out on high school because they had no winter boots, got pregnant, barely survived residential schools. For the literacy and English as a second language classes, they got me, newly arrived in Halifax, needing an evening job while I worked on my adult ed degree, determined to transplant *educación popular* from Guatemala.

Althea was in that first literacy class, with her friends Lynn and Paula. Exhausted, determined single moms, trying to make a life for themselves and their kids on half enough money. Leaders just waiting to bloom. They brought their kids to class with them — distracting, but no other option.

What do our children need? In a few weeks, we had organized a playroom for the younger ones, a couple of early childhood education students on field placements to organize and supervise, a homework room with tutors for the older kids.

What do our children need? By that summer, there was an outdoor playground, and in the summers after that, a recreation program. The next fall, the literacy class had graduated into a new community leadership course.

What do our children need? Access to doctors and dentists. That was more challenging until Jane Norris came along, newly retired from family practice but with too much energy and love for her profession to putter in the garden.

What do our children need? To be out of poverty. By then there was a large group of leaders. They had a Community Council and were fighting for better social assistance rates and affordable housing. That's when Judith joined us, during her student term at the Legal Aid clinic. Those women were good at inspiring allies like Jane and Judith. Like me.

It's getting dark now. Those heady days feel like ages ago and, at the same time, just yesterday. It's been, what? Twenty-five years? No, twenty-six. Jane Norris is dead. Lynn married again and moved to Dartmouth. Didn't work out too well. Paula fared better with her choice of new husband, moved to Spryfield. Judith is still at it. Althea is queen bee of the St. Marks hive. And Lucy? Broken down, crazy, hiding under the back outside stairs.

Gravity takes me downhill, from one pool of streetlight to the next until they run out, then through the noisy dark under the bridge ramp and down into the woods. Headlights sweep up the concrete curve, reflected on the tops of the trees. I check; no voices, no fire, no one there. I crawl into my hidden spot against the dockyard fence and wrap myself in my sleeping bag.

A stone grinds into my hip and the sleeping bag is damp again. Voices in the dockyard. Car doors. Farther away, lap of water. Slowly, slowly, the cold creeps in despite my warm clothes. There'll be no sleep again tonight. But then, hey, when have I ever slept more than a bit here and there? It's been years.

Wish I was back in Judith's basement on that crib mattress. Wish I *were*.

CHAPTER FIVE

Long, long night. Must have dozed, though, because I start when the sun touches my face. Chilled right through, I crack the rust in my hurting joints, roll over. I push the bag into its sack and pull it behind me by its rope strap, out from under the bushes.

I walk along the harbour side of Barrington Street waiting for a chance to cross, but it's rush hour. I retreat under the giant footings of the bridge. The cables take off from the concrete above me. They look delicate from a distance, but they're massive from here. Not many of the people crossing in their cars will be thinking about what's holding them up. A huge, grey boulder meets the bridge footing like a big chair, out of sight, out of the wind but warmed by the sun. I sit on my rolled sleeping bag and lean back against the concrete.

Choppy water, blue to match the sky. I close my eyes. The Beast growls, hundreds of cars for his voice. If I close him off, listen under him, there's water slap-slapping against the shore below. Bet I sound like that inside. Just a big bucket of held-in tears, slopping around when I breathe.

I could just float away. No dramatic leap from the railing above. Just a quiet swim from the rocks under the bridge, swim and swim 'til exhaustion takes me. Ha. That blue stuff is ice cold. How long would it take to get too numb to feel it? My luck, I'd get rolled under by some big container ship leaving the Bedford Basin.

When the traffic slows, I cross. In the lane behind Susan's Place, two voices, chatty and cheerful. I stay in my alley, press my fat, old body into the shadows. Not-Gord and a female voice, young. Is Gord there too? Can't tell.

Hinges on the restaurant's back door creak. "Hey! What are you doing there?" That same rough voice. Susan?

Bang. Lid of the green bin, dropped in surprise. Not-Gord starts in, "Hi. We're just looking …"

The young female voice, "We're hungry."

Pause, then the woman's voice again, softer, "You kids are looking for something to eat? What, you got no place to go to?"

So, what are the freegans going to say to that? Way they dress, bet they've got mommy and daddy or a university residence to go home to when they get tired of green bins. But it's the young woman who answers. "My parents've thrown me out."

"For what? You look pretty well-off to me. And you boys? Your parents throw you out too?"

Not-Gord says, "Not exactly. We can't go home for other reasons."

"Other reasons."

The girl: "But it's garbage, isn't it? You're finished with it."

"I don't want you making a mess out here for my employees to slip and fall."

My employees. So it is Susan.

Not-Gord, eager, "You haven't noticed any mess here for the past couple of weeks, have you?"

"You've been eating here for two weeks?"

"And there's other people come here for food too."

She lets out a big sigh. "I do hate the waste. The inspectors make us throw everything out that's been on a plate, even packets that've never been opened." She pauses, then, "I'll tell you what. How about we put the good, clean stuff separate, in a plastic bucket?"

Young voices tumble over each other. "That'd be great …"

"Wow, thanks …"

"If you don't come for it by the end of the day, though, it goes into the bin."

"We understand …"

"Like, of course …"

"And no mess, okay?"

"No mess."

"We promise."

"And *do not tell anyone*. I don't want every starving person in the city coming here, and if wind of this *ever* gets to the inspectors … *Do you understand?*"

They reassure her in as many ways as they can think of. The door hinges creak and, a few minutes later, creak again. "There you go," Susan says, and the door slaps shut.

"Holy cow, look at this," Not-Gord says. "A feast."

A feast? I can't help myself, peek around the corner. Gord spots me. "Hi." First time I've heard his voice.

Not-Gord's head whips around, bouncing the mass of dark curls. "You hungry?" He holds up a paper plate of food. Must have had paper plates in their pockets like last time. I hobble up to him and take it. He does a sort of court gesture with his hand, offering a seat on the restaurant steps. They're all sitting on the cracked concrete, where it should be warm in the sun but isn't because of the stiff breeze channelled down the lane.

The young woman's watching me, eyes big. Slight with fine, straight blond hair cut off square at her chin, pixie kind of face, snub nose, freckles. Norman Rockwell, except I don't think he painted young women in jeans and nylon jackets.

Not-Gord pulls a plastic fork out of his pocket and I eat, too fast to even register what's there. "Hungry, eh?" he says, amused, and starts to eat from his own plate.

We're slowing down, sharp edge of hunger worn off. Tall Gord has no hood on today, and his tumble of scraggly blond hair falls forward over his glasses.

"My name's Robin," says Not-Gord. "This is Gord, and this is Bara. What's your name?"

I tell him.

"Hi, Lucy," he says, like we're in AA instead of Starvation Anonymous.

"Hi, Lucy," the girl echoes, and Gord just nods. Man of few words, our Gord.

The guys say they have to leave, gather up their stained paper plates and put them neatly in the bin. "You gonna be okay?" Robin asks the blond girl, and now I see it, a big, yellowing bruise on her cheekbone. But she nods yes, thanks them, waves them off.

After they go, a tall man in a white cap and apron comes to the restaurant door, plate in hand. He sees us, holds it up. Two doughnuts, one with a bite out of it. The kid is quick onto her feet to fetch it, thanks him. She takes the one with the missing bite. We sit in silence, enjoying our dessert.

"So, what did Robin say your name is?"

"Bara. B-a-r-a."

"What kind of name is that?"

"Icelandic, actually. They put an accent on the first 'a' and pronounce it *bough-ra*. It was my great-grandmother's name. It means 'wave.' Like, ocean wave, not wave goodbye."

"So, your parents made sure you'd have to spend your life spelling your name."

"Actually, I did. My parents named me Barbara and call me Barbie."

"And that's too plain for you?"

She gives me a look just short of sighing and rolling her eyes. "Barbie is a *doll*. With, like, if she was real, forty-inch boobs and an eighteen-inch waist."

I laugh. "Got a point."

"Hey, there's a cat with no ears." Bara's looking down the lane. Old Raggedy is making his way nonchalantly in our direction. "Here kitty, kitty," she says, laying a pinch of doughnut on the concrete in front of her. Kitty, kitty? Battered old thing like Raggedy? He comes straight to her and gobbles the scrap. She picks something out of the bucket and he chews it down, cautiously stretches forward to sniff what's inside. She finds another bit. He bolts it. "Sorry, boy, that's all I've got." He seems to understand and forgive, because he rubs back and forth along her knee, purring loudly. She strokes him.

"I call him Raggedy."

"Hey Raggedy." She reaches out, makes a little kissy sound, and Raggedy goes to rub his back on her hand. After a minute, she asks me, "Do you, like, have a place to sleep?"

"What are you doing here, anyway? Good clothes, new knapsack. You don't look like your family's got no place to live." Didn't mean to sound quite so sharp.

She laughs, sort of. "Hardly. My parents have a big house in Bedford. My older sister and brother have gone away to university, so, like, we rattle around in it."

"So why aren't you up there in Bedford rattling around in it now?"

"They threw me out." Oh, right. That's what she told Susan.

There's a long silence while she strokes Raggedy. What on earth did such a nice, middle-class kid do to get thrown out by her parents? Hit, too, by the looks of it.

"Where do you stay, Lucy?" Bara looks at me hopefully.

I shrug my shoulders.

"You homeless?"

"Guess you could say that." I've been hit by the sleepiness that follows food these days. I start thinking about a nap and a change of clothes. "You know what time it is?"

She pulls back the cuff of her jacket and checks, really does have a watch. "Five thirty."

Too late. I look up. Yeah, getting on toward evening.

"So, like, where are you going to sleep?"

I put my hands on the gritty concrete to help shift my weight away from the wall. Pain shoots through my arms, shoulders, hips. I think my feet are past feeling.

"You okay?" Bara's eyes are big. Did I groan out loud?

"Could use some help."

She's a nice kid, leaps to her feet and takes both my hands, helps lever me up, looks worried when it takes a while to get myself straightened, even more when my first attempt at a step turns out to be a stumble.

I lead her into the shelter of the alleyway, with its overhanging roof.

"Cool," she says looking around. "Hey, what's that?"

I follow her finger. The pile of soggy newspapers has something on top. She goes to investigate and comes back with a big piece of cardboard, broken down box by the look of it. She folds it into a sort of bench and we settle ourselves, leaning against the brick wall with my sleeping bag over our knees. Raggedy follows us and curls up against my thigh, purring himself to sleep.

"So, why'd your parents throw you out?"

She looks at me, and I can see she's struggling to keep her eyes open. Poor kid is beat.

"You didn't sleep last night, did you?"

She shakes her head. "Did you?"

"I hardly ever sleep anyway."

She's surprised. Too young to imagine a life devoid of sleep.

We are quiet as the alley slowly darkens and cools. I pull the sleeping bag up around our shoulders. Her head nods forward. She catches herself with a little snort, then starts to slip away again. Soon she's slumped against me, snoring gently. After a little while, I put my arm around her. She flinches a little. Bruises there too? Through her jacket, she's all bones. Bones and bruises.

CHAPTER SIX

My arm around Mía's shoulders, nothing but bone, in contrast to her round pregnant belly. "He'll come back," I say, but she knows. Not so naïve by now, I know too, but the learning came too late. I've made a stupid mistake, and now the paramilitaries are watching San Marcos. I can feel them somewhere out there, pure evil. A dark cavern of dread opens up in my chest, because of what I've done. Mía isn't safe. None of them safe. Or their babies.

"Ow. Are you, like, trying to suffocate me?"

I jerk back as the young, blond one pulls away, fear and outrage on her face. Where am I? Brick wall. Light seeping in from above. Alley. Sleeping bag. I try to catch my racing breath.

"Lucy?"

She has a strange name.

I can speak now. "Sorry."

"What happened?"

"Nightmare."

She looks doubtful.

I reach out my hand. "Help me up." And she does, holding me up until a little feeling comes back into my legs and feet.

Bara checks out the lane before we emerge from the alley. "Coast clear. But no bucket yet."

"Susan's Place is barely open."

"There's lots of noise in the kitchen."

"Yeah, but no leftovers yet."

Bara opens the bin.

"Anything worth eating?"

"It's all jumbled together. All I can make out is ... hey, part of a loaf of bread. Want that?"

We stand by the bin and rescue what we can, tearing off the crusts stained with other unidentifiable foods. The middle of most slices is bearable.

"You should go get a proper breakfast at the drop-in at St. Marks."

"What's a drop-in?"

"Holy cow, where have you been all your life?"

"Bedford."

"Right. The drop-in is a place for homeless people to go during the day, since most of the shelters are only open for the evening and night. There's coffee and sandwiches, those breakfast cereals in little cardboard boxes, a toaster with bread. They serve a hot supper around five o'clock."

"Like, free?"

"Yup."

"So, let's go."

"I can't, but you should."

"Why can't you?"

"Long story and not your business."

She's frowning again.

"And why aren't you at the youth shelter, anyway?"

"Where's that?"

"It's called Horizons, and it's just a few blocks from here. Come on." I turn and begin to hobble toward the street. She follows.

I stop half a block short and point. "See the blue house with the big veranda? That's Horizons. Just go in the front door and tell them you've got no place to stay."

"Why can't I stay with you?"

"You just can't, okay?"

"But, like, where are you going?"

"*Like*, not your business."

She hesitates another moment, then turns and trudges toward Horizons.

She is not my problem.

Must be out of here by five. Judith is famous for working all hours. Once she told me she can only get her research done after client interviews, witness preparation sessions and meetings are over for the day. But officially, she's off at five.

My clothes dried while I walked around today, but I pull the damp sleeping bag out of its sack and hang it over the pipe, piling up the clothes I left here before. I spot a box of blankets. The one on top is old but nice, thick wool. I lower the crib mattress and curl up, chant in my head, "Wake up at four. Wake up at four. Wake up at four." God, my feet hurt. No wonder the shelters and the clinic are always so concerned about homeless people's feet. "Wake up at four. Wake up at four." I'm good at this. Never needed an alarm clock.

Except this time, it fails me. The basement windows are just faintly lighter than the dark stone walls. Damn. What time is it? I heave myself to my feet, lift the crib mattress back up against the wall, fold the blanket and lay it over the arm of the padded chair, push my lovely sleeping bag back into its nylon sack. I pull the string to turn off the light, make my way to the outside door, click off the light just inside. I've opened the door a crack when I stop.

Click, click, click. Women's dress shoes. Coming up the walk. I freeze in place.

Damn it. Judith. I can hear her humming to herself as she walks up the front steps.

There's a faint thump just inside the front door. Must have dropped that big briefcase she carries everywhere. I wonder if there's a downstairs bathroom. If she goes upstairs, I can slip out. I open the door further, ready to escape.

Footsteps coming toward this side of the house. Damn, damn, damn. A bright yellow square falls across the yard from the window above, blocking my route to the sidewalk.

Judith must have kicked off her shoes. I can barely hear her steps, but the refrigerator door opens and closes, cupboard, drawer, cupboard again. A pot clanks, grinding sound of a can opener. Kitchen must be right above me. Going to have to wait until she goes upstairs.

I gently close the door, lower myself to the hard floor and tuck my skirt up around my waist. Using the faint light coming through the dirty windows, I crawl, slowly, on hands and knees, stopping every now and then to feel what might be in my path, back to the crib. I try to lower the mattress without a sound, but the plastic cover slips out of my hand and it hits the floor with a gentle *whump*, sending up a puff of dust. A sneeze rises up the back of my nose. I pinch my nostrils and screw my eyes shut.

When my heart slows back to normal, I crawl onto the mattress and turn myself over to sit. I'm hungry again, but my bigger problem is I have to pee. Try to think of something else, anything else. Judith runs the water in the kitchen sink. Oh dear. If I pee on my skirt, I'll be really cold when I get back outside. That's when I notice that, like most basement floors, this one slopes gently down to a spot somewhere on the other side of the furnace.

Judith's feet pad toward the front of the house. I heave myself back up on hands and knees, tuck my skirt again, and use my crawl-and-feel method to work my way toward the furnace, letting the slope of the floor guide me. The path to the furnace is wider than most. Someone must come in to service it.

My eyes have adjusted to the darkness. Beyond the furnace are more boxes, more furniture, but a path winding through and, yes, almost to the back wall, the concrete eases down to the black hole of a drain. I squat over it, using the wall to hold myself steady.

Judith listens to CBC radio. There's a certain tone to it. That's what I used to listen to when I was home, at least when there wasn't someone there who had nowhere else to go. Wish I could hear what they're saying.

Maybe she stays up late. Hopefully she watches TV and turns the volume up really loud, though really loud would hardly be Judith's style. In fact, TV probably isn't Judith's style.

By the time Judith is washing her dishes, I'm lying down with the blanket from the arm of the chair more or less spread over me.

She sits down at her table. I can hear the chair pulled out, then in. What is she doing there? Why doesn't she go somewhere else, like upstairs? The furnace grumbles beside me. I'm warm, dozing off. I barely register when she shifts the chair again and turns off the radio.

CHAPTER SEVEN

———————

Drifting between sleep and waking. Thin blanket on a dirt floor. Talk and laughter through flimsy cornstalk walls. Clank of pots; chickens foraging in the street; voices, talking, laughing; rich, earthy smells of sweat, mould, damp earth, piss. Then, woodsmoke and coffee, the thin, bitter coffee the *campesinos* make from the shells left after hulling the beans. They tend the plants, pick the berries, spread them to dry in the sun, hull the beans, carry the huge sacks down the mountains on their backs. It's some of the best coffee in the world, but they never taste it.

Brisk slapping. Rosa making tortillas. Sizzle as she drops them onto the pan over the fire. Swishing sound as she moves them around, turns them with her bare hands. Hard, brown hands.

But wait … no. Where am I? Grey shapes all around. Water gurgles down a pipe somewhere near. *Information Morning*. Oh my God, Judith's basement.

Could use a pee, but not urgently enough to risk making noise, as long as I stay lying down. Refrigerator door opens and closes in the kitchen above me. God, I'm hungry. Close my eyes again, drift.

Wreaths of mist, woven among impossibly blue-green hills. Waiting for the afternoon rain, a little break as everyone takes shelter. They laugh at me. You people from *el Norte* always talk about the weather. "Nice day." Of course it's a nice day. "Looks like rain." Of course it looks like rain. Rains every afternoon, like clockwork.

I am new, working for the church in a town almost as new as I am, carved out of the jungle. Sitting on a bench in the square, preparing a lesson. Stopping to marvel at plants I know only in pots, a few inches tall, here grown into trees towering over my head. And the birds. Thousands of them. Singing, calling, voices strange to me.

A woman walks by, coming from the guest house with a huge basket of laundry on her head. I admire her brilliant *huipil* and skirt. Its pattern declares where her family comes from, but I just think it's pretty.

Something is up with the birds. Shrieking and calling out, alarmed. Abruptly, they fall silent. And then a rumbling sound, deep and strange, far off, coming closer. I stand in alarm, gather up my papers.

The ground began to pitch and roll. Waves of earth just like waves on the water. My feet fly out from under me. I bounce around, bruising my bottom. I see the laundry woman bouncing too, a few yards away. Her basket leaps away from her, sheets dancing like cartoon ghosts, spreading in a widening circle around her.

Rolling over onto my belly, I scrabble in the dirt, trying to grab it, hold it still, but it flies out between my panicked fingers.

I start awake. Where … ? Oh, Judith's basement. Dug into solid Halifax Ironstone. Safe. That first earthquake, I didn't know it then, but it was telling me what was coming. Terra firma. Gone. Forever.

Got to move, now. Judith, please go.

No radio. No sounds. Did I miss her leaving? Can't wait, anyway. Throw off the blanket and crawl through the narrow paths back to the drain. Haul myself up with the stones of the basement wall. Relief.

Quiet upstairs. Make my way back to the crib. Still silence. The house even feels empty somehow. I move quietly, but now I move. Fold the blanket, prop the mattress against the frame of the crib, pack my sleeping bag into its sack. Blessedly dry.

Pause again. Nothing. Open the basement door. No one in sight. I stumble, squinting, into daylight. Must never, ever do that again.

Bara sits on Susan's back step, eating right out of the plastic bucket with her hand. She grins when she sees me, rummages in her pocket with her clean hand and comes up with a crumpled napkin. She flattens it on her knee and starts to ladle food onto it, scrambled egg, a toast crust. "Excuse my hand," she says, and I want to laugh but I'm too hungry.

She's dirty, hair clumped in knots, dark circles under her eyes. Feels me looking, glances at me from under her bangs. "Tried to sleep in the alley." Points with her chin. "Sat up all night." She starts to lick the mess off of her fingers.

"Why weren't you at Horizons?"

"They don't want me there."

"What do you mean, don't want you there? Did you go in, tell them you don't have a place to stay?"

She shrugs, intent on licking butter off of her thumb. A shiver travels through me, little skinny thing like her, alone in an alley at night. What if the wrong person found her? Who would even know she was gone?

She looks down pointedly at my sleeping bag in its nylon sack. "So, where did you sleep last night?" She watches me lick up the last rubbery scrap of egg on my napkin. "And if there's free meals at that St. Marks place, like, why aren't you eating there?"

I glower at her, but she ignores it. "Like, where did you get that?" She points at the sleeping bag.

"Stop that.'"

"What?"

"Saying 'like' every damn sentence." She goes back to licking her fingers.

I don't want to snap at the poor kid. I'm afraid for her. Can

I keep her with me? I think of Althea's donation closet, the shelf of sleeping bags. I wipe my fingers on my skirt and hold out what's left of the napkin. "Okay. Put this in the bin and follow me." She tidies up our "dining room" while I lumber to my sore feet.

❦

"Lucy, watch it." Bara's hand on my arm. Stepped in a pothole, nearly took a header. "You're looking in every direction but where you're going."

That's exactly what I'm doing. I know too many people in this neighbourhood. We come out of a laneway across from St. Marks. I step out onto the sidewalk and nearly run into John. Damn.

"Lucy, m'dear."

I cross my arms and turn my back to him. "I'm not speaking to you."

"Don't think you have much choice, love. And who is this?"

Bara looks at me, but I stay silent, so she introduces herself. He's checking her out pretty closely.

"I think you'd both better come to my office." He makes a motion like he's ushering us down the sidewalk. Damn. He's right. There's really no choice. No escape, either. He lets me lead, keeping an eye on me from behind.

❦

"Have a seat, Lucy." He nods at one of the client chairs, pulls another one out of a corner and offers it to Bara. He rolls his own chair out from under his desk, following the grooves it's made in the linoleum. When he sits, his belt disappears into the folds of his belly. If he'd gotten this fat when he was a cop, they would've put him at a desk in the back room until he lost weight.

"You know I have to call your parents, m'dear," he tells Bara.

She has been looking around the cluttered office, everything slightly green from the florescent lights, but now goes absolutely still, staring down at her chapped hands in her lap.

"I can get the number whether you give it to me or not."

Can he? Looks like someone's jolly uncle, but he's a wily old fox.

"Yeah? Whatever. I don't care." She rattles off the number.

He dials and, after a minute, introduces himself. "I have your daughter here," he says. His bushy eyebrows go up. He holds the receiver away from his ear. Male voice. We can hear the bang as the phone's hung up.

"Guess you're not going home."

"Told you," says Bara.

"What'd you do to make him that angry?"

"John — " I start in.

"Okay, okay." He holds up his hands to fend me off. "She's going to tell me it's not your fault," he says to Bara.

"And it's not," I tell her, although I'm glaring at John.

Bara's eyes travel back and forth between us as if watching a tennis match.

"She wants me to say it: it's not your fault. All right, Lucy?"

I nod.

"All right." He turns back to Bara. "What I would like you to do, young lady, is go up the street to St. Marks Church and talk to the social worker there. She'll help you apply for social assistance, figure out a place to stay, get you back in school. Her name is Althea."

Bara looks at me, alarmed.

"It's okay," I tell her. "Althea's an old friend of mine."

"Are you coming?"

"Lucy and I need to talk," John says.

"I'm staying with her," Bara says, chin set.

"Then you'll have to go out to reception. We need to talk privately."

Bara looks at me doubtfully.

"Go," I say.

John rises and holds the office door open for her, pointing down the hall to a row of chairs along the wall opposite the reception desk.

He closes the door behind her and drops back into his chair, driving it a couple of inches along the grooves. "She's too naïve to be on the street."

"I know." That fearful shiver travels through me again.

"So, Lucy. Why are you angry with me?"

"You know."

"No, actually, I don't. At least, not the specific cause, this time."

"For God's sake, John. The letter. So I can apply for the Guatemala accompaniment program."

"Lucy, m'dear, you know you can't leave the country until you're off probation."

"It's just the application process, John. They know I have to finish my probation before I can go."

"Even then, Lucy. I read the description of what they'll be doing. It's going to be tough, physically and emotionally. Lots of unknowns. Danger. Miles of walking. Do you really think you could do that now?"

He studies me, and I study him back. When I met John, his face was beefy in a bully kind of way. Now it's soft and puffy in a tired kind of way. "Well, maybe not now. But by the time I'm off probation, I can get myself in better shape."

"You can do that anyway, without actually having an application in."

"But I need it, John. Something to hope for. A reason to stay on the straight and narrow."

"It's a worthy goal, m'dear. And there's nothing to stop you from working toward it. I just can't write you a letter now, while you're still on probation and not ready to go."

I cross my arms and stare hard at the ratty linoleum floor to keep my eyes from filling up.

There is a silence, broken, finally, by John. "Want a cup of tea, love?"

I shake my head no. It'll just be John's lukewarm, Styrofoam-tasting tea.

"Oh come on." He goes to plug in the kettle anyway. When he comes back, he opens his desk drawer and takes out his lunch box. Is it lunchtime already? He lifts out a sandwich and a paper napkin, which he spreads in front of me and lays the sandwich on it. "God knows I don't need it." He pats his belly. "I've got you to thank for this."

"What?"

"You and Judith and those women on the Community Council, when you made them start the Community Offices."

"Nobody *makes* the police do anything."

"Don't undersell yourself. You went public in a smart way. They'd have lost face."

I shrug and notice a whiff of rotten old body smell coming from the neck of my coat. It's hot in here, but I keep the coat on and buttoned anyway.

"I know you didn't want me in that job," he grins, "And you were right. All I wanted was a steady day shift."

"I *knew* it."

"But later I got into it, you know? Community policing. It's important work. If the police departments did more of it, they'd have less of the other kind to do."

I pick up the sandwich and take a big bite.

"So, Lucy, where have you been the last couple of nights? Magdalen House called, wondering where you were. We've all been worried about you."

Another bite, fill my mouth.

"Lucy, m'dear, what do I need to do to get you to keep your conditions?"

"I don't want to go back to that place."

"As long as you …" A suspicious look crosses his face. "Lucy? What have you done?"

Damn. Why did I say that? Maybe the florist shop woman didn't call the police after all. I focus on finishing the sandwich. Wish there was another one. Wish there *were*.

"Lucy, I know it's not the most comfortable thing, me being your probation officer, where we've known each other all these years, but I'm here for you. Althea and Judith too. We want you to keep your conditions, earn your way out of this system. The 'injustice' system, as you love to call it." He grins. "And we want you living somewhere safe and comfortable in the meantime." He gives my sleeping bag, on the floor by my feet, an expressive look.

"You mean Magdalen House, where the nuns can make sure I don't do anything crazy."

"Not what I meant, Lucy."

"Well, I won't do anything crazy. For sure I wouldn't if you'd write me that letter."

"All in good time, Lucy, and as long as you take your meds." He looks at me from under those bushy brows. "You are taking your meds, aren't you?"

I reach under my coat and pull the bottle out of my skirt pocket, hold it up.

He takes it from my hand, picks up his reading glasses from the desk and looks at it. "Nearly out." He glances at his watch. "My day's almost finished here. We're making a trip to the drugstore before I let you go." He hands me back the bottle. "Now let's see if you've still got a bed."

He calls Magdalen House. Yes, my little room is still mine. "I know you're not that fond of nuns and rules," he says, "But respect the staff, m'dear. They mean well."

As he starts to dial the drug store, I say, "I'm not your dear." A ritual between us. I protest, and he says all Newfoundlanders of a certain age say "love" and "dear." John's of a certain age, all right. At least he's never called me "my trout."

Bara gets up from one of the hard chairs in reception and falls in behind us as we walk to the drugstore. John turns to her at the door and says, "We'll be out in a minute." She gets the message and waits on the sidewalk. John pulls a stack of small bills out of his wallet, pays for the prescription and hands it to me along with the rest of the cash.

We part outside. "I'll see you soon, love, but check in now and then anyway, just so an old man doesn't have to worry about you."

"Hate to have you worried about me."

He gives Bara a little bow, then turns back to me. "And *stay out of trouble*, okay?"

I watch his bulky back disappear up the street, but as soon as he is well out of hearing, Bara is on me. "You're on probation."

"So."

"What did you do to get sent to jail?"

My face gets hot. "You little sneak."

She has the grace to blush. "Sorry, Lucy. I guess I kind of, like, listened through the door."

"I guess you did."

"But really, what did you do?"

"It's not your business."

"And what kind of meds are you on? Are you crazy?"

"It's not your business." She shrinks away from me. "We walked by St. Marks, so you know where it is. Now go and talk to Althea. She'll take care of you." I start to walk purposefully along the sidewalk, although I have no idea where I'm headed.

"But where are you going?"

"Away from you."

She follows me. "But this Althea, she's your friend. Can't you come with me?"

"You're a big girl. Go talk to her yourself."

"She won't want to talk to me."

I stop, face her. "What?"

She turns and begins walking in the other direction. "I'm going back to the alley. Maybe see you there."

Now it's me following her, anger drained, replaced by that creeping dread. "No, you're not. You're going to talk to Althea. She'll take care of you."

She stubbornly keeps on walking, though not quickly.

I grab her arm, realize that I was walking in the direction of St. Marks in the first place. "Come on, then."

She stops but doesn't turn.

"Okay, I'm coming with you."

She takes another moment or two but finally turns and walks with me. "You can let go of my arm now."

CHAPTER EIGHT

"Hey, Lucy!" I jump, then remember I'm not hiding now, and anyway, it's just Cindy. On our way upstairs to talk to Althea, Bara spotted the free clothing depot and I remembered I want a nylon jacket. I've been browsing along the rack, looking for something big enough.

Bara stops pawing through a bin of sweaters to stare at Cindy, who is bursting with a huge grin, holding up a pair of the longest, skinniest spike heels I've ever seen, bright red. "Look at these kick-ass shoes." Little silver dragons wind up the back of each heel.

"Some creepy john shows up, how're you supposed to run away in those?" I ask.

"Not gonna run no more."

"That a quote, from a spiritual or something?"

"Maybe. What I mean is I'm quitting street work. So's this girl here."

Cindy's friend Patty straightens up from a bin of children's clothing. Where Cindy is small and soft, Patty is tall and angular. Where Cindy is bubbly and talkative, Patty is quiet and dignified.

"Hey, Lucy." Patty walks over and takes my hand. "Cindy said she saw you. I'm happy you're out." She is trying not to look down at what I'm wearing and the sleeping bag in my hand, swinging from its makeshift rope handle.

I'm not so polite, and I survey her plain sweater and jeans, her long, dark hair pulled back in a ponytail.

She laughs. "No more beads, braids and feathers."

"You taught us all a lot."

"And still can. Believe me, I'm a proud Mi'kmaw woman. I just don't need to wear it on the outside so much now."

I can't look at a former student without remembering the moment the light went on. When they understand it's the world that's upside down, not them. For Patty it was a project she did on the residential schools. She wondered why her mother, a survivor, would spend hours cleaning the kitchen floor with a nailbrush. She asked, but her mother wouldn't talk about it. I gave her Isabelle Knockwood's *Out of the Depths* to read, and then she discovered the Nova Scotia Archives. She travelled from struggling with literacy to research at a university level without even noticing. As the class discussed what she found each week and listened to her pain, the questions shifted from "what" to "why." Those moments of blinding clarity, the world's lies whisked aside, fill me with awe. They clear the way for learners to see how smart they are, how powerful they can be together.

"We just had a long talk with Althea," Cindy says, setting the red shoes back in the footwear bin.

"You not taking those?" Patty asks.

"I won't be needing them."

"But hey," Patty shrugs her shoulders. "They're hot. When you going to see a pair like that again? Take them anyway."

Cindy grins and picks them up again, placing them in the bottom of the green garbage bag she's carrying.

Cindy and Patty met at the all-night drop-in for street workers long before they came to my literacy and community leadership classes. Now they lean, side by side, over the bin of boy's shirts while Cindy continues talking, almost faster than she can take in breath. "Althea's been working with us. We've got an apartment, sharing rent, social assistance. We've applied to get the kids back, going to share cooking and childcare, save on expenses." Her face is so hopeful, it shines.

An ache blooms in my heart. These girls try so hard. They get clean, get dragged back into the drugs; off the street, back on; get their kids back from Family Services, lose them again. It's like they're trying to walk out of a swamp. Every time they manage to lift a foot forward, the effort drives the other foot deeper into the mud. The swamp of poverty. These two are not my only former students to be sucked back in, over and over again. Some disappeared altogether.

I haven't said anything, so Cindy stops and looks up. "Honest, Lucy. It's different this time. We're doing it together, with a plan."

They pack their new-to-them kids' clothes into the garbage bag on top of the shoes while I go back for the biggest nylon jacket I saw, a dark blue one. I loosen the rope around the sleeping bag and add the folded jacket to the load.

"Want a cup of coffee, Lucy?" Cindy asks. Any other time, I'd go in a minute. Today, I want to get Bara up to see Althea before she leaves for the day, just in case she is going to leave for the day. More often than not she works overtime or stays for evening meetings.

Cindy and Patty don't argue, wave goodbye as they go up the stairs, arm in arm.

Bara watches them out of sight. She turns to me, opens her mouth, but a booming voice cuts between us. "Well, well. If it isn't my old friend Lucy."

I wince, see Bara catch it.

Reverend "Call-me-Peter" Cox is striding toward us, big hand out. "Haven't seen you for a while."

I stuff my free hand into my pocket, but he's already turned to Bara anyway. "And who's this?"

I do the introduction thing. "Hi there, Bara. Welcome to St. Marks." He looks at me. "Taking her up to see Althea?" I nod, and he turns back to the kid. "She'll fix you up."

"Gotta go now." I turn and take half a step toward the door.

"Wait a minute, Lucy." Why does he talk so loudly in such a

small room? Is the off-button gone on his sermon voice the way it is on my temper? "I've been hearing things about you."

Oh, great. Jail? Sleeping on the street? Blowing off in a florist shop?

"I understand you've done some preaching."

I gape at him for a moment, gather my wits again. "That was a long time ago. Let's go Bara." I start toward the stairs up to Althea's office.

"You wouldn't consider doing the sermon here one Sunday, would you?"

I think: you're crazier than I am.

He persists. "Is that a yes?"

"No."

"I've seen things you've written before. You're good."

I give him a bitter little laugh. "Like I said, that was a long time ago." I take Bara's arm, nearly drag her along with me.

"Well consider it, Lucy. I think you'd do a great job."

As we climb the stairs, I get slower and slower with every step. I have to drop Bara's arm. She takes the sleeping bag and jacket so I can concentrate on using the bannister to help lift my weight.

"First jail, then medication, then sermons," she says. "You are, like, too full of surprises. Is that the minister?"

"The Reverend Peter Cox."

"Doesn't look like a minister to me."

"He's different, all right."

"You don't like him."

I have to think about that as I catch my breath at the top of the steps. "He's annoying, for sure, but he has a half-decent analysis. St. Marks wouldn't survive without him. He talks the national church into funding the place every year, and he does the job for free."

"How can he do that?"

"Gets paid to teach theology at the university."

"I think he's creepy. Like, fake. What's he in it for anyway?"

When I don't respond, she narrows her eyes at me. "Are you a Christian?"

I have to laugh. "Why? Are you?"

"I ... was."

"What are you now?"

To my surprise, her eyes fill with tears. "An abomination."

I process that for a moment.

"My best friend ... we ... I mean, *girlfriend* ... That's why my parents threw me out."

"Oh. *That* kind of Christian."

"What do you mean, *that* kind of Christian?"

"The literal kind. Fundamentalist. Hates gays." She frowns at me. She has an odd way of wrinkling her snub nose at the same time. "So, how'd your parents find out?"

"She came for a sleepover. We were ... you know."

"Making love?"

Bara blushes a furious shade of red. "No. Just kissing. My mom walked in. Hit the roof. Told my dad."

"They'll get over it."

"You don't know my parents. They said they'd rather I was dead." Shiny eyes again.

Can't help glancing at the remnants of the bruise under her eye. "Is that why you think no one will help you?"

She nods, a tear overflowing out of each eye, trickling down her cheeks. She gathers the end of her jacket sleeve in her fist and uses it to scrub her face.

I reach out and take her wet hand as she lowers it. "Oh, my dear. Not everyone thinks like your parents."

"But this is a church."

"Not even every church."

"Your friend Althea, she's a social worker, but she must be a Christian to work here."

"She is, but not ... *that* kind of Christian."

"I only know one kind."

"Then we need to show you another one. Let's go see Althea."

"You're, like, sure?"

"I'm sure. Althea's office is just down here."

She brightens. "Hey, those girls at the free clothes place."

"Cindy and Patty?"

"Yeah. Are they, like, together?"

I bark out a laugh. "Hardly. Just really good friends, practically sisters."

"Oh."

"Lucy," says Althea as we appear at her door. Her eyes flick down, pause at the sleeping bag, come back to my face. "Where have you been? Magdalen House called."

"I know. I just saw John. He talked to them."

"So you'll be back there tonight?"

I nod.

She wants to ask more, I know, but she turns to Bara. "And who's this?"

I make the introductions, tell Althea Bara needs a place to stay.

"Welcome to St. Marks, Bara." They disappear into her office to talk in private. I should leave, she's not my problem, but I need to see her safely through the door of Horizons, or wherever Althea gets her a bed. I sit down in one of Althea's waiting chairs.

I can hear Reverend Call-me-Peter's voice through the wood of his office door. Is he talking long distance to China? I can't help thinking about his invitation to give a sermon. Ridiculous, given where I am now in life. On the other hand, I've got some things to say.

I hear the tail end of Althea's sentence as she opens the door. "If you change your mind, let me know. I'd be happy to talk to them. Lucy? You take care of yourself, and come and see me soon."

I lead the way out, pause on the sidewalk. "You hungry?"

She looks back at St. Marks. "Isn't that where the free supper is?"

"Yeah, but John gave me my social assistance money."

"He keeps it for you?"

"It's called a trustee. So, want to have a real supper? I mean choose something we want, from a menu. My treat."

Bara grins. "Sure."

We start out toward a little family-run Lebanese place on Agricola Street.

"Althea trying to get you to go back to your parents?"

"Everyone seems to think they'll get over it."

"Did you tell her about the abomination stuff?"

"Yeah. She got the point after that, but she still thinks maybe she could, like, talk to them."

"She's pretty good at it."

"Thanks, but no thanks."

"So did she get you a bed?"

"Yeah. That Horizons place. She doesn't think it'll make any difference that I'm …"

"It won't. In fact, bet you won't be the only one."

The minute our plates of shawarma are set in front of us, Bara starts to vacuum it up.

"Hey, slow down. When you're that hungry, it can make you sick."

She looks up at me briefly through her too-long bangs, smiles and goes back to eating, although she does slow down.

Later, over blessedly hot mugs of tea, I ask, "So, what would it take to change your parents?"

She lets out a bitter laugh. "But they're *that* kind of Christian."

I shrug. "I was *that* kind of Christian."

She nearly slops her tea on the table. "You were?"

I laugh. "I was overseas as a missionary before I even questioned what kind of Christian I was."

"Like, saving souls?"

"Don't look so shocked."

"Yeah, but, like, where?"

"Long story. Point is, I changed."

Her eyebrows rise, inviting explanation, but I don't have the energy. "Your parents can change."

She shrugs. "Whatever."

It's dark outside when we leave, a cold wind nipping at us. I accompany Bara to the door of Horizons. "Where will I see you?" she asks.

"St. Marks? I can't afford restaurant suppers every night."

She grins and doesn't hesitate as she goes up the steps and through the door.

I turn away, walk from streetlight to streetlight for the two blocks to Magdalen House. It will be the night staff on by now. They're not as grouchy as the day staff.

As I walk, my mind circles back to *that* kind of Christian. The church made us take an orientation course before going overseas. A whole month. I hung out with the other Bible-thumpers, totally bored. What did "cross-cultural sensitivity" or "colonialism in Latin America" have to do with us? The liberal Protestants were scary; the Catholics were terrifying. They were priests, mostly little brown guys with accents. We were pretty sure they were communists. And it was definitely suspicious how much fun they had.

And then they would surprise us, get antagonistic and scrappy. "Stop saying 'under-developed.' Say 'exploitation.' Our people were the richest in the world when your people came and took everything. Call it 'theft.'"

"Who do they think they are?" we'd whisper. "They blame white people for everything bad that's ever happened in the world."

"So arrogant."

"They don't have a personal relationship with Jesus."

"We must react to their anger with love. Turn the other cheek." We nodded to each other, smug. What good people we were.

CHAPTER NINE

I wake into consciousness gently, no dream. Nice to sleep in a nightgown in a room that is, for now, mine. A few of my clothes, a couple of my books. What passes for home. I linger in my warm bed. Swimming around in my mind is "turn the other cheek." Maybe Reverend Call-me-Peter would like a sermon about that.

I was annoyed at someone. A market woman? I thought she was rude to me. No, Nicolás said, I'd picked up something from her stand with my left hand. When there's no running water, no soap, no toilet paper, no toilet for God's sake, the right hand becomes the clean one, for touching people, food. The left is reserved for toilet tasks and anything else that will make you sick. "In *el Norte,* you've got so much soap and water, you've forgotten," he said. "It's *mano derecha, mano izquierda* in most of the world, and has been, probably always."

Damn, I thought. Nothing's good about *el Norte,* but he had more to say. "That passage about turning the other cheek? It doesn't say the *other* cheek. It says, 'If someone slaps you on your *right* cheek, turn and offer him your *left.*'"

I didn't believe him until later, when I checked my Bible and saw for myself. How can you misread a line like that all your life? How can a whole culture misread it?

"To us, you see, when someone hits your left cheek with their right hand, it says 'I'm angry with you,' or 'I challenge you,' but I recognize you as my equal. Hitting the right cheek with the left hand says, 'You lowly scum.' So Jesus told them, if someone, a Roman soldier say, hits you with his left hand, challenge him to hit you with his right. Force him to make a choice, recognize you as his equal or back down. Classic non-violent resistance, see?"

I didn't, for a very long time.

Sadness fills me. Nicolás, where are you? Still with the villagers who went into hiding, constantly on the move in the endless jungle? Did you go over the border to the camps in Mexico? If only John …

Stop it. Get up. Get something to eat. Get out of here before the day staff comes on. I look at the little travel alarm on my bedside table. Too late.

I can hear women talking, moving around on the ground floor, but there's no one in the kitchen. Sun pours through the window, spotlighting a bowl of fruit on the table. Bunch of bananas on top. Room begins to fade and melt. My vision narrows, down to a little sticker on a banana. Del Monte, Guatemala.

Lucy, don't. Walk away.

Can't help myself. Hand reaching out. Slow motion. Closing around them. Blood bananas. How many died so *el Norte* can eat these? So Del Monte, once United Fruit, can make a profit? How many more suffered under the vicious dictatorship the CIA brought them? Does no one remember? Does no one care?

I hurl the bananas, as hard as I can, against the kitchen wall. They're overripe and squish as they hit, a brown smear down the wall as they fall to the floor. The walls are closing in. Have to get out of here.

"Lucy!" Sister Marie, filling the doorway. Big woman, straight, plain-cut grey hair, big cross hanging around her neck. I take a run at her, hands up. Her breath goes out with a *whumpf* as she comes up against the far side of the hallway, a dull *thunk* as her head hits the wall. I take a step toward the front door, but stumble, breathless and dizzy, barely aware of other residents peeping around corners, drawn by the fuss. A social work student steps in front of me, just as Sister Marie's strong hand closes on the back of my sweater. What have I done?

Moments later, Sister Marie is looking at me across her big wooden desk. Her eyes are the same grey as her hair. "You understand what this means, Lucy."

"I'm out."

"You can apply again in a week. We'll consider you."

The social work student brings a bag of ice wrapped in a towel, hands it to her, leaves without a glance at me.

"I held your room for three nights as a favour to John, with no idea where you were, when, or if, you were coming back. You know we need every bed. Someone went without a safe place to stay while your bed sat empty. Oh, and there's this." From the papers on her desk, she picks up a small pink slip. "The psychiatrist's office called yesterday, wondering where you were." She looks up at me again. "You know I have to call John."

Damn.

I make my way down the steps into a cold, sunny day wearing the blue nylon jacket, the few clothes and books I had in my room packed into my small suitcase. Sleeping bag and old wool coat rolled together in the other hand. Now what? She'll have called John by now. I'll have to face him.

Cindy and Patty told me where their new apartment is. Can't feed me, but maybe they'll make me a cup of tea and help me think of someplace to go.

High-rise. Buggered elevator, of course. Can't speak when Cindy opens the door, gasping for wind after climbing the stairs.

What sweet girls they are. They invite me in, make tea. Nice to see them relaxing in their own place. Jeans, sweatshirts, no makeup.

Cindy sets a steaming mug in front of me. Relief just to put my hands around it. "Sister Marie threw you out? Lucy, what did you do?"

I tell them the story.

"You should talk to Judith," Cindy says. "She's helped us out every time we've been busted."

"But what she can do about this? Probation is probation. 'Keep the peace and maintain good behaviour.'"

"Oh no. Another thirty days in Burnside? Couldn't Judith get you sent somewhere else? One of the small jails? Guards are a lot nicer there."

Patty joins in. "Psychiatric hospital?"

"God no. That would be worse."

"But seriously, Lucy, when you do these things, do you know what you're doing?"

I close my eyes briefly, think back. "I guess I have to say yes."

"But you can't stop yourself?"

"It's just that I look at what's in front of me and see what's behind it. No one else seems to see it. It infuriates me, and the words just come out."

Patty reaches over the table to take my hand. "Lucy, you taught us all how to do analysis, looking deeper, asking: Why? Who benefits? Who has power? But don't you remember the other steps? Find a community of common interest, share what you see and feel, decide together what you want and what you can do to get there, pick a good first action, support one another and do it."

Cindy picks up the litany I've repeated so often, to so many cohorts of community leadership students. "Then learn from what you've done, decide your next action … You know that expression 'Physician heal thyself'? Not sure how you say that to a teacher."

"You say, 'Thank you for all you've done for us,'" Patty smiles at me. "Now you have to do it for yourself."

Cindy rises to fetch the pot of tea from the stove. "Warm up?" she says, holding it up.

"Sure."

She tops up our cups. "That thing with the bananas at Magdalen House …" She returns the pot to the stove. "You said they were from Guatemala. That's where you were, weren't you?" She comes back to the table, looks at me. "It's a big thing in your life, isn't it? But you've never told us anything about it."

"It's where I learned how to teach literacy and community leadership."

"Yeah, that Latin American popular education thing." Now she quirks me a grin. "It took a while to catch on here, though, didn't it? Remember that time, at the Single Parent Centre? You were trying to get a group of us to 'share our lives,' and no one would talk?"

I try to remember.

"Someone was brave enough to tell you how we were all having to do illegal things to get by, boyfriends staying over, bits of money under the table, and because of that we couldn't trust each other. Somebody might squeal, and we'd lose our assistance."

"Oh yeah. I remember."

"You were shocked."

"I was. Despite … well … I was still a naïve, middle-class white girl."

Patty sighs. "Lucy, back when I was still with my husband, did you catch on he was beating me?"

I think back to that time. Tall, dignified young woman, before the leadership course, before the "beads and feathers" phase, barely said anything. "No. Don't think I did."

"Guess I hid it pretty well." A quick, bitter half-smile. "You know, after I left him, I really hate to say this, but sometimes I'd think about going back to him. He just beat me up once a week. Poverty beats me up every day."

There is a pause while we all look into our cooling cups. The ache starts up again in my heart. "So, how are you doing?" I ask them. "Really?"

They look at each other, faces grim. "It's hard," Cindy says. "Even sharing like this, it's a full-time job to make ends meet."

"Meet?" Patty's eyebrows go up. She looks at me, eyes pained. "You know about assistance rates. It's barely enough to survive, as long as you don't need glasses, or furniture, or a deposit, or money for a school field trip, or a phone, or a repair to anything, or a prescription."

"As long as you don't want to feed your kids any protein," Cindy adds bitterly. She picks at a loose thread on her cuff. "It's so tempting to go back on the street, when you know you can make two, three hundred in a night."

Patty picks it up: "You tell yourself, just one night a month would make ends meet, and then you kick yourself, 'cause there's no such thing as one night, even if you could stay away from the drugs."

"The plan you made with Althea, moving in together, is it making a difference?" I ask.

"Of course," Cindy says. "Just not enough."

There's a pause, then Patty adds, "The worst thing is, we fight about money."

Cindy looks really sad. "And it's been so good up to now." She reaches out to take Patty's hand. "You know we're a couple, Lucy?"

So, Bara. You knew better than me.

The apartment door bursts open to admit a noisy, tumbling mass of little boys. Where has the day gone? Patty goes to the hall to referee. They line up in front of me, politely, to say "Hello Ms. Chambers," as they've been taught. I greet them back. Rodney, Amos, Kip and Leo. Good thing their mothers said their names over and over again during the day, or I never would have remembered. I ask about school. Apparently, it's "okay." Patty shepherds them off to change out of their good clothes.

Cindy says what I was both hoping and dreading to hear: "Why don't you stay here tonight? Sort it out tomorrow."

"But you're on assistance again. Can't let you feed me."

"It's not fancy, Lucy. Wieners and beans. We can stretch it a little."

"Stretch it a little" means Cindy and Patty get about two spoonfuls of beans each, no wieners. They try to give me a decent serving, like what they give the kids. I say I'm not hungry. Don't think they believe me. I eat about three spoonfuls of beans, reach over and put the chunks of wiener on the girls' plates. They pass them on to the boys, where they disappear fast. I actually think longingly of the bucket at Susan's back door.

With supper cleared away, three of the boys spread out around the kitchen table to do their homework. Leo settles beside me on the chesterfield to read me a chapter about ancient Rome. He asks me what various words mean. I ask him why there's nothing there about the women. Patty laughs and says, "Never too young for critical thinking."

"What's that, Mom?" says Leo.

Patty waits for me to answer, but sees I am waiting for her. "It means you not only read what's there, but think about what's not there, and think about why some things are there and other things aren't."

"Oh," says Leo, clearly wanting to get back to the drawing of a battle.

Cindy announces that her two boys will sleep on the floor, so I can have the foldout couch. I refuse. "They need to be alert for school tomorrow. I don't do anything useful." They laugh, then argue. In the end, we use my sleeping bag to make a pad on the floor with one of the boys' blankets to cover me. Sure beats cardboard and concrete. Even that thin crib mattress in Judith's basement.

Patty's right. Why have I forgotten my own lessons? Find a community of common interest, share what you see and feel, decide what you want and what you can do to get there. But I haven't forgotten. I just come up against a wall of pain each time. It's been there for years, but there used to be space in between, room to maneuver. Over time, it's moved so much closer.

Very early in the morning, the pitter-patter of little feet hits the ground. The smallest one, Kip, just misses my face as he jumps off of the chesterfield, then, startled, trips over me and crashes to the floor, howling. "Shut up," says his big brother Leo, glaring at him, "or I'll make you sorry." It works, and in minutes all four are running around, bouncing on and off their squeaky old couch, swearing and shrieking at a pitch guaranteed to punch out your eardrums.

I crawl to my feet, back and knees aching. Cindy appears in the doorway, sleepy and rumpled, wearing a pink Daisy Duck nightshirt. Don't imagine she wore that when she was working. "Shut up!" she yells, an echo of older brother a few minutes before. "We've got a guest."

They do, although as they go about their morning business, Amos punches Rodney and the whole circus is off and running again.

Patty arrives via the front door. She reaches into a plastic shopping bag and, grinning, holds up a small package of bacon. Once she gets to the kitchen and sets the bacon down on the counter, her hand goes back into the bag and produces a can of frozen orange juice. I'm touched. I know these special treats are because of me. Also because their cheques came last week. Later in the month, the feast will have to be paid for in days of oatmeal for the kids and nothing but instant coffee for the moms.

When the door slams shut behind the boys as they leave for school, silence descends. Patty drops into the chair across from me at the kitchen table, heaving a weary sigh. "Sometimes I wonder if they are better off with us," she says. "They're out of control half the time."

"One of many things I learned from you in the community leadership course was how the residential schools destroyed thousands of years of passed-down knowledge about how to raise children."

"It's so true. All my parents knew was dormitories and a dining hall with not enough food, getting locked in closets and scrubbing floors, abuse. They had no idea how to raise us, even when they were sober."

Cindy checks the coffee pot. Finding it empty, she sets her cup in the sink and joins us. "I'm no better. The Home for Colored Children looked about like that too."

I reach for Cindy's hand, squeeze it. "Are the two of you getting help with this?"

"Althea's great, and the staff at the Single Parent Centre. But they can't be here every time we need to know what to do or say. Things keep falling apart."

Cindy looks over at Patty, takes her hand.

Patty meets Cindy's eyes, her face determined. "I just want so, so much for it to work this time."

They have made their own private world as they hold each other's eyes, but Patty slides her other hand across the table in my direction, where it rests palm up, strong and brown, wrist decorated with an eagle feather tattoo. As I close the circle, I feel a current flowing through us, equal parts strength and despair.

CHAPTER TEN

I'm barely out the main door when I spot a uniform coming my way, young, scrubbed and cheerful. Damn. Caught. Don't want to talk to John. Not yet.

He walks right by. Doesn't even look at the fat, messy old lady standing right in the open. Delicious invisibility, but I won't count on it. John will ask them to look for me sooner rather than later. I have to figure out what to say to him.

I have no reason to be here. Shouldn't be here. It just feels so hidden. Safe. I've lifted the bedside table, or whatever it is, off of the seat of the padded chair, leaving a darker square on the upholstery. I sit, sinking in, leaning back, feeling warm. I've gone to earth like a rabbit. There's even safety in knowing Judith's life is lived upstairs, however little I know about it and however sorry I would be to have her know I'm here.

So warm. Tempted to pull down that mattress again and have a nap but, remembering last time, I don't dare.

I can feel my boxes sitting in the shadows, so close. My books. So many have gone through my hands, borrowed from the library or friends, or bought and then given away. The few I kept are the precious ones, page edges worn and grubby from rereading, scanning, searching for something half-remembered.

Most precious of all, Nicolás's Bible. Corners turned. Notes jotted in his small, precise hand. Is it here? It must be. It was on the shelf. No reason Judith and Althea wouldn't pack it with the others. My heart beats more quickly. I want to see it, touch the soft leather binding worn from his beloved fingers. I can see them, slender, brown. Feel them. My eyes begin to blur. Nicolás. I want to come and find you. Now, as the Peace Accords bring an end to the war. Give your Bible back to you after all this time.

Maybe the Bible will lead me back to Nicolás. Magical thinking, I know, but I sit up anyway. I can just make out my boxes in the chaos of things pushed aside to make room for them. And behind them, one of the dusty windows. It's darker than it was when I came. What time is it, anyway? I don't want to get caught again. The light by the door is still on. I use the chair arms to push myself to my feet, shuffle to the light, yank its dangling string. Darkness. Can't see to search for the Bible now, though I ache for the feel of it. But I must go. I promise myself I will come back tomorrow, earlier in the day.

Bara, Gord and Not-Gord, I mean Robin, are standing in the lane behind Susan's Place, heads together. Bara's face lights up. "Lucy, where have you been? The nuns said you're not there anymore. I couldn't find you."

"You're not my keeper."

"We've just decided to go downtown to eat," Robin says. "Want to come?"

"Downtown? Why?"

"The really good stuff's in the bins behind the expensive restaurants."

Bara looks at me. "What about it, Lucy? Aren't you tired of all-day-breakfast leftovers?"

"Not enough to walk downtown. Go without me. I'll be fine here."

"But Lucy, why not? Like, what else have you got to do? The walk'll do you good."

"The hobble, you mean."

Bara frowns. "Are you staying out of sight again?"

"Not your business. And I'm not walking all the way to Spring Garden Road."

"Okay, part way, then. Come on, it's a nice day."

She's right. It is one of those days when late fall is remembering summer. And, much as I hate to admit it, I like their company. And I'm hungry, maybe for something more than scrambled eggs. "Just part way," I say. The young people hide my suitcase and sleeping bag in the alley.

People down here are well-dressed, self-absorbed. The crowd breaks around me, giving me lots of space. Huge shopping bags from pricey stores. All along the sidewalk, high-class window displays, expensive restaurants. Anger starts to seep up from deep inside. I will write a sermon for Reverend Call-me-Peter. About how poor people die for our endless consumption. Immediately it starts droning around and around my head like a stuck record.

Bara tugs on my sleeve. "Lucy? You okay?" I shake her off. As I turn away, my eyes are hooked by mannequins in dresses, some kind of sparkly fabric, in the window display. The sermon in my head speeds up, and all I can see is my own scowling face reflected in the glass.

Then my face is melting, shrinking, becoming Rosa's face, weathered and brown, framed in the brilliant colours of her *huipil* and headdress. Her daughter Marta appears just behind her, then Adela, Mía, Emilia. A crowd of grieving women. Large, dark eyes, tears all cried out, they reach into my heart and wring it the way their strong hands twisted the water out the laundry they washed in the river.

They fade, disappear, and there are the glittery fake women in the display again, behind them the people jostling around inside, buying things. I can hear my heart pumping. Lucy, don't.

And then I'm on the move, my hands driven against the big glass doors. They give, and I push my way into the crowd. Bara's behind me, her voice miles away. "Lucy? Lucy, where are you going?"

I come up against a display of perfume. Now there's a useless luxury. Bottles arranged on some kind of satiny material draped around a wooden box. Bara's hand is on my arm, her voice frightened. "Lucy? Lucy? Robin, Gord, help."

I wrench away from her, pull the wooden box off the counter, shake it free of the fabric. Perfume bottles fly in all directions, breaking against the glass case, the floor. The woman behind the counter ducks as one hits her. The smell rises in a cloud, flowery, choking. I drop the box to the floor and step up onto it, hand on the glass counter, in the puddle of perfume escaping from a broken bottle.

"Waste and greed," I shout. The bustle abruptly stills. Shocked faces look at me, turned up slightly because of my box stage. Bara is one of them, her eyes and mouth frozen open. Gord's behind her, face equally shocked.

"People all over the world are hungry and sick," I shout. "Why? Because we, with money bulging our pockets, buy up their land, their metals, their trees, their crops, their oil to make all this …" I wave my hand at the glittering displays around me, "… junk."

Someone tugs on my sleeve. Robin. "Lucy, it's great, what you're saying, but — "

"People all over the world are killed by militaries and paramilitaries to keep them silent in their suffering, keep them sitting quietly at sewing machines."

Robin pulls my sleeve again. I shake him off.

"To keep them on electronics assembly lines, on bulldozers and loaders, making these shiny piles of stuff."

"Come on," Robin says, urgent, his hand hooked in my elbow. I try to push his hand away, but he pulls me firmly off of my box, catches me when I stumble. Gord hooks my other elbow and they pull me along. I sputter, but they're young and strong.

I twist, catch a glimpse of Bara running back the way we came, toward a cop about to step through the door. She points at something behind him, out on the street. He stops, swivels to look up and down the sidewalk.

"Lucy, come. Now," Robin hisses and I start to co-operate. People stare, but step aside. A few counters from the perfume, crowds are intent on their shopping as if nothing happened. The boys take me to the side wall, Robin glancing over his shoulder before pushing me through a big steel door behind a display. He guides me through a dark space and then all three of us tumble out into the alley beside the store. "Come on," Robin says and drops my arm, leading the way toward the back of the building.

Behind the store, there's a row of huge dumpsters with lids. Robin opens one, pulls out a few garbage bags and drops them beside the bin. He and Gord more or less lift me in. I land on something squishy. Robin vaults in beside me, a stick in his hand. Does he think he'll fight off a cop with a stick? No, he arranges it on the metal edge of the dumpster so that it props the lid open a crack. Feeling around, he finds an intact garbage bag and slides it over for me to sit on. He finds one for himself too. He's done this before, I think. Gord has disappeared.

We crouch in stinking darkness. I get alternate whiffs of garbage and the perfume from my hand. Don't know which is worse.

Voices. "They can't have gone far. It's just been a few minutes." Robin's hand on my knee in the dark. Does he think I'm so out of control I'll say something?

Another voice, just outside our bin. "No one here."

First voice again, "This is a waste of time," moving away.

After a while, Robin whispers, "You okay?" Touches my knee again. I'd slap his hand, but I'm too busy holding on to the garbage bag I'm sitting on. It keeps threatening to slump to the side and dump me into unidentified smelly muck.

"Get me out of here," I say.

"It'll be dark in an hour." He looks up toward the crack where he propped the lid. The light falls on his earnest narrow face, dark stubble on his cheeks. "Can you wait that long?"

"No choice."

"That was cool, what you said in there. It'll get you in trouble pretty quick in a classy store like that, but you were speaking truth. You're one brave lady."

"Don't have to tell me I'm in trouble. Or I'm right."

"So what, like, got you started?"

"Don't you start up with that 'like' thing."

He chuckles, then waits for an answer.

After a pause, I try. "It's like looking through something and seeing the whole story behind it. Like floating in a boat. Everyone else is saying how beautiful and calm it is, clouds and blue sky reflected on the water, and all you can see are the rusty cans and broken bottles on the bottom, covered with slime from the pollution. I want to wake them up, show them. The lake is dying. Do you know what I'm talking about?"

"Uh, no. Can't say I do."

"All those clothes in there. They're made in Bangladesh, Vietnam, Central America, where they can pay the workers a few dollars a day and not worry about sick pay, or pensions, or health and safety regulations.

"In Guatemala once, a friend plucked at the fabric of my sleeve, asked me, 'Where did this come from?' I had no idea, never thought about it. Later, when we were travelling, he asked a friend of his to give me a tour of a sewing factory. Row after row of young women bent over their machines, fingers cracked and aching, eyes squinting in the poor light. They were paid by the piece. To make enough for their families to live, they had to work twelve, fourteen hours a day, as fast as possible, until they sewed their hand into a seam or lost a finger to the cutter. The air was full of cotton dust.

Ever heard of 'brown lung disease'? And the noise …

"Those shoppers in there, they're not bad people. They don't want to force people all over the world to live in poverty, suffer ill health, die young, but why aren't they asking, 'Where did this come from?'"

I can feel him nodding in the smelly dark.

Light's fading. I try to get my feet under me. Can't feel them. I think I've pissed myself, but who'd know? "Get me out of here."

"Wait," Robin peeks out through the crack under the lid. "Okay, then." He lifts it open carefully as he can. It squeaks, and he pauses, waiting, but there's no one in the alley. Embarrassing to have him help me out of there, stiff, cold and filthy, but I can't hold myself up without him.

We make our way slowly through the growing dark back to the lane behind Susan's Place. Bara looks up from sorting through what the staff have left in the plastic bucket. "About time," she says. "Anyone see you?"

"Nope," Robin assures her. "Stuck to parking lots and alleys." He helps me sit on the restaurant's back step. "Got to go," he says to Bara. "You okay to take care of her from here?"

She nods, and he takes off with long strides. She begins arranging food on scrounged napkins, brings one to me. "You stink," she says as she bends to put it in my lap. I'm too tired to care what I smell like or what I'm eating.

Bara helps me into the alley, finds several layers of cardboard to sit on and urges me to lie down, but that doesn't feel right. I lean on the cold bricks of the wall and she wraps my sleeping bag around me. Next thing I know, she's climbing under one side of it, leaning against the wall and my shoulder.

"No, no, Bara. You have to go back to Horizons, where you'll be safe."

"And you'll be safe? Here, alone?"

"Safe enough. No one will see me."

"Then they won't see me either, will they?"

"You'll lose your bed at Horizons."

"I don't like it at Horizons."

"I can't take care of you."

"Then we'll just have to take care of each other, won't we?"

I feel something against my leg. Almost push it away before I hear that raucous purr. Raggedy has curled up on the sleeping bag between us. Bara strokes him a few times, her hand gradually slowing, finally coming to rest. The cat's purr fades off into sleep.

Nicolás liked to call on his vast network of friends to give me tours of the places the *campesinos* went to work in the off season or after they lost their land. The lucky ones, that is. I saw bananas harvested, coffee beans loaded onto ships, vegetables graded on endless conveyor belts, workers in pharmaceutical plants completely covered in paper suits. Before long, I couldn't look at anything without asking where it came from, who made it, who made money from it.

Nicolás could never have gotten me into the Inco mine, though. The offer of that tour came from a Canadian engineer when I was still a harmless missionary, long before I learned to ask who profits and who pays. Although, even then I felt uncomfortable when he called nickel "the metal of war."

"It makes steel harder and rust-proof," he said. "The price is depressed right now, but all we have to do is wait for another war and the price will soar again." And he laughed.

My eyes are closed, and in the darkness behind my eyelids, I'm suddenly there again, sitting in a jeep, breathing red dust, looking down into a vast, barren amphitheatre, a disappearing hillside, sloping downward to the sparking blue waters of *Lago Izabal*.

Every few minutes, a battered bulldozer appears at the lip of the hill. They look old to me, and small, left over from the 1950s. I hold my breath as they tip over the edge and plunge down at an impossible angle toward the lake below, pushing red earth in a cascade in front of the blade. They look to me to be on the verge of tumbling blade over treads. "Is that safe?" I ask him.

He laughs. "Looks scary, doesn't it? But it's perfectly safe. We work to Canadian health standards here. Men line up for these jobs, you know. Three hundred men are employed here. There was desperate unemployment in the region before we came."

I open my eyes. No, Nicolás did not arrange that tour, but years later, he introduced me to the people who made me understand it. The part about creating desperately needed jobs? That was after the government expropriated hundreds of square kilometres for the mine, land that used to grow food for several thousand people. And after the tailings from the mine poisoned the fish in the lake. The fishery had supported almost a thousand people. When people resisted, the government assigned the job of "pacification" to General Osorio, who later became president and introduced the whole country to the brutal genocide he perfected while he was "making the highlands safe" for Inco. By then he was called the "Butcher of Zapata." Turns out even that plunge down the hill wasn't so safe, after all. The workers' lives meant nothing to the company.

I reach into my pocket, fondle the key to Judith's basement. Warmth. Safety. Wish I was there. Wish I *were* there.

CHAPTER ELEVEN

As soon as grey light begins to seep into our alley, Bara stirs. She crawls out from under the bag and fumbles for something beside her. She holds up the bucket.

Her face blurry in the faint light, or maybe with dirt and exhaustion, she grins. "I brought it in here last night, so it didn't, like, get dumped into the bin." She looks inside. "Not much left, though. What time does the drop-in open?"

My body's turned to wood. I grunt as I try to shift my weight.

She frowns at me. "You okay?"

"No. Didn't sleep a wink. And I can't go to St. Marks."

"Why not?"

All my attention is focused on ploughing through the pain to sit up a bit straighter.

"What happened at Magdalen House?"

"Is there anything at all to eat in there?"

She pokes at the contents of the bucket. "Not really."

"We'll just have to wait then. Dump that thing into the bin and put it back by the step."

"You're hiding again, aren't you? You're in trouble. Not the thing yesterday at the store, because you didn't get caught. Something else. Something John will find out about."

"Elementary, my dear Watson."

"Lucy, whatever you've done, you know you have to talk to him sooner or later."

"They'll charge me again, send me back to jail."

"Yeah." She says it with that up and down slide the young people use when one of us oldies is being particularly obtuse. "As long as you keep doing nutty things."

"It's not that easy, catching the words in my head before they fly out of my mouth."

"I'm going to stick with you, keep you out of trouble."

"You're going back to Horizons."

"No, I'm not."

"What's wrong with it?"

"It's what I am."

"A lesbian?"

"Don't say that." She actually looks behind her, toward the opening of the alley into the lane.

"God, Bara. There's nothing wrong with being a lesbian, and the staff at Horizons have lots of gay kids there all the time."

"Well, tell that to the other kids. There's a couple of bullies there. They get their nasty jabs in when the staff aren't around." She looks miserable, tired and frightened.

"All right. Tell you what. Let's go see John together. He'll report me, but you're right. Got to talk to him sooner or later."

"At least he doesn't know about what happened yesterday. Thanks to us."

"Yeah, you're right. Thanks."

"So, we'll both go to John and … ?"

"We'll ask him to get us in somewhere together."

"They're just too strict there," I tell John, after the lecture about breaking my conditions again.

"Way I heard it, you assaulted Sister Marie."

"I didn't hurt her."

"Lucy, m'dear, you pushed her into the wall. Don't you think that might be a bit threatening, given what you did to Dell?" He stops, glances at Bara. She is busy staring at me with big, round eyes.

"I didn't hurt Dell either."

"Well, I can't send you back there anyway. Let's make a couple of calls, see where else we can get you a bed."

At least he doesn't seem to know about the missed psychiatrist appointment.

Bara pipes up. "Can I go with her?"

"But you've got a place at Horizons."

"It isn't working out. The other kids are mean to me."

"The staff should deal with that. We can't be hunting for another shelter bed just because you don't like it where you are."

"I want to go with Lucy. I'll keep her out of trouble."

John arches one thick eyebrow at her.

"I can," she nods earnestly.

He's on the edge of laughing at her but doesn't. Then, his expression shifts. He shrugs his ample shoulders. "Well, who knows? Maybe you can take care of each other."

Bara looks at me with a half-smile.

A couple of phone calls finds us two places at Fresh Start. "Those your things?" John is looking at the sleeping bag and suitcase sitting on the floor beside me.

I nod.

"Bara, your things are at Horizons?"

"I don't have things."

John looks at his watch. "Well, it's almost time for my lunch break. I'm going to take you both over there." He picks up my suitcase, leaving Bara to bring the sleeping bag. Just before we step out into the hallway, he turns to face us. "This is just to see if you really can keep each other out of trouble, okay?"

We both nod.

"And you," he directs this at me, but stops again.

"It's all right. She knows."

"All right, then. Take your meds."

72

Fresh Start is in one of those flat-roofed Edwardian duplexes that are everywhere in Halifax. The reception room still feels like the living room it once was, except for the big reception desk at one side. I study the once-classy hardwood as the young woman at the desk writes our names in a ledger.

"The only beds we have are cots in the overflow dorm, in the basement," she says. "You'll have to sleep there until rooms come free." She opens the bottom desk drawer, pulls a plastic bag out of a neat row of them, holds it up. Soap, shampoo, toothbrush. "Either of you need one of these?"

Bara takes one.

She takes my pills and puts them in a locked drawer. I'm supposed to ask a staff person for them morning and evening. She gets towels for us from a closet and lets Bara look through a box of used PJs. She picks a pair of blue flannel ones with snowmen on them.

We follow her to the basement. It's bare, linoleum tiles and painted walls, a row of cots down one side. There's a lump of blankets on one cot, lightly snoring. The rest are made up with worn but clean bedding, an extra blanket folded at the foot of each one.

"Bathroom's down there." She points at an open door at the far end.

Feels good to have a toilet, brush my teeth at a sink. I look over the big, old-fashioned bathtub. Actually big enough for me to get in and out of. While Bara uses the bathroom, I sit on the edge of my newly assigned cot. Exhaustion takes over every fibre of my body, making my limbs heavy and loose as rags. I tuck my jacket, sleeping bag and suitcase under the bed, spread the extra blanket on top and crawl in under it with my clothes on. The last thing I remember is looking up at the small high windows and thinking of Judith's basement. I don't even hear Bara come back from the bathroom.

CHAPTER TWELVE

When I wake up, Bara is curled up under the blanket on her cot, fully dressed and sound asleep, towels, plastic bag of toiletries and snowman pyjamas tossed on top of the blanket. It takes me a while to sit, then stand up, my body creakier than the metal cot. Holding my weight on the side of the mattress, I manage to bend and pull my suitcase out, flip it open. Inside, a small tangle of clothing and two of my books, read many times. I need to go back to Judith's basement. I close the suitcase, push it back, fish out my jacket.

I heave myself up, but my weight raises the far side of the cot and it bangs back down on the floor. Bara starts awake and sits up. She looks around, sheds her grogginess as she figures out where she is. Without a word, she gets up and heads to the bathroom.

By the time she comes back, I have my jacket on. She pulls hers out from under her bed. "So where are we going?"

"What do you mean, where are *we* going?"

"I'm keeping you out of trouble, remember?"

"Wait, wait. You're not thinking you're going to follow me everywhere, are you?"

"How else am I going to keep you out of trouble?"

"But I need my own space. So do you."

Bara shrugs her shoulders. "So, what do you want to do today?"

"I want to read." Damn, can't go to Judith's with Bara tailing me. I'll have to wait for a chance. "Hey. Do you want to go to the library?"

"Sure. The downtown one?"

"I was thinking of the North Branch."

"Let's go downtown. You can find a book and read while I, like, check out those dumpsters behind the expensive restaurants."

"Too far." My excuse, but I feel fear for her rising into my throat.

"But it's a nice day, we've got lots of time, and maybe I'll find us a treat. Something special."

"Bara, listen to me. Those guys who hang around the drop-in at St. Marks, some of them live by dumpster diving. They're territorial. Those downtown dumpsters, they'll fight over them."

"I'll be careful, make sure no one's around." She looks so eager, and young and quick.

"All right, but I'm coming."

I'm slowing her down, so I point out community services as we go — Uniacke Square Tenants Association, Legal Aid, the Community Clinic, Native Friendship Centre, Mi'kmaq Child Development Centre across the street. "Did you and Althea start all these things?" she asks.

I laugh. "Goodness no. All kinds of people were involved." I tell her about the Community Council.

"Is it still there?"

"Not formally. There's a network of community leaders working away, but it's harder now. There used to be grants for this kind of work, people in government assigned to help, on their paid time. Other institutions too, like universities ...."

As my voice fades, she glances over at me. By now we're in sight of the North Branch Library. I make one more attempt to convince her to go there. "Too nice out." She hooks her arm through mine. "Let's go."

At the bottom, Gottingen slopes up past the police station, turning left below the grassy flank of Citadel Hill and then swoops down to join Brunswick Street. As we turn to skirt the harbour side of Citadel Hill, I spot a row of limousines parked along Duke Street, uniformed drivers chatting in groups on the sidewalk. On the corner, there is a sign on a stand: Mining Association of Canada. It points down the hill toward the Trade and Convention Centre. Men in suits are making their way up the hill. I stop, squint my eyes to see if any match the photos of Inco executives in their annual report.

I start across the street. Bara calls my name, but it's lost in the screech of cars avoiding me. The suit men are scattering along the line of limos, drivers opening doors for them to get in. I'm trying to see their faces. Damn these dirty, scratchy old glasses.

A driver steps in front of me, radio aerial poking out of his pocket. "Can I help you?" he says, just as Bara, right behind me, says my name.

She grabs my arm and speaks to radio guy. "It's okay, she's a little crazy sometimes, but harmless. I'll take care of her."

He nods, hurries away to open a limo door.

Bara pulls me away.

I yank my arm out of her hand. "Crazy? Harmless? Is that what you think of me?"

"No, Lucy. I just wanted the guy to forget it and leave."

"Those guys in suits, they're mining executives."

"So?"

Most of the cars have left. Over her shoulder I see the last of the men getting into back seats. I shout at them. "How do you live with all that blood on your hands?"

Bara grabs my arm. "Lucy, calm down." She sidles me over to the Metro Centre steps, where I collapse onto the bottom one. As I catch my breath, Bara eases her hold on me. "What were you trying to do?"

"I was looking for the ones from Inco. When they put their mine in Guatemala — "

"Is that where you were a missionary?"

"The constitution was suspended for them, congress dissolved, new mining code brought in, land expropriated from the peasants. Then, to make the area 'secure and stable,' 6000 people were killed … I had a chance to prod the conscience of a killer!"

"But Lucy, you're on probation, remember? You can't afford to go on a public rant."

"I don't want you following me around, interfering."

"Interfering? Lucy, what are you thinking?"

"I'm thinking we need to fight for justice, whenever we get the chance."

She gets to her feet. "Whatever. Go back to jail if you want. Maybe I'll visit you there." She spins on her heel and begins walking furiously away, north.

The anger flows out of me, replaced by exhaustion and panic. Can I even get up off these steps? Let alone back to the North End?

I'm just about to call out, grovel for help before she disappears, when she stops and turns around anyway. "Shit," she says. "What am I doing? I brought you all this way. I can't just, like, leave you here."

She strides back to me, anger written all over not only her face but her jerky way of moving, and puts out her hand. "Come on, then."

I take it and she helps pull me to my feet. She hooks my arm through hers, roughly, but taking part of my weight. She refuses to look at me.

We sit at one of the long tables in the basement at St. Marks, trays of stew and bread in front of us. "Why do you fly off the handle like that?" Bara says between bites. "Are you mentally ill?"

I lower my spoon with a clatter. "Why is it that the minute someone is passionate about justice, they're mentally ill?"

"But yelling at guys in suits getting into limos?"

"They're thieves and murderers. Innocent people die so they and their friends can get rich."

"Okay, those guys maybe, but ordinary people, shopping?"

"It doesn't bother you? All those people with too much stuff shopping for even more, when so many have nothing?"

"But people shopping don't make other people poor, do they? They create jobs."

"Not if they don't ask for, and pay for, things made by people with a proper income, benefits, pensions. Bet there isn't a thing in that store not made in some place where people are wretchedly poor and getting poorer."

"Shhhh, Lucy." Bara glances along our table. A man and woman at the other end have stopped eating and are watching us.

I lower my voice to a whisper. "*We* buy the stuff that keeps the whole system going. It's produced for *us*."

"Us? But I own, like, a knapsack and one set of clothes."

"You're still a North American. We have to organize, change our culture into something that will let the rest of the world live." I'm still whispering, but it's full of "s" sounds. More people look our way.

Bara is thinking hard, judging by the deep crease between her eyes. "So, like, you obviously expect me to know all this. Did you, when you were my age?"

I have opened my mouth to say more, but I stop, close it. "No."

"So can't you say it so it makes sense to someone like me? So it doesn't look like you're attacking people? Why is it so … personal?"

I feel like the floor is sinking away under my feet. Sadness. Helplessness.

"Lucy? You okay?"

I have no more energy for eating. I set my spoon down.

Bara sighs loudly, rising and gathering up our trays. "I guess I just don't get it."

At Fresh Start, the first thing Bara does is ask the woman at the desk for my pill, and then she fetches a glass of water so I can take it. She digs my toothbrush, toothpaste, nightgown and soap out of my suitcase for me, grabs a towel from her bed. While I brush my teeth, I look longingly at the bathtub, but I have only enough energy to take the steps between the bathroom and my cot.

"I just don't get it." I said that to Nicolás in exactly the tone Bara used, more than once, as he tried to explain things to me.

Once, I complained because his literacy students said terrible things about the United States. "Why do you encourage them to hate another country?" I asked.

"I'm just helping them tell their stories."

"Well, the United States comes out as the bad guy in every single one."

Nicolás sighed. "If you came into my room one day while I was away and took something important to me — not that there's much to steal in my room — but, say you came and took my Bible that my sister gave me when I was ordained. Let's say lots of people saw you do it, so I knew you had my Bible. Now, let's say I came and challenged you for taking it and asked for it back — would you say I did that because I hated you?"

"No, I'd say you just wanted your Bible back."

"Think about it, Lucia. It's the same thing." We were walking down a path from one of the mountain villages. That's when he began to tell me the story of the 1950s: the hopeful times, when the elected government of Jacobo Arbenz nationalized a tiny portion of United Fruit Company's unused land to distribute to poor peasants, and the terrible times, the US-sponsored coup to overthrow Arbenz, the military dictatorship and all the suffering that came with it.

"But I'm not American," I said.

"Canada does it too," he said. "It's all *el Norte.*"

He continued on in silence and I followed behind him, frowning with the effort of figuring out what he meant. "I just don't get it," I said.

I remember how it felt to be so ignorant and confused. It hurt. I was trying so hard. So is she. I need to find my patience again, teach her.

CHAPTER THIRTEEN

My internal alarm wakes me just as the high little windows are lightening to grey. Bara is a mound of blankets, rising and falling with the breathing of deep sleep. I manage to sit up, gather the pile of discarded clothes on the foot of my bed and make my way to the bathroom without waking her or anyone else.

I let myself into the jungle of Judith's basement, pull the cord for the light closest to the door. Damn, I need a bathroom again. If I just needed to pee, the drain behind the furnace would do, but it's more than that.

The night I was down here while Judith moved around upstairs, I heard a toilet flush on the main floor. Can I get up there, use it and come back without leaving any sign? Have to.

The path to the furnace has a branch that leads to a bare-bones set of wooden stairs. At least there's a railing. I pull myself up to the door at the top, crack it carefully open an inch, listen to the house. Completely still.

The door leads into the kitchen, a plain, nineteen forties affair, cupboards painted white, walls a dark, gold yellow. Absolutely clean and tidy. So, she doesn't keep people away because the place is a mess. This is more like her office, the orderliness of papers and thought that help make her a good lawyer. And she is a good lawyer, a famous one, in my circles anyway. In other circles, infamous. Poverty law takes sides.

What was obviously once a pantry has been converted into a small laundry, apartment-sized washer and dryer, a few shelves holding soap and a laundry basket. A door framed in dark wood leads into the dining room. Another gives onto a short hallway leading to the front door, where a pair of wooden arches face each other from either side. Above the basement stairs, another flight rises to the second floor, but there, to the left of the door from the kitchen to the hallway, is exactly what I was hoping to find: a bathroom.

It's tiny, just a toilet and sink, probably added by taking a chunk out of the living room. It's almost empty, soap in a little ceramic dish, a hand towel on a rack by the sink, a glass shelf holding a precise row of things — brush, nail clippers, file, bottle of hand lotion, a couple of lipsticks.

There's a mirror over the sink. I look away. In that store window downtown, I saw the women of San Marcos: Rosa, Mía, Adela, Marta, Luisa, Carmella, Julia. The ones who died that day, the ones who went into hiding, the ones left behind to grieve. I've seen them in windows and mirrors before, brilliant cloth headdresses identifying them not only as *Quiché* but from their village. They were so clear and vivid, I wondered if they were really there, spirits, looking back at me.

I hold my breath hard and look up, but nothing happens. Just my own wrinkly, weather-beaten, old face. There's dirt in the droopy creases of my neck. How did I get this ugly? I was pretty once.

I use the toilet. There are only three pieces of toilet paper left. I daren't leave it empty. Judith's definitely the sort of person who would notice. I wipe myself with the hem of my skirt. Lucky it's brown. I wash my hands and dry them on the other side of my skirt, then walk out holding it carefully, like a nineteenth-century woman in a floor-length dress, lest it touch the fern-patterned wallpaper in the hall.

There is a small, elegant half-table just inside the front door, under a big, oval mirror. Beside it, a boot tray holds snow and rain boots, lined up equidistant from the back rim of the tray. The table holds a pottery dish with a small arrangement of beach objects: a sand dollar, a sea urchin, a starfish. Among them, several keys labelled with cardboard disks. Two read "Front Door," one says "Garage" and another, like the one in my pocket, is labelled "Basement."

From the hall table, I can look through the wooden archway into the dining room. It has two large windows and the upper part of the walls is painted a cream colour, but the room still has a gloomy feel because of its dark wood wainscotting. A plate rail high on the wall holds old-fashioned serving plates and there are more in a nineteen forties–era china cabinet. I walk over, skirting the dining table and chairs to peer through the wavy glass. There is a full set of china dishes in there, white with a small rosebud design. I think Judith has mentioned these before. Her grandmother's? A conversation about how our generation prefers sturdy mugs and pasta bowls, leaving these lovely old things to collect dust? One shelf holds a collection of fine cups and saucers, the kind our grandmothers would never be without. In fact, do I remember there is a cup in here that survived the Explosion? On the opposite wall, a sideboard holds the silver, tarnished serving dishes, coffee set and the kind of wooden box that will hold silver cutlery.

Across the hall from the dining room, a matching wooden arch opens into the living room, smaller than the dining room, probably because the downstairs bathroom was made from one of its corners. The wallpaper is light green with a small floral print. There is a comfortable-looking chesterfield, a reading chair with a floor lamp behind it, a rocking chair, a few small tables and a television in its own wooden cabinet, old enough to have a dial for the channels.

At the bottom of the stairs to the second storey, I tell myself to leave — now — but curiosity takes over my feet. I remember that this is one of the largest houses the Relief Commission built. The second level has a generous landing, a bathroom with a big, old-fashioned clawfoot tub, four bedroom doors and a set of stairs leading up to yet another level. I don't climb these but crane my neck enough to see that it's not an unfinished attic, but a room, with painted plaster walls and a window with a set of curtains. I can't see any furniture, at least from here.

There is a dresser on the landing, just outside the bathroom, with a lace runner, a neat row of toiletries and a mirror. Odd place to put it. Even odder, three of the bedrooms are almost empty. Their doors are wide open, so I can see that each has a bedstead, one assembled, its mattress bare, the other two taken apart, nothing but head and foot boards leaning against the walls. Each room has a bedside table and dresser, clearly just parked there. There are darkened squares on the walls with tiny nail holes but no pictures. Come to think of it, there are no pictures anywhere in the house.

I am brushed by an old anger. I took in so many homeless people over the years, a few nights here and there while we arranged a bed in a shelter, a few weeks, a few months in some cases. There were nights I housed whole families and slept on the floor. Judith had all this space, and she would never share it. Lame excuses, though I knew it was something deeper. I never even tried to pry. None of us did. At least, before today.

I must leave, but the last doorway beckons even more strongly just because it is closed. I expect it to be Judith's bedroom, as orderly and monastic as the rest of the house, but what I find makes me take in a sharp breath. The room is as chaotic as the basement, only instead of discarded household goods, this is a landscape of piled papers. They surround a computer on a big wooden desk, many bent back on their staples and festooned with sticky notes. They rest in piles on the shelves lining the walls, interspersed with the books. Stacks cover the floor except for a narrow trail from the door to the desk, just like the trails in the basement. Open books sprawl in a semi-circle around the computer chair, several layers thick, hung with torn paper markers. A thick tome, opened roughly to the middle, hangs over the edge of the desk, threatening to fall and start a paper landslide below. Even the wall is tiled with sticky notes, stuck all higglety-pigglety, circling and overlapping, each bearing a note in Judith's precise hand.

What is this? Surely her legal research is in her office at Legal Aid. I'm so much wider than Judith, I might trigger a collapse if I step in, so I hold the doorframe and lean around it, trying to see the titles on the shelves beside the door: *Common Land and Enclosure in England, A Social History of the English Countryside.*

I lose my balance and step into the room. Well, now that I'm here, I scan some titles on another shelf: *Stolen Continents. Drumbeat: Anger and Renewal in Indian Country.*

The light is oddly filtered. I turn. Sunlight coming through the window shines through a free-standing bookcase with a space behind it. I take another two steps, as carefully as I can, along the path to the desk. Now I can see another trail branching off, leading around the shelves to a small, single bed under the window. This one has a mattress and is neatly made up. A bedside table holds a lamp and three books with markers partway through. With all the space there is in the house, it seems Judith chooses to sleep in this cramped corner, hidden among her papers and books.

My skirt brushes a stack of papers. It jiggles. I hold my breath. The pile doesn't fall, but I've left a distinct brown streak across the page on top. Oh dear. I pick it up. "Levellers, Ranters and Diggers." I read the first few lines beneath the title, but the print is tiny and by now my head spins with hunger. I put it under the next one in the pile. I have the feeling that, even in all this chaos, Judith will notice.

I lumber back down the stairs. There's something intense about that room, like it's alive. As intense as, well, Judith.

As I pass the little bathroom in the front hall, I glance in, catch my reflection. My hair. What a mess. Something a mouse could nest in, a whole family of mice. How long has it been since I brushed it, anyway? Can't remember. Before I think, I'm standing at the vanity. I pull mismatched hairpins out of the tangle, yank out a rotten old elastic, and grab Judith's brush. It does feel good, and then I panic. Judith's brush is full of long, greasy, grey hairs.

I pull my mop back into the elastic and pin it up fast as I can, rake my fingers through the brush. Where to put the hairs? There's a little garbage pail under the sink, but it's perfectly empty and clean. I try to stuff them into my pocket, but they keep popping back out, caught on the rough skin of my fingers, dropping all over the white-tiled floor.

When I think I've captured them all, I put the brush back carefully, exactly where it was. I'm breathing hard by now. On the way back through the kitchen, I feel like I'm shedding dirt and hairs. I look behind me, but with my glasses so scratched and dirty, I don't know how I'd see bits of me on the floors anyway. I hold hard to the railing, lumber back down the basement stairs.

The Bible. I came here to look for Nicolás's Bible, but I'm rattled, can't think clearly. I'm also hungry. Maybe I'll go to the drop-in for a sandwich and then come back.

All the way down Gottingen, Brunswick, I worry about the brush. So many hairs, so clearly not Judith's shiny brown ponytail. Wonder if she dyes it? She's a decade younger than I am, but that still puts her into her fifties, old enough to be turning at least a little bit grey.

I'm sure I left a trail everywhere I went. When I go back, dare I go upstairs and check again? Or will I leave more evidence than I remove? Funny, if I'd been this dirty in my old life, it would have driven me crazy until I could get to a shower. Now, I barely notice. Except now I'm thinking about the bathtub at Fresh Start.

CHAPTER FOURTEEN

——————

At St. Marks, breakfast is over, but there's a nice pile of fresh sandwiches wrapped in plastic film. I take one and pour myself a cup of coffee. Three old guys sit a couple of tables over, two talking, one asleep with his head on the table, stringy, white hair fanned out around his shiny, bald head.

Bara appears in the doorway. "Lucy! Where did you go? Are you okay?" She is wearing a red-and-white, woolly toque with a big pompom on top and "CANADA" knitted around it. She sees me looking, pulls it off to show me, her hair flying around with static electricity. "I found it in the clothing depot."

I spare her a lecture about identifying with humanity, life and the land rather than nation-states. "Looks warm."

"It is." She holds it out. "Would you like it?"

"I've got my own." I hope it's still in my jacket pocket, where I put it when I arrived in Judith's basement. It is. Mitts too. I offer them. "Do you need these?"

"Got my own." Bara pulls a pair out of her pocket. That's good. Mine are filthy with a hole in the tip of the right hand. She sets her toque and mitts down on the table, slings her jacket around the back of a chair and goes for a sandwich and coffee for herself.

I watch her consume the sandwich in seconds. "Shouldn't you be going to school?"

She shrugs. "I've missed most of fall term now. I could start again in January. Besides, I have to take care of you."

I harrumph.

"You're, like, going to argue that you don't need someone to keep you out of trouble?"

I check my coffee. Gone cold. Take a sip anyway.

"Lucy? When you went to Guatemala, is that where you got so … political?"

"There's no such thing as not being political. Everything we do is political."

There is a short silence, then: "Should have known you'd say something I don't understand."

I cringe, remembering my resolution to recover my patience for teaching. "Sorry."

She looks up, surprised.

"Yes, Guatemala is where I came to see that everything we do, no matter how small, changes the world for better or worse. We have that power, whether we want it or not, especially us in the rich countries. And having, using power, is what political means."

"Oh. Are you a communist?"

I smile at her. "People have said so."

"But, do you say so?"

"I prefer the word socialist, but both are critical of capitalism."

"Can you, like, explain capitalism to me?"

"It's a long story."

"And we're in a hurry to go where?"

I sigh. "I'll try."

"Go straight for the heart of it."

"Okay, the heart. That would be private property."

"Like my knapsack, clothes?"

"No, that's personal property, just the things you need to live. Private property means land or money — things you could use to make or grow or extract other things. Ever heard of 'the means of production'?"

"Karl Marx. We studied him in my economics course in high school. The teacher thought he was, like, pretty bad."

I laugh. "I'm sure he did. Marx was the first to … I was going to say, 'see all this,' but lots of people saw it. He was just the first to write it in a book with his name on it. Anyway, the point is, in capitalism, the means of production — also called wealth, also called capital — can be owned by private individuals who can hire others to do the work, but they keep the profit."

"So, like, that saying, 'the rich get richer and the poor get poorer,' that's about capitalism?"

"Well, the point's for the rich to get richer all right. Money makes money. The poor getting poorer is more like a side effect."

"In economics class, the idea was if the rich get richer, so will everyone else."

"You really listened in that class, didn't you?"

She shrugs. "It was interesting."

"That's what a capitalist would say. A socialist would say when the rich get richer, it's because they've taken what should belong to all of us."

She thinks a while, the crease still there between her eyes. When she gets older, it will be permanent.

"So how did you get from saving souls to being a com — socialist?"

"That's a long story but, short version, a friend. A very dear friend. He even thought Jesus was a socialist. You know 'For unto every one that hath shall be given, but from him that hath not shall be taken away even that which he hath'?"

"Another way of saying the rich get richer and the poor get poorer?"

"Exactly. Jesus was born in the second or third generation after the Romans brought the idea of private property to Palestine, and my friend thought he saw, even then, how the rich were getting richer and the poor, poorer. And many at the time would have seen that as sinful. Do you know about the Year of Jubilee?"

She shakes her head.

"It's in Leviticus. 'The land cannot be sold outright because the land is mine.' Crops could be sold, but not land. If a family was so poor they had to sell their land, the new owner could only have it until the Year of Jubilee, every forty-ninth year, when all land reverted to the original family that farmed it. It was a system that made it hard for the rich to get richer and, therefore, the poor, poorer."

"Your friend, was he a missionary too?"

"No. He's Guatemalan. I guess you could say he is one of the people whose souls I was supposed to save."

"So did you give up on saving souls?"

"After a while, I didn't know what that meant any longer. I had changed so much I didn't even recognize myself, and there was no way back home."

"I know exactly what you mean."

"You come from the same kind of home I did. So after that ... no, not after that. It had happened long before I even came home. I had ... I guess you'd call it a breakdown. I was depressed for a long time. Only came out of it after I moved here and got involved in community organizing."

"And then you broke down again."

"Yeah. Only, maybe, worse. More out of control."

"So what happened? You had all these great things going and then ended up on probation."

"I found myself in a situation that looked a lot like the other one ... though, not on the outside.... It's hard to explain."

I am turning my empty coffee cup around and around, my sadness closing in on me again.

"John said you're supposed to be seeing a psychiatrist."

"When you were listening through the door."

"Sorry about that. But you are, aren't you? Like, supposed to be seeing a psychiatrist?"

"He's just a drug pusher. Not to mention a voyeur. 'Tell me all about it. You can't heal unless you talk.'"

"And isn't that, like, true?"

"Well." I pause. "Maybe. But not for *his* entertainment."

"You could tell me."

I look at her, startled.

She sighs. "Okay, okay. I know. 'It's a long story and not your business.'"

God, she does sound just like me.

"But, you have to see him to stay out of jail, right?"

"Yes."

"So when's your next appointment? I'm going to make sure you get there."

"Now Bara, you can't be following me everywhere, all the time."

"I promised John I'd keep you out of trouble."

"I'll tell John to get you back in school."

"I'm learning a lot more from you than I ever have in school." She gets to her feet, holds her hand out to me. "Come on. Let's go back to Fresh Start. Didn't you say something about wanting a bath?"

I groan but reach up to take the hand she offers. She pulls and pushes me to my feet, then clamps my arm under hers as we begin our slow journey up the hill.

Water thundering out of the tap. What a lovely sound. Steam. I peel off my sweater and turtleneck, step out of the baggy, brown tweed skirt. Everything looks ragged and filthy on the white tiles of Fresh Start's bathroom floor. Oh dear. I knew I had started to stink from the little puffs that seeped out from under the layers, but the bathroom fills right up, choking.

When I put my poor, rotten feet into the hot water, they hurt like crazy. I have to hold my breath, trying to stand it. Eventually I get out again, run some cold water. Thank goodness there is a bar to hang on to.

As soon as I lower myself into the water, the clean bubbles are beaten back by a grey, greasy film spreading over the surface.

I lie there for a while like a beached whale, one from very deep in the ocean, pale from lack of sun. There's a big bar of industrial-strength soap. I use lots of it, and it feels good, until my skin starts to peel, ribbons of it coming right off and floating around.

There is a timid knock at the door. "Go away," I tell whoever it is.

Later, another knock. "Go away," I repeat.

A few minutes later, another knock. A firmer one. "Lucy, you okay in there?" Bara.

"I am."

"Okay, but it's been a while and other people want to use the bathroom."

I don't respond.

"If you need help, you call. Okay?"

I ignore her. Her footsteps eventually move away from the door.

I stay longer than I want to, the water getting miserable and cold, just because I dread struggling to my feet. Finally, there is no choice. I use the bar to heave myself up, the side of the tub to balance while I dry myself. Then, I'm faced with a raw, naked, hurting body, a pile of filthy clothes topped with an equally filthy towel and a bathtub that looks like someone put it under a car to drain the oil. I scrub the tub as best I can, given the difficulty of bending over that far, with scouring powder I find under the sink. Smear it around, more like.

Fortunately, I thought to bring my nightgown with me — not clean, but passable. There's a basket for dirty towels. I gather up my clothes and clutch them to my chest as I walk out.

Bara glances up from the paperback novel she's reading. "Feel good?"

I'm too tired to answer. I toss the dirty clothes under the cot and sit down.

"Oh Lucy."

"What?"

"Your feet. What's wrong with them? They look sore."

I look down. They do look pretty bad. "Althea wants me to go to the Community Clinic."

"They have a clinic in a van that comes here once a month."

"How do you know that?"

"People talk. I'll find out when it comes. Got to get you something for that."

CHAPTER FIFTEEN

My inner alarm clock wakes me early. I haven't encountered the day staff at Fresh Start yet, but I avoid them on principle. Day staff in shelters do more than just keep an eye on things. They ask questions, push programs, check up on appointments. Not to mention I'd like to shake Bara and head for Judith's basement to find Nicolás's Bible. And some clean clothes. The ones in my suitcase are for the warm end of fall. I find a clean turtleneck, but have to pull the brown sweater and skirt from under the bed.

Damn. The cot beside me creaks as Bara sits up, rubbing sleep from her eyes.

After breakfast at St. Marks, I suggest the library. The *North Branch* Library. Bara doesn't object. There, the sun pours in through the big glass windows onto the warm, scarred wood of the shelves and tables. It's blessedly warm, quiet and almost empty, just us and a young woman hunched over a large book spread open on a table, toddler asleep in a stroller beside her.

The catalogue cabinet takes up most of a wall, rows of little wooden drawers hiding ranks of file cards. "Find me something to read, Lucy," Bara whispers. "Something political."

"What about poverty in Nova Scotia? Homelessness?"

"Yeah. Okay."

The catalogue drawers give off a comforting smell of varnish and old paper when I slide them out. I try "homelessness" and "poverty." Bara leans on the cabinet, watching me. Then an inspiration, a book I've used in classes. A little out of date in its specifics, maybe, but it explains the process of political analysis, step by step, and has a chapter on housing. I scrawl the call number on a paper square and hand it to Bara. She goes to find it.

I think of Judith's study, brown streak on a white page. No entries for Levellers, Ranters or Diggers. I go to the desk and register for the public computer, get one right away. Levellers, Ranters, Diggers. Resistance movement. 1600s. Also, Fifth Monarchists, Baptists, Quakers, Muggletonians, Seekers, Anabaptists, Familists. Good at names, these guys. What were they resisting? The "extinguishment of the rights of common." Of course, the beginnings of private property.

I have a sudden, vivid image of Judith the first time I saw her, younger, even thinner than she is now, sitting on the end of one of the benches near the law school, slightly hunched over, face as pale as typing paper.

I was working at Walford College, developing the community education program. It was a nice day and I had walked across to the benches with my lunch. "Like to share my sandwich?" I held half of it out to her.

"Ooooh, no," she said, turning away so she didn't even have to look at it. "I mean, thanks, but ..."

"Are you okay?" I asked her.

"Not really." She did look wretched.

That's honest, I thought, and gave her my full attention.

"I'm a law student," she said and glanced at me.

I hadn't taken her for a student, but no surprise. Lots of people study law after another degree and some life experience.

"You're going to think I'm crazy."

Funny she said that. Who's crazy now?

"Probably not," I said.

She studied me for another moment and, for some reason, decided to confide in me. At the time, I had no idea how rare that was. I've never asked why she did it, although once, much later, she did mention how desperately isolated she felt in law school. Until her last year, when she did her placement at Legal Aid. "One of this year's courses is property law. The professor keeps going on about private property, how wonderful it is, how much prosperity it has brought us, how it has allowed us to develop Western civilization beyond any other human culture that's ever existed …" She paused, looking to see if I did think she was crazy. I nodded to show I certainly did not, so she went on. "And I keep thinking, *this is where we went wrong.* Today I got so tied in knots about it, I got sick, had to run to the bathroom." She gave me a bleak look.

"I think I'd do exactly the same thing."

"Really?" She studied me with new eyes.

By now, Bara is slouched in a reading chair with *Getting Started on Social Analysis in Canada.* I move to the table where the day's papers are spread out and begin to flip through them, searching for any information I can find on the Guatemalan Peace Accords.

Once, Nicolás and I came upon a ruined police station in a village destroyed by the paramilitaries, concrete walls shattered, despite being thick enough to hide screams. Nicolás showed me the torture room, the wires hanging from the walls. He started to tell me, but I couldn't listen. As we walked away, he said, "Jesus is crucified every day."

I glance at the librarians' desk. No one's there. I help myself to a whole handful of little paper squares from the wooden box on top of the catalogue and one of the stubby yellow pencils. I take myself to the farthest table and sit down with my back to the room.

It's been ages since I've tried to write. My rough old hand doesn't work right. I cross out my first scribbles and begin again, printing carefully, like a child. "Who dies for our sins?"

Bara comes over to my table, book in hand, her stopping point marked by a scrap torn from the edge of one of the newspapers.

The light has changed and there are some school children in the library, their teacher and a librarian talking to them in low voices. She looks at the pile of little squares on the table in front of me, reaches to pick one up. I snatch it out of her hand, but she is already reaching for another one, and then another. "Is this the sermon for Reverend Peter?"

"Elementary, my dear Watson."

"I think you need a proper pad of paper."

I rise and gather my bits of paper, stuffing them into my skirt pocket, the one that does not hold Judith's key.

"You hungry?" Bara asks me.

"There's picnic tables out back. Feel like checking the bucket at Susan's and meeting me there?"

"You should go and see John, get some more of your social assistance money."

"Didn't Horizons help you apply for assistance?"

"I wasn't there long enough."

"You need to see Althea. But first, lunch."

"Okay." She begins to slide her book into her knapsack.

"Wait. You have to check that out."

"Oh yeah. But, I don't have a card here."

"I do, but it's back at Fresh Start in my suitcase and we can't get you one without proof of where you live."

She leaves the book on the table. "See you out back at the picnic tables," she says over her shoulder.

I wait for a few minutes, then leave the library. The wind is bitter with a skiff of snow skittering along the sidewalk. I bend into it and hold my jacket tight under my chin.

There are several boxes marked "Lucy — Books." I open the one on top, a box that once held canned peas, and squint at the books neatly arranged inside, barely able to see them in the dim light.

The ones on top are lying flat. *The Pedagogy of the Oppressed, Educating for a Change, A Popular Education Handbook, Pragmatics of Community Organization,* my copy of *Getting Started on Social Analysis in Canada.* I pick that up and set it aside. Under them, the box is packed from side to side with the spines visible. More popular education, all my anti-racism books. Fortunately, I know most of them by shape and colour. It strikes me that these were all on the bottom shelf. Trust Judith to keep them in order.

I need to find the top shelf. I repack "Canned Peas," then realize I should have lifted it down when it was half empty. Beside it sits "Lucy — Bedding." That I can probably handle. I set it on the floor so I can slide "Canned Peas" sideways. I open the next box down. It once held tomato sauce.

Not the top shelf, but the title that meets my eye, printed in white letters on a stubby, battered paperback, is *The Wretched of the Earth.* I pick it up. It holds together. Amazing. I read this book half to death.

I turn it over. *"Written in anger, this book by a distinguished Negro psychiatrist ... "*

"Negro?" I flip to the copyright page. 1963. I'd forgotten that Frantz Fanon was a psychiatrist. I think I need to reread this.

There is a gentle knocking sound, close by. I yank the string dangling from the light. I'm standing in the dark, holding my breath, when the knocking comes again, a bit louder, definitely coming from the door right beside me. Damn. Judith. She's home for some reason, saw the light in the basement windows. My heart starts pounding.

"Lucy?"

I gasp in a breath. Not Judith.

The door opens a few inches. Why didn't I lock it? A slight figure is outlined against the sky, wearing a toque with a big pompom. "Lucy? Are you here?"

My heart pounds out a leftover beat or two as I reach up and click the light back on. "You nearly scared me to death. What the hell are you doing here?"

"You're, like, not that hard to follow."

"Go away." I try to push the door closed.

She leans her shoulder against it. "I've been waiting out here for you for ages. I'm frozen."

"You can't come in."

She is small and slight, but has no trouble pushing the door open despite my efforts. "Just a minute. To warm up." She steps inside. "I'm sorry I scared you."

Where did I drop my coat? On the big stuffed chair beside my boxes.

Bara starts to follow me.

"No. Stay right there. We're leaving."

I stuff Frantz Fanon into my skirt pocket. Several little squares of paper pop out, drifting to the floor in front the chair.

Bara is there, stooping to pick them up. She squints at one. "'That's what we're taught,'" she reads. "'He died for our sins. Once.'"

"Give those back."

I stuff them back into my pocket and start to struggle into my jacket.

She is looking all around her with big eyes under her overgrown bangs and that ridiculous "CANADA" toque. "Look at all this stuff."

"Come on. We're leaving."

"What is this place?"

"Not your business."

"And why is your name on these boxes?"

"Bara. We are leaving. Now."

"Come on Lucy. You can't leave me in, like, suspense."

"I can, and I will. And if you say 'like' one more time, I'm going to put a sock in your mouth."

She laughs. "You sound like my mother. Not the sock part."

"Then she can't be all bad."

"She's not." There's a heavy silence, then a sniff. Damn. I've made her cry.

Bara flops into the big chair. A cloud of dust rises into the dim light. She puts her face into her hands.

I know from my search for warm clothes a couple of weeks ago that "Lucy — Nightgowns, etc." includes a pile of clean cloth handkerchiefs. And it's on top. I open it, dig by feel. Neat, carefully folded little squares. You can tell I didn't pack this stuff.

"Here." I hand her one.

She takes it and gives it a surprised look before unfolding it and wiping her eyes, blowing her nose. "Cloth hankies? That's old school."

I sigh. "I'm nothing if not old school."

She tucks the crumpled handkerchief into her pocket. "So, Lucy. Really. Whose house is this?"

"If you leave right now, I'll tell you."

"Okay." I hand her *Getting Started on Social Analysis in Canada*. "Can we go to the drop-in? I'm hungry."

CHAPTER SIXTEEN

We've both wolfed down our sandwiches and now Bara is picking up each crumb from her square of plastic wrap with the tip of her finger and eating it.

"The house belongs to my friend Judith."

"The lawyer?"

"How do you know that?"

"Sorry."

Right. My conversation with John.

"Other people around here talk about her too. So how come she has your stuff? That is, like, your stuff, isn't it?"

"When I was in jail …"

"You've never told me what you were doing there either."

"Having trouble keeping my conditions. You know all about that."

"But I don't know why you're on probation in the first place except John said something about Dell. Who's Dell?"

"Never mind about Dell. You asked about the boxes in Judith's basement." I explain about the rent, the landlord, Judith and Althea storing my things.

"Can you go there any time you want?"

"No."

"But you and her are friends, right?"

"You and she, and it's not that simple."

"But she gave you the key."

"Just to pick up a few things. She doesn't like people in her house."

"Sounds like she has something to hide."

"Judith? Goodness no. It's just … she's private."

Bara is reaching over eating the crumbs from my square of plastic wrap now. "Whatever."

A block or so from St. Marks, there is a newspaper box on the corner. I bend to read the headline. Federal budget. "Oh for God's sake," I say as I straighten up again. "Time for us to 'tighten our belts' again so they can cut rich people's taxes."

"Lucy?" Bara looks worried.

A man passes by, looks at me and gives us a wide margin.

"Cut taxes. That's all that's important, right?" I shout after him. "Public debt goes up. Have to cut services!"

Bara jerks my arm. "Lucy. Stop."

I am about to pull away when another voice says, "Lucy?"

We both turn. Oh my God, Judith.

She looks past me to where the man has disappeared. "Who are you talking to? Lucy? Are you all right?"

Now she is looking at me. I feel my face go hot, divert her by introducing Bara.

It doesn't work for long. "I'm glad I ran into you, Lucy. We need to talk."

"Sure, Judith. At the moment, Bara and I — "

Bara slides her arm out from under mine. "That's okay, Lucy. You go and see Judith now. There's something I need to do anyway. See you later." She doesn't pause for me to object. Just disappears into the flow of people passing on the sidewalk, her bouncing red pompom the last thing I see. Damn.

We run the gauntlet from the front door of Legal Aid to Judith's office.

"Judith, here's the file on the Parker case."

"Judith, here are your messages. This fellow's been calling over and over."

"Judith? Do you have time for a meeting this afternoon?" Judith. Judith. Judith. I follow in her wake. No one looks twice at me. It's not unusual for Judith to have a street person shadow.

As we go down the hall, a tall, thin man comes through an office door, bent over the papers in his hand, so intent he nearly bumps into us. Bob Cumberland, director of Legal Aid. "Oh, hello Judith," he says as his eyes focus on us, pushing big, out-of-date, dark-framed glasses further up his long nose. He stares at me, knowing he knows me.

"You remember Lucy Chambers," Judith prompts him.

Surprise crosses his long face, quickly suppressed. "Lucy. Yes. Hello." I can feel him staring after us as we continue down the hall.

As Judith drops her briefcase, it thumps the floor the way it does in her front hallway. Her office is as bare as her kitchen, but I don't know any of that, do I?

Judith perches on her chair like a bird. My sore knees drop me hard into mine. She takes her time, looking into my eyes for real information on how I am, not the swift down-and-up survey of my street-person fashion statement the way most people do. I force myself to look back. Her eyes are dark brown, large and clear.

"Lucy, dear, how are you?"

"Fine, Judith. I'm fine."

"Your application for the North End Housing Co-op is in the works. Sorry it's taking so long. They have a waiting list."

"Thanks. Yeah. That's good."

"In the meantime, is Fresh Start working out better than Magdalen?"

I nod.

"I gather from John that your friend Bara is staying there with you."

"She is."

"Lucy, you know there's a charge from the incident with Sister Marie, and it's a problem because it looks so much like what happened with Dell."

I nod again.

"But it's going to be a while before it comes before a judge. You did so well during your thirty days in Burnside. The librarian wrote a letter for your file about your literacy tutoring."

She pauses. That concerned look. It makes me want to squirm. Or cry.

"Lucy, I just want you to get through your probation, work with your psychiatrist, earn your freedom from all this, start to rebuild your life."

I hold myself in. There is so much caring in her voice, her eyes.

"You've got people on your side. We care about you."

My teeth are clenched so hard my jaw starts to hurt.

"Would it help to come here and see me from time to time?" Her eyes drop to her briefcase. Her daybook's in there. I used to carry a daybook, when every day had meetings and appointments. I know how full hers is. This is a generous offer. As generous as the key. Which she hasn't asked about.

I take a deep breath. "Sure, Judith."

I'm afraid she's going to push for a date and time, but I guess she knows my life doesn't work that way anymore. It doesn't for lots of her clients. "Just a brief check in, Lucy, so I know you're all right."

I let the breath out again. "Okay."

Bara is waiting just inside the door of Legal Aid, her knapsack at her feet, hanging open. She reaches into it and grins as she holds out a crisp, new pad of lined paper. "I got a couple of pens too."

"Good ones?"

"What do you mean good ones?"

"I mean pens that flow, not those scratchy ballpoint things." Is she too young to know what a fountain pen is?

"Oh. I don't know. You'll have to try them and see. Library?"

The library is quite crowded and noisy, for a library anyway. "Where did you get these?" I ask as Bara sets the pad and pens on the table in front of me.

"Convenience store."

Not sure I believe her. Both pad and pens are pretty good quality for a convenience store, but I don't ask, and she settles into one of the soft chairs, pulls my copy of *Getting Started on Social Analysis in Canada* out of her knapsack and starts reading. Maybe I'll just read Frantz Fanon for a while. But when I pull it from my pocket, a few little squares of paper drift to the floor at my feet. I push my chair out, but I'm too stiff to pick them up.

Bara notices and comes over. She bends to gather them, places them on the table in front of me. I quickly tuck them back into my pocket and check to see if the librarian is looking. As they cut up more little squares of used-on-one-side paper, they must have wondered where these ones went, since no one noticed a crowd of people all writing down Dewey decimals.

"I can't focus here," I complain to Bara in a whisper. "Too many people."

"But you already wrote the first part, didn't you? On those little squares. All you need to do is copy them onto the pad to get started."

I shoot a quick glance toward the librarian again.

Bara follows my eyes. "Do you really think they'll begrudge you some little squares of paper?"

I use the table to push myself to my feet.

"Now where are you going?"

"To a chair to read." Can you call it snapping if it's in a whisper?

The weak, early winter light comes through the window and warms me. It feels good.

"In the period of colonization when it is not contested by armed resistance ... the defensive attitudes of the natives give way and they find themselves crowding the mental hospitals. There is thus, during this calm period of successful colonization, a regular and important mental pathology which is the direct product of oppression."

A "calm period of successful colonization." That would pretty much describe Canada.

I drift away, don't wake up until Bara is shaking my shoulder because it's time to go to St. Marks for supper and then back to Fresh Start. The clinic van comes this evening.

CHAPTER SEVENTEEN

It's still dark as I quietly slip out. But then, the sun is rising later and later these days. And the sky is dark with clouds. As I walk, sleety rain starts to spit at me. The nurse gave me cream for my feet last night and they feel better already.

Judith's kitchen and hall lights are on. I back into a neighbour's overgrown bushes up the street and wait.

My eye falls onto the small garage beside the house. A small garage for a small car. Judith has an old, blue Morris Minor, although she hardly ever uses it. In fact, does she still have it? Or maybe the garage is as full of stuff as the basement, and the car's been buried.

I've clutched my jacket close around my neck and pulled my hat low on my forehead, but I'm shivering. Glad I'm not trying to sleep outside these days.

The kitchen light goes out. A few minutes later, the front door opens and Judith steps out. She turns to lock the door behind her before walking down the front walk to the sidewalk. In the lightening morning I can see her going away from me down the street, ponytail swinging from side to side in time with her brisk steps, lugging that huge briefcase in one hand and holding an open umbrella in the other.

The point is to find the Bible and get out again quickly, since Bara knows where to look now. The top "Lucy — Books" box, formerly "Canned Peas," now shifted to one side, held the bottom shelf of my bookcase, so it stands to reason that the top shelf might be in the box on the bottom, labelled "Canned Corn." They're heavy. I wrap my arms around "Tomato Sauce," the one Frantz Fanon came out of, and slide it to the edge but, when I try to lift it off, it crashes to the floor and splits along one edge. As the dust settles, I see that the corners of the books are poking out.

"Lucy?" The door hinges creak. Didn't I lock it behind me? Damn. "You okay?"

"I'm just leaving."

"Okay." Bara closes the door behind her and stands there looking at me and the box of books at my feet. "What are you trying to do?"

"Not your business."

"But if I help, we can leave sooner."

Why don't I want to tell her? "I need my Bible to be able to write the sermon. I think it's in that bottom box." I point.

"There's no Bible in the library? Or at St. Marks?"

I think about that for a split second. "Mine has all kinds of notes in the margins."

Bara gives me a skeptical look but easily lifts down two more boxes.

She steps aside, and I open "Creamed Corn." Bingo. Between the white-covered Bible I grew up with and my well-read copy of *The Theology of Liberation*, the dear, familiar, brown leather cover of Nicolás's Bible. Tears crowd in at the corners of my eyes, wanting to spill. I take in a breath and clench my teeth. I know I can't touch that soft, worn binding without falling apart. I pull out my childhood Bible instead.

"That's fancy," says Bara, nodding at the white leather cover closed by a zipper with a little gold cross on the pull.

Thinking again. "Yeah, too fancy to take out in this." I look up at the little window, high above our heads, where we can hear the tick, tick of sleet hitting the glass.

Bara is scanning the shadowy mounds of abandoned household goods piled around us. She reaches over and clicks on a second overhead light bulb, then walks toward the furnace and pulls the string of a third.

"Stop that. Someone will notice."

"Notice? On this little two-block street?"

"A neighbour. Someone walking by."

"Ah ha." Bara dives in among the boxes, shifting them as she goes. She pulls out an old vacuum cleaner and sets it, precariously, on a metal trunk. "Look." She is pointing at something. I take a couple of steps to see. An old table, not very big. Elegant in its day, with spindly turned legs and a drawer with a fancy brass pull. There are four boxes packed under it and as many on top. Bara lifts one off, sets it on top of another nearby.

"What are you doing?"

She ignores me, peering down into the box she has just moved. "Hey, look at this." She lifts out a cardboard photo sleeve and holds it up. A very young Judith, serious in a green jacket with a school crest on the pocket. Bara lowers it, looks again. "Wow. She was beautiful."

"*Is* beautiful."

She turns it over to examine the back. "It says, 'Havergal College, Grade Thirteen, 1965.' Grade Thirteen?"

"Ontario had an extra year of high school back then."

She turns it face up again, looks at young Judith. "Where is Havergal College?"

"Toronto. Private girl's school."

"I thought she grew up here. Why'd she go to high school in Toronto?"

"I didn't know she did."

She sets the grad photo aside, picks up something underneath. "This has got to be her parents. She looks just like her mother."

"I've never seen a picture of them."

"You didn't know she went to a private school in Toronto and you've never seen a picture of her parents? What kind of friends are you anyway?" Bara leans to hand me the picture, and I move to hold it under one of the bare bulbs.

It's true. Now that Judith is in her fifties, she could be the woman in the picture, except this woman has no warmth. She looks stiff and unhappy, as does the man, who manages to look rumpled even in his good suit. He was a lawyer, but the son and grandson of railway workers. Judith once said her mother always wanted to sell this house and move to the South End, but her father refused.

Oh dear. What am I doing? "Bara." I hold out the photo. "Put this back."

She returns it to the box it came from. While I was lost in the past, she had shifted more boxes. Now she can lift the table out. She carries it, miraculously missing the wobbly piles of things along the way, and sets it in the opening by the furnace. "This is your desk. Perfect spot to write a sermon."

"No. Bara, stop. We're leaving."

"Now we need a lamp."

"No. Bara, please."

But she is already climbing back in among the boxes, shifting them around, opening flaps. One of the boxes tinkles as she moves it. Glass. "You'll break things," I hiss.

She peeks under tucked cardboard flaps. "Ah ha."

She opens it, pulls out an ancient lamp, the gold paint chipping off of its metal stand, a pair of sockets holding old fashioned clear bulbs, a pair of dangling metal pulls with crumbling tassels on the ends. "I guess you won't be needing this." She holds up the ornate stained-glass shade that goes with it, and then sets it back into the box. "That thing's heavy. Now ..." She has turned her attention to the wall, holding the lamp in one hand, its plug in the other. "An outlet."

Even in this light I can see the cord is an old cloth-covered one, badly frayed, with one of those round plastic plugs, the wires inside covered only by a warped cardboard disk. "Don't you dare. You'll electrocute yourself."

"There." She clambers along the wall, stepping on and over obstacles. There is a rattling sound as she pulls out a metal coat rack, apparently on casters, hung with several garment bags. Then she is behind it, making a terrible racket.

"What are you doing? People down on Devonshire will be able to hear that."

She clicks on yet another overhead light and the thing turns out to be an old wringer washing machine. Behind it is, sure enough, an electric outlet.

"Stop. Please. Don't." I'm truly alarmed now, hold my breath as she pushes the ratty old plug into the outlet.

She clicks both of the pulls and doesn't drop to the floor dead. I let my breath out again. One of the bulbs comes on, a faint, flickering light. "Needs new bulbs."

"Bara, put that thing away. I am not going to be sitting down here writing a sermon or anything else."

"Judith is at Legal Aid all day, every day. You said so yourself."

"But there's nothing says she won't come home. She takes sick days like everyone else. In fact, more than most. Think she wears herself out. Speaking of which, let's get these lights turned off." I reach up and pull the cord of the one closest to me.

Bara walks as far from the outlet as the worn lamp cord will allow. Not far. "We need an extension cord."

"No, we don't."

She sets the lamp in the tub of the old washing machine where it beams its weak light upward, casting a distorted shadow of the wringer on the stone wall, and makes her slow and crooked way back to the little table by the furnace. Lifting it, she maneuvers it to a spot next to the washing machine and sets the lamp on top of it, then heads back along the wall. "There's three chairs over here. I saw them earlier."

Picking one up, she holds it over her head as she steps carefully back to the table. It's a spindly wooden thing, decorated with carved flowers and a faded needlepoint seat cover. She sets it down. "There. You are going to sit here and write a sermon."

"What do you think you are doing? I don't even have permission to be here, let alone move things around. You're putting it all back. Now. If Judith came home and saw this — "

"We'll turn the ceiling lights off. The lamp is not bright, and we can maybe use the shade after all. It'll be too faint to notice from outside, even if there was a window facing the front, which there isn't."

I look. She's right. The basement windows face the sides and back of the house except for one, which is blocked off on the outside, likely by the front step.

"I don't have the pad of paper with me, or a pen."

"Yes, you do." Bara picks her way back to her knapsack, sitting on the floor just inside the door, and pulls out the pad, pen clipped to the cardboard backing. She takes it over to the makeshift desk and sets it down.

"Lucy, listen to me." Bara's voice has taken on a sharp tone I've never heard before. "You feel safe here. I can tell. And I can trust you here on your own. Like, what do you do every time you're out of my sight? You head back here. At least it will give you a place to spread out all those bits of paper you've got in your pocket. I'll come back with something to eat midday and see how you're doing."

Bara returns to the box the lamp came out of and digs out the heavy glass lampshade. She turns out all the ceiling lights before she goes, leaving me in the dark except for a tiny pool of coloured light on the table.

I still have my childish, white-covered Bible in my hand. The box containing the rest of my old top bookshelf is on the floor in complete darkness. I kneel and reach inside, find the spine of Nicolás's Bible with my fingers, so soft and worn, so familiar. I rest my hand on it. My eyes fill.

I rock back on my heels, breaking the connection. Bara is coming back. I can't have her find me in fetal position on the basement floor, blubbering. And besides, I am going to Guatemala with Project Witness. I am going to find Nicolás. His beloved ordination Bible will lead me to him. I will put it back into his beautiful, brown hands. I will look once again into his expressive brown eyes. I will … I will work my way out of this damn prison called probation. I will keep myself busy. I will write a sermon for Nicolás. Jesus is crucified every day. He taught me that.

I had dropped my coat across the arms of the old padded chair. I pull a damp mitten out of the pocket, fish out all the little squares of paper and carry them to the pool of light on the tabletop, spread them out. They are crumpled and damp. I begin to lay them out, read what I can, squinting in the dim, multicoloured light.

"*Every day he is tortured for our sins.*"

"*Because he stood up to those who would take …*" Must be "his people's land."

I begin to make a pattern of them, a jigsaw puzzle, but a few minutes later, my mind wanders back to Judith's high school graduation picture. 1965. Wait. She's eleven years younger than I am. In 1965, she would have been twenty-one years old. Kind of late to graduate from high school if you're smart and the daughter of a lawyer. And then she didn't move back to Halifax until she turned thirty, 1974, when her mother died and left her the house, the year she started her law degree, the year I met her. All those years in Toronto. Years I know nothing about.

CHAPTER EIGHTEEN

I have begun copying sentences from the scraps to the pad when I hear Bara's footsteps in the cellarway. I get to my feet, switch on one of the overhead lights and hobble to the door. Someone coughs. Male. Damn. Plumber? Furnace repair guy? I look around for a place to hide, though moving that quickly and quietly is hopeless.

"Lucy?" Bara after all. When my heart slows enough to walk to the door, I let her in. A tall, skinny figure stoops through the door behind her. Oh dear God. Robin.

He steps forward. "Hi, Lucy."

Bara giggles. "Ever since that day in that store downtown, he calls you the Prophet."

"The Prophet?" I turn to Robin.

"You were great, speaking truth to power."

"More like foolishness to fools."

Bara moves past me to the upholstered chair and pulls the bedside table out from beside its arm. She produces three battered melamine cups from her knapsack and lays them out. "Borrowed from St. Marks."

"Borrowed?"

"I'll take them back when I find some for us." She also has three of the wrapped sandwiches from the drop-in and, finally, a shiny new thermos, which she holds up. "Coffee."

"Also borrowed from St. Marks?"

She grins and unscrews the cap. Fragrant steam rises and she fills the three cups. Robin, meanwhile, has fetched the chair from my "desk" and dropped the crib mattress onto the floor. "Hey Lucy," he says. "Want to see Bara blush?"

Bara stops pouring and glowers at him.

"Lesbian," he says, and Bara does blush.

She says, "Shut up!" just as I snap out his name.

We sit, me in my reading chair, Robin on the wooden chair, Bara cross-legged on the crib mattress.

"So, Lucy," Robin says, "all that cool stuff about consumption and poverty, you should write something for our newsletter."

"What newsletter?"

"We've started a newsletter for homeless people, every second week. Homeless people sell it on the street and keep half of what they make."

"Who's *we*?"

"A group of us that used to work on the university student newspaper. We use their press between issues."

"Are you a student?"

"No."

"You've got a degree, then?"

"A BA, for all the good it does me. Hey Lucy, what did the arts grad say to the tech grad?"

"No idea."

"'Do you want fries with that?'" He laughs.

"Oh for God's sake, Robin."

"My parents are desperate for me to go back to school, but that's their bourgeois values."

"Bourgeois values. Haven't heard that since the New Left used to spend more time calling each other bourgeois than working for actual change."

"You were part of the New Left?"

"No. Or let's say, on the edges. Not much room for women there, except to make sandwiches."

"Well, I don't believe in degrees or establishment shit like that."

"He lives in his parents' basement," Bara says, as if that explains something.

Robin looks hurt. "Well I *could* move out. I know how to survive on the street."

"Then you know enough not to choose it if you have a choice. Get as much education as you can. Then you can choose to be establishment or anti-establishment or just establishment enough to have shelter and food."

Robin looks at me, surprise on his face. "You sound just like my parents."

"People of good sense, obviously."

He finishes the last bites of his sandwich, wipes his hands on the thighs of his jeans. "So, Lucy, do you know what happened to the stuff in your office after the police took you away?"

Bara's head swivels toward me.

I go blank. "What are you talking about?"

"Your office, Lucy, at the university, after — "

I cut him off. "Why is this important?"

"Because you were doing really good work."

"Like the university wants to remember that."

"Probably not, but somebody put all your papers in the archives."

"And you went and had a look?"

"About time somebody did. Literacy, community development, co-op businesses. I'm amazed the university ever did that stuff."

"Don't worry, they came to their senses. Did you find my award?"

"Award?"

"Yeah, I won a national award. The same year they cut the program. But they kept the plaque next to the main office for years."

"No kidding!" Robin throws back his head and laughs, dark curls bouncing in the harsh light of the bare bulb.

"Yeah, well, and lots of good those 'accomplishments' have done me."

"But they have. What would you do now without St. Marks and the other community services in the North End?"

"And what makes this your business?"

"I want to know why you did what you did."

"Bara, what time is it?"

Bara has been staring at me with big eyes but now checks her watch. "One o'clock."

Robin persists. "It must have been something big."

Bara turns to him. "Geez, Robin, that's enough. People talk about things when they're ready."

Robin looks contrite. "Sorry, Lucy. I'm just interested."

Bara gives him a look. "You promised."

"Okay. But I want to talk again," he says to me.

Not if I can help it, I think as he rises to his full skinny height.

"Will you think about writing that article?"

"Get out of here."

Bara almost has to push him out the door. When she comes back, she puts the mattress and bedside table back into place and gathers up the cups, taking them behind the furnace. I hear running water.

"Is there a tap back there?"

"Yeah. Spotted it when I was peeing in the drain." She returns and packs the cups and thermos into her knapsack. "So, you were more than a community organizer. Were you a professor? Do you, like, have a PhD?"

"No PhD. It was a community-based program run out of the continuing education college."

"So what happened? What got you from there to jail?"

"Who just said people talk when they're ready?"

She blushes. "Right."

After she leaves, I disappear into timelessness in my little pool of dim light, hunting for scripture passages and scribbling on my lined pad, my hand finally warmed up and more or less working again.

I'm several pages in when the basement door creaks open again, and Bara is back.

"Did you leave the door unlocked?"

"You left it unlocked before."

"I didn't mean to."

"Right. Sorry. Look." She switches on the light nearest the door and, out of her knapsack, pulls a cardboard sleeve containing two light bulbs, holds it up. She turns off my desk lamp and screws them in. When she pulls the metal chains, the table is suddenly flooded with light, edged with the colours of the glass lamp shade. Light bulbs, the thermos. I don't ask where these things came from. Shoplifting? A first offence wouldn't get her much, maybe a couple of conditions. She might have to check in with John along with me. I swallow a smile. "What time is it?"

She looks. "Past three thirty."

"Oh my God. We've got to get out of here." I've stiffened from sitting so still but ease myself up with the edge of the table. Bara switches the lamp off again.

"We can't leave all this here." I indicate the table, my papers, the lamp.

"Sure we can. Who comes down here, like, ever?"

"Judith?"

"Doubt it."

"Furnace repair guy? Plumber?"

"Maybe, but they won't be going near that old washer. Watch." She pulls the rolling coat rack a foot or two until it covers the path she made to the washing machine, hiding the table from anyone traversing the main pathway from the door to the furnace.

I sigh, beyond arguing any more and urgent to leave. "Let's go."

Outside, everything is icy from the sleet earlier in the day. Bara takes my arm. We walk down the sidewalk opposite Judith's house in case she appears around the corner. Though, who could miss Bara's toque?

Once we reach Devonshire, the sidewalk is better. Bara doesn't let go of my arm, though, as we make our way to St. Marks.

CHAPTER NINETEEN

It takes two days to write my sermon. We've compromised about the door. I lend her the key, but as soon as she arrives, I hold out my hand for it. This time, she has an extension cord. She plugs it in, transfers the lamp's terrifying old plug to the other end and works her way toward my pile of boxes, threading the cord under and around things as she goes. When she gets to the padded chair, she sets the lamp on the bedside table beside it and clicks it on. It casts a nice, warm light on the threadbare upholstery, my coat flung over the seat and one arm, Judith's wool blanket folded underneath it. She looks back at me, waving her hand toward the comfortable spot she has created. "Voilá. Reading chair."

"But …"

"The chair was here anyway, right? The only difference is the table set on the floor instead of the seat and the lamp's moved. Judith's going to notice that in all this mess?"

"You don't know Judith. And besides, I'm not coming here anymore."

"But it's where you feel safe."

"Bara, the more I stay here, the more likely she'll come home and find me."

"And how will she know? She won't see the light from the front. You'll wait 'til she goes upstairs and, like, slip out."

I sigh and glance up at the windows, which are definitely darkening. "Let's slip out now." I gather up the final copy of my sermon, torn from the pad, and neatly fold it into quarters so it will fit into my coat pocket. "Will you put the pad and pen in your knapsack?"

"Sure." What is Bara doing? As I make my way to the main route through the basement, I see she is poking around in "Lucy — Sweaters," left open in the top row of boxes. "Weren't you going to get a change of clothes?" She holds up something dark, looks it over critically. "Geez Lucy, did you ever dress better than this? You must have looked like a street person even when you weren't."

"Thanks. Now give me that."

She does. A big, dark blue sweater, one I always liked. I take off the brown one and put the blue one on, begin to fold the brown one to take its place in the box.

"There's a washing machine at Fresh Start."

"I know."

"Have you washed anything in it?"

"I will."

"Then don't leave that here."

I let her take the brown sweater, which she folds and tucks into her knapsack. She nods at my skirt. "You should get something else and wash that too. Maybe a pair of pants. Don't you ever wear pants?"

"There's nothing here fits me anymore."

"You've got some of your social assistance money, haven't you? Or if you don't, you can get some from John. I think I should take you shopping."

I sigh. "I hate shopping."

"St. Marks clothing depot then." She steps behind me and rolls the coat rack into position to hide the desk while I put my coat on. She clicks off the light by the door and creaks it open.

"Wait." I've been trying to get her to check before going out, but she forgets. We pause in the darkness just inside the door.

"Listen," she says, and in a minute, I hear it. Sharp and clear on the concrete, that tap, tap, tap of ladies' dress shoes. They turn up the front walk. Damn. I put my hand on Bara's arm to make sure she doesn't creak the hinges again.

We stand like statues as Judith mounts the steps, unlocks and opens the front door, drops her briefcase in the hall. The first few steps we can hear, then silence. She's taken off her shoes. A pipe gurgles as she flushes the toilet in the hallway. Bara, thinking quickly, uses the sound of the flush to cover the creaking hinges as she closes the basement door until it just touches the frame, but she doesn't dare click it shut.

Silence overhead, then CBC radio comes on in the kitchen. Clink of something metallic, cupboards opening, closing.

After a few minutes, a series of creaks progress up the stairs to the second floor. "Now?" Bara whispers and opens the door a crack. Just outside is a square of light cast on the ground by the kitchen window. Another joins it as Judith switches on a light upstairs. I continue to hold Bara's arm, reluctant to cross that gauntlet of light lest Judith look out a window.

"All right, then," Bara says and, as quietly as she can, closes the door. She feels for my hand in the dark. "Carefully," she whispers, and I feel her moving past me.

"Where are you going?"

"Shhh." She leads me very carefully along our well-trodden path back to my boxes and the big chair. "Sit here," she barely breathes as she guides me into position in the seat. I hear a soft crinkle of plastic and smell dust. She has laid the crib mattress on the floor. A whisper of displaced air tells me she has folded her lithe frame into a cross-legged position just behind me and slightly to one side. At least this is more comfortable than standing in the cold draft of the slightly open basement door, and just in time. The sequence of creaks says that Judith is coming back down the stairs.

We can map her progress around the kitchen by the opening and closing of cupboard doors, clink of pots, rattle of cutlery, the soft scrape of a chair. Her feet are soundless. As I begin to doze in my soft chair, I picture her wafting about with her feet just off the floor, insubstantial, a will-o'-the-wisp. It's not a new thought, I realize.

I emerge back into the present when I feel the blanket on the arm of the chair gently pulled out from under my elbow. Bara is breathing over me in the darkness. She spreads the blanket over my knees. She moves again, to my pile of boxes. I hear one cardboard flap brush another. "Lucy — Bedding" is right there. Bara must have noticed. There is a soft crackle of plastic. Bara sits, then obviously lies down, arranging whatever she took from the box over herself.

Above, CBC is still playing. And now I can hear Judith's feet. Two, three steps, a pause, a much heavier one. Scrape of a chair, once, twice. Jerky.

Suddenly, there is a loud crash and clatter. I jump and hear Bara do the same. Scraping, more clattering, a couple of ragged thumps. I'm guessing a chair fell over and she's picked it up, clumsily. So unlike her. Another soft scrape. Faint thump. Silence again. Still CBC.

There is light in the windows. I am desperately stiff, but at least I dozed off — for quite a while, apparently. I turn my head to locate Bara. With a plastic crackle she sits up, lays a hand on my arm. "She's still here," she whispers. "But she's upstairs."

"How do you know?"

"I heard her go up, a while ago. Lucy, does she drink?"

"I don't think …" But I pause.

"Because I'm sure she was staggering."

"She's not all that well, sometimes." It sounds flimsy, even to me.

Bara is silently making her way toward the furnace, disappears behind it.

When she comes back, she holds out her hand. "Your turn?" She helps me up, steadies me. "Want me to come with you?"

"No." I make the word sound indignant, although once I'm

behind the furnace, supporting myself against the rough stone wall as I squat over the drain, I'm almost sorry.

It is very still upstairs. Carefully, listening at each step of the way, we gather our few things and slip out. I glance up at the windows from the yard. All dark.

After a quick breakfast stop behind Susan's Place, we head for the library. As we pass in front of Legal Aid, I pause. "Wait here," I tell Bara. "I'll be right back," but she follows me through the door and up the steps into the lobby. I ask for Judith at the front desk. They say she's called in sick.

I still have Frantz Fanon in my skirt pocket and settle into one of the reading chairs while Bara bends over the newspapers spread out on their table.

"Under the German occupation, the French remained men; under the French occupation, the Germans remained men. In Algeria there is not simply the domination but the decision to the letter not to occupy anything more than the sum total of the land.

I wonder if Doctor "Tell-me-about-it" has even heard of Fanon. Imagine, a psychiatrist who saw the pain of the world breaking through sensitive individuals and thought about how to end the pain instead of how to fix the individuals.

"Colonialism contents itself with bringing to light the natural resources, which it extracts, and exports to meet the needs of the mother country's industries."

Nicolás once said he thought of earthquakes as the misery of the land breaking through.

Earth pitching and rolling. On the ground, painfully bouncing, trying to grab the dirt. My solid world, breaking open.

Judith overhead, clumsy, stumbling. So unlike her.

CHAPTER TWENTY

When Bara asks for my morning pill, the worker wants to know where we were night before last.

"She fell asleep on a park bench," Bara tells her. "I couldn't wake her up. That happens sometimes with these pills. I had to stay with her to keep her warm."

The woman looks skeptical. I can feel her eyes follow us as we put on our coats and boots.

Outside, Bara turns to me. "Library? Or Judith's?"

"Library. Judith might still be home." I almost say, "home sick," but it sticks in my throat.

"Okay, library," Bara says, and starts off. As we pass Legal Aid, however, she says, "Wait here," and bounds up the concrete steps.

In a minute, she's back. "Judith's here."

"Oh." I pause.

She turns and starts walking north.

After another moment, I follow.

"Got enough to read?" Bara asks me.

I'm settled in the stuffed chair, blanket over my knees, rickety lamp with its bright new bulbs beside me, Fanon in my hand and a newspaper on the arm of the chair. I frown at it. "Where did that come from?"

"Lucy, you're out of it. I picked it up in a bus shelter. You, like, saw me do it."

"Oh."

I pick up the paper, scanning, just aware of Bara's steps

disappearing down the walk. I flip through to the international section, near the back, and my eye catches on a headline: "Accords Promise End of Civil War." I lean sideways to hold it directly under the light. Nicolás, I'm coming.

I throw off the blanket. "Lucy — Books, Creamed Corn" is still open on the floor. I lift out Nicolás's Bible, return to the chair. I curl both hands around the worn leather cover, feel for the invisible prints of Nicolás's fine-boned fingers. I lift it to my face and breathe in, remembering his scent of earth and woodsmoke. The edges of the pages, once dyed red, are faded now, some more worn than others. I slide my finger in where the colour's worn right off, knowing what I will find.

"Bienaventurados los pobres" Blessed are the poor. He has crossed out, *"en espíritu."* "In spirit" was added later, he told me, by monks copying the text in the Middle Ages. They had wealthy patrons, the church rich by then too.

"Bienaventurados los que tienen hambre y sed de justicia." Those who hunger and thirst for justice. Could anyone hunger and thirst more for justice than my Nicolás? *"Porque ellos serán hartos."* They shall be filled. With what? Bullets?

There are tears on my face. *"Bienaventurados los que lloran,"* Blessed are those who grieve. *"Porque ellos recibirán consolación."* So comfort me, Nicolás, Jesus, somebody.

The ground has a thin layer of snow sparkling in the sun, but the wind is cold. Good. I pull my jacket tight across my chest, lower my head and plough uphill to Fort Needham Park, heart and lungs making drum music in my ears.

Jesus and Nicolás, such saints, *bless* the poor, *bless* the righteous, *bless* those who grieve. I like damnation better myself. *Damn* those who think enough is too little; *damn* those who take what belongs to everyone; *damn* those who celebrate their "successful investments" when that profit comes from poor people's labour; *damn* those who buy cheap and never ask why it's cheap; *damn* the kings and the merchants and the Beast.

Gasping for breath, I stand at the top of Needham Hill. The sun is trying to warm the concrete face of the Halifax Explosion Memorial. I lower myself to a rim of crackly brown grass in the shelter of the tower and lean against it.

Speaking of blessed are the poor, between the park and the harbour sit the bleak human warehouses of Mulgrave Park public housing. How many times have the tenants tried to organize that place? Brave, creative, determined leaders. They all made a difference, but it's so hard to keep going in the face of people's despair and the absolute control of the Housing Authority.

Directly below me is the tower called "A Block." The buildings have names and the Tenants' Association has made valiant attempts to encourage their use, make the place sound less like a prison, but the residents, the city, everyone slides back into "A Block," "B Block," all the way to "W Block."

My eyes wander down to the blue sparkle of the Narrows, soaring bridge on either side. Right here, in front of "A Block," sat Pier 6, where the *Mont-Blanc* came to rest, burning and loaded with too much ammunition. Explosives meant to kill *them*, a good thing, right? Not *us*.

I close my eyes, feel the weak sun on my face, but it has given no heat to the concrete behind me. I'm slowly freezing from my back forward. Time to go somewhere warmer. I look around for something to grab, lever myself up. Nothing. Flat concrete wall, grass, sloping back down to the walkway. I try to rock forward, get to my feet that way. I'm too stiff. Damn. No one around. Not long ago, I wanted to freeze to death. Now, I clutch my jacket closer and try to push panic away.

Bara's face is close to mine, red with both cold and anger, judging by her eyes, just visible under her bangs and toque. "I've been looking everywhere for you. Good thing there was some snow on the sidewalk and at the entrance to the park."

"Help me up." I hold out my hand. She plants both fists on her hips.

"Is it too much to ask you to stay where you're warm and safe?"

"Sorry."

She gives me another couple of minutes to suffer, finally offers her hand. "Your teeth are actually chattering."

She has to swing her whole tiny weight back to even begin to help me up off the ground. My ass is so frozen I can't feel it. Legs, too. I can't even walk without Bara's arm around me.

We've pretty much finished supper at St. Marks before I begin to warm up. I let Bara refill my coffee, even though I don't want to drink it. It's just to wrap my hands around. She is doing the same thing with hers and her face is still red from cold. I wonder how long she was walking around on the hill looking for me.

I'm about to ask, but she speaks first. "Lucy, are you in love with Judith?"

"What? Where did that come from?"

She shrugs her thin shoulders. "You were pretty relieved when we found out she'd gone back to work this morning."

"Well, yeah. Of course."

"So, are you in love with her?"

"No."

"Maybe not *in love*, then, just *love*?"

I sip my coffee. She's watching me.

"Judith doesn't let anyone love her. I mean, she doesn't let anyone get close."

"Yeah, well, you know all about that."

"That's not true. I have lots of friends."
"So does Judith."

As the weather gets colder, the basement of Fresh Start is filling up. They've offered me a room, but I won't leave Bara down here in the ever-changing population of the overflow dorm. As I lie in the dark, pretending I'm asleep, I can hear women moving about, the creak of springs, whispered conversations, the bathroom door opening and closing, toilet flushing. Bara is just a pile of blankets, breathing deeply. What an odd kid. Do I love Judith?

CHAPTER TWENTY-ONE

Bara is digging through a box marked "Lucy — Books." Not "Creamed Corn," still sitting on the floor, Nicolás's Bible safely tucked between *Marx and the Bible* and *The Theology of Liberation*. This one held Lipton Soup and is filled with novels. "You sure have a lot of books, Lucy. Have you read them all?"

I nod. "Most more than once."

"So, what would you like to reread now?" She starts to read off titles.

"But I know how they end."

"Every single one? How about … *The Bean Trees?*"

"That's one you should read, if you want something 'political.'"

"Yeah?" She takes a closer look at the cover, then sets it on top of a neighbouring box. "Okay. So how about *This Place?*"

"I don't want to reread that. It's about women in prison."

"Happy ending?"

I pause. "No."

"You don't sound sure. You don't remember, do you?"

"It's several women's stories, different classes, races. I know what happens to a couple of them. But the others? Actually, I can't remember."

Bara hands me the book. She peers into the shadows and stands up on her toes, looking over the garment rack that hides the path to the old washer. The elegant little table and its equally elegant little chair are still there, the lined pad and pen she found for me. She frowns. "Lucy, you finished writing that sermon, didn't you?"

I nod.

"Where is it?"

I have to think. I folded it, in quarters. "Look in my jacket pocket."

She pulls out a wet mitten, reaches in again, produces a crumpled, dirty square of paper. "Oh, Lucy." She unfolds it, peers at it in the dim light. "I can barely read it. What is supposed to happen with it? Do you just tell Reverend Peter you're ready?"

"Am I ready?"

"It's a sermon, isn't it?"

I shrug my shoulders. "I think he wants to see it in advance."

"Then you'll have to copy it over." She hands it to me.

I sigh.

There is a tinsel garland around the door to the child care room in the basement at St. Marks, pinned at the corners by slightly crumpled fake poinsettias. Is it that time again already? Christmas always gives me a deep desire to hibernate. I can hear women talking in there, Cindy, Althea, Judith and another familiar voice from a long time ago, Lynn Daley. Bara stops at the doorway, says hello to them. "Is that Lucy with you?" Althea says. "Get in here, girl."

Bara waves goodbye. "See you downstairs. Don't forget the sermon, Lucy." She nods toward my pocket where the newly copied sermon nestles, then disappears in the direction of the drop-in.

Lynn rises to throw her arms around me.

In a minute, I hold her at arm's length so we can look at each other. Whatever she sees, it doesn't dim her delighted smile. She hasn't changed since she was Althea's classmate in the first community leadership course. No missing, though, that she is tense and weary. She turns to indicate a young woman sitting beside Cindy. "Lucy, remember my daughter, Rosemarie?"

"Of course. One of our little people who inspired the first playroom." I take Rosemarie's hand and get a brief, half-hearted smile.

In her late twenties now, I realize. She, too, is tense and weary, and she's wearing too much makeup.

"Sermon?" Althea asks.

"Reverend Peter wants me to preach."

"And you've written it?"

I nod.

"That's good," says Lynn. "You used to do that. I always liked what you had to say."

It's becoming obvious I'm avoiding Judith. I force myself to look into her eyes as we greet each other, remind myself she doesn't know.

"So where've you been since the night you were at our place?" Cindy asks.

From the corner of my eye I see surprise on both Althea's and Judith's faces and drop my gaze to the floor where Cindy's little one — Kip? — is playing with a plastic truck in front of a Christmas tree hung with battered decorations.

"I've got a bed at Fresh Start."

"I hear that's a good place. Pretty relaxed."

"Okay then." Althea gets to her feet. "You three …" She nods to Judith, Lynn and Rosemarie. "The small meeting room is free." They stand up, Judith picking up her big briefcase from the floor beside her chair. Althea looks at me. "Lucy, come with me. I've got something to show you."

Uh oh. What now?

Passing Reverend Peter's door, I knock. No answer, so I push the folded square of paper through the crack underneath. My name's not on it, but he'll know.

Once we've settled in Althea's office, she pulls open a drawer and lifts out a thick package of newsprint, yellowed on the outside. "Remember this?" she says. I watch cleaner paper emerge as she opens fold after fold. She is bent over, spreading it on the floor, when I see what it is. Childlike drawings face in four directions, artists coming at the paper from all sides with coloured markers.

"Where did you find this?" I say.

"I was cleaning out my cupboard."

"Last time I saw it, it was on the wall of the Public Housing Tenants' Association meeting room."

"That's the room we were in when we made it. Remember? Part of that first planning workshop you led for the community leadership class." Althea grins at me.

"And then we went back to it every time we sat down to check where we were, plan the next steps."

"For years."

We fall silent, looking over the chaotic and faded drawing. Grass and small gardens surround gaily painted houses. Parks, playgrounds, basketball courts, a pool, a large community garden, even a greenhouse. Althea points at an oddly shaped building housing a daycare centre and clinic. "Well, we got some of this stuff started."

I nod agreement. "Some other things, not so much." I point at the swimming pool and rows of affordable housing. By now public housing is crumbling and bursting at the seams, desperate parents waiting for years to quit couch surfing with their kids, hoping they get a place before they run out of friends with couches.

There is a gentle knock on the doorframe and Judith steps into the room, as straight and graceful as always, but I notice her eyes are sinking into a network of lines that didn't used to be there. Not laugh lines. Sad and worried lines.

"Plans coming together?" Althea asks, and Judith nods.

I am checking the feel of my face, hoping it looks normal in Judith's presence and hating myself for it, but she is looking down at the drawing on the floor. "Oh my. What a good memory. You've kept it, all this time."

Althea nods. Judith pulls up one of the wooden chairs from

beside Althea's desk. She looks so small and trim between Althea and I, well-dressed, that modest touch of lipstick. We are both what you might call substantial women and about as far from fashionable as you can get.

All three of us study the vibrant community spread at our feet. Stick people chat over fences, walk dogs. There are children everywhere — playing, working, talking, reading. Toward the edge, a group of adults and children pick apples on a field trip, yellow school bus parked beside the orchard.

"Donna drew that," I point to the school, bustling with people of all ages. "No desks in straight rows for her."

"Toni drew this," Althea points to a large community garden, green twisty lines spotted with red and yellow fruits of some sort — tomatoes? We had one for a few years, but now it's gone back to grass.

"I think that's supposed to be me." Judith points at the Legal Aid office, where two stick figures sit beside a desk in one of the upstairs windows. In other windows, consultations are going on, research at tables in the library, a group sitting in a circle in the meeting room downstairs. "I love the way the community has taken over the whole block." Storefronts all along the sidewalk contain co-operative businesses: a house painting company called "Roller Girls"; a beauty salon specializing in braids, extensions and weaves; a shop selling Black hair products; another for second-hand children's toys and clothes.

Althea looks up at me. "Did Dell change, or did she always think differently from the rest of us?"

"She believed in what she was doing." I note Judith's use of the past tense.

Althea persists. "Her economic development projects, sometimes they seemed to fit with everything else we were doing. Other times it felt like, I don't know, it was bringing in different values."

"Doesn't it always?" I say. "When you put the focus on

individual income instead of community services, it's going to benefit a smaller group. Hard not to get into competition, who deserves more, all that."

"Of course, these are all important services as well as income-generating projects," Judith says.

"True," I say. "It's just that maybe for the rest of us, the service was primary and for Dell …"

"I always felt she looked up to you," Judith says to me. "Thought of you as her mentor."

"You were her mentor too," Althea says to Judith. "I'll bet you still are."

"After defending Lucy?" Judith says.

"I'd say all of us were." I look at Althea. "But then she moved on. To a different kind of mentor."

Judith nods and Althea chuckles, looks at me. "Thank God it was a flimsy old window."

I can see it coming, Althea's laugh, the one that starts deep in her awesome chest and spreads upward, finally booming out, doubling her up. I can't help myself. I never can in the face of that laugh. I join her.

Judith looks appalled for a moment, then a smile creeps onto her face. And then she is laughing too. Is it ethical for my defence lawyer to laugh at my crime? I hope so.

Althea finally runs dry, sputtering to a stop, wiping her eyes. She leans over to place her dark fingers on the drawing. "Well, we did some good work, even Dell."

I nod. "The two of you still are."

Judith looks like she is about to say something comforting to me, but Althea starts in first. "Well, the heart of it was always the low-income women who were on the Community Council and now do their organizing and lobbying through the tenants' associations and ad hoc committees."

"We should all be proud that the people involved keep

changing," says Judith, "There are those who move, marry or are taken by death, of course, but think how many have gone on to get education and jobs and then were able to raise kids who got education and jobs."

"Including me," says Althea. "The education piece was yours, Lucy. I'll always be grateful."

Judith nods.

We work together to fold the drawing along its well-worn lines.

"Will you keep it?" I ask.

Althea sets it on the corner of her desk. "We should get everyone together to look at it again, evaluate where we are and what still needs doing. Maybe you'll be up to organizing that soon, Lucy?"

I shrug.

"How did you learn how to do all this stuff, anyway? You always say you brought it back from Guatemala, but you've never said how you learned it."

It is Judith who speaks into the pause. "You're going to get clear of your probation, Lucy. You're doing so much better lately. Which reminds me, you have a court date coming up in January. We need to do some preparation, right after Christmas."

"And I have to not do anything crazy in the meantime."

CHAPTER TWENTY-TWO

Rich, thick music pours out of the sanctuary. The organist practising Christmas music. Real Christmas music. Not the saccharine carols the malls will wear ragged by the time December 25th rolls around. I decide to go in and listen, but I stop at the doorway. Something's caught my eye, dusty half-light on a head of blond hair. Bara, standing perfectly still, looking through the main doors, up the aisle toward the altar.

I step through the door and she starts, turns, relaxes when she sees who it is. "Hey Lucy."

"You're not all mushy about Christmas, are you?"

"Something tells me you're not." She pulls the sleeve of her jacket down over her hand and takes a swipe at her face with it. "I'd like to see my brother and sister. They'll be coming home from BC and Ontario."

"Wouldn't your family welcome you this time of year? No matter what? Christmas spirit and all that?"

"You told me you didn't fit in at home anymore after you came back from Guatemala. But did you go home for Christmas?"

"No. I wasn't welcome and didn't want to anyway."

"Well, then, you know what it's like. My mom might want me there, I guess, but she won't go against my dad."

Her sadness seeps into me, mingling with mine. What is it about this season anyway? Just the sentimentalism pushed at us from every direction? Or something much older?

The smell of food is drifting up from the drop-in. "Want to come down for supper?"

Bara has set a brochure on the table beside her tray. I try to read it upside down.

"It's about people starving in East Africa." She holds it up. Children with their bones showing, big pleading eyes crusty, flies. "My parents donate to campaigns like this at Christmas and send gifts to the children they sponsor."

"That's what we used to call 'development pornography.' Makes the people of the South look like helpless charity cases, so we can feel big by giving them a few of our excess pennies."

"But don't they, like, need help?"

"What they need is for us to stop making them poor. The people of Africa are some of the world's best farmers. They're perfectly capable of feeding themselves."

"But the drought ..."

"They've had those for thousands of years. That's why they were nomadic. They followed the rains. Now they're hungry because the world's richer people buy up their land, or just take it, and turn them into trespassers. They have to stay in one place and then we force them into trade relations where they have to sell their products cheaply and buy back what they need for many times more." I place my finger on the brochure. "This is charity."

That little frown appears between her eyes. "Isn't charity a good thing?"

"For the givers, sure. For the receivers, it's a Band-Aid on a cancer."

"Okay. Okay. I've got the point. So we need to give people back their land and resources, right?"

"Right. Justice instead of charity."

"I am learning, you know."

"I know."

"Sometimes I wish I didn't have to, though. Once you

make me see this stuff, I can't un-see it, ever. I feel like Humpty Dumpty."

I smile at her. "Good image."

"So who made you see? Your friend in Guatemala? The one that thought Jesus was a socialist?"

"He didn't just make me see. It was more like an earthquake. It broke me open."

"Before you said 'breakdown.' Is that the same as broken open?"

I stop eating to think. "There are people that break open and then somehow make a new, bigger self. But some of us are ... brittle." I study her earnest pixie face under its ragged bangs. How does someone so young have so much wisdom? "So, Bara, does Humpty Dumpty want to be put back together?"

"Just the same as he was?" She grins. "No."

I turn my attention back to the stew. It's a bit watery, but hot, and tasty. The bottom of the bowl appears quickly. Bara is already done, waiting for my bowl. She takes our tray back to the kitchen window and returns with two mugs of tea. It's hot. I hold my cup, waiting for it to cool a bit. "Are you going back to school in January?"

"Did Althea tell you?"

"No, just asking."

"Well, I am. Althea helped me register."

"Good. You trust me on my own?"

"No ..." She slides the word out. "But you're doing better."

"Have you been talking to Althea about me?"

"Maybe." She grins. "A little."

"Plotting against me?"

"Plotting *for* you." She takes a careful sip. "Lucy, I need you to explain more about capitalism and socialism."

"Why? The social analysis book?"

"That, and I met some students from the art college. They throw these words around, neoliberalism, deregulation, commodification ..."

"Ask anytime."

"Yeah? Until you, like, bite my head off."

"I'm sorry. It's just, sometimes I feel so crabby with the world. No, crabby's not the word. Disappointed, maybe?"

The crease disappears, and a grin breaks out. "You're okay, Teacher Lucy."

I lie on my cot listening to the night sounds of the other women in the Fresh Start basement. Althea, this afternoon. "You never said how you learned."

The first time I saw Nicolás in action, I thought I had never seen anything so useless in my life. For a long time, I'd wanted him to take me with him on one of his trips to the villages in the mountains. I was curious. People talked about his literacy classes with excitement. They never talked like that about mine.

He said no. I figured he didn't think I could keep up. But then, some of the women in the villages were asking for a female teacher.

When he finally invited me to come, I pushed my legs beyond collapse just to prove I could climb any mountain he could, literally gritting my teeth. We got to the village after dark. Because of how worried people were, I knew I had, in the end, slowed him down.

It was Nicolás's first time at that village. After breakfast, everyone gathered around a large tree in the central square, just a patch of dust. Nicolás began: "The topic of this meeting is 'What do your children need?'"

There was a long discussion. I looked around at the children. Some played around the edges of the adult group, a few of the younger ones right in the middle of the circle of adults. Many sat on laps, leaned against adult knees or sides, or one another, listening. A bedraggled lot — thin, ill-dressed, sickly, dirty bare feet. A lot of runny noses.

The people broke up into smaller groups to discuss what the children needed most. They came back together, made proposals and — I couldn't believe it — they decided what the children needed most was a statue of the Virgin Mary.

I looked at Nicolás. He was perfectly calm. Where could they get a few bags of concrete? Who knew how to cast it? I barely listened, struggling to believe what I was hearing.

Next day, on the trail again, I challenged Nicolás. "What on earth are you up to? Those kids need food and medical care, not a statue of the Virgin Mary. I don't think this is what your donor organizations have in mind. Are you cheating them?"

Nicolás kept on walking, slender brown hands tucked into the straps of his backpack. When I ran out of breath, he said, "Wait and see."

Weeks later, the new statue of the Virgin Mary stood on top of a hill beside the village, shiny white and new-looking. A little rough, but I had to give the villagers credit — it was pretty good. Certainly easily recognizable as the Virgin Mary, head bowed and hands spread in the traditional gesture.

The villagers gathered on the hillside below her. They vied to tell us how they had worked together to get what they needed to construct the statue. It was a celebration, and I felt out of step. The children were certainly happy along with the adults, but they were still thin and sick.

When the story was told and the people settled down a little, Nicolás addressed them. "Now that the children have a statue of the Virgin Mary, what do they need next?"

No need even to break into groups and discuss it: "Vegetables."

"What do you need to grow vegetables?"

By the end of the meeting, the villagers had figured out where to get seeds and tools, and plans were underway to build terrace gardens up the hillside all around the Virgin Mary's feet.

"See?" Nicolás said on the trail home. "If I had said, 'No, your children don't need a statue of the Virgin Mary,' that would have been the end of it. An outsider knows what they need more than they do. Instead, they proved to themselves what they can do together."

"But what does any of this have to do with literacy?"

He stopped, brown eyes totally focused on me. Shivery feeling. Was that the first time I felt it? "Literacy — words — are the heart of empowerment. What you can name, you can act on."

"Okay, but how do you get from growing vegetables to reading and writing?"

"At some point, they will need to read to keep going. Maybe when they need more information about soil, or the vegetables they want to grow, then they will want literacy classes. Then they will start to explore more of their world."

CHAPTER TWENTY-THREE

Legal Aid takes a break over Christmas, including Judith. We hang out at St. Marks and the library, Fresh Start in the evening. Bara talks me into going to the Christmas service, where Reverend Peter gives a pretty good sermon on the social status of carpenters in Jesus's time, how it wasn't the professional trade we think of. On the way out, he catches up to me. He likes "Who dies for our sins?" Would I consider preaching one Sunday in January?

The prospect of me standing in the pulpit, along with Bara's plans to return to school, prompts a trip to the clothing depot, but there are no pants big enough for me and nothing "cool" enough for her. She gathers up some of our social assistance money and drags me off to Sears. The Central American Solidarity Network has its office upstairs in this mall, but I usually scoot as quickly as I can from the doors to the elevator. It's been years since I've actually gone shopping. Mostly, I hole up in the change room and Bara drops things over the top of the door. I hate it, but I survive and go home with a pair of navy wool slacks I actually like. Bara chooses two of the skinny, odd outfits women her age wear these days.

On the first Monday after New Year's, Bara dresses in her new clothes and goes to school. I feel at loose ends without her, but I have my own fish to fry, my court date coming up. Have I been a good enough girl? Will Santa give me freedom from probation?

I show up at the Legal Aid reception desk to see if I can get an appointment with Judith. The woman gives me one, written on a little card, but says, "You should check the day before, in case she isn't back."

"Isn't back?"

"She's out sick. I'm sure it's just a winter flu or something. She'll be back for your court date."

John pulls out my file, scans the papers on top. "There was the incident at Magdalen House. Don't get me wrong, m'dear, that was serious, but you've been doing much better at Fresh Start. Just a couple of nights when you didn't turn up. What was that all about?"

I hear Bara, that innocent voice to the worker at Fresh Start. "Sometimes my pills make me sleepy. I drifted off on a park bench."

"You could have frozen to death."

"Bara stayed with me, kept me warm, got me back to Fresh Start when she could wake me up."

"She did say she could keep you out of trouble. And the other night?"

Now I have to fall back on "I don't remember."

"I'd be happier if you had another visit with the psychiatrist. Shall I make an appointment?"

I nod, and he makes a quick call. Second little card I've collected today.

He takes another page out of my file. "Now here's a police report I kept. Older woman, dressed like a street person, gets up on a box in a downtown store and starts yelling at people. Politics sound suspiciously like yours."

I look as innocent as I can.

"Apparently, she got away."

I'm fascinated with the grooves his chair has been digging into the linoleum. There is a rustle as he picks up the page. I look, expecting to see him slide it back into the file, but his hand has moved to the edge of the desk. The paper floats downward into the trash can. I look up. He's smiling.

"So, m'dear. Looks like a better report for the judge than last time. We'll see what he says."

"And if I get off probation, you'll write a letter to Project Witness?"

"We'll see."

Damn. He softened me up, then "We'll see." My plan was to go to the library and read, but now I feel the need to walk, sore old knees complaining but pushed ahead by anger. This is dangerous. I don't want to do something stupid so close to my court date. I force myself to slow down, walk normally, breathe.

I still end up north of Needham Hill, small houses in narrow residential streets. I am just about to turn around when I see an old blue Morris Minor like Judith's. Not a common car. It is going slowly and, approaching an empty parking space, pulls over. A slight figure steps out, shiny ponytail swinging with the motion.

I step between two parked cars and crouch. My vision distorted by several rear windows and windshields, I watch her walk around to the trunk and open it. She looks both ways up and down the street, also takes a careful look at the houses nearby. She lifts out a large, blue recycling bag, sets it down on the curb beside one that was already there. I glance along the street. Every house has at least one. I duck because Judith looks around again before getting back into the car and driving off. I straighten, feeling slightly dizzy, and walk over to look, although I've already guessed. Bottles.

I see Doctor "Tell-me-all-about-it," who is surprisingly uninterested in hearing all about it this time. Maybe he's given up on me. Congratulates me on doing better with my meds, writes another prescription.

It's hard to work with Judith when she returns to Legal Aid, feeling the weight of my secret and hers, but it's she who seems distracted. She fiddles with her elegant fountain pen as she goes over John's report, briefs me on what she plans to say. Her main concern, too, is Sister Marie.

That, as it turns out, is the judge's concern too. It looks too much like what I did to Dell. He congratulates me on doing better and gives me another six months' probation. That evening, at a table in the sitting room at Fresh Start, I sit beside Bara as she does her math homework. Those rows of figures down the page I hated when I was in school. Beside her notebook is the calendar she uses to keep track of assignments. I flip the pages, counting weeks. July.

I set up a meeting with Carmela, coordinator of Project Witness, and ride the bus out to the Sears mall. She pulls my application out of the file. No, no letters yet, I tell her, explain about getting six more months of probation. "*Lo siento*, Lucia. I'm so sorry," and her round brown face tells me that she is. "The first group has been chosen, anyway. They are preparing to depart. But there will be more."

"Does anyone need practice speaking Spanish? I could help."

"Everyone in this first group is fluent. But maybe some of the people who have applied for future groups …" She looks thoughtful. "Say, Lucia, would you consider helping us with something else that requires fluent Spanish?"

"Of course."

"You know about the children? The ones that were taken …"

"And sold. I know."

"Their parents, the ones that are still alive, will always grieve for them, but it might help them to heal if they know where their children are. The children too, many would like to know where they came from. As part of the Commission for Historical

Clarification, the Guatemalan government has agreed to open their adoption records. We have a package of papers for children who came to Nova Scotia, and there will be more as the process continues.

"By coincidence, Nova Scotia started an adoption registry this spring, where children who were adopted and parents who gave children up can fill out a form and the government will try to match them up. It's an opportunity to maybe find some of the Guatemalan children, put them back in touch at least with their country, if not their parents. They are, in a way, exiles too."

"And you need someone to translate the Guatemalan documents?"

"It won't be easy. They will be sad, the stories."

"I know, but yes, I would like to do it."

Carmela finds a zippered portfolio to protect the documents. On the way home on the bus, I rest my hand on its anonymous plastic side and, for the first time in a very long time, think of my Guatemalan baby. I wonder what would have become of her.

Everything in Judith's basement is just as we left it before Christmas, the lamp sitting on the small table beside the reading chair. I have brought the Guatemalan adoption files with me, along with my half-used lined pad. I balance the pad on the arm of the chair, lay my pen on its clean, white surface, open the zipper, then pause, feeling the grief, the tragedies, the loss inside, Mía, Adela … perhaps I said yes too quickly.

I reach inside. My fingers close around the first few sheets of paper, stapled together in one corner, and touch a small square, thicker than the rest, shiny on one side. Oh dear, there are photos. I pull the report partway out into the dim light. I can see most of the top page. It won't take long to translate, a small scattering of words. Quick peek at the photo, scrawny, sickly little body, wearing nothing but a cloth diaper. I push it back out of sight, my vision blurring. I did say yes too quickly.

I get to my feet, pace the trail from the chair to the door and back. Bending over the box on the floor, "Creamed Corn," I open the flaps, lay my hand on the spine of Nicolás's Bible, but it just brings more tears. Before Christmas, Bara had pulled out my copy of *This Place*, left it sitting on top of the boxes. Reading about women in prison won't be any less emotional, but at least it's closer to the present. At least it's anger.

I take the book to the chair, open it and stare at the first page, but the words just swim around, refusing to sit still long enough to be read. And now I become aware that I need a bathroom. Beyond what the drain behind the furnace can handle. Well, I made it up to the bathroom under the stairs before and apparently left no trace. Nothing she noticed.

I check the small bathroom in the front hall very carefully before I leave. I can't see any trace of my little invasion. As I begin my retreat to the basement, my stomach grumbles. Is it really that late? There will be a sandwich in my coat pocket, put there by Bara as she does each day when she makes her own lunch. My hand is on the knob of the door back to the basement when I remember. Bara didn't have time this morning. She apologized, suggested I pick something up at St. Marks before coming here. Damn.

In Judith's refrigerator, I find a row of small yoghurts, perfectly straight, of course, three quarters of a President's Choice frozen lasagna, tired bag of salad greens. Enough yoghurts that, if I spread them out a bit, surely there's no way she'll notice one missing.

I borrow a spoon from her drawer, take a few stale crackers from a box in the cupboard, and eat the yoghurt. I wash the spoon, put it away. The empty yoghurt container, even the foil lid, go into in my pocket. All I leave in the kitchen is a wet spot on the tea towel, but that'll be gone by the time Judith gets home.

Just before I disappear back into the basement, on an impulse, I check the cupboards under the sink. Sure enough. Bottles. Not just wine, but Scotch too.

CHAPTER TWENTY-FOUR

"Tomorrow Christ is coming, as yesterday he came.
A child is born this moment, we do not know his name.
The world is full of darkness, again there is no room ... "

The organ booms into the gothic beams of the sanctuary roof. A scattering of people stand in the front pews, mostly my friends — Cindy, Patty, Bara, Robin. Judith's neat dress suit stands out, but not her hat, which is small and plain compared with most of the others in the congregation. Althea's wearing a great, flowered creation with a brim that hides her face when she looks down at the hymnal. A few of the homeless guys from the drop-in are here, sporting clouds of greasy hair, tied in ponytails or flying about. Everyone is holding a hymnal and singing, but I can't hear them. None of them knows this hymn. That was one of Reverend Call-me-Peter's objections to it. I insisted.

"There will be no tomorrows, for many a baby born;
Good Friday falls on Christmas ... "

Dressed in my new navy slacks and a robin's-egg-blue blouse Bara located in one of my boxes, washed and pressed, I stand beside Reverend Peter behind the pulpit, in front of the empty choir stalls. Despite his resistance, he booms out the notes beside me. He must have learned it between Wednesday and today.

And then the last note flies away into the rafters. There is a brief shuffle of people sitting down, expectant faces turned up to me, smiling encouragement. It's been a long time since I've done this. I wonder if anyone can hear me over my pounding heart. I take a huge breath. "That cross behind me, what's missing? The torture victim. The Catholics kept him, but we Protestants like our crosses bare. Still, the central image of our faith is an instrument of torture.

"Think it happened once, do you? Not surprising, that's what we're taught. He died for our sins. Once. But that's not true. Every day he is tortured for our sins. In a concrete cell, in a clearing in the jungle, with a rubber rod, with electrodes and a car battery, because he stood up to those who would take his land to grow our coffee, our bananas …

"Our sin. Our greed. Our ignorance. Our desire not to know."

Reverend Peter shakes my hand and then claps me on the back so hard it nearly knocks the wind out of me. "Well done, Lucy. Now I think you should write one about capitalism as the Beast in Revelation."

My eyes jump up to his face.

"You said that once. Remember?"

I said that? Out loud? To Reverend Call-me-Peter?

"Consider it," he says, as he moves on to greet someone else.

I get warm thanks for my words from everyone, a hug from Althea, Judith's hand laid briefly on my arm, a hug and some tears from Cindy. Robin tries for a hug, but I sidestep.

And later, I can't help myself. My mind starts to turn it over. Capitalism as the Beast of Revelation.

Judith's basement is darker now. The snow is piled against the grubby windows like a cutaway geology model, alternating layers of packed snow, ice and black city grit. It makes my reading chair feel even safer, the circle of light cast by the stained-glass lampshade cozier. I hold Nicolás's Bible once again, run my thumb over the edges of the pages, moving toward the back of the book.

Revelation. Nicolás once called it the Bible's horror movie. The margins are full of his spidery notes, different ink at different times, but very few in John's psychedelic vision of the end. Halfway through: "*Un exceso de guerra, venganza.*" I agree, too much war and vengeance. Next to the Whore of Babylon on her seven hills: "*Roma*" and "*Porque mujer prostituta?*" Why indeed?

As the Whore of Babylon falls, Nicolás underlined a series of passages: "*the Kings of the Earth … wallowed in her luxury … the sea captains and voyagers cried out, 'Alas for the great city, where all who had ships on the sea grew rich on her wealth' … the merchants of the earth will weep and mourn for her, because no one any longer buys their cargoes of gold and silver, jewels and pearls, cloths of purple and scarlet, silks and fine linens … scented woods and ivory … slaves and the lives of men.*" "*The lives of men*" is underlined twice.

So what happens to the Beast in the end? I've forgotten. I turn pages. There: "*Taken prisoner and thrown into the lake of fire with its sulphurous flames … .Chained up for a thousand years.*"

After supper, Bara and I sit at opposite ends of the table in the sitting room at Fresh Start. She is working in pencil, more lines of numbers, every now and then sighing and rubbing something out. I hold a pencil too, given to me by the woman at the front desk when I couldn't find my pen. I consider the clean top page of a new lined pad Bara lent me.

Beast of Revelation. Capitalism. Too "normal" to see. "Can a fish see water"? Until someone challenges him. Rises up, roaring.

I grind to a halt, losing my thread. "Can I borrow your eraser?"

Bara slides it across the table without looking up, that small frown between her brows.

I erase, start again.

The Beast of Revelation. What is he? Violence. War. "We" win or "they" win. It doesn't matter. The Beast wins. That's the whole point of non-violent action. We withdraw our participation in the Beast, deny him life, because he has none without us. He responds with violence, of course, showing himself for what he is, a killer of innocents. This calls up all that is decent in those who look on, forces them to choose.

"Lucy." Bara's eyes are on her page, but she is holding out her hand for the eraser. I slide it back and she attacks her page with it.

Bara and I have fallen into a habit of meeting at St. Marks drop-in for supper. Today she is clearly excited, waves a piece of paper in front of me. "Hey Lucy, look."

I catch "Halifax G7 Summit."

"This meeting they're having? They're going to build a barricade around the waterfront, with concrete and razor wire, bring in loads of police." She hands it to me. It's a black-and-white, photocopied brochure. The G7 is meeting in Halifax this spring and the non-government organizations are planning a parallel "People's Summit."

"This here," Bara underlines a sentence with her finger, reading aloud. *"Fundamental reform has never been so urgent. The policies of the World Bank, the International Monetary Fund and the World Trade Organization are having devastating consequences on our lives.'* So, like, what are these, anyway?"

"They're big international financial institutions, formed by the rich countries to keep the Global South in line by loaning them money with lots of conditions attached."

I move her hand aside so I can read. *"Those in the South are increasingly marginalized and insecure; Canadians are reeling from cutbacks and job loss; workers in G7 countries are scrambling for diminishing work. And Indigenous people, people of colour, and women bear the weight of the financial gains of the few."*

Bara reaches out to point at "the financial gains of the few." "This is, like, what you talk about, isn't it?"

I keep reading: *"It is time to put the G7 'rich men's club' back into the hands of the people of the world. The present economic system is demonstrably failing to provide for people, failing to measure the pressures on people and the planet ..."*

"This is, like, your thing."

"Yes, it is." I give up on reading, drop down the page to scan the list of events: a day of activities and speakers on the Halifax Commons, followed by a march to the barricade protecting the meeting location on the waterfront, a whole week of evening speakers. I look at the list of names and photos. Impressive. People whose books I've read for years. "Where did you get this?"

"I have a friend. She goes to the art college, and they, like, talk about this kind of stuff all the time, the same things you talk about. They were passing these out. So, we'll go, won't we?"

I look at her flushed face, a mirror of the excitement I'm feeling myself. "Definitely."

That evening we sit working at our opposite sides of the table. I think I'll ask Reverend Peter if I can give my Beast as Capitalism sermon during the G7 Summit. The Beast, after all, has seven heads, for seven kingdoms.

CHAPTER TWENTY-FIVE

John congratulates me for being halfway through my six months without breaking my conditions once and, finally, we have a truly warm day. Spring is upon us. I still have my jacket on, but I walk from John's office to St. Marks with it open to the breeze.

The drop-in is packed but weirdly quiet, like a funeral. People whisper in groups around the tables, nursing their coffee. In the lineup at the coffee machine, I begin to catch phrases.

"So young."

"On the street."

"Sad."

"Who was she hanging out with?"

Someone has left a newspaper on a table, folded back to show a headline. I crane my neck. "Body Found in Alley." I head out to look for Althea.

I find her with a group of women in the Single Parent Centre. When I catch her eye from the door, she comes over. "I just got here, Althea. What's happened?"

She moves into the hall with me. "It's Lynn's daughter, Rosemarie. She'd fallen in with one of the gangs, working the streets."

"I wondered when I saw her here before Christmas."

"That's when Judith was helping them figure out what to do. Rosemarie's pimp was going to move her to Toronto, and she told her mom. The Safe House Network had a place for her in PEI. They were going to slip her out of here today, but she didn't show up and now her body's been found in an alley, stabbed."

"Wrong person found out?"

"That's what we're thinking."

"Oh God, Althea." I put my arms around her and hold on. After a few minutes, she pulls away, smiles sadly and pats my arm, then turns to rejoin the group in the Single Parent Centre.

I retreat to Judith's basement. I've been getting sloppy about checking the house. I'm into the yard before I notice the kitchen light is on. I step back quickly, then cross the street and stand where I'm hidden by someone's overgrown bushes. Every room on the main floor is lit up.

Bara comes looking for me. She immediately sees the lights, stops on the sidewalk. I hiss to get her attention. She crosses, slides in among the bushes with me. "Is she there?" she whispers.

"Must be."

I turn to suggest we leave, but Bara isn't there. She's gone back across to Judith's yard, under a tree with spreading branches. A moment later, the crazy child is climbing the tree.

I look up and down the sidewalk. No one coming, but the neighbouring houses all have lights on, and since the tree is winter-bare, anyone who looks to see why the branches are bouncing could see her. I am relieved when she drops back down onto the lawn and scurries quickly back to my hiding place.

"She's there."

"What's she doing?"

"Sitting at the kitchen table."

"Eating?"

"No, Lucy. Drinking. She's got a bottle of single-malt Scotch. I recognize the label, Lagavulin. My dad drinks that to show off. She's still in her office clothes, with a glass in front of her, and she's just, like, drinking."

I stare at her, but I'm searching my mind for memories of Judith drinking.

"You don't believe me?"

"Of course I believe you. After that night when she sounded so clumsy upstairs and ..." Bara gives me a curious look, but I've remembered that she doesn't know about the bottles on the street and under the sink. "It's just not something I knew before."

But I have found a memory. Judith and I at my apartment, a bottle of wine with the meal. She kept refilling her glass and mine. My head began to turn in those big, slow circles I hate. I tried to refuse. She topped my glass up anyway, so I slowed down, a token small sip now and then. She didn't. I remember something she said as that evening went on, "Stay away from me, Lucy. In the end, I'll hurt you."

Another memory comes back, a party, election night. A friend, dedicated community worker, ran for office and lost dismally. Judith couldn't walk home. Bob Cumberland drove her.

The downstairs lights are still blazing, but now an upstairs one is on as well. Judith's study.

The next day I ask for her at Legal Aid. Called in sick. After school, Bara walks up to the house. She reports that the kitchen light was on, but switched off while she watched, and a minute or so later, the same upstairs light came on.

The next day we walk up to Needham Street and watch for a while from our hiding spot in the bushes. "I'm worried sick about her, Bara."

"Is there anything you can do?"

"Knock on the door, you mean? Or maybe pop through the door from the basement and ask if she's okay? Scare her to death on top of whatever else is going on?" I'm trying to lighten us up, but it has the opposite effect. I suppose I could knock on the front door and say, what? That I hear she's been sick and ... what?

There is a big funeral for young Rosemarie, lots of people, photos in the paper. Cops will be watching from the back pews, like they always do when a murder's unsolved. I need something smaller, quieter. I wait a few days for the memorial that the Street Smart drop-in organizes for the other street workers.

I hear Judith was at the funeral. As soon as I arrive at Street Smart, I scan the room for her. It's crowded, about thirty people arranged in a double semi-circle in what was once the living room of an old house. Althea is sitting near the door and pats an empty seat beside her. She lays her hand on my arm, squeezes and leaves it there.

I've spotted Judith through the heads in front of me, sitting in the front row partway around the circle. She is dressed in suit and heels, as always, hair shiny and brushed under her modest hat. Her head is bent, but in the brief moments when she looks up, I can see how haggard she looks.

The Chaplain, a short, plump woman with curly grey hair, is on her feet. "Jesus said: 'I am the Resurrection and the Life ...'" She is dressed in gown, stole and clerical collar. Street Smart memorial services are formal and dignified at the beginning. Most of the street workers won't go to a regular church, but say the traditions are comforting.

After the readings and prayers, there is an open session where anyone can contribute memories or whatever else is on their minds. One of the young men working Citadel Hill talks at length about how he took Rosemarie under his wing and tried to protect her. I lean toward Althea and, very softly, whisper into her ear, "Judith looks terrible."

She brings her mouth close to my ear. "She's been home sick all week."

I check at Legal Aid for several days after the memorial at Street Smart. I don't need to bother the woman at reception. Little magnets on the board beside her indicate who is in. Judith is there. Now that the weather is warmer, I can spend more time outside, but my peaceful place is Judith's basement, the reading chair, the coloured light of the stained-glass lamp, my books, Nicolás's Bible.

I shouldn't, but I've also been visiting Judith's mysterious study. I'm fascinated with how the piles of paper shift and move, especially the books. Big, dusty tome with a faded cover perches just beside the keyboard and then another day it has joined the semi-circle of paperbacks on the floor around the chair. A slow-motion party for books. Open one with a red cover chats with a tiny one in blue. Faded brown one gets into serious conversation with the computer. One with a picture on the front flutters its sticky notes at a journal. An exhausted one collapses face-down on the carpet, its own weight marking its place, while two hardcovers whisper together in a corner.

It's odd. Whole weeks go by when I don't see Judith, but I feel as if, whatever it is she is doing here, these visits to her study are an ongoing conversation with the inner workings of her mind. I always lift the paper on top of the pile next to the door to see if the "Levellers, Ranters and Diggers" are still there, complete with brown streak on the top page.

Bara is rarely at St. Marks for supper or in the lounge at Fresh Start in the evenings. She has friends now, and they're involved in preparing for the People's Summit. I haven't worried about her since we moved into Fresh Start together, but now I find myself thinking about the barricades, the rumours that there will be an attempt to breach them.

One evening she turns up at the Fresh Start sitting room with Robin in tow. I take in his clothing, every scrap of it solid black.

"Oh no. You're not …"

"I've joined the anarchists."

"Oh for God's sake. The G7, you're not … ?"

"Planning something? I'm not free to say."

"If your group is going to spoil a peaceful protest by bringing violence into it, shame on you."

"Lucy, don't you get tired of peaceful protests that take months to organize and then the media doesn't even bother to mention them? No one wants anyone to get hurt, but a little property damage, a little 'getting out of hand' …" He makes quotation marks in the air.

"Do the organizers know?"

"They know. There's all kinds of negotiating going on, because they don't like it, but the streets are public space, man."

"That's not fair. It gives out the wrong message."

"Nothing else gives out *any* message."

"You're maddening."

"And you're mad."

"Robin!" Bara gapes at him, shocked.

"He's not as well brought up as you," I tell her.

"Are you kidding?" says Bara at the same time as Robin roars with laughter.

"Robin," Bara takes him firmly by the elbow. "I think we need to talk somewhere else."

She pulls him toward the front door. As he leaves the lounge, he says over his shoulder, "Nice to see you too, Lucy."

CHAPTER TWENTY-SIX

"The Beast Comes Back." That's what I call the sermon I give at St. Marks on the Sunday before the G7. Two New Testament readings, from Revelation, ending with the Beast thrown in the sulphurous pit for a thousand years. And then: "For the man who has will always be given more, and the man who has not will forfeit even what he has," as it says in the New English Bible. But I use the King James Version, because I can't imagine this passage any other way, always with an echo: "*Porque a todo el que tiene, más se le dará; pero al que no tiene, aun lo que tiene se le quitará,*" then Nicolás's notes in the margin: "Jesus understood private property."

I use the images I've used for years in my teaching to explain structural violence; my favourite, a huge clock, built centuries ago by a master clockmaker. It runs, but no one needs to wind it, or even think about it. Just so, those conjoined twins, capitalism and colonialism, gears operating in the background, eternally taking from the many, giving to the few. The Beast, invisible until it's challenged. Then it lashes out. I explain non-violent action, peaceful challenge, forcing the Beast to either back down or visibly attack innocents in a way decent bystanders can't ignore.

My friends are there, Althea in another huge Sunday hat, smiles encouragement. Robin, dressed in black, grinning at me. Bara with that little frown between her brows and a group of friends, presumably her art college circle. Judith is not there, an empty space much bigger than her physical self.

⟿

Later Bara confesses that she didn't understand everything. We sit in the lounge at Fresh Start, the new lined pad filling with Bara's ragged script, an essay she is trying to write on the choices faced by women in the time of Jane Austen. We talk about women as property until she heaves a sigh. "I have to get back to Jane's ladies."

"Sure." I move my chair back from the table.

"Lucy."

"Uh hmm?"

"Why do you only talk about, like, big ideas? You learned all this somehow, and you care about it, a lot. I see your eyes fill up. I see what happens when … anyway, why don't you talk about the stuff you've actually seen and done?"

"Now you sound like Doctor 'Tell-me-about-it.'"

"Maybe Doctor 'Tell-me-about-it' isn't so far off."

There is a heavy moment of silence. "Perhaps not. You know that silly expression 'water under the bridge'?"

"What's silly about that? It just means you can't change the past."

"Except it makes it sound like the past goes away."

She's watching me. "He wasn't just a teacher, was he? The one in Guatemala. Or even just a friend."

On cue, my eyes fill up. I use the table to push myself to my feet and retreat to my bed in the basement.

Not just a teacher, not just a friend. And Doctor "Tell-me-about-it" isn't so far off. After Ramón, that terrible day when I knew I'd killed him, Nicolás asked me why I didn't wail and cry with everyone else grieving his loss. "We don't do it like that in North America," I told him.

"Then how can you ease your grief? How can you share it, carry it together?" And then he surprised me completely. He said, "No wonder you don't know what your companies and governments are doing."

"What are you talking about?"

"You are hiding your deepest feelings from one another. Shame keeps you apart, so you also can't really talk. You can't figure things out together. It makes you easy to control politically."

It was many years before I even began to figure out what he meant, and I still haven't learned.

I love it. Sunny May Saturday, Commons like a carnival, crowds of people in sun hats, carrying skateboards, pushing bicycles and strollers, eating fries, listening to speakers and music. For once, it's not me ranting about greed and power. Speaker after speaker talks about who has and who hasn't got access to the world's resources. Bara walked down to the Commons with me, then took off with her new friends. They're moving around, handing something out. I find myself a curb to sit on near the main stage, where I can hear the speakers.

Bara turns up at my elbow. She hands me a leaflet: "**World for Borrow Only.** *At the Youth Perspectives on Our Global Future workshop we expressed our ideas and put them into action.*" A list of headings follows: "Poverty and Employment," "Cultural Diversity and Peace." At the bottom: "Written by a coalition of youth participants."

Bara's head is cocked back, staring at the speaker, her eyes travelling up and down the woman's brilliant sari. "Who is she?"

"Vandana Shiva, scientist and activist, wrote ..."

"She's gorgeous."

Bara's friends are moving off. A short, brown girl turns and beckons her to come. "Gotta go, Lucy. See you later."

"Wait, Bara ..." I try to get my feet under me, eyes fixed on Bara's friend. Young, pretty oval face, brown skin, long black hair tied with a bright, handwoven scarf, definitely Central American. Is it Guatemalan? I need a closer look at the pattern. "Bara, wait ..." But the crowd has closed behind them.

I turn back to Vandana Shiva. Small farmers in India ransacked and burned the offices of Cargill, protesting the company's tactics to make them dependent on patented seed and agricultural chemicals. In Europe, there've been enough demonstrations against genetically modified organisms to force their governments to ban them. "The multinational corporations have to grow or die," she says. "Anywhere we can stand in their way, we set them back."

The Raging Grannies take the stage. Oh my God, I know almost all of them. Old tunes turned into new protest songs: "*My eyes are dim, but I can see, I know something about the economy.*" Comic hats, long skirts, looking like, well, me. "*There are suits, suits, exploiting the grassroots, in the world, in the world....*" Good thing I'm lost in the crowd. What would they say if they saw me now?

Soon after they leave the stage, I find out. A voice, right behind me: "Lucy?" Jeannie Wright, but they all gather around me, old anti-war, anti-racism, anti-poverty activists — Susanne Collier, Linda McLean, faces I can't put names to right away, all older than I remember.

"Lucy, it's been ages ..." Sheila, with the hyphenated last name. Voice trails off. You don't say, "What have you been up to?" to someone who looks like me. Grace Colpitts, looking old — but then, she is — steps back a bit, smiling stiffly.

"Do you still see Dell Compton?" one of them asks.

Before I can say no, someone else says, "She hasn't been out to anything like this in a long time."

"Yeah." A woman whose last name is MacDonald, which narrows it down to half of Nova Scotia. "I heard she had a nervous breakdown or something." She heard it was Dell that had a "nervous breakdown"? That's interesting.

A scruffy young man steps up on the stage, a bullhorn in his hand. "Please listen to the marshals," he bellows. "We're identified by yellow armbands, like this." Holds up his arm, then makes it into a people power fist. Laughter in the crowd. "They've barricaded the whole waterfront, so we won't get anywhere near the conference centre. When we reach the wall, the bulk of the demo will spread out and sing to the police. The marshals are handing out the song sheets. The civil disobedience groups will move according to plan."

"I wish they wouldn't do that," says that really short woman who doesn't see very well, Cathy something. "It always gets violent."

"It's only them ever get hurt, though." Barkhouse — Jane, June, Jan?

"They get the media out." Suzanne Collier, sounding like Robin.

The guy with the bullhorn is still trying for order. "The Raging Grannies will lead the singing at the barricade, so be sure to let them through to the front." People turn to look at us, a smattering of applause.

"You'll come with us?" Jeannie Wright says to me. I start to protest, but the crowd picks us all up and sweeps us along. "*Hey hey, ho, ho, rich and poor have got to go!*" As always, the spirit of so many united voices fills us, inspires us, carries us forward.

Susanne falls in beside me. "I'm letting the young ones do the chanting now, save my voice for the singing."

"Good idea. There's enough of us this time, not the usual hundred or so trying to sound like more." We both laugh.

"I haven't walked with this many people since the March Against Racism five years ago," Susanne says.

"That was one of these moments, wasn't it?"

"Though a hundred can sometimes be as powerful as a thousand, especially when things are happening out of public sight. I don't think many people knew how many Canadian businesses were investing in apartheid before we demonstrated against them. That was only a few of us."

"Helped that it was coordinated across the country."

"Like the marches for the Mohawks at Oka, part of something national."

"Or the gay pride marches, small but mighty."

"I only went to one of those. Too scary, the people heckling along the sidewalks, and those young men that took a run at us with their car."

"But isn't that why it's important that allies come out?"

She sighs. "You're right, of course. And the bigger they get, the safer. Like this. No one could hear a heckler on the sidewalk even if there was one."

The waterfront looks like a big prison, a row of cops in riot gear in front of a concrete barrier topped with a slinky of razor wire. The crowd spreads out in the middle of the street, Raging Grannies in an intersection, facing the demonstrators. The tallest of the Grannies, a younger woman I don't know, has the bullhorn now. Songs more yelled than sung. The crowd roars back. As probably the only Granny on probation, I keep my eye on the police line and stay out of sight behind the others. Feels good to be just one ranting old lady among many.

The cops move closer together, plastic shields touching. They remind me of old Colgate toothpaste ads, people with clear shields around their heads, smiling. These guys are *not* smiling, though how would I know? Can't see their faces. Might be grinning like maniacs.

Gathering tighter right in front of us, they leave bigger spaces off to the sides. That's where the first civil disobedience group rushes the wall, trying to get over fast and run toward the conference centre. All hell breaks loose, cops inside and out running to grab them, throwing them down on the pavement, cuffing them. A whole row of paddy wagons up a side street start their motors. Hadn't noticed them before.

The front one pulls up. Jeannie, beside me, flinches as they throw a handcuffed young woman back over the barricade. Her breath is knocked out of her as she lands hard on her back, her hands under her. Second later, cops on our side are stuffing her into a paddy wagon. Her nose is bleeding. Others follow, many wearing black. I begin to search the crowd for Bara, but I'm being pushed here and there. I have to concentrate on keeping my feet under me and my panic contained. Where is she?

The first line of paddy wagons moves off. Small groups of kids in black are still trying to storm the walls, hitting in different places, wherever the police line gets thin. The police start arresting anyone young and wearing dark clothes. They make a pen out of steel barricades, herd them in like so many cattle. Jeannie shouts beside me, "Hey, that's my niece."

The whole thing is breaking down. A cop yells over our singing, "Get back!" He has a bigger bullhorn. "At least a hundred yards from the barricade!" A hundred yards? The street isn't that wide. "Disperse now, or we'll start gassing."

"We're going to escort you back farther," a young woman in a yellow armband says. A group of them circle the Grannies, me too, and start maneuvering us back into a side street against the force of the crowd still pushing forward. Just as I lose sight of the steel pen, I catch a glimpse of Bara and her friend inside, arms around each other, looking scared.

My heart is pounding. I try to move toward Bara, but I can't fight the current. After a few minutes we're back between buildings, and a little while after that we break through to where the crowd is thinner, people heading away from the scene. "You'd better go, before they get serious about gassing," says the marshal woman. She and the others disappear back into the thick of the action, toward the police.

"I'm not leaving my niece and those other young people in there," Jeannie says and begins to march along a street parallel to the one where the confrontation is taking place. In a moment, I am right beside her. The older Grannies begin to disperse, but the rest fall in behind us.

We come out right in front of the pen where they're holding the young people. Down the street the crowd has backed off, not a hundred yards, but there's open pavement in front of the police. Not here. The crowd mills right around the metal barriers. Jeannie spots her niece. "Watch the cop," she says to me, nodding at the uniform guarding the pen, only one. "Tell me when he's not looking." She looks around at the Grannies. "Bright clothes," she says. "Gather up bright clothes."

They immediately start taking off all the bright things they can spare. Down to essentials, they approach other people in the crowd wearing bright colours. Sweaters, jackets, hats are passed toward the pen.

The cop is overloaded, watching what's going on behind the concrete wall, standing by to open the gate for new arrests and keeping an eye on the kids already in the pen all at the same time. "Now," I say to Jeannie, then "stop," when he looks our way, then "now," again.

Jeannie pushes bright clothing through the metal bars. Her niece slips out through a small gap the kids have made in the back of the pen. As she runs into the chaos, making her way toward the side street, she strips off her borrowed red jacket and passes it back.

"Now," I say. Another two brightly dressed kids slip out. Back come a bright blue hoodie and multicoloured scarf to be pushed between the bars.

"Now." A couple more slip out.

"Lucy!" A hiss at my elbow, Bara, clutching her friend's hand.

"Jeannie, over here." I grab the rainbow tie-dyed T-shirt and green coat that come my way, push them through the bars at Bara, watching the cop. "That way," I point to the gap. Damn. Uniform sees me. His eyes follow my finger.

"Get back here," he yells at a skinny young man trying to climb out. He pushes his way around the outside of the pen, leaving the gate. Immediately young people are slipping away through it, including Bara and her friend.

The young man straightens up, clutching a yellow shawl around his shoulders, black jeans and T-shirt underneath. Too late to run. Cop has him by the arm.

An empty paddy wagon pulls up. More police jump from the cab to help shove the captive into the back. The yellow shawl falls to the ground, trampled. As they push his head down to avoid banging it on the frame, the young man looks back. Robin.

I've lost track of Bara and her friend, scan the crowd for any sign of them. Just then, I hear the telltale rattle of a metal canister on the pavement. Tear gas. Innocent-sounding name for something that grabs your throat, claws your eyes, puts you in an instant panic because you can't breathe. Jeannie yells to the Grannies to skedaddle. We begin pushing our way into the open. Next moment, I'm holding my breath, sleeve over my mouth and nose, staggering into a fog of my own streaming tears.

Coughing painfully, I have that urge to go to ground. After a mass arrest like today's, Judith won't be home until late. Moments after I arrive, so does Bara with her friend, their arms around each other's shoulders, coughing as deeply as I am. "Can Cat stay here with us?" Bara asks.

Cat? She studies me with big, serious, dark eyes. She has a face that belongs to the whole world. She could be Aboriginal, or a light shade of Black, what they call "high yellow," or she could be biracial. She could be white with a darker heritage, Pictish maybe. She could be Italian. She could be Jewish, or high-caste Indian. She could easily be Latin American. In all the confusion she didn't lose the hand-woven, Central American scarf that holds back her thick, black hair. I look at the end hanging over her shoulder. Quetzals. Guatemalan.

"Who are you?" I ask her.

They stare at me.

Bara speaks, sounding defensive. "We're, like, girlfriends. As if it's your business."

I drop my head into my hands, screw my eyes shut. Brown skin, dark eyes, oval faces, looking up at me, eager to learn. Mía, Adela, Marta, Emilia. Hair wrapped in bright, woven scarves.

"Lucy? Are you okay? You're acting really strange."

I shake my mind clear, look at Cat again. "How old are you?"

"Lucy? Geez. What's wrong with you. You're being, like … *rude*. Come on Cat."

"Where are you going?" I hear panic in my voice.

Bara ignores me. They make their way to the door.

"No! Don't go." Now I sound whiny.

Bara pauses, looks around at me. "This is so weird," she declares finally and, turning, heads for the door.

Damn.

CHAPTER TWENTY-SEVEN

It takes a couple of days for my cough to disappear. Bara's too. I hear her at night, barking away in the cot next to mine. No one complains about us that I know of, but I'm sure we keep people awake.

As a few days go by, she softens about Cat, answers a few of my questions. They're in love, as if anyone who saw them the day of the G7 demo could miss it, and now it doesn't take much more than Cat's name to bring a rosy flush to Bara's pale little face. "It took a while to admit to each other we're queer."

"Queer? Where did you come up with that?"

"It's what people like us are called."

"Really? Isn't that an insult? In my day it was."

"Haven't you heard of taking back a slur and making a joke or compliment out of it to defuse its hurtful power?"

"Wow. Where'd you pick that up?"

"Cat's art college friends."

"She's a student there?"

Bara nods.

"Is she from … somewhere else?" I ask.

Bara gives me a strange look. "I don't know. She lives with her grandmother. She's the only person in her family that isn't white."

"She's adopted?"

"Yeah." That sliding up and down "yeah" that tells me I've just asked something stupid. As if I didn't know the moment it was out of my mouth.

"Does she want to know where she comes from?"

"Her grandmother won't talk about it, but the government's just opened up its adoption records. She's put her name in."

"What is her name? A form of Catherine? Catalina, maybe?"
Bara frowns at me, and I can feel my face begin to heat.
"Geez, Lucy. What is going on with you?"

﹌

Robin turns up a week later. "So, you're out," I say. "I've heard
most of the people they arrested are still being held."

"Yeah, I'm out on bail. My parents." His face twists into some
sort of wry apology. "I've got a curfew and I have to wear this."
He pulls up his pant leg to show me the high-tech monitor on his
ankle. "It means a lot more conversation with my parents lately."
He rolls his eyes.

"That's good for you. You won't always have them."

﹌

John counts the weeks out on his calendar. Just four left. Thank
goodness I didn't get caught at the G7 demonstration. "So, John,"
I say. "My letter?"

He looks puzzled.

"To apply to for the accompaniment program? In Guatemala?"

"Lucy, m'dear, you might be more stable psychologically, but
have you noticed how you're walking? From what I read, the
accompaniment volunteers walk for miles and miles, over rough
terrain. Do you really think you can do that?"

"Touch of arthritis. Doesn't stop me going anywhere. I'm so
used to it, I barely notice."

He lifts his bushy eyebrows. "What do the others say? Judith?
Althea?"

I shrug. Must speak to them. And I must get at those adoption
files. I've been avoiding them.

﹌

I meet Bara on the street outside St. Marks, both of us heading to the drop-in for supper. In the echoing hallway, we come upon Judith and Althea talking at the bottom of the ornate wooden staircase that rises to the second floor. They fall abruptly silent, then jump to greet me at the same moment.

I look first at Althea, then Judith, who looks terribly tired. They both look embarrassed.

I weigh my options, decide to confront. "Talking about me?"

They look at each other.

"Sorry Lucy," Althea says, "But we were."

I wait.

Judith gives me her concerned look. "We're on our way to a meeting about the social assistance education policy. I was saying to Althea that I would love to have you there. You probably know more about it than anyone else …"

My eyes have filled. Can she see it in the darkness of hallway, or does she just know?

"Lucy, dear, none of that was your fault. You did everything you could to help those students pick up the pieces."

Bara's Humpty Dumpty comes to mind, only, in this case, a literal fall.

"She made her own decision," Althea says.

I should have taken the avoidance option.

Judith reads my mind. "Your probation ends in a month or so, doesn't it? I'd like to talk about what you want to do once you're free of it." She pauses. "Not so much as your lawyer, but as your friend. I might be able to help."

Did John say something about Project Witness?

"What was that about?" Bara cuts up a slice of chicken properly, fork left; knife right. It's been a long time since I've done that.

"Not your business."

I switch my fork to my left hand. Pick up my knife.

"You can't tell me you didn't come pretty close to crying."

I take a bite, chew slowly.

"And you say Judith has too many secrets to have real friends."

I sigh and set the knife down again on the edge of my plate. "Most of my students missed out on their schooling because they were poor when they were kids. They were sick all the time, or didn't have winter clothing, or they got pregnant too young. Some were in the residential schools. Our program helped them get their GED, but it was a dead end. If they tried to go to community college or university for more than a short occupational course, they'd lose their social assistance, and none of them could afford that.

"We were working to change that policy — as you just heard, they're still at it — but in the meantime, we added university-level courses to our program. Professors volunteered to teach. The students didn't have to travel across the city and could continue to bring their kids to our child care. We supplied sandwiches and cookies, because they often came too hungry to learn. We helped them borrow their tuition under the student loan program, so they could register properly, for credit.

"But then the college I worked for changed. Every program had to not only pay its own way, but also make money for the university. Our adult learning program closed, leaving the students in a more desperate situation than they were in before, no credential, no way to pay back their loans." It's as far as I get before my eyes fill again.

"From what Althea said, I'm guessing one killed herself?"

I can't speak, and after a moment, Bara says, "I'm sorry, Lucy."

We empty our plates in silence, and Bara goes to fetch two hot cups of tea.

"Maybe this isn't a good time, but Lucy, I've got something to tell you."

I raise my eyebrows and wait.

"You know how a couple of times Fresh Start had private rooms come up, but you said no because I couldn't stay there too?"

"Uh huh."

"You know what's her name, on the main floor, got a unit in a housing co-op? She's leaving."

"I still won't take a room without you."

"Well, now that I'm going to school, Althea says I can get a shelter allowance."

"You know I'm on the waiting list for the housing co-op. What if I were to apply for a two-bedroom unit? We could share."

That little frown appears between her brows. "Actually, Lucy, I was thinking of an apartment of my own."

"You're going to move out?" I hear my voice begin to rise.

"Your probation will be over very soon, and you're doing really well. You don't need me."

"But you'll be on your own. Who'll look out for you?"

"Cat."

I stop, pieces falling into place.

"You're moving in with Cat?"

She nods, watching me closely.

Damn. Well, maybe it's time for me to think about an apartment again, if the co-op housing unit is going to take much longer. There's something to talk to Judith about.

"You're both so young."

Bara grins. "We'll be all right, Lucy. I'll, like, visit you really often."

That evening I walk into the Fresh Start lounge, determined to start translating the file of Guatemalan adoption records I carry under my arm. Bara and Cat are there, their homework spread out on either side of a corner of the table, but they aren't doing homework. They are, as we used to say, "billing and cooing."

I clear my throat, and they leap apart.

Bara's features settle quickly from shock to annoyance. "It's you."

"Hi, Bara; Hi, Cat."

Cat nods, looking as annoyed as Bara does.

I seat myself at the other end of the table. "So, I guess I see why you need a place of your own."

"Good." Bara says, and sighs as the two of them settle back into their books.

I should leave, but I am looking at Cat side-on and find myself studying her profile. It's a large nose, curved slightly. Could you say it's Mayan? Maybe. Crossed with something else. A Mayan nose is so distinctive.

"Lucy." Bara snaps at me.

"Okay, okay." I get up to go. Just before I leave the lounge, I add, "I know it's hard to believe, but I was young once too."

Bet they go right back at it the moment I'm out of sight.

There's no one in the kitchen. I take a deep breath, pull out the files. I turn under the stapled corner of the top page, hiding the thin, sad baby in the little photo. I forgot the pad, but I'm determined to start. Working in pencil, I begin to jot English words between the lines.

Why do I think of my baby as "she"? Because all babies start out female, and she didn't have time to turn into a boy? I sometimes even think of her as Nicola.

We were so young, and so in love. I used to wonder why moths fly into open flame. Why would God create such a powerful urge when it can lead to nothing but destruction? After Nicolás came into my life, I still didn't know why, but I knew exactly what the moths were feeling.

It hurt so much, aching to be near him when I was away from him, and then trying to behave as if nothing was going on when he was there, except when we were alone, which was so rare. Tiny things would make me melt: his long eyelashes, dirt in the creases of his knuckles. Surely, everyone could see me eating up my own heart. Surely, they could see it in his eyes too.

We resisted for a long time. We should have parted never having touched, would have, I'm sure, if life hadn't become so fragile and precious in that place and time.

My chest hurts. Something swelling, trying to get out. A sob. I grab it, hold on. Won't let it escape.

CHAPTER TWENTY-EIGHT

Judith and I have an appointment to talk about what I'm going to do after probation. Now that Bara is moving out of Fresh Start, I want to know where I am on the housing co-op waiting list and ask her for a letter for Project Witness. I sit in the waiting area, bracing myself to see Judith, and not an ever-shifting dance of books and papers in an upstairs study. A law student comes instead, hands me a message in Judith's neat, fountain-pen cursive, asking me to come to Althea's office.

I falter when I see her there. She looks distracted and deadly serious, as does Althea. Is this about Judith's basement? Have they found out?

Then I see Patty, red-eyed and ashen.

Judith sees me. "Lucy, there you are. Have you heard?"

"Heard?" I step through the door.

"Cindy's in Burnside," Althea tells me.

"What?" My memories of the place shudder through me. "Picked up for communicating?"

Tears spill down Patty's cheeks, obviously just wiped dry from a previous flood. "She's been off the street since we got the apartment and the kids back."

"Then what?"

Althea answers. "She tried to steal a chicken from Sobeys."

Patty grabs another tissue from the box on Althea's desk and blows her nose. Her voice, usually so deep and clear, has been reduced to a shaky whisper. "She had to get a prescription for Leo.

We've been out of food money for over a week. Cindy talked about maybe going out on the street. 'Just once,' she said. That's what happened last time she lost the kids. She went out 'just once.' 'Just once' for sneakers. 'Just once' to get them into hockey. 'Just once' for school books. I talked her out of it. There's no 'just once,' and she knows it. We had some pasta and stuff set aside and got a bag from the food bank, but the boys were hungry."

"So she tried to take a chicken?" I say.

Patty nods, miserable. "She didn't think ahead or anything. She saw it and thought about the kids and how long it's been since they've had meat."

"Was a store detective watching?" Althea asks. It was she who taught me, a long time ago, about how store detectives follow Black people.

Patty shook her head no. "Didn't need a store detective. She had her wool skirt on. It's full, you know? She put the chicken between her thighs."

"Ooooo," Althea winces.

"Yeah. It froze her thighs. They were all red and swollen. Couldn't feel if she was hanging on to the chicken or not. As she tried to walk out the door, it fell on the floor."

"And they put her in jail for that?" Althea's eyebrows shoot up. "What's a skinny Sobeys chicken worth? Twelve dollars?" Patty reaches for another tissue. Althea pushes the box closer.

"I think Sobeys wants to make an example of her," Judith says. "Stores sometimes do that, and in this case it's a bit easier for them because of her record."

"Bail?" I ask.

"The judge set it high. She hasn't turned up in court a few times when she should have."

"Are you going to defend her?" I ask.

"Of course, though there is no real defence. They caught her red handed."

I catch a glint in Althea's eyes, and guess she's thinking what I just thought: red-thighed.

"Cindy wants to make a moral point. We will to go to court and the media and argue that the chicken is a little thing to Sobeys, but a huge thing to her boys. The scales of justice are being asked to weigh the lives, health and future of two young human beings against a couple of dollars of profit for a national grocery chain. We are thinking we could calculate the profit on the chicken as a proportion of Sobeys annual income and Cindy's, get Cindy on the stand to talk about what they can afford to eat, what happens when there is a special expense like winter boots or a prescription, ask the boys to testify about how tired they are at school, how often they're home because they're sick. What do you think, Lucy?"

Althea is nodding in agreement and Patty's big moist eyes are on me. "What a brave woman she is," I say, and Patty's eyes start to flow again.

"We'll plead guilty and get her out. There will be a fine, but I'll keep it as low as possible. I'll make all the points I can about poverty. There are good 'whereas' points about the mandate of the *Employment Support and Income Assistance Act* and the *Human Rights Act*."

"And her kids?" says Patty. "Will she get them back?"

I close my eyes a moment. Those kids are the most important thing in Cindy's life.

"As soon as we get her out," Judith says, "we'll go to work on that."

Althea offers to care for Patty's boys, so she can go with Judith out to the jail. Patty turns to me. "Come with us."

"You need your time with her." My heart is beating too fast.

"Cindy thinks the world of you, Lucy. She'll want to see you, and she'll be happy you're helping with this."

Judith is watching with those clear, direct eyes of hers. She knows how I feel about Burnside. I give her a little nod.

Althea folds Patty into the nest of her strong arms and holds her like a small child. Patty breaks into tears again. I get a giant Althea hug too. Her soft bosom always seems to say, "I'm the Mother of the World and everything will come out fine."

On the way out to the industrial park where the jail is, Patty rides in the front seat. From my spot in the back of the tiny car, I can see Judith's eyes in the rear-view mirror. They seem larger. Has she lost weight? I try to remember. I think she has. Maybe she should be eating something more than yoghurt. Or maybe someone else is eating her yoghurt.

Judith presses the button on the intercom, says who she is. We stand in front of the big glass doors waiting for a guard to let us in. I'm shivering, and it's not the wind blowing across the desert of the industrial park. "I've changed my mind," I tell them. "I'll wait in the car."

Judith's eyes fill with sympathy. She'll release me, but Patty speaks first. "Please, Lucy. For Cindy's sake."

My heart and my lungs are both making noise, like someone drumming in a big, hollow cave. I picture a big hand pushing down my panic. It looks like roiling black water, or sludge maybe, sewage. I take a deep breath, stay with them.

Click of the guard's key in the lock. Excuse me, "correctional officer." We step into a small lobby almost filled by a metal detector. More locked doors. A receptionist behind what looks like bulletproof glass, a little slot to pass things through, Judith's ID, Patty's driver's licence. I don't have anything. Judith has to vouch for me, sign me in.

Another officer comes to get Judith. He unlocks the door under the sign that says, "Professional Visitors." "Wait here," he says to Patty and me.

Judith disappears. There is a click as the guard locks the door behind her. Hearing my deliberately slow, deep breathing, Patty looks at me with concern, takes my arm as I lower myself onto the cold plastic. That proud eagle feather tattoo on her wrist. I touch it, smile. She smiles back. Both smiles brief.

I read the visitors' rules, slowly: *"Purses, knapsacks and bags must be placed in locker before entering visiting room, including keys, money and cell phones. If metal detector is triggered, the visitor will be subject to a manual search. Visits are limited to fifteen minutes. Do not try to touch the prisoner or pass anything to the prisoner. Conversations with prisoners will be monitored. Any visitor who does not co-operate with these rules will not be allowed to visit."* Visitor. I'm just a visitor. I can leave anytime I want. It helps, for a while.

Judith returns with a guard at her elbow, a woman. I recognize her. Rhoda? Rhonda? She knows me too. She stares but doesn't say anything.

"They'll give you each fifteen minutes with Cindy," Judith says.

"I'll give my time to Patty," I offer.

"No, she wants to see you too."

"Five minutes, then. Can I give the rest to Patty?"

The guard gives a single nod and watches with a stony, suspicious face as I struggle to my feet.

Cindy just cries and cries, her nose running into the telephone on her side of the glass. "I know you know what it's like in here," she says. "Pray for me?"

"I could get myself back in, keep you company."

That gets a smile, but then she says, "The boys are back in foster care" and starts weeping again.

"Judith will help you get them back once you're out."

Cindy nods.

I reach out toward the thick glass. Rhoda or Rhonda snaps, "Do not try to touch the prisoner." I put my hand in my lap.

I keep repeating, "Judith will get you out and get the boys back."

⤚

It's dark and raining when we come out. As we drive through Dartmouth, we're quiet, except for Patty sniffing in the back seat. The streetlights, each in turn, toss their yellow glow across the front seat, broken by the slash of the windshield wipers. Each flickers for a second across the tired, sad lines in Judith's face.

Questions march through my head. Do you see your drinking as a problem? What were you doing all those years in Toronto and why didn't you graduate from high school until you were twenty-one? What are you doing with the Levellers, the Ranters and the Diggers?

Patty's sniffles fade into loud, even breathing. "She's fallen asleep," I tell Judith.

"Good. She's exhausted."

"Judith, do you ever feel like giving up?"

Streetlights pass. The windshield wipers flop back and forth. I think she's not going to answer, but then she does. "Sometimes, I long for a place to go where no one can find me, where I could just sleep and read crime novels for a while. Is that the same thing?"

"You read crime novels?"

"When I can, which isn't very often. I love the feeling of knowing the crime is going to be solved by the end of the book." Is there a streak of grey in the hair pulled back from Judith's temple, or is it just a trick of the passing lights? "But do I want to give up permanently? No. What else would I do?"

"Become a regular lawyer, write wills, help people buy houses, stuff that wouldn't regularly break your heart."

"It wouldn't feel real. I'd still know all this is going on, but I wouldn't be doing anything about it." The next streetlight picks up the network of fine creases that appear around her eyes when she smiles, but in the next one, it's gone again. "My heart does get broken, though, so often it doesn't have time to mend in between."

I hold my hand out, hard, weathered palm up, where the next light can slide across it. She glances down. "You're no stranger to a broken heart yourself," she says. Then, a few moments later, lifts her hand off of the steering wheel, placing it in mine. The bones are fine and breakable, but the squeeze is firm. And she leaves it there, driving left-handed until we get to the bridge tollbooth, where she has to fumble in the ashtray for a token.

CHAPTER TWENTY-NINE

Cindy pleads guilty, and they let her out. Judith will make her arguments at the sentencing hearing. Robin writes an article for his homeless people's paper, and the regular media pick it up. Bara starts coming home with papers full of letters to the editor about poverty and food. Judith is interviewed on *Information Morning*. More letters to the editor. Something's going on. Sometimes, after years of work on an issue, it suddenly catches fire — or, perhaps a better image, reaches a tipping point. You take what seems like a small action, or something just happens, and you find out it's that last grain of sand that causes a landslide, the proverbial last straw. I hope that's what this is, but I won't let myself count on it quite yet.

Judith, at least, is on fire. She is spending hours on Cindy's case and looks so much better, alive. I've seen this before, when a case really challenges her sense of purpose. Although, I wonder if she's sleeping at all. Because somehow, she still finds time for the Levellers, Ranters and Diggers. I know because the papers and books in the study continue to move.

More reporters show up for Althea and Judith's press conference than they expected. The program room at the library is full, standing room only. I see Robin, Gord and Bara in the crowd. Reverend Peter sticks up above the people around him. Patty and Cindy sit in the front row, a respectable distance apart. Bet they'd like to be holding hands right now.

John works his way through the crowd toward me, smiling. He

holds out his hand to shake mine. "Congratulations, m'dear. You are a free woman."

I take in a breath, counting days in my head.

"Today, Lucy. It's your last on probation." His grin is taking up most of his face. When I smile back, he pulls me forward and gives me what can only be called a bear hug. "I can give you back control of your money now, if you want."

"Sure, and John? The letter?" But he has already turned to greet someone else. Better to talk about it in his office anyway.

A circle of microphones, cameras and lights are focused on the tiny, bright spot that is Judith, although I'm always impressed by how she can look bigger than she is. Maybe it's the posture and clothes. More likely it's the intense way she speaks, an inner furnace raging through her politely restrained voice, correct grammar, academic language.

"What do we value?" she says. "How did we get to the point where our laws protect a national grocery chain worth four billion dollars against a worried mother who can't afford twelve dollars and forty-five cents worth of chicken to feed her children?" She pauses. That's another thing she does, leaves silences, just a beat longer than you'd expect. "We say we live in a country that protects the weakest, that has a safety net for those who fall through the cracks. The introduction to the legislation that mandates our social assistance programs says that the Province 'shall furnish assistance to all persons in need.'

"And then there is our human rights legislation. John Humphrey, a Canadian from New Brunswick, wrote the Universal Declaration of Human Rights. He was, in part, responsible for its adoption by the United Nations. One of the basic rights in the Declaration is freedom from hunger."

"We're still talking about theft here," says one of the reporters.

"We have two conflicting laws," Judith said, "One says that my client committed theft. The other says that we, Canadian and

Nova Scotian society, have failed to protect her human rights and those of her children. It is not unusual for two laws to come into conflict, and when that happens, we have to choose which one represents our more deeply held values, the kind of society we want to live in."

Bara comes back early with the newspaper the next morning, its headline blaring: "Sobeys Chicken Case: Lawyer says theft justified."

Saturday afternoon. I follow the giggling and find Bara and Cat looking at a newspaper spread on the table in the lounge. Classifieds. The giggling stops. I nod at the page where they've circled several ads. "Are there some you can afford on the shelter allowance?"

"Cat's grandmother will pay her share."

I nod. Pretty clear I'm not welcome here. "Good luck," I say, walking away.

At Legal Aid, there is no receptionist, but a passing law student tells me that he saw Judith earlier, thinks she's there working on Cindy's case. She has been using the quieter time on weekends to prepare for the sentencing hearing.

I feel better the moment I step into the dusty darkness of Judith's basement. I feel for the nearest light cord. Familiar clutter springs into light and shadow. I start. Someone is here. "Bara?" But even as I say her name, I know it's not her.

Judith stands in the main path to the furnace, her eyes hollow shadows in the overhead glare.

"I've come to pick up some of my things." I hold up the key, its cardboard tag dangling, as if to say, hey, you gave it to me. I hope she can't hear my heart beating.

Slowly, mechanically, she looks down at the reading chair, with its side table and lamp, the crib, wool blanket folded and hanging over the frame. Then she raises her eyes, following the trail to the table in front of the derelict washing machine, papers and books on its surface. Finally, her eyes return to me, her hard look, reserved for power company lawyers, racist employers, slum landlords. "I trusted you." Her voice cracks.

My heart flutters around my chest now like a trapped bird. I had thought about it, what I would say, but it's all turned to ashes.

"You know how I feel about this house."

I can't hold her eyes. I look down at the ragged sneakers on my feet, scuff my toe in the dust on the floor.

"How long?"

"Since that time on the street, before Fresh Start."

"Bara too?"

I nod, feeling miserable. "It was warm here, Judith. Safe."

She holds out her hand. "The key, Lucy."

I feel panic. "These boxes," I nod toward them. "There're all I have left of my old life."

"I know. But now I need you to return the key."

Reluctantly, I place it in her palm. She closes her hand around it, then closes her eyes, taking in a shaky breath.

When she looks at me again, the anger has drained away, leaving just hurt.

She takes another deep breath, releases it, turns and starts along the side path to the stairs. "Well, since you've already been in my kitchen, stay and have tea with me."

I'm so shocked, I don't move until she looks back to see why I'm not following.

I watch Judith move about the kitchen, making tea. Even her casual, at-home clothes are dressy, camel slacks with a crease, a soft blue and beige tartan flannel shirt over a tank top, immaculate loafers. She moves as if she's exhausted. I sniff the air, searching for wine or Scotch, but don't smell anything.

There is so much I want to ask her. About the drinking, the full basement and empty upstairs, the years in Toronto. Why do you sleep in your study, Judith? And why is it full of Levellers, Ranters and Diggers?

"I figured it out today," she says. "That you'd been in the house." She searches a shelf in one of the cupboards, produces an opened package of digestives. "It was the hair."

I cringe.

"At first, I thought they were mine. I am getting grey ones, as you may have noticed. And then this morning I picked one up for a close look. It was too long, too thick and too curly to be mine."

"Did I frighten you?"

"Not after I figured out whose hair it was. More a feeling of … betrayal."

She hasn't looked at me once since we came upstairs. As she pours the tea, she becomes businesslike again. "Your probation is over, Lucy. Congratulations. And you've done well at Fresh Start, although I know it's been hard. Bara has helped, hasn't she?"

I nod.

"I checked with the housing co-op a few weeks ago. You're high on the list."

She sits, pushes an old-fashioned matching milk and sugar set in my direction, along with the digestives on a plate. "If I were a real friend, I guess I would have invited you to stay here until you could get your own place."

I catch my breath.

She watches my surprise. "It's an old habit, keeping my home to myself. You know that."

"I truly didn't mean to hurt you."

"I know." She looks so sad, sitting there with her hands cupped around her tea. "You're my friend, Lucy. And now I feel I can't trust you."

I look into my half-full cup for a moment, back to her eyes. "But am I? Your friend?"

Now she looks startled.

"I mean, we've spent a lot of time together, worked together, but I don't know you. I don't know anything about your family, your life before I met you, how you feel about things, what you do when you're not working."

"My family just wasn't like that. You know, sharing personal things, feelings. And besides," She gives me a humourless smile. "You're one to talk."

I sigh. "That psychiatrist I have to see is always after me to tell him about my past."

"Me too."

"You have a psychiatrist?"

"Not a psychiatrist, but at law school we could ask for a certain number of free counselling sessions to deal with the stress."

"Did it help?"

"No. More my fault than the counsellor's. I wouldn't talk, not really."

"People are sometimes puzzled by you, you know. You're so warm, up to a point, and then they hit the wall of your secrets."

"Look who's talking, Lucy."

I have to laugh.

She relaxes a bit, smiles back.

"Are they right, Judith? Would we be better off if we talked about the past?"

"The theory makes sense, that telling the story of painful times is part of the healing. It's just so hard. Hard to do, and hard to trust someone enough."

"And now, whatever trust you had in me is broken."

Now she looks at me. "Do you trust me, Lucy?"

"More than anyone else I can think of, except perhaps Althea."

"Would you ever consider telling me your story? Your whole story?"

"I sometimes wonder if it wouldn't make me feel less … lonely."

"You feel lonely too?"

I nod.

She takes in a deep breath. "I don't know, Lucy."

"Is it something we should try? Maybe set aside an evening?"

"Not now. I'm preparing for Cindy's sentencing hearing."

"After that?"

"I've been thinking about taking you out for supper anyway, to celebrate the end of your probation."

I can't imagine we'll actually go through with this. Our shells are too old and thick. But somehow, even talking about it makes me feel changed. Just a little bit.

Judith looks different too, the warmth back in her eyes. "I'll drive you back to Fresh Start."

CHAPTER THIRTY

"Hey, Lucy." It's Robin, in the basement hallway at St. Marks, still dressed in black but now dotted with bright spots, explained by the paintbrush in his hand. "Look what we're doing." I follow him, noting that the monitor is still on his ankle.

On the floor of an unused room, young people kneel in a rough circle, bending over squares of cardboard. There are paintbrushes in their hands and more resting in cans with bright colours dripping down their sides onto the concrete floor. Bara waves with a stapler. Cat, just behind her, looks up. When she sees me staring at her, she steps in behind a big guy in black. Bara bends back to her task, stapling a placard to a wooden picket.

"There's going to be a demo outside the courthouse during Cindy's sentencing hearing," Robin explains.

Finished placards are stacked against the far wall. I read them upside down.

"Need not greed."

"Food before profit."

"Freedom from hunger is a human right."

Many show chickens, alive or roasted, on platters. They're well done, many striking and beautiful. I remember Cat's crowd are art students.

Someone takes over Bara's stapling task while she comes over to greet me. "Cool, eh?"

"It is."

"You've been doing demos all your life, but it's my first. Whenever there were marches and things on TV, my parents would say the people were, like, misfits or 'professional agitators,' but that's not true, is it? It's just people who care about something."

I give her a smile. "How is the apartment hunt going?"

Her face falls, and I'm sorry I asked. "There's not much that we can afford. Mostly really dirty rooming houses. Places that don't even feel safe."

Cat straightens, pushing her cuff back and holding up her watch. "Bara, look at the time."

"Sorry Lucy, we gotta go. But you'll be at the demo, right?" It isn't a question.

"Hey guys," Bara announces to the room. "Everyone who's coming to the planning meeting at the art college, it starts in fifteen minutes."

A third of those present jump to their feet, pushing their paint cans closer to those who are staying, scrambling to find their sweaters and shoes.

When I get to the law courts for Cindy's sentencing hearing, I can't believe the scene outside. It's not just the art students. The street is full of people. I make my way to the steps and climb up where I can read the signs. Some were painted in the basement at St. Marks, but there are many, many more:

"*Mr. Sobey, do your children go hungry?*"

"*Hunger,*" with a red circle around it and slash through it.

"*Right to food,*" a picture of Justice with a hungry child on one side of her scales and on the other, the Monopoly banker with money falling out of his pockets.

Inside, the place is packed. A young man gets up and waves his hand toward his seat. I squint at him, decide I don't know him. Black clothes, big grin. Buddy of Robin'? Thinks I'm Lucy the Prophet? I take the seat. Up ahead I see Reverend Peter, his height making him stick out.

The prosecution case is quick, since no one's denying Cindy took the chicken. The judge calls on Judith and she stands, tiny in her black gown and crisp white tabs. The judge, of course, knows what she's going to try to do. Everyone does.

"Miss Maidstone," he says, looking down at her over his half glasses like a caricature of his profession. "I will not entertain arguments that are not directly related to the case."

"Yes, Your Honour." She nods to him. "I would like to call Miss Beals to the stand."

Cindy looks small and grey, circles under her eyes. Yes, she took a chicken out of the freezer. It was for her boys. She didn't intend to eat any herself. What would she have eaten? Pasta, with margarine. How often do they eat pasta with margarine? Late in the month, every day. The day she took the chicken, how long had it been since the boys had eaten protein? A couple of weeks.

Judith was refused permission to put the boys on the stand. "I would like to call Professor John Collier," she says.

"What is your intention in calling Professor Collier to the stand, Miss Maidstone?"

"Professor Collier is an expert on international treaties, Your Honour."

"And what do international treaties have to do with this case, Miss Maidstone?"

"Canada is signatory to eight international treaties guaranteeing the eradication of poverty, Your Honour, beyond our own four pieces of legislation, eight legislative guidelines, three Orders in Council — "

"Miss Maidstone, I know what your strategy is. You have made it perfectly clear in the pages of every newspaper in the country. I, however, fail to see the relevance of international treaties, the introductory paragraphs of various pieces of legislation, and statements of intent from the various levels of government to the simple theft of a chicken. If you wish to make a challenge regarding the constitutional rights of your client, this is not the place to do so."

Never veering from her calm, polite respect toward the judge, never raising her voice out of its even, cultivated diction, never showing a ruffled feather, Judith fights. She makes every point she can, obliquely or straight on, packing extra words in wherever she can like the long-ago lawyers who were paid by the word. Anywhere else, we'd be cheering.

When she can't filibuster another word, the judge makes her sit down and lectures her about taking up the court's time with ridiculous grandstanding. "I could have you indicted for contempt of court," he says, but doesn't. Judith had warned us that, with all her prior convictions, Cindy could have been given some jail time, but she gets probation. The bad news is that her boys will stay in the foster home until she completes her probation.

Judith goes out on the courthouse steps still in her black gown. A stiff breeze off the harbour flaps it around her ankles. Someone hands her a megaphone. With Cindy and Patty standing behind her, openly holding hands, she makes the rest of the case she would have made in the courtroom to the people gathered outside. We all cheer and boo and yell "Shame, shame," at appropriate moments.

And then the crowd begins to move, flowing down Spring Garden Road to Barrington, chanting *"No more hungry kids."* A few blocks along Barrington, the crowd turns, descending Prince to Granville and pouring into the grounds of the provincial legislature. Gathered around the front steps, the chant changes to *"Hey hey, ho ho, poverty has got to go."* Placards catch my eye — *"We love all our kids,"* with a big red heart; *"Mr. Sobey, how long since you last ate?"* Some have artwork good enough to be on someone's living room wall.

A face I recognize moves into my line of vision, handsome, smiling. "Lucy Chambers? Ned Fielding." He puts out his hand. "Art college faculty. Remember the meetings about saving the departments the university tried to cut in 1990?"

"Yes. Of course."

"I thought your Dean was going to have a heart attack that day you joined in with the theatre and drama students, that demo with the coffins. Her face was so red." He laughs. "So, what do you think of this new generation? Remember we used to joke that the art college should grant degrees in activism?"

A young person comes up beside Ned Fielding, says something to him. He turns to listen, and I move closer to the legislature steps, into the dense centre of the crowd. When it gets too packed to move any closer, I look around and realize that Robin is close by, watching me.

Several students speak, as earnest as can be, but we're all waiting for Judith. There is a stir as she is pushed and pulled through the cheering crowd and up the steps. In front of the legislature's imposing front door, she looks tiny and her tailored suit makes her look like a society lady out for afternoon tea, until she opens her mouth.

Then out pours the pure, concentrated fire of Judith's passion. "Poverty in Canada is no accident, no aberration, not a case of a few people 'left behind.' It is a deliberate creation of legislation, indispensable to the political and economic system we live in. It is a choice." I imagine her channelling something massive and powerful that hovers, invisible, just behind her, an energy, an irrefutable truth. "Poverty does not exist for its own sake, because we are somehow an unfeeling society. No, it's a by-product, collateral damage, of the policies that benefit those who would accumulate more than their share." The students cheer and bob their placards up and down.

After Judith steps down and disappears among the chanting students, I wiggle out of the claustrophobic pack of human bodies and find a bench nearby. In a few minutes, Robin sits down beside me. "Hey Lucy the Prophet, not going to get arrested today?"

"No, are you?" I look down pointedly at the bulge the monitoring bracelet makes in the cuff of his pants.

"Yeah, well, that was a deliberate tactic, planned ahead. I wasn't just yelling at people in a store."

I snort.

"Oh come on, Lucy, tactics like ours have led to revolutions, changed governments, forced dictators to back down, forced multinationals to give up plans to privatize water."

"And then what happens?"

"What do you mean?"

"Capitalism is insidious. It just finds a different costume, different words, and sneaks back in through a different door."

"'Insidious.' That's good. That professor from the art college, he's got quite the rep as a radical. You knew him back when you were on campus?"

"Not well, and Robin, I wish you'd stop calling me Lucy the Prophet."

"It just means I think you're honest and brave. What you did at the university, lots of people think you're a hero."

"Lots of people?" Over his shoulder I see Bara detach herself from the edge of the gathering and head in our direction.

"Well, some people."

Bara sits down on my other side. "Lucy? You okay?"

Robin rises. "See you later," he says as he heads for someone he has spotted in the crowd.

Bara is frowning at me. "Had enough of crowds and noise? Do you want to go and sit for a while in Judith's basement? That always calms you down."

"Oh, Bara. I haven't had a chance to tell you. She caught me."

"In the basement?"

I nod.

"Was she upset?"

I nod again. "I can't go back."

"But she's doing interviews with reporters. And after that the demo organizers want to talk to her. It'll be a long time before she goes home."

"She took back her key."

There is an odd silence beside me.

"Bara? What?"

She lifts her ever-present knapsack onto her knees, unzips a front pocket and produces a shiny new key.

"Is that … ?"

She nods.

"How did you … ?"

"That day I got the extension cord."

"I don't believe you did this to me. Can't I trust you at all?"

"About as much as Judith can trust you."

Did she mean that to hurt? "All right. Give it to me. I'm going there to pick up a few things and then I'm going to destroy it."

She hesitates.

"Wait. Have you been there without me?"

Her silence gives me the answer.

"Oh, Bara."

She sighs, hands me the key.

I must work quickly, collect a few precious things. My eye falls on the crib mattress, flat on the floor, a couple of blankets tangled in a heap. Bara, Bara, Bara. I'll fold those and put them away before I go. Thank goodness Judith didn't catch them.

My knees are so sore from the uphill walk, I can't bend down to the box holding my precious top shelf books. In fact, I'm exhausted. Just a few minutes in the reading chair. I turn out the light, just in case.

Ned Fielding. That day the front steps of the university arts centre were crowded with faculty emerging from the hall. We had been summoned, all however many hundred of us, to be told that the university's purpose was no longer education, but money. Well, the president didn't put it quite like that. There was lots of blah, blah, blah about "excellence in education," "rationalizing programs," "doing more with less," "working smarter," but at the heart of it was an announcement: programs that couldn't pull their financial weight — like drama and music — would be chopped or have their primary mandate changed to producing revenue for the university — like continuing education. As we came out onto the steps, a sombre procession of drama and music students approached along the sidewalk, dressed in black, heads bowed, pacing slowly to a dirge played by a brass band. In their midst, two coffins, riding the shoulders of pallbearers in black top hats, "drama" and "music" written on the sides. I joined them. Interesting that Ned noticed Dell's reaction.

I'm not sure how the drama and music people knew it was coming. In continuing education, we had heard vague rumours but no real warning. But then, their Dean was on their side. I still thought ours was, but she wasn't speaking to me much at that point. I was slow to grasp how much she had changed.

I start awake when the front door opens upstairs. Damn. Darkness has fallen outside and it's completely black down here.

The briefcase thumps down on the floor in the hall. A minute later the toilet in the hallway bathroom flushes, gurgling in the pipes. CBC comes on in the kitchen. She'll want to hear what the media says about the day's events. I certainly do. I hear cupboards open and close, the metallic rattle of cutlery, a pot set down. Now what? I daren't move.

And then there is a crash, a chair clattering across the kitchen floor, a soft thump right above my head. Then, breathless silence.

CHAPTER THIRTY-ONE

———————————

Judith lies on the tiles, curled around the legs of the chair she knocked over as she went down. Her hair has come out of its ponytail and is spread in an aura around her head. Using the table for support, I lumber into a kneeling position beside her. She's breathing hoarsely through her mouth, alive — a relief — but unconscious, which in some ways is a relief too.

I lever myself up and head for the front room, call 911 from the phone sitting on a side table. They say to stay on the line, but I don't want to leave Judith alone. They tell me to unlock the front door.

Returning to the kitchen, I remember to shut off the radio and the soup heating on the stove before lowering myself to my knees again. I should maybe have left the radio on. All I can hear now is Judith's laboured breathing. "Judith, hang on, they're coming." Her face is a bluish greyish colour and her hand lies, loosely curled, under her chin. I take it in mine, hold it firmly. "Judith, stay with me. You'll be all right. Just hang on."

Where are they? It's taking forever. I look up at the clock on Judith's kitchen wall. Big help. I don't know what time it was when I called, but now I hear the siren far off, quickly coming closer, stopping abruptly in front of the house. In seconds, two big young men come through the hall into the kitchen.

"We need some space," one of them says to me. Picking up the fallen chair with one large hand and taking my elbow with the other, he helps me sit. They set to work with their stethoscopes and machines, one of them reporting every move into a radio on his shoulder. In a few minutes one of them leaves, comes rattling back with a stretcher on wheels.

"We'll need her purse," one of them says to me. Remembering the thump of her briefcase hitting the hall floor, I get to my feet. Suddenly breathless and dizzy, I have to pause for a moment, supporting myself with the edge of the table.

Judith's briefcase sits beside the hall table. I pop the catches open. It's stuffed with papers, but in the front compartment there's a leather clutch. I flip it open. All her cards and things are neatly arrayed in pockets.

By now, they've lifted her onto the stretcher, wrapped in a blanket, her face hidden under a mask, and they're wheeling it into the hall. "Good," says the young man, seeing the clutch in my hand. "Do you want to come with her?"

I nod and stumble along behind, gripping the clutch to my chest. I remember to shut the door behind me.

The paramedics go through a series of quick, clattering maneuvers with the stretcher and slide Judith into the ambulance. As one goes forward to the driver's seat, the other helps me in and seats me on a stool. The door clicks shut and we're off, jostling over uneven pavement, veering around corners, siren wailing.

"We're on our way," the guy beside me says into his radio, followed by a steady stream of words in a language I don't understand, a lot of numbers. He reaches for Judith's clutch. I hand it to him. It takes only a second for him to locate her health card and driver's licence. He speaks into the radio again: birthdate, October tenth, nineteen forty-four, name, Judith Selene Maidstone. Selene?

The ambulance stops howling and comes to halt. The doors fly open. One coordinated lift and they're rolling Judith along a concrete platform. I'm almost bumped aside, but someone grabs me, guides me through a sliding glass door into a hallway. The two paramedics run ahead with Judith, turn a corner and disappear. People in pastel scrubs converge and follow. I'm suddenly alone in this bright, barren place and my knees have gone trembly. Right in front of me is a small, green plastic chesterfield. I stagger to it and collapse.

I hear voices from around the corner, muffled, but it sounds like someone barking out orders. A little while later, I hear something metallic coming. It's the stretcher from the ambulance, empty, pushed by the paramedic that did the driving. He sees me and comes in my direction, parking the stretcher against the wall in front of me. He sets about putting a fresh sheet on it.

"Are you a relative?" He has a kind voice.

"Friend."

He crosses the straps on top of the sheet, folds the blankets. "I'll let the charge nurse know you're here." He disappears around the corner again. A few minutes later, an efficient-looking woman comes, the paramedic behind her. "Are you," she checks a clipboard in her hand, "Miss Maidstone's next of kin?"

"Friend." The paramedic winks at me as he rolls his stretcher away toward the ambulance dock.

The nurse consults her paper again. "Do you know Robert Cumberland?" I nod. "Is he a relative?"

"Her boss."

"Do you know where he lives?" I shake my head no. "All right, no problem. We'll find him." She moves past me to another set of glass doors. "We have a family room where you can wait. I'll see if it's free." She pushes through. Obviously, I'm to follow.

This hallway is as blank and empty as it can be, only two doors, solid and closed. She knocks on one of them. No response. She pushes it open a crack, looks inside, then opens it wider. "You can wait here. There's a phone with an outside line, if you want to make any calls. We'll let you know what's happening as soon as we can."

There are some comfortable chesterfields and chairs in the room, the same university-dorm green plastic upholstery as the couch in the hallway. I drop myself into one. There is a window here. It's dark outside, but the building I'm looking at has towers and satellite dishes on the roof, all lit up. The CBC building.

Beyond that, a parade of lights moves along the street, coming and going from the Willow Tree intersection. The walking paths on the Commons are lit but empty.

I'm startled when someone rattles a huge metal cart past the doorway. I look at the phone. Should I call someone? I'd love to have Althea here with me, but I don't know her home number.

I wonder what time it is. The energy that carried me upstairs to Judith, to the telephone and back to the kitchen, has long since drained away. I close my eyes. Dear Judith, please be okay. Dear Jesus …

How very, very long it's been since I've even tried to pray. When I think of Jesus, all I can see is Nicolás, intense brown eyes in his brown, Indian face, full of the love we weren't even supposed to name, let alone act on.

Voices outside. The door opens, and the nurse shows Bob Cumberland into the room. He looks even more like a scarecrow than usual, quickly dressed in jeans and a plaid shirt, hair sticking out in all directions. His face is stubbly and gaunt in the harsh florescent lights, as grey as Judith's was, lying on her kitchen floor. That picture, now, without the urgent need to do something about it, makes my eyes blur.

"Hello Lucy. They said you were here, that you were with her …" I nod. He looks around, his eyes puzzled behind his thick glasses, as if he's just landed on the moon.

"Sit down, Bob."

He does, running a long hand through his dishevelled hair. "What happened?"

I tell him — leaving out the part about being in the basement, of course.

"Oh dear," he says. "Oh dear. She's been working too hard. She always works too hard. Oh dear."

He falls silent, his long frame bent forward, bony arms propped on equally bony knees. Every few minutes he runs his hand through his hair again, making a worse mess of it. "Oh dear," he says each time.

He looks up at me. "Were you at her house for supper?"

I nod again. I was, after all.

$$\approx$$

Much, much later, a short, dark man in scrubs comes, his hair hidden in a round blue cap. He introduces himself as the doctor in charge of Judith's trauma team, sits on the edge of a chair facing us. He mostly talks to Bob.

Aneurism, he says, arachnoid something or other, intracranial pressure, ventricular drain, SAH, vasospasm. They might do surgery tomorrow, but for now she's stable. They're going to take her up to the ICU, where she'll have a nurse monitoring her through the night.

"Is she conscious?" I ask.

He turns toward me, and I see how tired he is. "No."

"Will she ... be okay?" The first word that had come to me was "live."

"We don't know. She may regain consciousness, but not tonight."

He suggests we go home, tells us how to visit the ICU tomorrow, fifth floor, phone on the wall, direct line to the ICU reception desk. Tell them who you are and who you're there to visit.

$$\approx$$

A nurse leads us through another glass door into the public waiting room, where people are scattered around the rows of plastic chairs, bored, sleepy, miserable. Bob turns to face me, looking haggard and haunted. "I'd take you home, Lucy, but I'm completely wiped, and I have to be in court in the morning. Can I give you money for a cab?

He pulls a couple of crumpled bills out of his pocket and helps me find the cab company's direct phone.

$$\approx$$

Bara's things are at Fresh Start, but she isn't. Did they find a place to live today? Surely, they couldn't get a bed and everything that fast. Could they? Although, some boarding house rooms are furnished. I roll up my sweater and skirt and push them under her covers, plumping everything up so it looks like she is there, then crawl into my own. For the second time in one night, I pray. God, Jesus, whoever, whatever is there, please bring Judith back.

CHAPTER THIRTY-TWO

On the fifth floor they are wary of a "friend," or maybe it's just the look of me, but Bob has put my name on their list.

A circle of glass-walled rooms surround a busy hub, a nurse at a little desk in front of each room. One of them guides me to Judith, laid out on her back like a sacrifice on a raised bed. She's hooked up to all kinds of tubes and wires, curling off in every direction, clipped to her fingers, bandaged to her hands, disappearing under the crisp sheet that covers her. A plastic mask covers the lower half of her face, a ridged tube in her mouth. Half of her head is shaved, and a tube emerges from her bare scalp.

The nurse is explaining. Endotracheal tube. Cerebrospinal fluid. I'm not hearing much besides her voice, efficient and kind. She stops. "I know. It's a lot to take in." She finds me a chair, tells me I can stay with Judith as long as I want. I'm relieved when she goes.

I can see daylight through a cheerful print curtain covering a window in the back wall, but the room is dim. The machines whirr and click. One wheezes in and out. It must be the one breathing for her. There are small screens with moving lines on them, different coloured lights. In the middle of it all, Judith looks oddly peaceful. Someone has brushed the hair on the side of her head that isn't shaved. It falls, smooth and shiny, brown with a streak of grey, across the pillow, away from her still face.

So it wasn't a trick of moving streetlights and falling rain, those grey streaks at her temples, the night we drove back from Burnside in the dark. Funny, I never noticed them before. When Judith is animated, sending the power of her mind into the world through her well-chosen words, you don't notice the details somehow. She's pure energy. Lying here, tied up in tubes, she looks so vulnerable. And that drain thing, stuck right into her brain. Sharp, brilliant, amazing brain. A shudder passes up my spine. Her hand lies limp on the sheet beside me, the one with only one tube stuck in it. Gingerly I pick it up, hold it in mine. It's cold.

In Judith's kitchen the saucepan of soup is still on the stove, bowl set beside it, cutlery on the table. I turn on the heat. I meant to go to St. Marks for supper; I need to see Althea. Bob said he would call her first thing this morning. I'd like to find Bara too, but my feet just kept walking north. Good thing I came; I'd left the front door unlocked.

Restless, I wander the old-fashioned downstairs rooms, looking at the china in the cabinet, a delicate vase on the living room mantle, the orderly row of toiletries in the small bathroom. Returning to the kitchen, I eat the soup and some crackers I find in the cupboard, a container of yoghurt for desert. Then I clean up, wash the dishes and put them away.

Upstairs, I look inside the bathroom, admiring the big clawfoot tub. Ornate hooks just inside the door hold a flannelette nightgown and a plush bathrobe. I peek inside the medicine cabinet above the sink. A couple of boxes of expensive soap, shampoo and conditioner, a prescription pill bottle. I turn it to look at the label. Trazodone. "Take at bedtime."

I run the tip of my finger over the row of things sitting on the dresser just outside the bathroom door — antique silver mirror, brush and comb set, matching tray holding a bottle of foundation, a circular container of powder, a couple of lipsticks. I open the top drawer a couple of inches. Neat piles of panties and bras. I close it quickly. The next one down holds tank tops, a couple of clean nightgowns. I close it as well. I shouldn't be doing this, but I need to find Judith.

I try the closet in the almost-empty bedroom between the bathroom and the study. Tailored suits give off a faint whiff of dry cleaning fluid, sober grey, blue, brown. She's been wearing these same suits since I met her. Either that, or when one wears out she buys another one exactly like it. There are several silk blouses, dove greys and browns, mint green, one flowered. What was she wearing when she collapsed in the kitchen? A dark blue suit, I think. What happens to the clothes a person has on when they go to the hospital in an ambulance?

Beside the suits hang three soft flannelette shirts and several pairs of pants, including the camel ones she had on when she made me tea in her kitchen. A shelf below the clothing holds several pairs of shoes — dress ones with high heels and those comfortable brown loafers. The plaid flannel shirt she wore that day hangs beside the camel pants. I pull it toward me, bury my face in it, but all I get is a faint whiff of laundry detergent.

I stand in the doorway of her study. The papers and books are in yet another arrangement. She had continued to work on the Levellers, Ranters and Diggers even while preparing for Cindy's sentencing hearing. I check to see if the brown-smeared paper is still the second one from the top of the pile right beside the door. It is.

I gather up my skirt and pick my way along the path to the computer but turn off before that, taking the route to the neatly made bed. It's a cozy space, between the bookshelf and the window. The bedside table holds a lamp and a murder mystery with a bookmark partway through. My eyes are suddenly swimming. Will she find out who did it? There is a small box of tissues on the bedside table. I help myself, blow my nose.

The pillow is sitting on top of the blankets. I can't help myself. I lie down on the bed and bury my nose in the stiff, white linen. There is a faint, faint smell of her here. I breathe it in, feeling comforted, although tears begin to trickle down my cheeks and into the fabric of the pillow case.

In the morning, I leave by the front door. There are two envelopes on the floor under the mail slot. Bills. I gather them up and set them on the hall table, leaning them against the pottery bowl. There is a ring of keys in it, obviously dropped there when Judith came in and set her briefcase on the floor. I check the tags on the single keys in the bottom of the dish. The one I've had in my pocket all these months is there, its tag — dirtier than the rest — labelled "Basement." Two say "Front Door." I pocket one.

"I'm so glad to see you, Lucy." Bob Cumberland's a tall man, but right now looks like a scared boy playing lawyer behind his big desk. He has to peer at me around stacks of files, and he never stops shuffling through them as he talks, though he can't be seeing them. "Have you been to the hospital?"

"Right after this."

"I have to go to court this afternoon."

"They said you're her next of kin."

"Legally, yes. I'm her guardian in health care and I have an enduring power of attorney from her, a will and living will too. I'd be executor if it comes to that."

"Doesn't she have a family?"

"No one she cares to be in touch with. Ah." He pounces on a file, stuffs it into his briefcase. Hope he has the right papers when he gets to court.

"Why don't you come to the hospital after court?"

"Yes, yes. Good idea. I'll do that." I wonder if he's forgotten where he's going, but he suddenly strides toward the door. A stray paper is sucked from his desk. It swoops gently back and forth toward the floor. I pick it up, but there's no place on the desk to put it. I leave it on his chair.

CHAPTER THIRTY-THREE

Judith is barely there, a scrap of life surrounded by a fortress of clicking, humming steel creatures. All I can see is the upper part of her face above the plastic mask and tube, white as paper; the shiny, exposed side of her head; and a delicate hand on the crisp sheet, with two tubes bandaged to it. Tubes, tubes, on her, into her. A giant space spider. I wince as one of them gurgles for all the world like it's hungry.

I decide to ignore them, search hard for the Judith I know. Really, her closed eyes are all I have. Studying them in the dim light, I see there are more creases than I had noticed before, a web of delicate wrinkles. Worry lines.

There are only three names on the visitors' list: mine, Bob's, Althea's. I wonder if anyone besides me knows that when she comes home from work she drops her briefcase in the front hall, kicks off her shoes and turns on CBC radio. Does anyone else know about the perfectly straight row of yoghurt containers in her refrigerator? The orderly bottles in the bathroom? The chaotic basement and empty upstairs rooms, the bed and stacks of papers in her study?

Bob and Althea come together. The nurse finds two plastic chairs. Bob nods at me. He looks pretty ghostly himself after a night in emergency and an afternoon in court. Althea reaches over to take my hand. She folds it into hers and her warmth travels up my arm. We sit like that for what seems like a long time.

I jump when Althea speaks. "Aren't you supposed to talk to people in a coma?"

I see Bob's eyebrows go up.

Althea shrugs. "I'm sure I've heard that sometimes people can hear even if they can't respond." She leans closer to the bed. "Hey Judith, honey, we're here, Bob and Lucy and me. We're hoping you can come out of this." She shoots me an uncomfortable look. "I mean, you are coming out of this, back to us."

She shifts her generous hips forward to the edge of the seat, lowers her voice even more. It comes out in a syrupy rumble. "How about that leisurely coffee we've been talking about? We've been bad girls, not making time for friendship. Soon's you're better, that's what we'll do, coffee at someplace nice, that pastry place in the Hydrostone."

She pauses. The pause goes on. She looks at me, pleading. I'm thinking like crazy, but nothing pops into my head. She looks at Bob. "And we're taking care of things for you, Judith. Bob's taking over your students and your cases, including Cindy's. Tell her Bob."

Bob looks like he's having a panic attack. "Judith? Can you hear me?"

"Just assume she can," Althea prompts.

"Okay, if you can hear me, I'd sure like you to come back. How am I supposed to add your caseload to mine? I guess I knew you were going a few extra miles, as they say, but I didn't realize just how many." Althea scrunches her face at him.

Althea lifts her free hand as if scooping something up. "Positive," she mouths.

"So, hey, that young guy doing research, Brian. Is he always this whiny? How do you get him off complaining that all he gets are the most boring cases and make him actually do some research? Maybe I should give him Cindy Beals's file, the whole national and international history of assistance and human rights legislation?" Althea winces. "Kidding, Judith, kidding. Now, what case is Brian on? Oh yeah ..." Bob gives us a glance. "Althea and Lucy are here, so I can't talk about anything confidential."

Althea shifts back into the molded plastic seat, lets go of my hand to check her watch. "That's okay. I've got to go anyway. Meeting in half an hour. Lucy? Come with me for a minute? We'll let these two talk professional secrets."

My knees have stiffened. I have to rest a minute, hanging on to the chair back. As we go, I look back at the machines circled around, Judith a wisp on the high bed. Bob, long and awkward, leaning toward her. At least he's talking now as if she really can hear him.

Outside the ICU, Althea turns to me. "I'm organizing a community meeting at the North Branch Library on Wednesday evening. There's a real head of steam built up over Cindy's case. Time to channel it." She grins.

"Like old times."

"So you'll come?"

I look at the door to the ICU.

"You can't sit with her all the time. She needs rest too."

"All right."

"Great." She glances at her watch again. "Bob will have to go back to Legal Aid soon. Will you sit with her a little while after he goes?"

I look around at the comfortable seats in the waiting room. "I guess I can wait."

"Why don't you go down to the cafeteria and have a bite?" She gives me a shrewd look, sets her huge purse on the arm of a chair and digs through it. "Here." She holds out a ten-dollar bill. I hesitate, but she gives it an impatient shake. I take it.

When I get back upstairs, Bob is gone. Judith lies slightly to one side, looking like she's having the most peaceful sleep in the world even with tubes coming out of her in every direction. The machines tick and hum, squiggly lines jagging up and down. They're watching too, and they don't feel friendly. I think they'd like to throw me out of here, leave Judith for them to suck dry.

I carry one of the smaller plastic chairs around to the side of the bed she's facing. Now that I'm alone, it's not hard at all to talk. "So, Judith, in all the excitement around Cindy, the end of my probation slipped by. You said you would take me out for supper. I'll hold you to that, as soon as you're out of here.

"Another thing too. There's this project sending volunteers to Guatemala. The Peace Accords were signed in December, and they need foreigners to accompany the people who've been living in exile, keep them safe while they travel home and rebuild their communities. I won't leave you here like this, Judith. But as soon as you're better, I need a letter saying I'm off probation and okay to go."

There is a nurse behind me. She's come up on those silent, rubber-soled shoes they wear. I hope she didn't catch "I'm off probation." She ignores me, looks at one of the screens with the squiggly lines for a few moments, picks up the clipboard attached to the foot of Judith's bed, writes something. I turn to look up at the screen too, not that it tells me anything. She smiles at me. "It's good that you're talking to her. Most of the time, when people come out of a coma, they don't remember what people have said to them. Probably because of the sedatives we give them."

"She's on sedatives?"

"It helps with the irritation from the tube in her throat. But sometimes people can recall at least part of what was said, although they often remember it as a dream. So keep talking."

A minute later she's gone. I stare at Judith. "Can you really hear me?"

For the first time, I walk up to Judith's front door. I dig into my pocket, latch first onto Bara's copy of the basement key, then the one with the "Front Door" label. A car door opens and closes out on the street. I pay no attention until footsteps come up the walk behind me. Instinctively I glance around for escape routes. Best bet, look perfectly normal, like I own the place.

I turn. Bob Cumberland's eyes fall on the key in my hand. "Oh. You've got a key to Judith's house?"

"I — "

"Have you been staying here with her, then?"

I open my mouth, but nothing comes out.

"Because that would solve a problem. Her enduring power of attorney makes me responsible for the house and the insurance company wants to raise the rates if it's empty. But if you're here …"

"Well, I — "

"Do you pay rent or share costs?"

"Well, I … I'm not … at the moment …"

"I see," he says, with a glance at my clothing that he probably can't help. "Well then, that's fine. When the bills come, bring them to me and I'll pay them from Judith's account. And if anything needs fixing, let me know, all right?"

I nod. Wow. Lucky day, I think, followed by a sharp stab of guilt.

"I'll let the insurance company know it's occupied." One side of his mouth quirks up. "That Judith. Full of surprises." He turns to leave.

"Oh, Bob, wait." I put the key in the lock and turn it, praying it works. The door opens. I scoop up the bills on the hall table and hand them to Bob. He glances at them, tucks them into an inside pocket of his jacket.

Dear Judith, thank you for thinking of everything. When you get out of hospital, I'll take care of you, I'll —

"Hey, Luce." I start. Robin. He and Bara are sitting at Judith's kitchen table.

"What are you two doing here?"

"How is she?" Robin asks.

"Out cold."

"And you, Lucy. How are you?" says Bara. She gives me a worried once-over. "You look exhausted. Here, sit down. Tea?" She holds up Judith's old Brown Betty teapot. "I found some in the cupboard."

"Bara." I put my hesitation into my tone.

"If she's out cold, Lucy, she's not coming back soon, is she?"

I sit down heavily in the third chair. Bara puts the kettle on.

"How did you get in?" I ask her.

"Basement door," she says. "You didn't lock it."

I didn't? But time has already split into before and after that soft thump above my head, my memory of before gone fuzzy.

"Who was the guy at the door?" Robin asks.

I tell them about Bob and the house.

"All right!" Robin says. "We can move in, like a co-op house."

"You will not!"

"Just kidding, Luce."

"Very funny."

"Sorry, bad timing. But you'll come and live here?"

"I don't think so."

"But that Bob asked you to, or you'll invalidate the insurance."

I look at Bara.

"It's okay, Lucy," she says, pouring three mugs of tea. "Cat and I will keep on looking. Meanwhile, I'm okay at Fresh Start."

Robin stands at the sink, suds billowing out onto the counter, washing up the mugs while Bara walks to Fresh Start to get my things. He rattles on about Wednesday's meeting at the North Branch until she comes back, my small cardboard suitcase in one hand, tightly rolled sleeping bag in the other. When they've left, I turn on CBC radio, but it brings a wave of sadness. When I switch it off again, silence comes to fill every corner of the house. It's going to be a few weeks before Judith comes home, at least. I head upstairs.

It's a shame to bring the Lucy disorder into such a pristine space, but I open my suitcase on the bare mattress in the only room that has one and pull everything out. Frantz Fanon, *This Place*, a pile of clothes. Most are clean. Bara has kept on top of that. I notice she has also washed the sleeping bag. It smells good.

I consider the clawfoot bathtub for a moment, but I'm too tired. I drop the clothes I'm wearing into a pile on the floor, find my nightgown and pull it over my head. I find my way along the narrow path between the books and papers and crawl into Judith's bed. It does smell of her. Just faintly. I can feel the books and papers all around me, waiting for Judith. She's coming back, I tell them. Soon.

CHAPTER THIRTY-FOUR

They have moved the breathing tube to a heavily bandaged patch on Judith's throat. Talking to her feels more normal without that thing going into her mouth. However, today the fluid in the tube draining her head has tiny flakes in it. "Is that supposed to be like that?" I ask the nurse, pointing.

"Hmmm," she gives it a quick glance. "That's normal."

"When she comes out of this …" I stop, thinking, *if* she comes out of this.

The nurse is a small woman with large brown eyes, familiar looking, but I haven't had the energy to learn any of their names. She's waiting patiently for my question.

"Will she be all right? I mean, can a brain heal from a … whatever it's called?"

"Subarachnoid hemorrhage. It's really hard to know." She's giving me a sympathetic look, which scares me. "There will be damage. Brain cells don't heal like other cells do, but how much damage there'll be, what will be affected, there's no way to know in advance."

When she's gone, I can't stop staring at that horrible tube, the little dust mote things moving slowly along in the yellowish fluid. That's all draining out of Judith's brain. She can wrap her head around massively complicated ideas and then — how often have I seen her do this — she can boil them down to something crystal clear, so that someone with a Grade 3 education gets excited about them. I feel as if it's all draining out of her, her ideas, her thoughts, her mind.

My eyes prickle and I tear them from that hateful tube, reach out and stroke Judith's pale hand. No response. Speak to her. Among the eavesdropping machines, it's hard to start.

"Bob's taking care of everything, Judith, for when you're well again. It feels a little odd, him being your next of kin. I mean, not odd in itself, he's a great person to take care of things, but … your family. Aren't there relatives, somewhere? All these years we've worked together, been friends, and I don't know."

I've stopped anyway, but now the nurse slips in. She checks things, gives me that sympathetic look again. I stretch out my pause until she walks away.

"But then, if it were me lying there, you wouldn't know anything about my family either, would you?"

I'm searching for more words when Judith's eyelids flutter. I suck in my breath, hold it, watch. Did I imagine that? No, it happens again. "Nurse!" I'm on my feet. "She's coming to."

The little nurse with the brown eyes comes in. "Judy?" She shakes Judith's arm.

"She's called Judith."

"Judith?" The nurse pats her cheek, firmly.

No response.

The nurse straightens up, eyes still on Judith while she speaks to me. "That can happen." Now she looks at me. "It's good you called, though. It can mean something." She checks all the tubes before she goes.

Strange, the nurses are right there, just the other side of the glass, but when they're not actually in the room, it feels private, just Judith and me.

I tell her about the meeting coming up at the library, watching her eyes. They don't flicker again, but they are moving under her eyelids.

⤜

Almost a hundred people show up. Cindy talks about her experience with the legal system, and then Althea takes the microphone. "The judge did what he had to do. His job is to uphold the letter of the law. Although in this case, who among us can claim this is justice?"

The crowd takes over, chanting "*Justice, justice, justice,*" until they run down. Althea is asking for silence with her hands.

"So the problem here is the law. And who can change the law? We can, the people, the electorate, the voters. Elections are a big opportunity, but there are other kinds of pressure we can put on our lawmakers in the meantime."

She breaks us into small groups. The old hands step in to facilitate the discussions. Been a long time since I've done this. It feels good.

All the same old ideas go up on the flip charts: letter campaign, endorsements from organizations, visits to MLAs from their own constituents. We keep doing these things because they're all we've got and, if there are enough of us and we're clear and persistent enough, sometimes they work. Who knows someone in Pictou East? Kings? Guysborough-Sheet Harbour? People volunteer for working groups to write model letters, create a mailing list, organize visits to the minister.

Patty comes to sit with me a while. "I'm sorry about Cindy's boys," I tell her.

"We miss them, but their foster family is good to keep in touch, and we've still got my two."

"And Cindy's will come home soon."

"It feels great to see all these people here. They care about what's happening to us."

I think: Maybe.

"They really want to change things."

I think: Maybe.

When did I get to be such a cynic? It used to be me saying, "Of course it's going to take decades, but if we don't push, it won't change at all," or "We never know what little thing is going to circle around and get bigger. How much change was Rosa Parks expecting when she wouldn't give her seat to a white man on the bus?" or "If you're not part of the solution, you're part of the problem."

"Judith should be right here in the middle of this. We're really worried about her."

"Me too." I reach over and put my hand on hers.

There is a large group of the art school students at the meeting. They want to design a logo and make T-shirts to wear in the legislature gallery. By the end of the evening, they're on the floor in a corner, Bara and Cat among them, sketching on flip chart paper and laughing.

Most of these people will dribble away, of course, once the real work starts. There I go again.

The day after the meeting, Bara turns up at my door with a couple of Superstore bags. "Not Sobeys," she declares, holding them up.

"You think Superstore wouldn't have done the same thing?"

She shrugs and sets to work making a lovely pasta dish and salad. She also cleans up and puts everything away in the right places. When she offers to prepare more meals for the two of us, I give her my social assistance food money. And then I give her the other key to the front door from the pottery dish in the hall.

The next night both Robin and Bara show up. In the centre of the table two of Judith's casserole dishes sit on hot pads, one filled with a mix of vegetables, steaming and topped with cheese, the other with rice. Bara is arranging an interesting platter, a pork chop in a tomato-based sauce, a slice of tender roast beef with a pastry crust, a piece of salmon with a glaze on it and a chicken breast stuffed with something green and white. I poke at the green and white stuff with my fork.

"I think it's, like, goat cheese and spinach," Bara says.

"You didn't buy all this on our social assistance money."

The two of them break into laughter. "We went foraging," Robin says. "The good dumpsters behind the downtown restaurants."

I sigh. "Moms on assistance go hungry to feed their kids, and people leave goat cheese on their plates."

"You don't have to eat it, Lucy," Robin says.

Bara is bent over the platter dividing each treat neatly into three and transferring them to our plates. She sets them in front of us. "Dumpster mélange."

"You should have a TV cooking show," Robin says, chewing.

"Don't talk with your mouth full," I say before I can help myself.

"Yes Mom," he grins, with his mouth full. He turns back to Bara. "You could call it 'Gently Used Food.'"

"Street Eats."

"Dumpster Cuisine."

"Found Food."

"Bin Chef."

Hilarity breaks out. They laugh helplessly, tears in their eyes, until I have to join them.

Serious again, I remind them it's not always safe around those bins.

"It's okay, Lucy." Bara waves my concern away. "There's two of us and we went after dark. I found a flashlight in one of Judith's drawers. Most of the divers are, like, drunk or in the shelters by then, and that's when the fancy restaurants are throwing out the best stuff."

Bara rises to clear the table while Robin is still working his way through a second course of rice and veggies.

"I thought you were living with your parents," I say.

"I've got a room in their basement. Fixed it up myself."

"If your parents have room for you in their basement, what's wrong with their table?"

"The arguments around it. My parents don't agree with much of what I stand for."

"But they'll feed you."

He shrugs.

When Robin's plate is finally clean, he leans back in his chair and pats his stomach. "That was really good, Bara."

She turns from the sink where she is washing dishes. "Thanks. For the compliment and the help foraging."

CHAPTER THIRTY-FIVE

Althea and I sit on either side of Judith's bed telling her about what has now been named the Campaign to End Hunger in Nova Scotia, although even before we left the library that night, people were calling it the Chicken Campaign.

When we run out of news, the sounds of the ICU take over, machines beeping and blipping, nurses talking softly outside, people coming and going from the other rooms.

"Lucy," Althea is speaking to me now. "You never actually told me the story of what happened that day at the college — I mean, apart from what was said in court. Of course, you might not want to. I know how bad a time it was for you, after they cut the support for single moms in the degree program."

"Oh, Althea. You understood right away exactly what was wrong with the university making a 'revenue stream' out of a program that was meant to give back to the community. You and Judith. You knew what it would mean for the students who couldn't pay. And you know what it feels like, your heart breaking every time they get knocked down again."

"It's a pretty big love."

I let out a sigh. "I confronted Dell about what she used to stand for. She said I was stuck in the past, accused me of thinking I was better than my colleagues who were knuckling down to 'market' their courses."

"I can't believe she said that to you. She changed direction, sure, didn't need you anymore, and you became a problem, but she knew what you did and why and who for. She used to believe in all that too — or said she did. Did she get a free lobotomy with her

MBA? And surely, the university has ways to ship people out when they're not needed anymore, pay them off or whatever."

"Yeah, they do. In fact, the faculty contract says they have to. But by then, the college's purpose was to make money. If they handed out a severance package, they had to find a way to pay for it and still make a profit. Apparently, no one gave any thought to the contract, not to mention that the salaries were much higher than any new business would be paying."

"So was she trying to push you so hard you'd leave? Deliberately?"

"It crossed my mind, but I found it hard to believe. Of her, anyway. Others in the administration, not so much."

"Even if she was doing others' bidding, so what? She was doing it." Althea studies me for a moment. "So, what finally broke you? That day. Not the day before, or the day after."

"I don't know, Althea. It's not as if she said anything she hadn't said before over and over, or as if I was more tense that day than any other time she called me to her office. Maybe I just, as they say, 'reached the end of my rope.' There was a humming sound. I think it was there for a while, but I suddenly noticed it. And ... it's hard to describe. She was standing in front of me, and she looked like ... no, more than looked like. She had *become* every rich, powerful oppressor that's ever hurt or exploited anyone I care about. I felt like I left my body. I watched myself grab the lapels of her jacket ..."

I am reliving it as I speak, the view from somewhere above my own head, watching myself break. My stomach is all clenched up.

A nurse leans into the cubicle and makes a shushing motion, finger in front of her lips, then looks at me with a little frown. "Excuse me, are you all right?"

"We're just going." Althea gets to her feet. "Come on, Lucy."

I follow her out, trembling.

It quiets down by the time we're in the lobby. Althea faces me and takes my arm. "Are you all right?"

"I think so."

"Sure?"

I nod.

She guides me to a seat in the waiting area. "I have to go, but you sit here for a while before you go home. Okay?"

I nod again.

Where am I? I look around, puffing with effort. Parking lot, Citadel Hill. Tour bus parked on an angle, bus driver leaning on the open door, watching me and smoking. Looks away when I look back.

I don't know how I made it up here. Now I need to sit. There's a lookout place, a bench at the head of the path down to the clock. I make it there, sit. My chest aches as I try to grab hold of my breathing.

"It's a pretty big love," Althea had said. It's sometimes more than I can stand, aching for all my students, in Halifax, in Guatemala. Even before Nicolás taught me how to spark their critical thinking, unleash their power to act, back when I was parroting Bible stories and verb tenses, even then it was a pretty big love.

The downtown spreads across the hillside below me, steep slope to the harbour. Metro Centre, shiny office buildings, a few remnants of an older Halifax tucked into the shadows between. Traffic bustles up and down, and many people. People going somewhere, people in offices, pubs, the legislature, going about their business, not thinking about what makes all this commerce go. The Beast.

I use the railing to pull myself to my feet and, clutching it, lean forward and shout at the city, "Wake up! Wake up! Goddamn it, wake up!"

Steps behind me. "Lady? You okay?" A uniform. I start down the stairs away from him before it sinks in: I'm no longer on probation and he's the bus driver.

"So, like, do you think she can hear you?" Bara says.

"Hard to tell."

"Do you think it could actually help her come to?"

"She could come back here and live with us," Robin sits across the table from me, cleaning his wire-framed glasses with a paper napkin.

"Us?"

Robin cocks his eyebrow at me. He looks oddly naked without his glasses, so young.

So, what will happen if Judith, *when* Judith, comes home? She'll need care for a while, won't she? I guess that will be a long time off, but perhaps I should prepare her.

"Judith, I don't know if Bob's told you, but I'm living in your house. Keeping it, like, for the insurance company." Oh my God, I sound like Bara.

"Judith." My voice chokes off as my eyes fill. I fumble in my pockets. Nothing. There's a small box of tissues on the bedside table. I help myself. Nose blown, I feel I can finish my thought. "Please come back, Judith. I miss you so much. And we need to talk."

CHAPTER THIRTY-SIX

"What's this?" I say, coming through the front door.

"Paint," Robin holds out a canvas bag to show me several spray cans.

"Red, judging by the blotches."

"Lucy, we need a lookout." Robin wears the black anarchist outfit he had on for the G7 demonstrations. "Gord? Show her."

Tall Gord greets me with a grin as he comes into the hallway from the kitchen. He carries a battered artist's portfolio, which he opens to show me plastic stencils in three sizes. They're all of a picture I saw on several placards the day of Cindy's sentencing hearing, a child and a chicken on the scales of justice, only this is a more stylized version.

"We're going to paint the town red," says Robin.

"It's late, and I'm going to bed."

"It won't take long. You'll like it," Robin takes on a wheedling tone. "We'll go slow."

"I don't need anyone to go slow for me."

"Okay then, we won't. Please, Lucy. We really need the help."

Ahead of me, Robin carries the portfolio. Gord comes behind with the paint cans. How did I get talked into this, walking the dark streets with these lanky creatures? I'm glad my feet aren't like they were when I tried to survive on the street, although there is enough pain in my knees. It must have been the "we need you" line.

And they do actually need me. We stand in the shadow of some bushes looking at the entrance to the Public Gardens, a busy area even in the middle of the night. Their goal is the brick pillars on either side of the iron gate. "Stand out on the corner and look homeless," Robin says.

"Not funny."

He grins. "Just tell us when a car or pedestrian is coming."

Gord holds up a stencil, hands protected by plastic gloves. Robin pulls a spray can from the bag, but before he can start, a pair of lights turn into Spring Garden Road. "Car!" I announce and start to move slowly along the sidewalk like an old homeless woman with sore knees. The boys melt into the greenery.

When the car has gone by, they reappear. Gord's black sleeves turn red from the elbow down as Robin sprays. In minutes both pillars are decorated with bright red symbols. They'll shine in the sun come morning.

"Car," I announce once again, and we all step back into the shadow of the legislature fence, out of range as the headlights slide past us. We've worked our way across town, decorating strategic surfaces as we go. They spray twice more, on either side of the gate into the legislature grounds.

"Okay," Robin says. "That's enough for one night."

Gord carefully slides the stencil back into the portfolio and hands it to Robin. He strips off his paint-covered gloves and shirt, bundles them into a plastic shopping bag he produces from his pocket and vanishes. Robin dumps the can back into the canvas bag and we hustle away in the opposite direction.

"It's a rush, isn't it?" Robin says.

"Sure, if you're young."

"Oh come on, Lucy, you love it."

The next morning the paper displays a large version of the Chicken

Campaign logo on the side wall of Province House. I describe it to
Judith before I start reading aloud. Letters to the editor section has
gone crazy. Some are copies of letters people have written to their
MLAs. The politicians are starting to squirm, government side saying, "Poverty is a clear priority," opposition parties crowing about
what *they* would do if *they* were the government. Okay, so I was
wrong about people drifting away. So far.

The living room is full of young people when I get home, and a
smaller group in the dining room are setting the table with Judith's
good dishes.

"Bara!" I head for the kitchen.

Several young women, working at the counter and table, turn
to stare at me. Cat is there, but steps back out of my line of vision.
Bara stands at the stove.

"What the hell is going on?"

"This is the Chicken Campaign Coordinating Committee,
Lucy. We're having a potluck to celebrate."

"Those dishes in the dining room. They're old, Judith's grandmother's."

"There's not enough of the ones in the kitchen. We'll be careful, Lucy. We won't hurt anything." She turns back to the pot she
is stirring.

"Just be sure you don't."

"We won't."

"And clean everything up and put it back just the way it was."

"Yes, Lucy."

I do have to admit the food smells good.

Bara keeps her word. Before she and Cat disappear into the night
with the last of their friends, the kitchen and dining room are

spotless, every dish put away. I tour around to be sure, turning off the ground-floor lights as I go. In the front hall, I start. Judith's briefcase is gone. So is her ring of keys.

At the bottom of the stairs, I see that one of the upstairs lights is on. Strange. At the top, mystery solved. "Robin!"

Bold as brass, he's sitting at Judith's computer, one of her files on his lap.

He looks up. "Lucy, have you ever heard of 'the extinguishment of the rights of common'? Listen." He starts to read from the file: "'*The heart of the Enclosure Movement was the "extinguishment of the rights of common," the destruction of a system of rights that allowed peasants to take the necessities of life from, even live on, land that they did not legally own. In the new system, landlords could punish as poachers those who tried to take fish and game, as trespassers those who tried to collect herbs and berries and as squatters those who lived on the land.*'"

My dear boy, I think, I have *lived* the "extinguishment of the rights of common." What I say is, "Robin, put that down."

"Is this a thesis?"

"Judith doesn't need a thesis. She's got the education to do what she wants to do."

"Then is she writing a book?" He looks down, turns over a page. "This is really cool. Listen: '*The sixteenth-century flood of gold and silver from the Americas caused inflation, making tenants' rents worthless. Meanwhile, markets sprang up for metals, slate and wool.*'"

"Robin! Get out of there."

"Okay, okay, Lucy. Keep your hat on." He places the file back on the desk.

"I hope that's *exactly* where it came from."

He rises from the chair, points to the floor beside the desk. Second mystery solved. Judith's briefcase sits there. "I put her keys inside it. I started to worry about them, keys to every door in the house, the garage, the car, the Legal Aid office."

I nod. "Thanks Robin."

He looks over toward the bed. "Are you sleeping here?"

"Not your business."

"Is this Judith's bed? In her study?"

"Robin, get out of here."

"It must be." He finally comes out of the study. "Because all the other rooms are pretty much empty. Why is that, Lucy?"

"Robin, you're not welcome up here."

"If you're going to live here until Judith comes back, we should set up a real bedroom for you."

"No, you won't. Now just go."

He swings his lanky frame around the top newel post and onto the top step. "You don't fool me, Lucy. You're not the grouch you pretend to be."

He laughs as he bounds down the stairs and, a minute or so later, out the front door.

My eyes are swimming. Judith, I'm so sorry.

CHAPTER THIRTY-SEVEN

"Oh, look, a card from someone." I pick it up from the cluttered little stand beside Judith's hospital bed. "There's a painting on the front, a woman, sitting in a window seat, looking out, thoughtful." I open it. A sudden chill. It's from Dell. I almost say "damn," stop myself, set the card back where it was.

I pull the plastic chair close beside the bed and sit, but my eyes want to wander back to the card. "What made Dell change so much, Judith? Wanting to be the first woman dean? The money? Her new circle of colleagues with their big ideas about the college bringing in thousands from corporate training? Only Althea saw through her right from the beginning. Not long after they met, she said Dell was 'slumming it.'

"I don't think I would have been so hurt if she hadn't been a friend and ally before she went away to do her MBA. As you said not long ago, we were her mentors until then. After that, she didn't need us. I felt so betrayed. I know I reacted … strongly … but it wasn't the first time I lost a place in life where I felt I really, truly … *belonged*."

Althea and I are in Bob Cumberland's office. He has papers spread out on his desk over an open file folder with Judith's name on the tab. He is not looking at them, though, or us. He has his desk chair angled slightly toward the window and seems to be watching the people passing on the sidewalk below. "Her doctor asked for a meeting yesterday. He says she's levelled off, not getting any worse but not getting any better either. The scans and tests say there is activity in her brain, whatever exactly that means, and her heart and kidneys are functioning. They don't know why she isn't waking up. They have to keep her on sedatives because of the ventilator and there is a possibility that's holding her back. They want to try, as they say, 'weaning' her off of it, see if she can breathe on her own." Now he turns to look at us, his eyes pained behind his large glasses.

"And if she can't?" I ask.

"Then we'd have to decide whether to leave her on it longer or …" He pauses.

"Let her go," Althea fills in.

"The doctor says anything can happen. She might stop breathing right away or breathe for a while and then stop hours later, or days. It's a chance we'd be taking."

Althea nods at the papers. "I assume you've got those out for a reason."

"Yes." Bob moves his chair closer to the desk and bends over the papers, pushes his glasses farther up his nose. "She thought ahead, of course, being Judith. She's given us an advance directive." He selects a document, just a couple of pages clipped together with one of those blue, cardboard corner protectors law offices use. He clears his throat, begins to read.

"I, Judith Selene Maidstone, being of sound mind and rational thought …"

A thought pops into my mind: if I wrote a document like that, would it be legal? Would anyone believe at this point I could be "of sound mind and rational thought"?

" … voluntarily make this declaration to be followed if I become incompetent or incapacitated to the extent that I am unable to communicate my wishes, desires and preferences. This declaration reflects my firm, informed and settled commitment to refuse life-sustaining medical treatment if I should be in an incurable or irreversible mental or physical condition with no reasonable expectation of recovery."

Bob places his finger on the end of that sentence and looks up. "She doesn't specify who decides when there is 'no reasonable expectation of recovery.' The doctors, of course, but I guess, in the end, the guardian in health care and enduring power of attorney documents give the final decision to me."

He lifts his finger, carries on: "Although I do not want my process of dying to be prolonged, I do wish my physicians to take any measures to make me comfortable and relieve pain."

"So, Bob," Althea cuts in. "Is the doctor saying this is what's going on — 'no reasonable expectation of recovery'?"

"No, no, no." Bob puts his finger back on the document, shifts his feet. "It's just they want to try her without the ventilator, and there's a risk it will end her life sooner or later, and we ... I ... have to make that choice, and I thought it might be helpful to see what Judith wants, at least, wanted when she wrote this."

"It's okay, Bob. Don't get flustered. I just want to be clear. So if Judith can't breathe on her own, the ventilator could be considered 'prolonging her process of dying,' and she doesn't want that."

Bob calms, takes a breath. "Yes."

Another pause. Is he waiting for us to say something? Another breath, then he continues: "We can wait another day, of course, another week, another month, another year. There's no time limit."

My stomach sags, sick and heavy. I slide my eyes over to Althea. She looks like I feel. And why's he asking us anyway? He's the lawyer, with power of attorney.

"Do you think there's any hope?" he asks, eyes travelling from one of us to the other and back again. I glance at Althea. She's looking at the floor, her brow pinched into a deep fold between her eyes. "Okay," he says. "Let's wait a while longer."

"No." Althea looks up. Her face is ashen, but her back has straightened now. Bob's arm stops, curved across the top of his desk, about to scoop the papers back into their cardboard file. "No," Althea says, quieter this time. "It's already been a while. I can't imagine she's coming back. Even if she did, what would she be like?" She looks at me. I can see the pain I'm feeling reflected in her eyes.

She's waiting for some signal. Finally, I give her a tiny nod. She studies me another moment before turning back to Bob. "If she's out of it completely, wouldn't it be for the best? And if she's suffering, even better."

Bob straightens, leaving the papers where they are. His eyes are fixed on Althea's through his owlish glasses. A few moments go by. He looks at me. "Lucy?" My vision blurs, and I can't speak. He takes it for an answer. "All right." He sighs, folds his hands as if praying, his elbows resting on Judith's papers. "I'll talk to the doctor."

As we walk away from Legal Aid, Althea slips her arm through mine. "Lucy, do you pray?"

"I used to, and I seem to be doing it again lately, but basically I stopped when … I came back from Guatemala. You do, though, don't you?"

"Oh yeah, when I sing with the gospel choir, when I'm helping a single mom appeal an assistance decision, when I hug my grandchildren …"

"Oh well, I guess if you look at it that way."

"But I pray in words too. Old fashioned, I guess, right down on my knees."

We've reached the door of St. Marks. "Why'd you ask?"

"Because I think Judith could use some prayer right now." She looks up at the big, old stained-glass window over the door, back at me.

"Sure, Althea. Why not?"

On the other side of the window, light streams in, splashing colour on the worn carpet. The cavernous sanctuary smells of dust and old varnish. We kneel before the simple wooden altar. Hurts my knees, but I do it for Althea … and Judith.

Althea's deep voice calls through the waiting space. "Dear Lord, hold our friend Judith in your loving hand. You know what a good woman she is, how many people she's helped. Now, please help her. If it's your will she live longer, then bring her back to us, all the way back. If it's time for her to go, take her into your glory …"

Her voice melts into echoes among the ornate beams. Is she waiting for me to say something? The pause goes on.

"And please, no pain," I say. "Whatever happens, if she goes or stays — and we'd like her to stay — if she's still Judith, that is — anyway, don't put her through any pain. We love her …" I fade, out of words, choking up anyway.

After a moment, Althea takes up my dropped speech. "In Jesus's Holy Name, we ask it."

I join her in a soft "Amen."

When I leave St. Marks, I'm restless, start walking with no particular destination, but my feet take me back to the hospital. Judith is slightly turned toward one side. I move the plastic visitor's chair forward. One hand doesn't have any tubes in it, though you can see the holes and bruises where the needles have been, the chapped squares left by the tape. I hold it between mine, a motionless little bird. I hear Bob's voice, "there is activity in her brain."

"Dear Judith," I whisper almost into her ear. "Bob showed Althea and me some of your papers today. You made a living will, do you remember? I hope it's still what you want. Bob's going to talk to the doctor. I think they'll take the tubes and things away. After that, if you want to live, you'll have to do it on your own."

A wet spot appears on the pillow just beside a strand of Judith's hair, dull and straggly now. The bare side of her skull is covered with downy fuzz. She always kept her hair so brushed and shiny.

"We promised each other we would talk about our lives. I want that, Judith. I want to know you. I do trust you … and I think I need to let some things out, hear myself say them, if I'm ever going to … be whole."

A nurse comes, an older woman, wheeling a cart full of plastic-wrapped packages and neatly folded towels. She sees me and stops in the doorway. "Oh, sorry," she says. "I'll come back later." She leaves the cart just beside the door, though.

I rub my hands over my tight face. They come away wet. There is so much more to say to her. It might be my last chance. But I'm so tired. I just sit, Judith's bony little hand in mine, and plop more dark spots onto the pillow.

I find Robin in Judith's study, this time reading her computer screen. "Robin! That's private. Shut that down immediately."

He starts, turns. "Just the book. Nothing else."

I start in along the trail between the towers of papers, ready to pull him out of the chair if I have to, but my skirt catches a pile of papers, slides it into my path.

"Lucy!" Robin leaps to his feet. In a moment he is kneeling in front of me, carefully re-piling the papers, checking that they're in the right order.

He shuts down the computer and leaves right after that, but I can't forget the look on his face. Horror and, what, possessiveness? I feel myself relax. Dear Judith, what happens to all this thought and work if you don't come home? Maybe Robin is the answer after all.

CHAPTER THIRTY-EIGHT

Althea and I sit in the family room while they disconnect the machines and take out the tubes. It's a familiar place now, with its dark green chairs. They're comfortable enough, which is good, because it takes a long time.

A nurse had warned us, but still we perch on the edge of our seats, if two women as well padded behind as we are can be said to perch. "I didn't know if I should say goodbye, just in case," Althea says. "Did you?"

"No, I guess I didn't. I held her hand for a while, though, had a cry."

"Yeah, me too."

Every time there's a sound in the hall, we turn to the door. Mostly whatever is making the noise just goes on by, but then the handle turns. I hear Althea take in a breath at the same time I do, but it's only Bob, in his usual breathless and disheveled state. "They told me you were in here," he says, setting down his brief-case and draping his coat over it. "Are they … ?"

"Yeah," Althea says. "They said it's a gradual thing. They'll turn the ventilator down a little and wait to see if Judith takes a breath on her own. If she does, they'll turn it down some more."

When the doctor finally comes in, we all search his face and know immediately that things are cautiously okay. "She's breathing," he tells us. "And her oxygen levels are all right. We've been decreasing the sedatives for several days, down to nothing. Now all we can do is watch and wait."

Judith looks naked without her tubes and machines, small under the sheet. It's good to see her face again, mask removed, although her lips look terribly chapped and sore. She has a peaceful expression, an unearthly Sleeping Beauty, translucent skin stretched over delicate bones. What's left of her hair is combed smooth, spread on the pillow. The drain is gone from the other side of her head, the spot marked by a white bandage nestled in the light-brown fuzz. Another big gauze patch covers the hole in her throat.

I hold her hand. A breath goes in. Pause. Out. After what seems like ages, in again. We hold ours, listening. This one will be the last. This one. This one. The space between is unbearable. Nurses come and go. Tears trickle down my face. I don't care. Althea's too. Eventually I notice a damp trail on Bob's cheek as well.

An hour later, my tears are finished. Althea's too. Breath in. Breath out. The doctor comes in several times. He feels her pulse, looks at Bob and shrugs his shoulders.

The afternoon crawls by. Breath in. Breath out. Lighter than a butterfly fanning its wings. Nurses come in and out. Another doctor comes, says she's stable. "Does that mean she'll continue breathing on her own?" Bob asks.

"No way of knowing," he says. "She could die an hour from now; she could go on for months."

When he leaves, Althea crosses her arms and raises her eyebrows at me. "So, when did they start graduating doctors at sixteen years old?" I give her a quiet chuckle. Feels good, like I've forgotten to breathe myself, for hours.

Bob looks at his watch. "I have to go. Will you call me?"

Althea looks at hers, sighs.

"Go, if you need to," I say. "I'll stay here." I'm getting stiff, but what if Judith stops breathing, all alone? Althea hugs me. Bob pats my arm.

I stay and stay. I think, okay, really got to go, but then think, what if I go and she dies? But, as the sixteen-year-old doctor said, she could go on for months.

⌇

Much later, they decide to move her out of the ICU. Three nurses shift Judith to a gurney and I follow. It's a much bigger room, four beds, only one occupied and the person doesn't respond as we come in. They put Judith in a bed by the window. The setting sun floods the room with a pinkish light. I look out. "You've got a view into the tops of the trees, Judith."

Breath in. Endless wait. Breath out. I stop talking because I'm listening. Breath in. Breath out. Uncomfortable metal and plastic chairs. I fetch one and sit beside her. It's nice to have just the intravenous pole, a feeding tube disappearing under the cover, the catheter bag hidden under the bed. There's still the occasional gurgle, but no ominous machines watching. Judith looks like a little bony bird the cat dragged in.

I think of the disorder I've brought into Judith's house. She'd be horrified, but it doesn't seem to me now that she'll ever know. Don't think that, Lucy. But it would take a miracle of some sort. But then, it's a miracle she's still breathing right now, even "stable," the young doctor said. Just not waking up, and they don't know why. "Judith," I whisper, "Wake up. Please wake up." Nothing.

It's the window that lets me know we've moved into night. "I'm sorry, Judith. I have to leave you. I'll be back, soon. Please don't die while I'm gone. I don't want you to be alone."

Breath in. Breath out.

⌇

When I walk into the kitchen, four young female faces turn to me:

Bara, Cat, a girl with short brown hair and one with red spikes sticking out from her head like she's suffered some kind of thought explosion. They have plates in front of them, smeared with the remains of supper. Cat gets to her feet and begins clearing, turning her back to me. No woven scarf, but shiny black hair in a long braid down her back. My eyes are glued to it.

"Lucy." There is a warning note there. Bara has circles under her eyes, a crease between her brows. "I think you met Carol before." The brown-haired one nods. "And Maggie." Red Explosion glances up. She looks like someone hit her in both eyes, but it's makeup. Bits of metal stick out here and there. "So, what's happening?"

"Still breathing."

Bara looks relieved. "Like, for long?"

I shrug. "Nurse at the station in the hall promised to call if it looks like the end, but it's looked like the end all afternoon."

There are footsteps on the stairs. Robin appears in the doorway, eyebrows lifted into dark parentheses above his eyes. I repeat, "Still breathing."

"Really? Wow."

"And where did you just come from?"

"Lucy, it's just — "

I put a hand on his arm. "It's okay, Robin. I've been thinking about it. We'll talk."

His face brightens. "Really?"

As soon as the dishes are stacked by the sink, Cat disappears down the steps to the basement. A few minutes later, Carol and Maggie follow.

"Bara gets to her feet. "You must be starving, Lucy. Sit." She gets up and lays out a place setting for me, carries a plate over to the pots on the stove.

Robin is still in the door, leaning on the frame. "We've been worried."

I frown at him. "You don't even know her."

"I feel like I do, reading her stuff. She's one amazing researcher."

I dig into the pile of spaghetti Bara has set in front of me to cover my blurry eyes.

"And we've been worrying about the house," Bara says as she straightens, looks at Robin. "Lucy, what happens to this house when Judith dies?"

The phone rings. I jump so hard I drop my fork, scattering bits of tomato sauce across the table. Robin disappears into the hallway. "Hello? Hey, Gord."

CHAPTER THIRTY-NINE

They've moved Judith to a small, private room one floor higher. Maybe they figure all our talking to her and each other will disturb other patients. There is a nurse sitting in the visitor's chair beside the bed. She turns when she hears me.

"Is she … ?" I can hear the alarm in my voice.

"No, she's pretty stable." She gets up. "I was just visiting. Here, take the chair."

"Stay if you want. Would you like me to go? I can come back later."

"No. My shift starts soon." She pauses, her sadness clear as she looks down at Judith.

I pull another chair over to the other side of the bed. "Did you … *do* you know her?"

She glances at me, drops her eyes to Judith again. "She was my lawyer once, before I got my LPN course. I wouldn't be here without her."

"She helped a lot of people."

"Sure did." There is a pause, then words pour out of her. "My first husband beat me. I had two kids, no money, no friends — he was possessive, he'd driven everyone away, my family too. I was terrified." She looks up, seems to pull herself back into the present, looks at her watch.

She checks the fluid in the plastic bag on the pole, smooths the sheet across Judith's chest. "I heard she was out of ICU. I just had to come."

"Did you talk to her?"

"No … oh … I guess you're supposed to, aren't you?"

"She'd like to know you remember. Come back. Tell her."

She gives me a ghost of a smile, another soft look for Judith. "I will."

Judith is lying on her side, one curled hand resting in front of her face like a small child's would. It's such a relief not to have the sound of the machines anymore. Just a slight whistle of wind rounding the corner of the building outside the window and Judith's breathing. I listen to it for a while, soft in and out, then get up to check the view from this new window. Looking down through the treetops I can see the grassy slope of the Citadel and a birds-eye view of the Bengal Lancers' riding ring. I describe the horses to Judith, tiny from here, going around and around, carrying children in proper English riding gear. How many cities have horses this close to the centre of town?

I am starting to describe the pedestrians and cyclists on the road around the Citadel when Althea arrives. "How is she?" She, too, bends over Judith to listen to her breathing. "Better?" She looks up at me.

"I think so, unless I'm imagining it."

"I think so too."

Althea settles herself into the chair the nurse was sitting in. I tell her about that visit. Althea nods as I talk, her eyes on Judith. When I finish, she takes a deep breath. "Judith saved my life, too. Did I ever tell you?"

"Is this about your husband?"

"Yeah, Darrell."

"He's in jail, isn't he?"

"Yeah. Finally killed someone. It could have been me. He threatened often enough."

"Oh, Althea."

"After I threw him out, Judith helped me get a peace bond.

It was still scary. He'd come home high as a kite, stomp up on the porch, bang on the door, try to break the windows. I'd call the police, and they knew to come fast. Judith made sure of that. When they came, I'd hold that peace bond up to the window. Quick glance and they'd take him away.

"He always said he'd kill the girls too. I had them trained to hide when he came, but if he'd ever gotten in, it wouldn't have taken him long to find them. I did it so they'd feel just a little bit safer, maybe so they wouldn't hear everything he said."

"Must have been a relief when he finally went to jail."

"Yeah, but it scares me to have Judith lying here like this. A life sentence isn't really life, as you know. He keeps coming up for parole. Judith goes to the hearing with me, helps me organize my statement, say the words the parole board will take seriously. He's up for parole again in the spring."

"Bob will help, if Judith …"

"Sure he will, but she's sort of like my guardian angel, you know? Makes me *feel* safe."

I'm wishing I were on the same side of the bed and could squeeze her hand. Instead, I run my fingers along the blue veins on the back of Judith's. "We all leaned on her, one way or another. But who did she have to lean on?"

Althea nods.

We leave together. In the lobby downstairs, we hold each other in a long hug. As we separate, Althea asks, "Did you ever hug Judith?"

"No. Strange, isn't it? Sometimes I think it's just how we women working in the community say hello and goodbye, but Judith's always kept a sort of distance."

"Uh-huh. Like she's made of glass or something. Might shatter."

"And you know, Althea, I've been thinking lately, how little I really *know* her. I can't tell you anything about her life before I met her, except that she grew up in the house on Needham Street, her dad was a lawyer and she spent some time in Toronto."

"Yeah, me too. I know she had some kind of break with her family when she was away, only came back to Halifax after her parents died and left her the house."

"But you don't know why?"

"No, do you?"

"No."

"Do you know about the scandal around her dad?"

"No … oh, wait, something about being accused of racism?"

"Yeah. He hired Edmund Smith, one of the first Black lawyers to be called to the Nova Scotia bar, with great fanfare, and then, a few months later, fired him again. Accused him of being incompetent and unethical. But Smith was well known even then and had a long career afterwards. Everyone knew it wasn't true."

"Edmund Smith didn't ever talk about it?"

"No. He never said anything. Neither did Judith's father, and the other lawyers in the practice were as puzzled as the rest of us."

"When was that, anyway?"

"Oh, a long time ago. My kids were babies. Early sixties? Judith couldn't have been out of her teens at the time." Althea slides her purse up her arm and begins buttoning her sweater. "The only other thing I know is that Ronald Maidstone was pretty well known as a drunk."

I swore I wouldn't do it again, but they "need me." And, okay, it is a rush. I'm a good lookout. Who'd suspect a lame, old homeless woman standing on the street late at night? Besides, it'll be a story to tell Judith.

"You'll like this one," Robin tells me as we walk south along dark streets, but he won't tell me where we're going. Many blocks later, I'm regretting coming when I notice we're on campus. And then we stop beneath a glossy new sign I know all too well: "Continuing Education. Learning Solutions for a Changing World." That useless slogan. They spent a fortune on an "image consultant" to come up with it. Enough money for four years of fully subsidized community leadership courses.

Just above is a ghostly name, faded into the bricks of the building: Walford College. It *is* a ghost, the college that died. Well, not the college itself — behold the glossy sign — but its original spirit. Dr. Walford and his colleagues were old-fashioned, social-democratic adult educators who cared about people who can't pay for education.

The side of the building is shaded from the streetlights by a row of trees along the street. Few cars here, more pedestrians, students on their way wherever after they should be in bed. Mostly they cut across the end of this side street, though, along University Avenue.

Working their way down the side wall, Gord holding the stencil, Robin spraying, it doesn't take long to decorate the side of the building from one end to the other. When Robin joins me, I'm grinning like a fool. "Like that, eh?" he says.

CHAPTER FORTY

Oh, how I hope Judith can hear me. She is lying on her back this afternoon, her mouth slightly open, lips cracked, although they've put something on them. I tell her about the Chicken Campaign logo, the length of the Continuing Education building. I am holding her hand and, in my pleasure, squeeze a little harder than perhaps I should. She squeezes back. Just a little spasm-like movement, but surely a squeeze. Was it a response to what I said? A sign that she's coming to? I press the call button.

A very young woman comes. Her name tag says RN, so I guess she's actually old enough to be a nurse. "Were you touching her palm?" she asks.

"I could have been."

"There's a reflex there. Sometimes coma patients squeeze if you touch it." She sees my disappointment. "Sorry."

After she leaves, I tentatively squeeze again. Nothing happens. I deliberately touch Judith's palm inside the curled fingers. Nothing again. What does that child of a nurse know? I prefer to think Judith is celebrating Chicken Campaign logos sprayed right over "Learning Solutions for a Changing World."

I've been silent for a while. Ran out of things to say. The room is small and, as the light outside fades, it feels more intimate. I get that feeling of travelling in a car at night, just driver and passenger looking out at the dark road, lights flickering by. Like you're not really talking to anyone, not accountable for your words. Judith's very stillness is a vast, quiet space, listening.

I take in a deep breath, hold it, let it go again. "Judith, we promised each other, as soon as Cindy's sentencing hearing was over, we'd talk about our lives. At least, try."

Silence. Even the city outside is quiet this high up and through thick panes of glass.

"I must've said it before, about growing up fundamentalist. Have I? Surely. But not everything …"

This isn't easy. "You know I spent time in Guatemala, because of my work with the Central American refugees, but did I ever say I went out as a missionary? There were lots of fundamentalist missionaries going to Latin America in those years. The Guatemalan government saw us as a calming influence, a belief system that would make people accept their lot as their villages were 'cleared' to make way for coffee and banana plantations, factories and mines. That is, violently destroyed. I was so naïve."

I watch Judith's eyes for a few minutes. They move now and then under her eyelids.

"Were you raised to be a justice activist, Judith, or did you come to it on your own? I never could have imagined becoming what I did, raised in a perfect, padded little world, my parents' beliefs like tinted windows, colouring everything. Well, I guess every set of beliefs is like that. It's just that some have clearer glass than others.

"So easy to be always right, with your very own personal Lord and Saviour. But he was more than that. I had a passionate love for the Jesus I grew up with. I was a quiet, obedient kid, lonely, but he walked right beside me, my ever-loving, ever-listening friend. Thin, blond and Anglo-Saxon of course. No wonder I got the missionary calling. 'Save' those poor benighted people. Be-nighted. Dark."

It's coming out all jagged. Bits and pieces. "You see, Judith, I was born born-again." Not the first time I've made that joke, but haven't for a very long time. "Good thing I've been born again and again and again ever since.

"But the problem with being born again is no one recognizes

you. When I came back to Canada, I had changed too much to go home. The church in Guatemala had written to my parents telling them I'd been brainwashed by communists. By the time I got back, they heard everything I said that way. They threatened to hire one of those deprogrammers, you know, the ones who work with people who've been trapped by cults? I had to leave. Came here. Amherst is only a two-hour drive away, but I never went home again. In fact, it was years before I stopped looking over my shoulder for the deprogrammer."

Laughter drifts up the stairs at St. Marks, along with pounding noises. I follow it to a formerly empty room in the basement and stop, face to face with a giant, newsprint person. Robin looks up, his arms sunk into a large plastic bucket on the floor, dripping white glop. "Hey Lucy, come and meet Mister Ten Percent."

The basement seethes with activity, Bara, Robin, Cat, their friends and all the art students that came to the meeting after Cindy's sentencing, plus a few. The glop, I see, is wallpaper paste. They are dipping strips of newspaper into it and handing it to a lanky fellow on a stepladder. He places each piece carefully on a big wire armature topped with a huge balloon.

There are a few chairs just inside the door. I help myself to one of them. I have to admit, it's like magic. Mister Ten Percent slowly emerges out of nothing but wire, paste and paper. The big balloon grows arching eyebrows and fat smiling lips. A smaller one taped on the front becomes his oversized nose.

His hands dry a few feet away. "They're going to be rigged on sticks," says a young creature with spiky pink hair. He or she, I can't tell which, has come to rest for a while on the chair beside me, a white crust drying on his or her arms. "One hand'll hold a big sack of money with a sign saying '94.6% of Canada's Wealth.' He's the richest ten percent of Canadians, you know?" I do know, but don't think I'm meant to answer. "It's for a demonstration next Saturday." I'd figured that out too.

A thin, brown young man comes and sits on the other side of me. "Are you the Prophet Robin talks about?"

I look around for Robin, but he is totally engaged in giving Mister Ten Percent an intricate ear.

As the young people disperse, Mister Ten Percent propped against the ladder in the middle of the room to dry, Bara confesses that our refrigerator is almost empty. Good smells fill the basement, coming from the kitchen at the drop-in. We decide to stay.

Bara tells me all about the plans for the demo as we eat, but after taking our trays of dirty dishes to the racks by the kitchen door and returning with tea, she becomes quiet, looking down into her cup. "Lucy, I've been thinking about something. That day you, like, yelled at all those shoppers?" She pauses, looks up. "Are people guilty of what they don't know about?"

"I know, they don't intend to harm anyone, but does that make any difference to the woman getting paid pennies to sit at a sewing machine making their clothes? Or starving because their coffee is grown on the land that used to grow her family's food?"

"But how are they … we … supposed to know?"

"The information isn't hard to find."

"But it's so big and complicated. Do you really believe you, personally, are responsible for what happens to people down there?"

My turn to look down into my cup. "You're right. It is big and complicated."

"Lucy? Are you all right?"

"I need to go home."

She smiles.

"What?"

"You're calling it home."

CHAPTER FORTY-ONE

"One of the young people involved in the Chicken Campaign asked me something, Judith, if I believe I'm personally responsible for the North's exploitation of the Global South. When is a person responsible for another person's suffering? A student who takes her own life, a village in Guatemala, a baby conceived at the wrong time.... You start out wanting to do good...."

There's a lump in my throat, but the story is rising up, trying to get out. I need to tell Judith so badly, I can taste the words.

"If I'm going to tell you about my life ..."

My voice comes out all squeaky. I clear my throat, start again.

"My friend, Rosa, in Guatemala, had a son named Ramón ..."

Again, my throat tightens around the words. I realize I have to back up, start at the beginning.

"In Guatemala, I was assigned to a church in a new town, built by a Canadian mining company for their employees. No way in and out but the company bus. Odd little place, a few square blocks carved out of the jungle. Roads that went nowhere, but full of great big old gas-guzzlers bought by the younger miners so they could race around those few corners, kicking up dust.

"Mostly I taught literacy. They sent me to a language immersion program when I first went so I could teach people to read the Bible in Spanish, but the church was also interested in 'lifting people out of poverty.'" I make the quote signs in the air, although she can't see them.

"That meant a 'job readiness' program, for men wanting to work in the mine. My assignment was to teach them to read some words in English. I can't dignify what I was doing with the name

'English as a Second Language.' It was just a few 'useful' things like 'Slow.' 'Stop at the white line.' 'Look both ways.' 'Caution.' 'Poison.' 'Do not open without permission of your supervisor.'

"The teaching wasn't going very well, in Spanish or English. At the same time, everyone was talking about this great literacy program in the villages, up in the hills. All kinds of people were learning how to read and write. It was always labelled communist, because it was 'out there' in guerrilla country. One day when the village teacher was in the town, I went in search of him and asked him if he would teach me how to teach."

My eyes have closed again and now, on my inner movie screen, I see Nicolás's face that first day, closed, suspicious. "He didn't want me anywhere near his program, but his method, *educacíon popular*, starts with the learners talking about their lives. There were a lot of things the women didn't feel comfortable discussing in front of a man. Not that I knew anything about the things they wanted to talk about either, female bodies, sex, pregnancy … but he took me out to a village where a new program was starting up and began to teach me how to teach."

I take a few minutes to watch clouds floating by the window.

"I don't know how to describe what happened to me. A revolution, a conversion, an earthquake. My world turned upside down. I certainly began to see the mine in a whole different light. The mission church figured I was 'going native,' turning communist. They were going to send me home. So Rosa, one of the matriarchs of the village of San Marcos, where I was teaching, took me in to live with her family.

"I should never have shown my face in Inco's company town again, but I got a message that the church was holding a stack of letters from friends and family back home. Rosa tried to talk me out of it, but I was homesick. I wanted them. She sent her son, Ramón, to walk with me. Once I got there, he was to stay out of sight, watch from a hiding place at the edge of the jungle.

"Oh, Judith, if a genie came out of a bottle and offered me three moments of my life back to do over, this would be the first one. The letter thing was a trick. When I realized this, I had to be quick on my feet to get away, and I couldn't do it alone. Ramón ran out of the jungle shouting and waving his arms to divert them. He got away with me, but he was recognized.

"Rosa turned pale when we told her. She knew, Ramón knew too, but they wouldn't say anything. It was Nicolás ..." My voice cracks again. I swallow. "He explained to me. Ramón was part of a group trying to organize the miners.

"He went into hiding in the hills, but a military patrol found him a few weeks later. I tried to comfort Rosa and Ramón's young wife, Mía. She was in my literacy class. I figured since he hadn't committed any crime, they would let him go. I was so, so naïve.

"Ramón's body was dumped in a field just outside the village. I won't even try to tell you what they did to him, Judith. No one should have that picture in their mind. I wish I didn't. I will also never forget Rosa wailing. I tore her heart out of her. I may even have pointed the paramilitaries toward San Marcos...."

I have no more words. If Judith can hear me, it's only sobbing now.

My need for Judith's quiet, hopefully listening, presence stays with me all through supper. I barely taste the soup and bread Bara serves me, barely look up at her. I know my eyes must be red. They feel like they're full of sand. She doesn't push, though. Just nods when I say I want to go to bed and rises to clear the table.

In the bedroom beside the bathroom, I expect my open suitcase to be sitting on the bare mattress, my small piles of ratty clothing ranged around it, but that is not what I find. The mattress has been made up. The bedside table has been set beside the bed, holding the lamp and box of tissues from beside Judith's bed in the alcove.

My suitcase sits, closed, beside the dresser. I pull open the drawers to find my clothes folded and arranged inside.

I turn to find Bara in the doorway.

"What have you done?" I ask her, my voice peevish even to my own ears.

"It's time you have a proper bedroom, Lucy."

I cross to the closet and pull it open. On the rail, only my navy slacks and spare skirt. "Where are Judith's clothes?"

"We moved them to the closet in the bedroom across the hall." She points. "We thought you'd be happy."

"I don't want the place to change. When Judith — "

"I know, but please don't worry. We'll put everything back the way it was."

I ignore her until she leaves, a terrible thought forming in my mind. As soon as she calls goodnight up the stairs, I almost run into Judith's study.

The bedside table has been cleared off. I open the drawer and find Judith's murder mystery, the marker, thankfully, still in place. But the bed itself is neatly remade, sheets and pillowcase clean. Tears starting again, I lie on top of the blanket, bury my face in the pillow. Nothing but laundry soap. I am sobbing again, picking up where I left off at Judith's bedside, but this time there are no tissues handy.

CHAPTER FORTY-TWO

The day of the demonstration is cool and windy, and my knees ache. Mister Ten Percent has a cloth body by now, his face painted. One of the taller young men carries the frame on his shoulders so that the puppet towers a good five feet above the crowd. Two young women manipulate his hands on long sticks, one holding his sack of money, the other a scroll labelled "The Law." And so Mister Ten Percent comes to life, dancing down Spring Garden Road, leering and rolling about from side to side, ruling the world.

Cindy walks along in front of him, waving to the crowd. She's a celebrity, moving in a knot of reporters and admiring young people. Her face is shining, but not as much as Patty's, hovering just behind her. Cindy doesn't see me, but Patty does, grins a bit wider and points at Cindy. I give her a thumbs-up.

I tell Judith about it, fresh from the excitement, winded from the walk. "Remember when we used to do that sort of thing? Poverty. Apartheid. Gay rights. I don't remember ever making anything like that Mister Ten Percent puppet, though. I walked behind him, watching him bob and bow to the crowd along the sidewalks. They made him look so scornful.

"Oh, Judith, it was loud and young, a whole new generation demanding redistribution of wealth. Good thing; it's a lot more concentrated in their day than it was in ours."

Robin has come out for the demo, but now that I have a bedroom, he's practically living in Judith's study. And I find myself drawn there, again and again, to hover at the door.

This time, he turns to look at me. "Lucy, stop fussing out there. Come in."

I pick my way along the path through the papers. Robin has been placing file cards on top of the piles, each labelled in black marker: Levellers and Diggers (England) 1649; Highland Clearances (Scotland) 1770s–1850; Northwest Rebellion (Canada) 1885; Michoacán (Mexico) 1869–1904; Women's Land Title (Tanzania) 1990–present.

I sit on the edge of the bed — a bit awkward, since we have to talk around the end of the freestanding bookshelf, but there is nowhere else.

"I'm figuring it out, Lucy. She's collected all these papers and books about people resisting privatization of land in different times and places, and she's writing case studies. Those are all in the computer."

"Any idea what she's after?"

"Well, there's an introduction, explaining that she's trying to answer her own questions about how and why corporations and governments force land privatization on people, and what works and doesn't when people resist."

"Robin, I'm uncomfortable with this."

He looks up at me, marking a spot on the page he's been reading with one long forefinger. "I'm not moving anything, Lucy." He waves his other hand at the piles on the floor. "Everything's exactly where it was."

I sigh.

"Don't worry."

I do worry, though. Maybe I should warn Judith.

I retreat to the living room and pick up the newspaper someone has left on the arm of the chesterfield. My eye falls on an editorial about the Chicken Campaign graffiti. After the first two or three nights, a week or so apart, there hasn't been any more. The editorial writer suggests that the vandals are getting bored with it. "It was fun on summer nights but now the weather is getting cooler." He, or she, even suggests that the police have gotten it under control.

Althea sits quietly in the plastic visitor's chair, back to the window, head bowed as if praying. She looks up when I come in. "Hi, Lucy, I'm glad you're here. I need to go." She holds out her hand.

I take it and squeeze. "Not talking to her?"

"I was. Ran out of things to say."

"I know what you mean." I squeeze her hand again, then move around the bed and sit down in the other chair. They have Judith lying on her back today.

"Do you know what she makes me think of?" says Althea. "One of those Egyptian mummies."

I lift my finger to my lips.

"Oh yeah." She puts her hand over her mouth for a second. "Sorry, Judith."

We sit quietly for another few minutes. What she said is true, though. Judith is drying up. Her skin kind of hangs over her bones. She's breathing through her mouth, which chaps her lips, and her teeth are turning brown.

I'm embarrassed to blather on in front of Althea the way I do when I'm with Judith alone, but Althea is on her feet anyway, gathering her things. She gives Judith a gentle kiss on the forehead, waves to me and then she's gone.

Judith's hand is under the blanket and I don't go after it, just talk. "Judith, I want to warn you about something, for when you're ready to come home. A young man who's involved in the Chicken

Campaign, Robin, he's interested in your research on land privatization. He's reading some of it. I'm letting him, because it's lighting some kind of fire in him. He's truly interested, and he's not moving anything out of the piles where you have them, and, well ... I trust him. With that, anyway. When you come home, if you want help with your research, I'm sure he'd do it, or if you want everything left alone, that's what we'll do."

I watch Judith. Her eyes twitch under papery lids. At least she won't be caught completely by surprise when she ... if she ... .

"Judith, last time I told you something I've never told anyone before, how my naïveté killed Ramón. It weighs on me, though not, in the end, the heaviest.

"Rosa continued to take care of me. She did it for the village. Ramón's death led to a bitter debate about whether I brought them danger by attracting the attention of the paramilitaries — they were getting closer and closer to the mine by then, burning down villages, murdering the people — or, and Rosa argued for this, my presence, as an outsider, a Canadian citizen, brought them safety. I was a witness. Nothing could be done to them in the name of a Canadian company with a Canadian watching. The debate went on, but Rosa was the matriarch of the village, they listened to her, at least then ... ."

My voice has creaked to a halt. I pause, taking in deep breaths to free it again.

"Mía disappeared, Ramón's wife. She was pregnant. I often wonder about that baby, hers and Ramón's...."

Now my voice gives out completely. The deep breath trick doesn't work, sounding more like choking, or sobbing.

On the way home, I think about the Guatemalan adoption files. They have been sitting in my suitcase since I came to the house, untouched. I could work on the dining room table. After all, we eat in the kitchen, apart from that potluck to celebrate the first graffiti night.

That plan falls apart the minute I walk through the door. There is an awful clatter in the dining room. A sewing machine, set up at the end of the dining room table, a head full of dreadlocks hunched over it, dark hands pushing fabric through the needle. Bara and the one with all the bits of metal in her face have fabric spread across the other end of the table and are going at it with huge shears. Two more machines sit on the floor, waiting for the cutting to be finished.

"What's going on?"

I'm not sure they can hear me, but Dreadlocks stops and looks up. Blessed silence.

"Hi, Lucy," Bara straightens from her work with the shears and brushes aside the blonde hair that has fallen across her face. She introduces the young women around the table, Jane, Alyson, whatever, whatever. The names slide out of my head as fast as they come in. "And, of course, you know Cat." But my eyes had found Cat long before the introduction. She looks up briefly and then bends again to her task of pinning red shapes to black cloth. Her already brown skin turns a shade darker.

"We're making Chicken Campaign flags." Bara picks up a big, bright piece of cloth to show me, the chicken on the scales of justice, neatly appliquéd. "Maggie found this article."

"For a paper, for my textile class," adds Metalface.

You sew? I think, without sewing yourself to the fabric?

Bara practically shines with excitement. "Some women in Norway, there was this referendum on nuclear power. These women were against it and the polls said most women were, but they were too shy to speak out, so they made flags. They ran the logo of the anti-nuclear campaign up every flagpole in Norway the night before the vote."

"And they won," says Metalface. The rings in her lip and eyebrow rise up and stand out when she smiles.

I retreat upstairs, but the noise follows me. "Lucy," Robin calls from Judith's office. He eases his long frame free of the computer chair, picks up something from the corner of the desk and comes to the door. "Who's this?" He holds out a photograph. I recognize the couple from the more formal portrait Bara found in the basement. The man we figured is Judith's father, too jolly, his clothes awry and his arm around the shoulders of the woman who must be Judith's mother. She is dressed for a party with jewellery and lipstick. She is rigidly straight, a tight smile on her lips, nothing in her eyes.

Robin looks at it. "I wonder if that's Judith's parents?"

"Where did you find it?"

"There are photos tucked in between some of the books on the shelves."

"That's odd." I scan the spines of the books, row after row, covering the walls.

"And this one, Lucy?" It's smaller, a casual snapshot of a little girl dressed in her Sunday best: a frilly dress and crinoline, Mary Janes. She smiles tightly, self-consciously at the camera. "Is it Judith?"

I look at the narrow, delicately boned face. "Could be." I take it from him. It's faded to the watery oblivion of early colour prints. When did colour film come along?

"Does Judith have kids?"

"Not that I know of."

"Must be her, then. And look at this one." He hands me a very small photo of a newborn. A girl, judging by the pink blanket. Coffee skin, Black features. It looks like one of those photos the hospital used to take in the nursery. It's been handled, the emulsion worn off along the bottom and right edges.

"A child of one of her clients, maybe? Or someone she worked with in the community."

"You should take these to the hospital, describe them to her. If you still think she might be able to hear you, that is."

"Hope so."

I place the photos carefully in my pocket. Back in my room, I sit on the side of the bed and take them out, look at them more closely. I think the little girl is Judith, and then I don't. The man and woman have to be her parents. At least, the woman has to be her mother. And if the man is her father, what was he like to inspire such discomfort, perhaps even fear, in her mother?

I spend the longest time looking at the small photo of the baby. Why keep a picture of a baby you barely know? Between two books? And handle it often?

CHAPTER FORTY-THREE

"The dress looks white now, but it might be yellow, or pink. It has, what was that kind of needlework called? On the bodice. And little, white ankle socks. It's what we all looked like dressed up back then. Smocking. That's what it's called."

Judith is on her side again, curled up a little. The sun falls on her returning hair, almost an inch long now, a lighter brown than I remember. An Egyptian mummy, Althea said. Or perhaps the extremes of human life, a premature baby or an ancient crone.

"Judith is this you? Can you remember being lifted up onto a chesterfield to pose?" I finger the photo. Or did you do the lifting?

"I was pregnant once, Judith. I almost didn't come home because of it. When I realized I wasn't missing periods because of stress, or how little food I was eating, I told Rosa.

"'Is that so bad?' she said. 'Many babies are born to single mothers. Go home. Your mother will care for you.' My eyes must have been huge because, in that moment, I saw it all, how my parents would react, especially my mother, if I came home pregnant, a 'fornicator.' And not just that, but the baby would be brown. I told Rosa I'd stay in Guatemala, since she'd just said there were many babies born to single women there."

I close my eyes for a moment, hit by that vivid memory, the sudden chill in Rosa's open kitchen, like an evening breeze blowing through. "'Those babies and mothers blend into the village,' she said, and suddenly I knew: my baby would be too brown for my home in Canada, too white for San Marcos. Meanwhile, Rosa had gone still, looking at me, until I understood something else. She knew who the father was."

A leaf skitters against the outside of the heavy double-glass window.

"The picture, Judith. Shall I leave it with you?" I look over the medical clutter on her bedside table. "No. It'll get lost here. I'll put it back where Robin found it." I slide it carefully into my pocket. "Yeah, that's what I'll do. Okay, Judith?"

The girls are working on their sewing machines. "Where did you get these, anyway?" I ask Bara. "We found the first one in the basement, and then that one," she points, "we got in a second-hand shop. We got the third one on the curb on a garbage night."

"Works pretty well for garbage."

"Cat knows how to fix them," Bara says.

Cat looks up. "My grandmother taught me. She does alterations, wedding dresses and that."

The table is piled with bolts of red and black cloth. "As soon as you start putting these flags up, the cops'll be looking for anyone who's bought a lot of black and red cloth lately," I say.

A hesitant little laugh runs around the table. "Cat's grandmother," says Bara. "No one bats an eye when she buys a whole bolt of anything."

"A red and black wedding party?"

There is a titter around the table again.

"She makes other things too, costumes for theatres and that."

"She know what it's for?"

"She's a friend of Cindy's," Cat says.

"Oh, what's her name?"

"Paula Thomas."

"Paula is your grandmother? I know her."

"Yeah, she says she was in a class with you. She says that's what made her believe in herself. It got her started on her GED and sewing business."

~~

In the morning, I take the Guatemalan adoption files out of my suitcase, tuck them under my arm. Bara said Cat put her name in the adoption registry. How is she or any of the other lost children going to find out where they come from if I don't translate these? Not to mention the gift it would be to any grieving parents left alive.

So much for my plan to work on the dining room table. I look in to be sure. The sewing machines sit in their nests of red and black fabric, silent but in undisputed possession of the tabletop. Perhaps it's time to work at the library again, although the house is silent. No Robin, and the girls are likely all at school. Why not the kitchen table?

I prepare and eat a bowl of cereal, then push the empty bowl aside, take a deep breath and pull the document on top out of the plastic folder. The photo of the emaciated baby is still turned under the way I left it the last time I tried to work at this. All I've done so far is pencil in some English words between the typed lines. So little information, the baby's name, the name of a man who drove him to the orphanage, the name and location of the orphanage. This one was in Antigua.

Do they all give the location of the orphanage? I pull the documents out and shuffle through them, avoiding the sad little photos, looking for place names. There is no standard format. I see some villages and towns — Cobán, Huehuetenango, Sololá — nothing near San Marcos, although would that matter? Who was the man who drove that little boy to the orphanage in Antigua? How far had they come? Who, and what, was he? Why was the baby with him? Did Mía have her baby in prison? Where was the prison? Did she even live that long?

Despite my attempts to resist, my eyes are drawn to the baby from Sololá by a bandage wrapped around her matchstick arm.

She was called Inéz, her file a single page, her medical report at the bottom. I see *herida*, the word for a wound made by a knife. Other words are obvious, like *anemia, malnutrición*. I will need a dictionary for others.

My stomach has clenched so hard it wants to send back the cereal I just ate. Maybe I can't do this after all.

Judith's hospital room is silent. The wind outside rattles the leaves on the trees below. There's no missing now that some are turning gold and orange. Judith is lying on her back, her knees propped up by a pillow under the sheet. Her hair has grown into a fine, silky brush cut on the one side, the hole where the drain was, a pink scar now, barely shows through. On the other side it's scraggly and lank, tangled on the pillow behind her head. There is a brush in the nightstand. I give the short side a quick, gentle once-over, then reach across to the other side. It sticks together in clumpy strands. I keep brushing, though, in a rhythm, for the comfort of it.

"It took a while to convince Rosa that my parents would not welcome a child. When she saw the spot I was caught in, she suggested a *curandera*. I was shocked. I might have changed a lot from my missionary days, but I still thought of a *curandera* as evil. 'Trust me,' Rosa said. 'When it's women's things, they know.'

"I resisted for a few days, hoping desperately on every trip into the bushes that I would find that blessed bloodstain. But no such luck. The *curandera* was ancient, exactly my picture of a witch. The fact that her little house was festooned with more crosses, crucifixes and statues of the Virgin Mary than I could count just made it worse, all mingled with the usual foil Christmas decorations and bright plastic tablecloths. Just one step inside the door, I lost my nerve and turned to leave. Rosa put a firm hand on my arm. 'At least hear what she has to say.' When I paused, she added 'How many choices do you have?'

"The old woman held my face between her hands and studied me with her raisin eyes. She spoke to Rosa. 'She's frightened of me.' Then she laughed, a dry cackle.

"'She does not want to have this baby,' Rosa told her. The old woman said something back in *Quiché*."

I glance down at Judith and startle back into the present as I realize that more of her scalp is showing through, pale white, on the side where the hair is still long. I stop brushing, look in horror at the clumps of hair tangled in the bristles. "Oh, Judith, I'm sorry." I glance over my shoulder, but no one is there. I pull the wad of hair free of the brush and drop it into the waste basket, repeat, "I'm sorry," but my mind is already flying back to that smoky, long-ago hut in the highlands of Guatemala.

"The old woman did some sort of ceremony with smoke and a handful of grass. It terrified me. I thought I was being cursed, which was silly, because I was already cursed by then. She assembled a packet of bits and pieces I couldn't identify. Plants, I hoped. They would 'send away the soul that wants to enter me,' Rosa explained, but also make me very, very ill.

"I carried it with me for the next month. I was still living with Rosa and what was left of her family, looking for someone to take me north to find … the people who went into hiding. I knew the journey would be dangerous, even without being pregnant. I would decide to take the concoction, open the packet, finger the bits inside. It smelled vile. I would prepare a tea to wash it down. Then I would decide to wait, just a bit longer. It would be a terrible sin, killing my own baby, though, if I were going to do it, I knew waiting would make it worse.

"The packet had become brittle and dirty when, late one night, I opened it, made the tea, said a prayer and swallowed it down. I was unbelievably ill. So much pain. And blood. Rosa nursed me through it, but after, she wouldn't let anyone take me north. It would not only be dangerous for me, she said, but for the people who were fleeing. And by then, she knew I couldn't keep anyone safe.

"That was the worst thing. I did it so I could go north, follow … Nicolás. I sacrificed the main connection between us to do it. I killed our baby. And then I lost him anyway."

The hairbrush is still in my hand, clutched so hard it's made a deep dent in my palm. I gulp in air, choking on held-back sobs.

———————

CHAPTER FORTY-FOUR

Later, the kids call it "the night of the flags." The place is milling with more girls than I've ever seen here before, plus a lad or two, talking, laughing, excited, dressed in black.

"You all joined Robin's bunch now?" I say to Bara.

She laughs. "We just don't want to be seen."

The flags are all set up properly with thick pieces of cord, wooden toggles. Each gets its own grocery bag. As if on a sudden inspiration, Bara asks if I want to come. Not sure she means it. I'd slow them down pretty badly.

Soon after, the laughter drains out of the house, just like someone pulled the plug. But the house isn't empty. As I pass the foot of the stairs I see the light pouring out of Judith's study broken by the silhouette of Robin's long frame and curly hair. He is coming down the stairs, a mug in his hand. He salutes me with it. "I thought they'd never leave."

I sit at the kitchen table while he fills the kettle and leans back on the counter, his hands hooked over its edge on either side of his hips. "Lucy, tell me what's so wrong with private colleges. The college gets paid; the student gets a course."

"But there's no subsidy. Government grants pay two-thirds of the cost in a public institution. In a private college, the students pay the whole thing, to the tune of $20,000 a year at the ones I'm familiar with, and that's just tuition. Low-income students can't hope to access them. Even middle-class students use all their savings and go into debt."

"Lots of students use all their savings and go into debt."

"But with realistic prospects. The private colleges I knew would lure students in with promises of six-figure salaries, assure them they'll be able to do the courses, whether they could or not."

"But if they've got the prerequisites — "

"No one was checking prerequisites. There were no registrars, just salespeople with quotas. Sign up three students this week or lose your job. Ten and you get a bonus. If the students couldn't keep up, bye-bye, too bad, no six-figures, work in a coffee shop 'til you pay off your debt. Some never will."

I am grateful that the kettle whistles just then. Covers the closing of my throat. Robin turns his back to shut off the burner and pour hot water on what looks like an already-used tea bag. Moments later, though, I have his attention again.

My voice is back. Anger helps. "The ones who benefit are the owners and shareholders. Some of them have a pattern. They start a college, collect the tuition, pay themselves well, and then, when the business goes bankrupt, they abandon the students and walk away with a big house all paid for."

"Are these what the university calls 'continuing education partner colleges'?"

I nod.

"But why did continuing ed get involved with them in the first place?"

"They gave the university half the profit in return for accreditation."

"Oh. Of course. Makes sense."

"No, it doesn't. In my day, at least my earlier days, the university knew a lot of research depended on information that came from people in the community. The point of continuing education was to give back, especially to people who didn't have access to the university any other way."

Robin spoons the tea bag out of his cup and flips it into the sink.

"Robin? How do you know about continuing education partner colleges? Been digging around in the archives again?"

Robin picks up his cup. "Oh. I didn't offer you a cup. Want one?"

I lower my voice a notch or two. "Robin. How do you know about continuing education partner colleges?"

He considers for a moment, then comes to the table and sits, letting out a breath as he lands in the chair. "My father."

"Who is your father?"

He is watching my eyes. "Warren MacIntosh."

"Oh, Robin." I have a dizzy moment, as though the floor has tilted under me.

"Yeah, I know. He was VP Academic when Walford College's mandate was changed. He was part of that decision."

"So why are you asking these questions? You know the answers."

"I know how he saw it: 'innovative partnerships,' 'efficient use of the university's resources.' For him it solved the problem of less grant money. Why do you think he went for the idea of partner colleges in the first place? And worked so hard to get their accreditation through senate? He doesn't think about the people you taught, what it meant for them. He probably doesn't know they exist, or at least he doesn't think they have anything to do with him."

"Did he invest in the partner colleges?"

"I don't know. He doesn't talk to me about his investments. To him, I'm a crazy, misguided kid going through a phase."

"Why did I never ask your last name? Why didn't you tell me?"

"Why would I?"

"I don't know. So I could have avoided you?"

"Exactly."

"Does he know you know me?"

"Why would I tell him that? He thinks you're crazy and violent. Not to mention a communist."

"So, his crazy, misguided kid is going through a phase with a crazy, violent old commie." I laugh.

Robin grins back. "His worst nightmare."

I actually hold the paper up for Judith. It's a big photograph of the flagpole in front of Province House. "Look Judith, one of the Chicken Campaign flags. They took it down pretty early, but the press photographers got there first. I guess they learned a lesson when no one but the student paper got a photo of the one in front of City Hall." I turn the paper around, look at it again myself. "Province House. Those kids must have climbed that horrible spiky fence."

I read her some of the letters to the editor. A nurse comes into the room, a plump woman, dark hair pinned up into a bun. "How are we today?" she says, addressing Judith.

I want to say, "*we're* fine," but instead I busy myself folding the paper. I guess it doesn't matter if she sees the Chicken Campaign flag on the front page. The whole city has, but I feel the urge to cover it up anyway.

The woman shifts the sheet aside, exposing Judith's thin body, outlined under the nightgown she is wearing, even the feeding tube that curls up her side and enters above her stomach. I'm shocked by how frail she is, flesh melting from the space between bone and skin, and a sour smell, stale sweat, dirty diaper. I want to cover her. She looks unbearably vulnerable. It only takes a minute, though, for the nurse to bend over her, a kind of hug, and turn her over, neatly tucking the sheet and blanket around her again.

"The girls are carrying the whole chicken thing, man." Gord stands outside the study door with two young men I don't know.

I hear Robin's voice from inside. "I'm busy with this."

"Aw, come on. We can't stop now."

"I thought you said it's getting harder for the paint to dry now that it's colder."

"Well sure, but who cares if it's dry? There's still some weeks before winter."

"You'll just have to do it without me," Robin says.

The boys look at one another. "Shit," says one. Gord shrugs his shoulders back. As they start down the stairs, Gord turns to me and grins.

The chicken logo starts to appear more around town, a graffiti hit one night, a flag the next.

CHAPTER FORTY-FIVE

Judith's room is as peaceful as always, morning light slanting through the glass, Judith curled, silent and still beneath crisp sheets, listening, I hope. "Those young women involved in the Chicken Campaign, Judith, one of them looks so Mayan. She's adopted, has no idea where she comes from."

I take a deep breath.

"After I recovered from losing the baby, there was no choice but to come home. There would be no guide for the journey north into the jungle and I could never find the people without one, if I even survived. It was becoming clear that I was a burden on Rosa and her family.

"The night before I began my long journey home, Rosa made enough tortillas to stuff my pack full. There wasn't much else to carry by then, an old shawl Rosa's sister gave me for the journey, a notebook and three small things that belonged to Nicolás, all that survived … .

"That evening I remember holding the shawl tightly around my shoulders, as if it could keep me from falling apart. I watched her pat the tortillas, flipping them around her battered black pan, and memorized every detail of the scene — Rosa's round, brown body, the beautiful fabric of her clothes, all woven by her own hands, the flickering light of the fire, fragrant woodsmoke, the frogs and insects singing outside in the darkness. I had lost Nicolás and my life in San Marcos, then the baby. The next morning, I would lose all that remained."

I pause for a moment, eyes closed, seeing, smelling, hearing that tiny lean-to kitchen.

"Rosa startled me when she spoke. '*Escucha*. Listen.' It was the way she began when she felt what she was about to say was very important. 'I know you want to help us and you're sad that your time to do that here is over, but your real power is not here anyway. It's in Canada. That is where Inco has their headquarters, where many of their shareholders live. Most Canadians are ordinary people, good people. I don't think they know what their company does here. If they knew, they would be angry. They would use their voices and their money to make Inco and the other big companies change. Go and talk to them. You're white. They'll hear you.'

"I was hurt at the time. It felt like a dismissal, a rejection. But I memorized it, along with everything else about that evening. It has defined my life ever since. I came to see that my knapsack held much more than a shawl, a Bible, a notebook and tortillas for the journey. It held powerful tools for changing people and, eventually, cultures."

Another breath.

"I had no money for a bus. Rosa found someone going to Guatemala City by donkey cart. It took a couple of weeks and felt like forever, jouncing along, my broken heart bleeding with each jolt. I replayed the decision to take the *curandera's* herbs over and over again. Maybe I could have taken the baby home. My parents would have rejected me, but they did anyway. It would have been a permanent connection to Nicolás. Now all I had of him was his three remaining possessions. I had found two of them in the charred ruins of his room in San Marcos and cleaned them up as best I could, his rosary and a small pottery figure of a peasant with huge, work-worn hands, praying on his knees.

"The third thing was the most precious to him, his Bible. When we were walking to the villages in the hills, Nicolás would carry the camping gear and I would carry the few teaching materials we had. When he went north with the villagers, he left without warning. Soon after, I went with the remnants of Rosa's family to her sister's house in San Piedro. I emptied the teaching materials out of my knapsack and left them behind, except for one notebook and a pen. That's when I discovered I had his Bible."

"In Guatemala City, I went to the mission headquarters for my denomination and threw myself on their mercy, 'confessed' that I was brainwashed, repented my sins, everything else they wanted to hear, so they would send me home. Before I left, though, I made a visit to the headquarters of Nicolás's order.

"During the journey from San Piedro, I had sat by small camp-fires in the evening, notebook in my lap, writing him a letter. I asked him to come to Canada. I would sponsor him. We would start a new life together. No one need know he's a priest … oh. I've said it. Now you know. Nicolás was a priest."

I watch Judith for a moment. Her collapsing face, the sheet gently rising and falling with her shallow breathing.

"Would he have left his order to come with me? His beloved Latin America? Who knows? Decisions made when any day could well be your last are different from other decisions. The paramilitaries were hunting priests and nuns by then. They would have killed Nicolás on sight, even before what happened in San Marcos. It made life so exquisite, so intense and precious. Even at the time, I knew we became lovers only because of that."

There are tears in my eyes, but I find I can still speak.

"The brother I spoke to said they didn't know where he was. He wouldn't have told me anyway, because of the danger. They would keep Nicolás's belongings for him, he said. I didn't dare include the letter and, God forgive me, when I took the rosary and pottery sculpture out of my knapsack to give to him, I left the Bible where it was."

A few steps out of the elevator into the second-floor lobby, I stop. From the hallway to my right comes a deep, rich alto voice:

"*Sometimes it causes me to tremble, tremble, tremble.*" Each word rolls out slowly, deliberately. I'd know that voice anywhere.

The sign on the wall says "Hospital Chapel" and points down the hall toward the music.

"*Were you there when they crucified my Lord?*" The varnished doors stand open, welcoming anyone passing by into a large, bright space. Chairs are set in rows facing a tapestry of a tree hanging on the front wall behind a simple altar. A cross sits beside a Menora and a sculpture I'm guessing is Buddhist. Muslim prayer rugs are piled in a corner.

"*Were you there when they nailed him to the tree?*" Althea stands facing the altar, arms spread out, hands open. A light above her polishes her corona of dark hair sprinkled with white hoarfrost. "*Sometimes it causes me to tremble, tremble, tremble.*"

I close my eyes and listen to the final verse. "*Were you there when they laid him in the tomb?*"

When the last note melts into the sunlit space, Althea slowly lowers her arms and bends her head. Praying? I wait until she lifts it again. "Althea?"

She turns, but her eyes are far away. "Hey, Lucy. I heard you talking to Judith. It sounded quite lively."

Oh dear, how much did she hear?

"I decided not to interrupt. I needed a bit of quiet anyway."

I take a few steps to the chair closest to the door, sigh and lower my weight off my aching knees. She comes over, sits down beside me. The windows look out into a dying fall flowerbed. Sitting on the broad window ledge is a small framed print of that old Holman Hunt portrait of Jesus that was on the wall of the Sunday school when I was growing up and just about every church or mission building I've been in since. "Althea, how do you picture Jesus?"

"How do I...?" Her eyes follow mine. She laughs. "Oh, that white, white Jesus. No, I never saw him that way."

"How do you see him?"

"Well, by now, Jesus is more like a presence, a whiff in the air, something I can feel but can't see. A spirit, you know? Like the Christmas spirit or the community spirit. Can't you just feel those in a room sometimes?"

"But didn't you have a picture of him, in your mind, when you were younger?"

"Guess I must have."

"Was he Black?"

She thinks for a few moments. "I guess so. Yeah, must have been. Why? Did you picture him like that?" She nods toward the Holman Hunt.

"I did. I even had a card with that picture on it between the pages of my Bible. That's who I talked to when I prayed. I carried that picture to Guatemala with me ..."

I can feel Althea looking at me. "And?"

"He turned into a small, brown man, slender, graceful, eyes that twinkled, though he could be sharp and fierce when he felt you needed cracking out of your naïve shell, a laugh that bubbled out of him, as easily as his tears ran ..."

My voice trails off into the silence of the chapel.

CHAPTER FORTY-SIX

As I hobble down the stairs, I can see the kids huddled in the living room, a big green garbage bag in the middle of their circle. "What's up?" At least a dozen young faces turn up to look at me.

"The Income Assistance Bill," Bara says. "It's coming up for first reading tomorrow."

"Oh." I step into the room. Gord unfolds his long frame from one of the chairs and makes me a little bow, sweeping his hand toward it. I sit down. "What's that?" I nod toward the bag. Metallic Maggie reaches in and pulls out one of those joke plastic chickens, plucked with the head and feet still on, floppy and gross. She grins. They all do.

The plan is that each of them will smuggle a chicken into the gallery over the legislature, under their coats. When the bill is presented, they'll toss their chickens down on the heads of the unsuspecting members, shouting ... well, apparently they haven't decided yet what to shout. That's the discussion I've interrupted.

"What was that chant just after Cindy's trial, when Judith was talking to the crowd?" I ask.

Bara answers. "*Rich country, hungry kids.*" They look at each other.

Judith's door is partly closed. I turn to a familiar-looking nurse sitting at the station in the hallway, alarmed. "It's all right," she says. "She's the same. Go on in."

I don't, though, because I've heard a big, deep laugh. "Do you

278

remember that Roberts kid? 'But I'm not racist.' Sure you're not. Your neighbours just happen to be the first Black family in the neighbourhood and you *accidently* burned a cross on their lawn?"

Well John, you old softy. I tiptoe away.

CHAPTER FORTY-SEVEN

The plastic chicken action creates havoc in the legislature. *"Rich country, hungry kids,"* the kids chant. Most of them are over the government benches, the better to land rubber chickens on ministers' desks. I'm on the opposition side, watching the reaction.

Cindy is in the thick of it. The attentive young people around her make her look like the queen in a hive of bees. The security guards are on the scene immediately. As they try to escort each demonstrator away, they go limp, forcing the police to carry them. The next time I look, Cindy is gone. She won't want to be arrested.

A few go to jail, Bob Cumberland and a couple of his students following the paddy wagon in Bob's old station wagon. Oh, Judith, that's where you would be, in the passenger seat, briefcase propped on your lap.

Later, when I read the newspaper's account to her, it's all about the chaos, the arrests. "Damn media. The kid's message didn't make it through. And it wasn't for lack of repetition."

Althea, sitting in the chair across from me, laughs. "Think of all the creative demos we've done. Remember when that community services committee asked for briefs about social assistance rates and we put up a clothesline around the legislature, pegged it full of panties with our feelings about assistance written on them? And the tent city on the boulevard above the old bridge when affordable housing was impossible to find?"

"Remember the day the tent city group tried to evict the MLAs from the legislature?" I chimed in.

Althea turns serious. "But where have we gotten to? Poverty's still a hard, old grind." She crosses her thick arms, looks thoughtful. "Where did that 'blessed are the poor' thing come from, anyway? Poverty is hardly a blessing, and poor people can be just as nasty as anyone else, put down anyone they can get a bit of power over. Older kids rip off younger kids; husbands control wives; neighbours take from neighbours."

"I had a friend once who thought it was about which side the church is supposed to be on."

"The poor instead of the rich? Huh. I wish."

"And it's the oldest sentence in the New Testament."

"Now, how would anyone know that?"

"There are scholars who study oral literature. It's different from stuff that was written down from the beginning. It's full of tricks to help people remember, like certain rhymes and rhythms, and a key word planted at the end of each section to remind you what the next one is. The Sermon on the Mount has more of those markers than anything else in the Gospels. So, they were passed down from person to person, maybe through the whole three hundred years it took to get the Gospels written down. If there's anything in there that the real Jesus actually said, it's most likely to be that."

"Really. Blessed are the poor. Huh. So how did you know that?"

"My friend."

"Same one who thought it's about what side the church should be on?"

"Yup."

"What are the poor supposed to get, anyway? You know, for being blessed?"

"They 'inherit the Kingdom of Heaven.'"

"So the poor will rule in Heaven? God help us."

"Or the poor will be rich in the things that really matter in Heaven?"

"Maybe we'll all be equally poor in Heaven."

"Like the vow of poverty monks and nuns take."

"Ha. We've had Ecumenical Action on Poverty supper meetings at the St. Mary's glebe house before. They eat — and drink — better than most of us."

"I guess the theory is they don't own any of it. Mother Church takes care of them."

"Wish she'd take care of me!" Althea's booming alto laugh fills the room.

Althea leaves before me. I have no energy to keep up one-sided conversation. I pick up Judith's curled hand from the sheet. It's so tight now, I can barely slide my thumb between her fingers and palm. I cup my other hand around her fingers and begin a gentle, circular rubbing, hoping they'll relax, just a little.

She's on her back, the head of the bed raised. One of the nurses explained that it helps her breathe. I study her face, so sunken now, skin hanging over bone, tendons in her jaw showing through. Someone once remarked on Judith's "aristocratic cheekbones." Now they're almost all that's left.

CHAPTER FORTY-EIGHT

"Hey, Althea."

She looks up from the papers on her desk and grimaces. "Funding proposals."

"Oh God. I remember. Hours assembling useless detail, just to have them most likely say no, even then."

"Uh-huh. Oh, Lucy, don't sit."

I arrest my motion toward the old wooden chair beside her desk.

"We're going out." As she swings her jacket around her shoulders, she slides something into the pocket, a booklet she picks up off her desk.

Althea settles herself at a table in a little neighbourhood cafe near the church, orders coffee and pastries.

"Now I'm curious," I say. "Since when don't we talk in your office?"

"Since I don't want Reverend Peter to come sniffing around while we're talking."

She chats about funding until we've had a few bites of our Danish pastries and a sip or two of coffee. Then she pulls the booklet out of her coat pocket and places it, facing me, on the table. It's an academic journal, theology. She places her finger beside one of the articles listed on the cover: "'The Beast Comes Back: Capitalism in the Book of Revelation,' by Rev. Dr. Peter Cox."

I look up into Althea's eyes. "Uh-huh," she says.

I open the journal to the page listed on the cover, begin scanning:

"What did the Beast learn from a thousand years in the sulphurous pit? How to be invisible, so 'normal' we can't see his violence against people, creatures and the earth. Especially us, members of a culture so individualistic that we have lost the concept of collective entities, structures that behave with a will. They are made up of many individuals playing the roles that animate them but are so much more than the sum of the parts."

I look up. "More or less what I said. A little more academic."

"Uh-huh."

I flip to the endnotes, peer at the tiny print. "Here are the writers I quoted and referred to." I work my way through to the end. "But not me."

"Uh-huh."

"Well, that sneaky ..."

"Ripped you off good, girl."

"For his academic career."

"Which is a bit better paid than yours just now."

"Damn."

After a silence, Althea asks, "What are you going to do?"

"I don't know. What can I do?"

"Surely something. Those are your ideas."

"Well, no. They've been written by others, and when I first heard them, it was from my friend."

"Yeah, but you put them all together. He just took it. There's a name for that."

"Plagiarism. A serious charge against an academic."

"Can you prove it's yours?"

I think, where did I write that? I see the pages I pushed under his door. "No. It was handwritten. One copy. He knew."

The cafe is filled with the soft chatter of people at other tables, the clink of cups and saucers. I quietly flip through the article, my eye catching on this word, that word, most of them mine.

Althea places her dark, strong hand over mine, stilling the restless flipping. "He won't get away with this. We'll think of something."

❧

I can hear Robin's voice out in the hall even through the hospital bustle. He is sitting beside Judith's bed, in the chair I think of as mine, a sheaf of paper in his hands. More paper sits in piles on the edge of the bed, all of them flapping with little yellow sticky notes. "Was it the same generation of Scots, the ones the lairds drove from the land during the Highland Clearances, that came here and took the land from the Mi'kmaq? Or was that later? Must check." He scratches a note in the margin of a page.

Judith, of course, just lies there, on her side at the moment, a skeleton with skin stretched over it, more tightly curled than ever. At least her hair looks a little cleaner. Someone has done whatever they do to wash the hair of someone in bed. In fact, she smells clean generally. I get so used to the slight spoiling body funk in the room, I don't notice.

"Hey, Lucy," Robin says, looking up. His face is haggard under curls gone wild from running his fingers through it. "You do think she can hear us, don't you?"

I pause. "I've been counting on it."

He goes back to studying Judith, his shoulders slumped more than usual. "There's so much I need to ask her."

I look around for the second chair, which seems to be missing. Robin jumps to his feet. "Here, sit in this one." He carefully sets the paper in his hands beside the others arrayed along the side of the bed and disappears into the hallway.

"Hello, Judith." I take her lifeless hand. "I see Robin has come to consult with you about … your book. You remember I told you he's looking at it? He says it's got the makings of a book."

Robin appears again, with a second chair. He is careful, but it clatters anyway. Plastic chairs do that.

We just watch Judith breathe for a while. It's the golden light of fall in the room now. I know if I were to look down from the window, it would be into bright, autumn leaves.

"I keep hoping she'll send me some secret message. Frown when she doesn't like something, speak to me in a dream, whatever." Robin gives me a wry smile. "Wishful thinking."

"Does it make things clearer in your mind to figure out what you'd like to ask?"

"Yeah, I guess, maybe. It does help to read it aloud, anyway."

I nod at the papers.

"Okay." He takes his time, picking up the piles of paper, one after another, stacking them neatly together. Creasing his brow, he flips through it, settles on something:

"*Word spread quickly around the village. Sheshatshit's oldest couple put on their coats and rainboots. A daughter tried to dissuade them from going. It was cold and wet, the eighty-year-olds might get sick, but time was running out for their people. Soon Mary Pasteen was shuffling beside her nearly blind husband, clutching him for support. The Pasteens and seventy other residents of Sheshatshit boldly walked past a startled security guard at the entrance to the air force base at Goose Bay. They had come to tell NATO their land is not for sale and Canada has no right to give it away.*"

I don't know how long Robin reads. Between the interesting content and Robin's smooth reading voice, the time slides quietly by. Eventually he stops. Silence again. Judith breathes.

Robin looks at me. "It's an awesome manuscript. So much information, all tied together into one package." He studies Judith again. "How does such a far-reaching mind live in such a small skull?"

If it is still living in there.

"It's like there's a huge aura or something, reaching out." There is another space of silence, then he turns to me again. "Where does it go, Lucy? I mean, when someone is unconscious or when they die, where does that big bundle of ... ideas ... mind ... whatever, go?"

"Into a book?" I say, and then feel stupid. I know his question is bigger than that.

Two nurses arrive to turn Judith. Robin gathers up his papers — Judith's papers — and leaves. They pull the curtain around her bed. I listen to their voices as they work and think back to where I left off in my story. Guatemala City. Nicolás's Bible. Tattered pages that fall open to beloved words. It is still in its box in the basement. Now that I have a bedroom, some privacy, I could keep it in the drawer of my bedside table. In the silence of the night, I would know it was there. I still can't help feeling the Bible can lead me back to him. As Robin would say, wishful thinking. And I'm not on probation any longer. But how can I leave with Judith like this?

"Bara's not home," Robin tells me. He is not in his usual habitat upstairs in the study, but in the kitchen, bending over a pot on the stove. "So it's just canned spaghetti and a salad. Hope that's okay." I glance at the table. Two places are set on either side of the salad bowl.

We don't talk much while we're eating, too much work getting the spaghetti to stay on our forks. As always, I put quite a lot of tomato sauce on the front of my sweater. Once we're into salad, it's easier. "Robin, is this book of Judith's actually close to being finished?"

He shrugs his shoulders. "I'd have to ask someone who knows more about the book biz." He looks at me, brightening. "I have a friend who edits for a progressive publisher. Would you let me take it to him?"

"I don't know." I push my plate aside. "Any chance of tea?"

"Sure." He gets up to put on the kettle.

"Robin, before you sit down, there's something I'd like to show you. Did I leave my jacket in the hall?"

He walks out there, calls back. "It's on the arm of the chesterfield."

"There's a journal in the pocket. Could you bring it here?"

He is back in a flash, journal in hand. In fact, he has already read the cover before the final bound into the kitchen. "Is this what I think it is? You got your sermon on the Beast published?"

"Not me. Look at the author."

"Oh." He is flipping through the pages to find the article. "Did he give you credit?"

He flops back into his chair. I let him scan the endnotes for himself.

"What? He credits everyone you quoted, but not you."

"Exactly."

"This is plagiarism. You should report him to the Academic Discipline Committee."

"Yeah, except I can't prove it."

"You don't have a copy?"

"No. I wrote it by hand."

"Oh." Robin is scanning the rest of the article, rubbing the dark curls hanging over his forehead with the long fingers of the other hand. "Maybe we could look back through his work and see if he's done something like this before, to someone who has a copy."

"And how long would that take? No, I've been thinking about it for a few days. I don't think there's much I can do."

"He's got to be accountable to someone for this, even without written proof. Hey." His face lights up. "I'll write an article in Streetlights. Lots of people heard you give that sermon. They'll go before the Academic Discipline Committee."

"Really?" I raise my eyebrows at him.

The light in his face dims. "Yeah, you're right. Hey." The bulb flicks back on. "We'll write a letter from some made up academic organization saying we're giving him a big award for his outstanding article and we'd like to present it on a Sunday morning at St. Marks so the whole community can appreciate his great talent."

I laugh. Not a bitter or cynical laugh, a merry one. Robin joins in. "But I'm serious, Lucy."

I laugh harder. "Robin, if I had a son, I'd like it to be you."

He sobers quickly. "Really, Lucy? Because I take that as a huge compliment."

"Oh, Robin." A minute later, the heart of his idea sinks in. "But you know, you're right. The real accountability is to the St. Marks community. He's supposed to be our pastor. No need for a fake academic organization. Maybe a few people who heard the sermon would be ready to go to his office."

"Confront him."

"Well, let him know we've seen him. Bear witness."

"The real accountability is to you, Lucy."

"Well, I think that would be enough for me. Let me talk to Althea."

CHAPTER FORTY-NINE

Judith is curled on her side, her back to me, every vertebra showing through layers of skin and sheet. She faces Robin, who looks so gangly in the hospital's plastic chair. It's not big enough for his long legs. Of course, mine isn't big enough for my fat ass. It always goes to sleep from hanging over the sides.

Robin bends over the stack of papers he holds reverently in both hands. *"In 1648, the disruptions caused by economic change and war were intensified by a disastrous harvest. People were starving. A writer of the time tells us that 'the poor did gather in troops of ten, twenty, thirty, in the roads, seized upon corn as it was carrying to market and divided it among themselves before the owners' faces, telling them they could not starve.' A Leveller pamphlet declared that 'necessity dissolves all laws and government, and hunger will break through stone walls.'"*

He has a nice reading voice, expressive. It's peaceful, being read to. I like not having to carry a constant one-way conversation, although I can feel more of my story rising in me like bread dough. I need to tell her.

Someone has cut the longer side of Judith's hair to match the short side, now grown out a couple of inches. It's actually a nice cut, framing her face as much as possible with the scrappy bits that haven't fallen out. Her ear looks sore, flattened and red.

A sentence catches my attention. "They called themselves the Diggers."

"Robin, my mind wandered. I missed the last bit. Can you read it again?"

He puts his finger on the paper to mark the spot and looks up at me briefly. "Sure." He slides the finger up a couple of lines.

"Okay. *'Against this backdrop, on Sunday, April 1, 1649, a band of about twenty poor labourers began farming common land on St. George's Hill, at the edge of Windsor Great Forest. They called themselves the Diggers.'* She's put a poem in here. Actually, she says it's a song. I'd love to know the tune.

> *"In 1649, to St. George's Hill,*
> *A ragged band they called the Diggers came to show the people's will.*
> *They defied the landlords; they defied the laws.*
> *They were the dispossessed reclaiming what was theirs.*
>
> *We come in peace, they said, to dig and sow.*
> *We come to work the lands in common and to make the waste ground grow.*
> *This earth divided, we will make whole,*
> *So it will be a common treasury for all.*
>
> *The sin of property we do disdain.*
> *No man has any right to buy and sell the earth for private gain.*
> *By theft and murder, they took the land.*
> *Now everywhere the walls spring up at their command."*

By the time Robin reaches the fate of the Diggers, I have tears in my eyes, for the Diggers and because this is just so Judith. And for Nicolás, and Rosa, Ramón, Mía, Emilia ...

> *"From the men of property, the orders came.*
> *They sent the hired men and troopers to wipe out the Diggers' claim.*
> *Tear down their cottages, destroy their corn.*
> *They were dispersed, but still the vision lingers on."*

Robin looks up to see if I've recognized the song. I shake my head. "Doesn't Judith credit someone who's recorded it?"

"She does. It's been recorded at least five times, but none of them seem to be still available."

"Nothing in Judith's study?"

"Not obvious, if it is. Of course, there's stuff there I haven't gone through. I've just looked at what was clearly connected with this research."

"It might be there somewhere. Or the library, did you try there?"

"I did. Never heard of any of these recordings. Obscure, lefty stuff."

We grin at each other.

"Bet she knows." He looks down at Judith, his face sad.

"Well, keep looking," I tell him.

I have the house to myself. I open the door to the basement stairs, make my way slowly down the steps, find one of the dangling strings and click on a light.

The basement is transformed. It's still packed with household goods, but everything is neatly piled, floor to ceiling, along the back wall. The space opened up by this rearrangement is divided into three alcoves, separated by walls of boxes. Each has a mattress, the familiar one from the crib and two I haven't seen before, a single and a double. All have sheets and blankets in various degrees of rumpled. In the middle of the double bed is a round nest curved around a furry bump. As I approach, it lifts a scarred and earless head. "You old rascal." At the sound of my voice, Raggedy leaps to his feet and disappears among the furniture and boxes.

The reading chair still sits where it was, in front of the furnace, but back by the drain and tap is a curtained-off cubicle with a chemical toilet. Quite the nest. How dare they? Little sneaks. It dawns on me that they've been coming and going through the kitchen door to the basement. I didn't give it a thought. And why haven't I heard them?

Milk crates serve as bedside tables, a different old lamp on each. One of a pair on either side of the double mattress holds a couple of sweaters I recognize as Bara's, neatly folded and stacked. There is a battered paperback book on the bedside table. I walk over and pick it up. Even with part of the cover torn off I see it features a woman with very few clothes on, hip thrust out, pouting in that way that's supposed to be seductive but just looks arrogant and spoiled. Why do girls read this crap? Then I notice a shadowy fig- ure behind the nearly naked woman in the foreground, watching her as if she's something to eat. Another woman. Oh my. Is that what young lesbians like? Something intended to turn on men?

I flip it open to a random page.

"Kim's arms were suddenly round her — she bent her head and kissed Audrey's mouth — a kiss like the closing of a sea anemone. It gave and took and sealed. Audrey sat there, still and calm, looking at Kim with half-tranced eyes, dimly aware of all the cruelty that she was bringing her, as some small furry animal is aware of the hand that is going to rip open its heart while it gazes, fascinated, with soft, unseeing eyes."

A kiss like a sea anemone? Half-tranced eyes? I toss it back.

The crate on the other side also contains clothing. I pull out a dress. Some sort of clingy knit material, nice sky blue, so skinny, it might just fit one of my thighs. Beneath that there's a pair of black tights, faded jeans.

My boxes form the wall between this alcove and the next. It doesn't look like anything's been poked into. The box I dropped months ago, with the split corner, sits on the floor at one end hold- ing just one other box, "Lucy — Books, Creamed Corn." Relieved that it isn't too high to reach or too buried to dig out, I retrieve Nicolás's Bible.

As I climb the stairs, I catch my foot on a step and go down hard, twisting my ankle. Pain spikes through it. Damn. I use the bannister to pull myself into a sitting position and slide down, step by step, until I'm sitting on the bottom one. I pull my skirt aside to look. My foot is in the right position, but it's swelling already. I gingerly put some weight on it. Spears of pain. How am I going to get back upstairs?

Above me the front door opens, accompanied shortly by cheerful whistling. "Robin!" I shout. The whistling stops. "Robin!"

Light pours down the steps as he opens the kitchen door. "Lucy, what happened?" He comes down the steps and squats a couple of steps above me.

"Did you know Bara and company are sleeping in the basement?"

"Yes. Didn't you?"

"No. How long has it been going on?"

"Since the beginning."

"Beginning?"

"When you started to live here."

"Coming and going through the basement door."

"There were a couple of keys in the front hall."

"And they just helped themselves?"

"Lucy, that's not your most serious problem at the moment."

"But they've moved everything around. This is Judith's house …"

"They'll put everything back the way it was."

I twist around so I can look at him.

He looks embarrassed. "Yeah. That story is getting a little thin, isn't it?"

It takes some time for Robin to tug and lift me up the stairs, since I can't put weight on the one foot and one arm is holding Nicolás's

Bible. Once in the kitchen, he can put his arm around my waist and I can put one over his shoulder. With him taking quite a bit of my weight, I hop to the living room chesterfield and flop down into its saggy cushions. He kneels in front of me, wanting to take my sock and shoe off. I pull my foot back against the upholstery.

"Will you let Bara look at it?"

"Who knows what Godforsaken hour she'll come back."

"They're already back. Listen."

Young female voices drift up through the open door to the basement. Robin is gone before I can stop him, shouting for Bara.

A few minutes later, she arrives, flushed. "Lucy, have you been snooping in our things?"

"I was looking for something of mine."

"And that requires pulling our clothes out, reading our books? Give you a little thrill?"

Robin breaks in. "Bara, you can deal with that later. She's hurt."

I hold out my foot, the ankle now about twice it's normal size.

She transforms instantly. "Oh, Lucy, what have you done? Is it broken?" On her knees in front of me, she eases off my shoe and sock, carefully feeling the bones under the swollen flesh, apologizing when I flinch. She asks me to wiggle my toes. "I don't think it's broken. Sprained, though. Robin, get all the ice in the freezer and put it in a plastic bag. Get a towel, too."

She wants to know if I can take a Tylenol with my other meds. My meds. I can't remember how long it's been since I've taken them.

Bara sits beside me while ice and a Tylenol ease some of the pain. "So, you didn't know we were downstairs? We haven't been trying to be quiet or anything."

"You could have discussed it with me."

"I thought you knew."

"And how long have you had that old cat in the house?"

"Raggedy? The vet said he hasn't got any teeth left. He was starving."

"You took him to the vet?"

She looks at me, exasperated. "How is this, like, any different from when you and I were down there, and Judith didn't know?"

"It isn't different. That's the point. This is Judith's house. We're changing it so much. We won't remember how it was."

She pauses, looks like she's going to say something.

I point at the bag of ice. "I can't feel anything now."

"You're right. That's long enough."

Robin helps me up the stairs. Bara turns down my bedcovers and finds my nightgown for me. After they've left, though, I don't bother with it, just crawl in under the covers and curl myself around Nicolás's Bible.

It's a terrible night. My ankle aches and I can't fall over the edge into sleep but rove back and forth, barely into dreaming, then back again to stare at the dark patch of sky in my window. It's been a long time since I've had a real nightmare, but each time I slip into the edge of a dream, I hear desperate weeping. I fumble through the darkness, trying to find whoever it is, offer comfort, but I stumble and fall onto my hands and knees. When I shift backward to get up, my hands are covered in blood. I know it is loved ones' blood. My heart is breaking.

CHAPTER FIFTY

The window is barely turning grey. I want to see Judith. I roll over, grunting as my ankle stabs me. I've also rolled over onto Nicolás's Bible. I pull it out from under the covers and put it away in the drawer of the bedside table.

Tap, tap on the door, "Lucy, how are you?" In pops Bara's head. "Do you want breakfast? I can bring it up here."

"No, thanks."

She pauses but then blessedly disappears. The door clicks shut behind her.

Tap, tap on my door again. I grope my way out of a sound sleep. Unlike polite Bara, Robin comes right in. "Lucy, look what I found." He holds up a cassette tape. "'The Diggers' Song,' recorded by a Vancouver group called Aya. The actual title is 'The World Turned Upside Down.'" He sets a small, black cassette player on the bedside table and pops the tape into it.

I struggle into a sitting position. Robin pulls my pillow up, so I can lean on the head of the bed. He presses the button and sits down on the edge of the mattress as three, clear, female voices rise into the room: *"In 1649, to St. George's Hill, a ragged band they called the Diggers came to show the people's will ..."*

Bara comes in, listens. "Hey, wow, what's that?"

Robin explains while I work myself to the edge of the bed and turn sideways. I try to rise to my feet but flop back in sudden pain.

"Lucy, be careful," Bara says. "Robin, help her up."

He does, and I even accept his support to reach the bathroom door. When I come back out, Bara offers to bring up a supper tray for me, but I've always hated the idea of eating in bed. "I'd rather go downstairs, but I'll need help."

Robin has disappeared back into the study. Bara calls him to help me down the stairs.

Bara insists I sit on the chesterfield in the living room after supper. She uses a towel to wrap another plastic bag filled with ice around my ankle. "That's cold." I sound whiny.

"That's the point."

"How long do I have to do this?"

"Until your ankle stops hurting."

I look around me. "This room is a mess."

"I'll get to it on Saturday."

"The dining room's worse." Through the arches on either side of the hallway, I can see the sewing machines in their nests of red and black fabric on the table. More red and black pieces hang from the backs of chairs and gather in little piles on the floor. Whole bolts lean here and there. Not to mention scissors, pins, tape measures, spools of thread. A plastic package lies open on the floor, metal grommets scattered on the hardwood.

"Hey," says a male voice from the doorway.

"Hey Gord," says Bara.

"Robin here?"

"He's gone down to the hospital," Bara tells him.

"That's where I'd like to be." I sit up, lean my weight on the arm of the chesterfield.

"You're ankle's too swollen. You have to rest it."

"But Judith — "

"She's got Robin reading to her."

"But — "

She puts her hand on my arm. "Lucy, Robin's taking care of her."

Bara turns to look at the doorway where Gord was standing, and my eyes follow hers. He's gone.

"Bara, did Robin leave the cassette player and that tape upstairs?"

"Probably. Do you want me to look?"

She comes back down with it, plugs it in and we listen to the song again. "Is that, like, where capitalism started?"

"One of many times and places. An important one, though, because it transformed England and paved the way for the industrial revolution, which spread colonialism and capitalism around the world."

"The stuff Robin's working on, up in Judith's study, is it going to be a book?"

"I don't know."

"I hope so. I want to read it."

❦

The pain has faded by the time Bara takes the ice off my ankle, although when I try to stand, it returns with a stab that sends me back into my seat. "This'll help." She has a roll of elastic bandage. She kneels in front of me and I have a sudden memory of Althea washing my battered, frozen feet when I was living outside.

"Not too tight?" Bara says.

I wiggle my toes.

"And wait there. I just remembered something."

She disappears into the basement. A little while later she emerges, grinning and holding a wooden cane, plain but well made, nicely curved handle. She helps me up and I experiment with it, hobbling up and down the hall. I discover that, if you get your timing right, it really can take a lot of the weight.

❦

"Hello, Robin." I'm standing at the door of Judith's study, a triumph of elastic bandage and cane, not to mention Bara's tending.

"Hello, Lucy." He doesn't even turn around. He's like a groundhog, burrowing through Judith's computer.

The piles on the floor are neater now, each with a file card label. "Have you been tidying up?"

"A little. Can't see what's here if I don't."

"Now, don't you be snooping into her private stuff."

He turns to look at me finally. "Hard to help when she stores her photographs between the books. I'm making a pile. There." He points.

I hobble over to find a small collection of old snapshots. Most of them are of Judith at various ages, from one labelled "eight months" to a teenaged Judith awkwardly hunched over tiny breasts barely visible in one of those ugly bathing suits we used to wear. There are square bangs and home perms, the grin with no front teeth, the family standing on the front steps, stiff and unhappy in their Sunday best. These are so much like my own childhood photos, left behind in my parents' house in Amherst. In every one of these images, Judith looks straight into the camera with those clear, intelligent but worried brown eyes.

Robin is standing beside me now. From under the pile of snapshots, he pulls a cardboard folder stamped with a photographer's name and address. Inside it has the gold-edged square mat that should hold a portrait, but instead it contains a small collection of yellowed clippings. He unfolds the top one, presses it flat so I can see. At the top is a photo of a striking, young Black man in lawyers' gown and tabs, a formal portrait. "Have you heard of Edmund Smith, Lucy? One of the first Black lawyers in Nova Scotia? Judith's father hired him."

"And then fired him."

"That's what these are about."

The clippings come from both Halifax papers of the time. They all have the same photo. Two, dated November 1961, announce that Mr. Edmund Smith is joining Maidstone, Parker and Wilson. The other two, dated July 1962, note that Mr. Edmund Smith has been dismissed from Maidstone, Parker and Wilson, accused of incompetence and unethical behaviour.

I refold them, tuck them back into the folder and replace it under the pile of photos. "We shouldn't be snooping into Judith's private things."

"When photos fall out, I put them in the pile. Other than that, I'm just assembling the book."

"So is it a book, then?"

"I think so."

"How much of it is there?"

"The more I search, the more I find. Every time I think I've got a handle on it, I find another whole piece she was working on. It's like a labyrinth."

"That's Judith's mind you're exploring."

"A labyrinthine mind, then?" That big grin of his.

"It … is."

His grin fades. "It does need some organizing. Lucy, my friend, the editor. …"

"But it's Judith's, Robin."

He sighs, turns back to the text on the screen.

CHAPTER FIFTY-ONE

It is such a relief to be back at Judith's bedside. My ankle is healing well, although the trip down here brought back the ache. I like the cane. Should have found one long ago to help with my achy knees. Robin has brought in the cassette player and placed it on the bedside table.

Judith is lying on her side. Her arm is on top of the sheet, the joints in her shoulder, elbow and wrist obvious, like a famine victim. I pick up her curled claw of a hand and try to pull it toward me. She resists, or her arm does.

I hear a nurse passing in the hallway. "Excuse me."

She hears me and comes in. She's one of the middle-aged ones, with more time for the likes of me. "Yes, the tendons get tighter all the time," she tells me. "Early on we try to work them, but by now …"

"Can I do anything about it?"

"Pull gently." I do. "Good. And when you meet resistance, pull just a wee bit more." I do. "Watch her face. She might grimace if it hurts." Nothing crosses Judith's wasted features.

"If I pull any more, I'll be using force."

"Don't do that. Just ease it as far as you can, maybe massage her arm. Like this." She puts her hands around Judith's bony forearm and skillfully rubs up and down with her thumbs, working her way to the elbow and back again to the wrist. "Or work her fingers a bit, just gently. Over time, it helps."

When I thank her, she says, "Judith has good friends," and smiles. That's because Judith was a good friend, I think. I mean, *is*.

As the soft soles of the nurse's shoes disappear, I try her

up-and-down rubbing technique on Judith's arm. I pause long enough to press the "play" button on the cassette player. The voices of Aya softly give us "The World Turned Upside Down."

"By theft and murder, they took the land ..."

A wet spot appears on the sheet beside Judith's swollen elbow. Tears are trickling down my face. I take a tissue from the bedside table, blow my nose and then click the machine into silence.

"He was a priest, Judith, and I was ... well, I was no longer a fundamentalist missionary, but I had some pretty deep beliefs about the sinfulness of sex before marriage. But there we were, teaching, talking, walking for days in the hills. We resisted for months, but we were melting. And the danger, the terrible thing closing in on the villages, just made us ... desperate. For life. For love. For touch.

"One evening Nicolás went for a long walk into the woods on the hillside above our campsite. I was worried. We hid our campsites well, and it was getting dark. It would be easy to get lost. Later, he said he was wrestling with an angel. When he came back, the tears were rolling down his cheeks. He put his arms around me and buried his face in my hair. When his tears stopped, the passion just seemed to rise up through him, as it did through me. The desperate love and fear we felt for each other just came pouring out. Neither of us had ever made love before, but it didn't matter. Pure passion drove us forward.

"It wasn't the last time he took a long, painful walk before making love, or sometimes after. It was his vows he was wrestling with."

My hands are tiring. I set down her arm, extended a little. It stays where I put it, looking naked and cold. I pull up the sheet and blanket to cover it.

"I've never loved anyone else, before or since, like I loved Nicolás. Have you ... ? My god, Judith. I don't even know if you've ever been in love."

I reach out to stroke the wispy hair covering the scar. It comes away with my hand.

༄

I can hear music from the sidewalk. As I come through the front door, I am assaulted by young talk and laughter. The sewing machines are sitting on the floor along the dining room wall, fabric folded and piled beside them. All of Judith's bowls are on the dining table, from both the kitchen and the china cabinet, plus some paper ones, all of Judith's cutlery, good silver mingled with plastic spoons, a mountain of paper napkins and, in the centre, Judith's wooden salad bowl filled with rolls. Across the hall in the living room, there are kids everywhere, every available seat, cross-legged on the floor, perched on the arms of the couch.

A visitor from a past generation would think this was a movie about another planet, the odd things they wear. Some outfits are too large, pant crotches and sweater hems touching knees, hands hidden in ragged sleeves. Others are too small, tights like a second skin, pant legs revealing calves, tops revealing bellies. And then there are the tattoos and bits of metal stuck everywhere. How do you blow your nose with a big stud of some sort sticking out of it? Eat with a ring in your lip? There's a lad in Judith's stuffed armchair doing just that.

Then I notice his sleeve, tight black stretchy stuff decorated with red blobs. Paint. Wet. As I watch he begins to lower his forearm toward the arm of the chair. Speaking of the movies, the scene flips into slow motion. "Stop!"

All noise halts, all faces turn toward me. The young man's arm comes down. Damn. I point at it with the cane. "Get your arm off that chair." He lifts it, looks, sees the red spots matching those on his sleeve.

"Get out of here." I say it first to the young man in the chair, then begin to swivel around, addressing all of them. "Get out." I wave the cane, symbolically sweeping them all out the front door.

There is a shift of bodies in the kitchen and Bara emerges,

surprise on her face. "Lucy? Put that down. You're going to hurt someone."

"Look." Using the cane, I point at the paint on the arm of the chair, then begin to see more, on the furniture, rug, even the walls. "There. And there. And there."

They follow with their eyes, dead silent except for the lad who just put red spots on the arm of the chair. In a small voice, he says, "Sorry."

They're gone, filing out quickly and quietly, except for Bara furiously attacking a sink full of dishes. She turns and, ignoring the big gobs of soap suds flying from her hands, crosses her arms in front of her. "Geez, Lucy. We'll clean up. Lots of people would have stayed and helped."

"And how much good would it do? You can't get paint out of upholstery."

"Sure you can."

"And then there's the layer of dirt under that. Have you seen how grubby that carpet is, where you've all been walking through?"

"I'll rent a carpet steamer."

I can see the bridge from the corner of Devonshire and Barrington, lights arching off into the dusk, reflected in the inky black water below. The Dartmouth end is hidden by the bulk of the shipyard. I crave my hiding place in the woods by the dockyard fence, but my new cane-supported gait won't take me any farther. The breeze off the harbour tells me my face is wet. I fish in my pocket for a tissue. Nothing, so I blow my nose on the sleeve of my sweater, scrub at my eyes with the other sleeve. Sniffing, I allow my eyes to follow the curve of the bridge. How long ago was it I thought about jumping? I'm upset, but I can't imagine doing that now.

I study the house from the sidewalk, lit up in the dusk, a whirring machine noise coming from the open windows, too loud to be the vacuum cleaner. I'd hoped to slip in and up to my room without being seen, but now ... Bara's slight form passes slowly in front of the living room window, bent over something.

It's a carpet steamer, adorned with a big sticker from Superstore. As soon as she sees me, she shuts it off, scans her work. "I think it'll look better when it's dry."

I use my cane to point at the china cabinet in the dining room. "And can we put the dishes back on the right shelves?"

She studies me, that little frown appearing between her brows. "Don't you, like, get it?"

"Get what?"

"Robin has told me what Judith is like now. She isn't coming back."

The tears that had stopped as I hobbled my way back start up again.

"Oh, Lucy, I'm sorry." She clicks the handle of the steamer upright, steps closer and puts her arms around me. There's almost nothing there, she's so skinny under her baggy T-shirt. Despite the chemical smell of the carpet cleaner, she smells like food.

CHAPTER FIFTY-TWO

Althea and I are in Bob Cumberland's office. Bob sits behind his chaotic desk, but this time there doesn't seem to be a particular file involved. "Did I tell you that the medical staff are looking for a nursing home for Judith?"

I look at Althea, who looks back, her face as blank as mine must be. "No, Bob," she tells him.

"It didn't seem imminent at the time."

"When was this?"

"A while ago. A few weeks."

"No Bob, you didn't tell us."

"I guess I let it slip my mind. Anyway, they're thinking this is going to take a long time, even if she ..." He pushes his dark-framed glasses up his nose. Behind them, there are dark circles under his eyes. "Hospital beds are expensive. A nursing home can give her the same care, or better, because there's things going on, music, volunteers to read to the patients, or whatever they call them."

"Uh-huh," Althea interjects, probably to encourage him, because he's floundering a bit.

"Sounds good," I add.

"The problem is ..."

We wait.

" ... it's the first bed that becomes available, no matter where it is."

Pictures of Judith's room flash into my mind, the cloud of conversation we've been creating around her, Althea and I chatting with each other, John's confession, Bob's accounts of cases and students, Robin reading aloud her own words.

"They just let me know that a bed will be coming up soon … in Bridgewater."

"But Bob, how will we get there to see her? I can't take a couple of hours out of my day to drive both ways, at least not very often. Lucy does most of the supporting, and she has no car."

"I know. I'm sorry. We'll see that you get there, Lucy." He thinks for a minute. "How would you feel about driving Judith's car?"

"I've never had a car, so I let my driver's licence expire."

"I wonder if you need to pass the test again to get it reinstated?"

"I don't know." I'm feeling so heavy I can barely speak, let alone think about finding out how to renew my driver's licence.

"Don't worry. We'll get you there somehow."

"Can't we object?" Althea says. "Ask for her to be in Halifax?"

"The system doesn't work that way. I guess we can apply to have her moved back here when a bed becomes available, but it all depends on whose case is most urgent."

"She's not considered urgent, huh?" Althea says.

"No." Bob looks helpless, and I guess he is."How soon?" I ask.

"I don't know," he says. "Soon."

"Does someone there have to die first?" Althea says.

Bob shifts uncomfortably behind his desk.

Althea looks over at me. I must look bereft, if I look the way I feel. "We'll just have to pray for long life," she says. "For everyone in that place in Bridgewater."

On my way to the hospital I spot Bara and Cat on the opposite sidewalk, going south. I slide in behind the thick trunk of a tree and watch. They laugh and talk, too much into each other to notice me.

When they are well past, I reverse my direction, though I stay on my side of the street. Blonde head, dark head, slender young backs, so animated. Cat sways her hips and waves her hand in the air, dismissive. A caricature. Bara laughs. They pause and talk facing one another, then turn and walk on. Cat's long, black braid bounces from side to side.

I keep pace, well behind. A man jostles me, and I mutter an apology. I keep them in sight, in sight, in sight, and then, oh no, they turn a corner. I hold my urge to step into the street long enough to look both ways. A car, coming south; two north. Go. Go. Get out of my way.

Finally, a space. I cross, hurry as fast as my cane gait allows to the corner where they disappeared. More slowly, I tap my way down the street a few blocks, pausing to glance right and left down each street that cuts across. No sign of them. Gone. I can taste my disappointment.

Judith is on her back. I find myself watching her rice-paper eyelids. In the beginning, you could see her eyes moving underneath. I can't remember when it stopped.

Althea sits on the other side of the bed. She's been explaining, in her deep, comforting voice, about the move to the nursing home. "It won't happen right away, but when it does, we'll still come to visit, often," she promises, with no grounds to base it on. I feel sick.

Althea looks across at me, and her tone lightens. "Hey, Judith, we've got something to tell you about. Our friend, Reverend Peter, has done a number on our Lucy here."

She tells Judith the story, her eyes on me. "You come up with any ideas, Lucy?"

"I have, in fact." I tell her about my conversation with Robin. The part about the fake academic organization prompts her rumbling laugh. The idea of getting together a group to have a serious talk with Reverend Peter, she likes.

Next thing I know, she's digging around in her huge purse,

pulling out a pen and an envelope. "Who was there that Sunday, Lucy?" We start listing names. She writes them on the back of the envelope, not everyone, but the ones we think might be up for a visit. We add people, cross others off, until we have a list we're happy with. There is a fresh box of tissue on Judith's bedside table. She pulls the cardboard insert out of the opening on top. Turning it over, she copies half of the names, mine to contact. She'll talk to the rest. We're a lot lighter by the time we leave, almost giddy. I hope Judith's been listening.

I've just heaved myself up the stairs on my way to bed. Tired, tired, tired. The light is on, as always, in Judith's study. "G'night Robin." It comes out automatically. No return goodnight. I pause and look in. Robin sits slumped in the chair staring at a massive block of paper set in front of the computer. "Robin?"

He starts, turns, grins his Robin grin. "Hey, Lucy. Look at this." He waves a hand theatrically in the direction of the paper. "The whole thing. I sorted out the order and printed everything off."

"Your friend, the editor. Is it ready to take to him? See if there's a book in it?"

"But you said — "

"I know, but I've thought more about it."

"Really? Can I take it to him?" He radiates the excitement of a kid.

I nod.

"Thanks, Lucy."

"What's that?" My eye has fallen on what looks like an old sepia print lying on the desk beside the manuscript. He reaches for it, holds it up. People in rags, men, women and children, huddled around a small fire on the side of a road.

"It's a detail of a sixteenth-century print," Robin explains, "Homeless families looking for food and work, living on the only common ground left, the verges of the roads. Judith spotted them, tucked away in a corner of an old reproduction, a drawing of a church. She thinks they're meant to glorify the church for helping the poor." He lays it carefully on top of the manuscript. "I figure, if this ever gets to be a book, the print might make a good cover."

He rests his long hand on top of the block of paper and his face drops again. "And what will I do with my time now?"

"I'm sure there'll be lots for you to do between now and its appearance in the bookstores, since you're the one that's read all this." I wave my hand at the stacks of paper on the floor. "So before you take this massive chunk of paper to your friend, are you going to show it to Judith?"

"Of course. Come with me?"

"Sure. So, there's nothing more to learn about resistance to land privatization?"

Robin brightens. "Of course there is. I've even been thinking about going back to school, although I hate that it'd be a victory for my dad."

"So it's all about being stubborn, then? Oh dear. Here I am siding with your parents again, you crazy, misguided kid."

He laughs again.

CHAPTER FIFTY-THREE

Bara is eating breakfast at the kitchen table. I am making toast, my back to her, trying to sound nonchalant. "You never told me what 'Cat' is short for."

I hear her push aside her empty cereal bowl. "Lucy, Cat thinks you were following us."

I freeze, mortified by a sudden image of myself through the eyes of the young and beautiful Cat: old, dishevelled, hobbling around spying on them.

"Lucy, it creeps Cat out, the way you stare at her. Maybe you're not quite so comfortable with dykes as you make out you are. Or maybe you just don't want me to have a lover."

I turn to face her. "Dykes? Where'd you get that word? And no, of course I'm glad you have a lover."

"Then why the staring? Why did you go through our things? Why were you following us? It's a problem, because I've decided she's a keeper."

"What does that mean?"

"It means we're going to start looking for someplace else to live."

"Last time you looked, you couldn't find anything you could afford."

"We'll figure it out." She rises and crosses the kitchen, placing her cereal bowl in the sink. She disappears through the basement door without another glance at me.

Behind me the toast pops.

"Judith, it's Lucy and Robin," Judith looks even more like a mummy, parchment stretched over bone. "Look, it's your book. Robin printed everything off." The stack of paper is packed in a cardboard box. Robin sets it on the bedcover. Judith's hand is curled into a stiff, bony fist, but I lift it gently and place it awkwardly on the package.

"I'm taking it to my friend." Robin says. "He's an editor. He's going to look at it, see what it would need to be published as a book."

"And Robin found a print in your study that might work for a cover," I tell her.

"You know, Judith? The dispossessed people you spotted in the corner of that old print of the church?" Robin adds.

We keep up a three-way conversation for two as long as we can. When it's time to go, I lift the husk of her hand off of the manuscript, set it down on the cool cotton of the bed. Robin picks up the package. He holds it reverently in front of his chest as we leave.

"At last, the manuscript you've been telling me about." Robin's friend is scholarly looking with his round glasses and slightly bent shoulders, clearly excited about the box Robin places into his hands. More excited than a few days of knowing about it would warrant, but I don't even cast Robin a sideways glance. It doesn't matter now. I've caught his excitement about the thought of Judith's work published as a book. To celebrate, Robin takes me out to lunch at Susan's Place, inside that is, at a table.

When we arrive home, Bara meets us at the door. "I've been trying to find you. Bob Cumberland called. He's at the hospital. Judith's struggling to breathe."

Robin and I go together. Althea is already there. Bob stands to greet us, hair as rumpled as his suit, face pale. He goes to find more chairs.

Judith is propped up on more of an angle than usual, and her face, ghostly pale for so long, is flushed. She is puffing, grasping for air through her mouth, her terribly deteriorated teeth exposed. And then she stops.

I look at Althea in alarm. "Wait," she says. "She's been doing this." And as the last word comes out of her mouth, Judith gasps, setting off another flurry of ragged breaths.

Bob returns with chairs. We form a tense circle, our eyes pinned to Judith's struggle.

"What does the doctor say?" I ask Bob.

"Pneumonia." He says it in an odd, breathless voice. I realize Judith has paused again and Bob is holding his breath with her.

"Is it something they, you know, can do something about?" Robin asks.

Bob glances at him, then to me, and finally Althea. "It's okay, Bob," Althea says. "Tell him about the non-resuscitation order."

"Oh," says Robin.

I glance at him. He understands.

"They've given her something for pain," Bob adds.

And now I realize I am holding my breath too, because Judith has stopped again. When the air rasps back into her throat, mine is so dry it also feels like a rasp.

I see a shine in Althea's eyes at one point, respond with a welling in my own. But then I dry up, waiting, listening, tense, finally sore. We are a circle of statues.

Bob is the first to leave, with a promise to return. Robin goes next. Althea holds Judith's hand on one side, me on the other. "Lord," she prays, "please release our dear sister from her travail." She pauses, Judith does as well. When Judith takes up breath again,

Althea takes up her prayer. "Fold her to your breast. Comfort her." Another pause, another gasp. Althea is swaying slightly, face raised and eyes closed. "Grant her the rest she so richly deserves. Reward her for fights well-fought."

I lean over and whisper in Judith's ear. "Dear Judith. It's time to go. We'll be okay." I pause, then add, "I love you."

As darkness gathers outside the window, I start awake. My chin has hit my chest. And still there is the fight for breath, given up, engaged again. Bob arrives, sets down his briefcase just inside the door. "Still the same?" he asks.

Althea and I nod in unison.

"I talked to the nurse outside," he says. "She's been through this before. It can go on for a long time. I think you should both go and rest. I'll call you if anything changes."

Althea and I consult with a glance. She looks terrible. We nod in unison again.

We take the bus, holding each other up with our well-padded shoulders propped together, saying nothing. I lie down on the chesterfield in my clothes, remembering all those nights on the street and in the basement of this house when I had no other choice. This time, it's because I might have to get back to the hospital quickly.

It seems only moments later the phone rings. Bob.

"Shall I come?"

He can't speak, just a squeaking sound.

"It's over, isn't it?"

I make my way to the kitchen, check the cupboard under the sink.

The bottles are still there. I take a juice glass out of the drainer, fill it with stale wine, sit down at the table. The clock says three thirty. Three thirty in the morning of the day Judith died. Who knows, she may have left us weeks or months ago, but this is the date we will remember for the rest of our lives.

I try to pray. How does Althea come up with all those formal phrases, pouring out of her so naturally? All I can come up with is *"Bienaventurados los que tienen hambre y sed de justicia."* Blessed are those who hunger and thirst for justice. *"Porque ellos serán hartos."* For they shall be filled.

CHAPTER FIFTY-FOUR

"I'm sorry, Lucy," Bob says, shedding jacket and briefcase in a habitual motion as he comes through his office door. I don't know if he means because he's late or because Judith's gone. He digs through the filing cabinet that stands beside his desk, the kind lawyers seem to like, with the files sideways. He finds what he wants, sits down at his desk. "Judith had a pre-paid arrangement with a funeral home to cremate her remains." He frowns at the papers in his hand. "And some interesting instructions concerning her ashes." He unfolds some kind of form, adjusts his reading glasses. "She wants her friends to scatter them from the Angus L. MacDonald bridge on a windy day, quote 'with a prayer for the end of private property and poverty. No God.' Do you know what that means? I was thinking of asking Reverend Peter to do something at the church but — "

"No." I say it so strongly that Bob gives me a curious look.

"All right, let's think about it. There's no hurry."

"Bob? Is her will there? What happens to the house?"

He turns over some pages in the file, all with blue, cardboard corners stapled in place. "It's here somewhere." He frowns. "My memory is she left the house to the Shelter Society, along with the funds to maintain it."

"I was going to ask my gospel choir to put together something rousing for her at the church." Althea screws up her face. "But it'll be on the bridge? And what on earth's a prayer without God?"

"Oh come on," says Patty. "People have memorials and

weddings, all kinds of ceremonies where they talk about what's sacred to them without naming it God." Her eyes are red around the edges. I glance over at Althea, eyebrows raised, but she doesn't see me. She doesn't look convinced by Patty's comment, either.

We sit in the old wooden chairs scattered around her office, the sun pouring in through the thriving plants on her window sill. Besides Althea and Patty, there's Bob, Robin, me and, of all people, John. He's retired, he announced when I greeted him. The way he fills his chair and flows over the edges, it's clear he's given up even the flimsy line he was holding against his weight. He looks happy, though. I wonder if he can still write me that letter, now that I'm free. Free of my probation, and now free … the thought comes with an intense mixture of sadness and relief.

Althea lays her hand on a dark-coloured cardboard box sitting on her desk. "She was a good woman." With a little jolt I realize what the box is. So small. There was almost nothing left of her at the end, but this wouldn't hold a pair of shoes. I miss her terribly. I hold my breath, feeling my eyes begin to swim. She'll never unlock the front door again, kick off her shoes and turn on CBC. And my story, what will I do with the rest of it? Having started, I can feel it bubbling up, wanting out.

"So what do people picture happening, with this prayer thing, I mean?" Bob asks us.

"A prayer without God," Althea snorts.

Robin's face brightens. "Judith did research on the Quakers. Why don't we do it the way they do, sit silently together until someone feels inspired to speak?"

"Really?" Althea looks skeptical.

"Up on the bridge?" says Patty.

"She's asking for a windy day," John joins in for the first time. "And it's November. Could be cool up there. And noisy."

Robin persists. "A modified Quaker thing, then. Like, we each share a memory of Judith, everyone who wants to."

We continue to talk, but eventually we circle back to Robin's idea. Out come the daybooks. Can't say I miss having one. Only one other person doesn't: John. Even Robin slides one of those free calendar booklets from Hallmark out of his back pocket. It has to be a windy day, though, so just like people set rain dates, we name a couple of "no wind dates."

"Shall I keep the ashes here at the church in the meantime?" Althea asks.

"No." I don't realize I've spoken until I hear my own voice. "I think …" I don't want to say, "take her home"; I'll cry. " … At the house," is what I manage to get out.

"That's a good idea." Althea nods. So does everyone else.

Robin volunteers to take them.

Afterward I ask Althea about Patty's red eyes and Cindy's absence. She shakes her head. "Not good."

"Breaking up?"

"Afraid so."

"Did Cindy get her kids back?"

"Yeah, but the break-up makes the whole situation pretty unstable again."

On the way out, I almost run into Reverend Peter at the bottom of the stairs. "Ah, Lucy," he says, in that booming voice of his. "I'm so sorry about Judith. Do you know her family? Will they be wanting a funeral here?"

I tell him briefly about the bridge and get out of there, thinking: And a group of us will be coming to see you. Soon.

I've been holding my breath over Bara's decision to leave, but when I get home she looks pretty settled at the centre of household life, as always. The kids are meeting, living room full, a few standing in the hallway. They make way for me, a smile or two. I sit on the second-to-bottom step to listen. I can see Judith's ashes on the old wooden mantle, dead centre. She'd like that.

They are talking about the flag campaign. What better memorial to Judith, they decide, than a Chicken Campaign flag on every flagpole in town the night before we scatter her ashes? She'd like that too.

The next morning the girls start sewing. Without the manuscript to work on, Robin is underfoot. "Get out of here," Bara tells him. "Get your stencils and paint out again, call Gord. We could use some Chicken Campaign graffiti that night too."

He's taken her seriously, stops bugging them. I feel a little underfoot myself. I guess I was spending more hours at the hospital than I realized.

I see Cat only once. Heart in mouth, I watch her. She gives me her darkest look. Finally, Bara gives me a fierce frown too. I leave, walking restlessly around the streets of the North End.

"Lucy Chambers? Gina's eyebrows shoot up behind her round glasses. She's always worn glasses like that. Make her look like an owl. I know the next line by heart. "I haven't seen you in a long time." And then the eyes flick down to take me in. She's standing on the front step with a bald, middle-aged man behind her. She doesn't introduce him, but he nods. He's got a clipboard. I let them in.

Bara, Robin, Cat, Carol and Maggie sit around the kitchen table. They are neatly dressed for a change, after a morning of furious cleaning. The sewing machines and every scrap of fabric are tucked away somewhere in the basement. Maggie has covered all the tattoos and bits of metal that aren't in her face. In fact, I realize some of the face ones are gone.

"This is Gina Rountree," I tell them, "Director of the Shelter Society."

Bara looks up with her sweetest expression. "We're youth in need of shelter."

"Oh?" Gina looks around at them.

"We were all living on the street, like, before here."

"And you've been living here? Did Judith take you all in?"

"Well …" Bara fades out.

"It's a long story," Robin fills in.

"Would you like a cup of tea?" Bara jumps to her feet and scoops up the teapot from the table.

"No." Gina glances at the man with the clipboard. "We're just here to inspect the house. It won't take long."

We sit quietly, listening to them move through the rooms, male voice, female voice, footsteps. We can't hear what they're saying. Bara makes a new pot of tea anyway, and we drink it, mostly for something to do.

Gina's cheerful when she stops by the kitchen door. "We're done then. We'll get out of your way."

"Wait," says Robin. "What's going to happen to the house?"

"I'll take this report to the board." Gina gives him a tight little smile. "It needs some renovation and it's small for a shelter, although, if the planning department would go for it, we could tear down that rotten old garage and put on an addition."

Bara says, "I mean it, you know. Like, we need a youth shelter."

"Well the board will make that decision, what type of shelter it becomes. If they decide on a youth shelter, you'd be welcome to apply, although we have a waiting list."

"But none of us has anywhere else to go, except Robin." Bara's tone is rising.

"Or, if we decide to sell it — "

"Sell it?" Several of the young people speak in unison.

"It's the board's decision," says Gina, turning to go.

There is total silence in the kitchen until we hear the front door click shut and their footsteps retreating down the walk.

"Shit," says Bara. "What do we do now?"

I glance at Cat and back to Bara. "Aren't you and Cat are looking for another place anyway?"

There is an awkward silence. Robin and Cat look at Bara, Cat expectantly. Robin appears to be angry. Bara's face has flushed.

"Oh." I've been slow to catch on. "A *youth* shelter."

Robin shifts uncomfortably in his seat, about to say something, but I speak first: "It's all right." I smile at him, then at Bara. "I'm hoping to go away for a while anyway."

I'm surrounded by a circle of surprised faces.

CHAPTER FIFTY-FIVE

I ask Robin to move Judith's ashes to her desk. The house is quiet, the young people gone in various directions. It's just a box of ashes, I tell myself, not Judith, but I still don't want to leave her alone. I settle into the chair in front of the computer. Since getting the manuscript off to his editor friend, Robin's tidied up the study. The books stand on the shelves and he's organized all the papers into a row of magazine filing boxes, labelled and arranged along a lower shelf. Judith's briefcase sits on the shelf beside them, light and empty since Bob asked for the files on Cindy's case. The bed is neatly made up in its alcove, all sign of Judith gone. The expanse of empty floor feels very strange. Even the square marks on the carpet have been erased by a zig-zag of vacuum cleaner tracks.

"Where are you, Judith?" I find myself speaking aloud to the dull, blue cardboard of the urn. "Have you flown away to Heaven? The Spirit World?" I think of Judith's high cheekbones and clear, fair skin. "Valhalla? You've taken all your secrets with you and left before I could finish my story."

I laugh. I've been talking to Judith for months, not knowing if she can hear me or not. Why not her ashes? I take a deep breath, as if I plan to swim a long distance underwater.

"The government of Guatemala was clearing the highlands of people, hundreds of square kilometres, a modern Enclosure Movement, Judith, a new version of Scotland's Highland Clearances. One day we arrived at a village where we were working, Nicolás and I, out at the edge of our territory, and found it in ruins, burned to the ground. All we could do was pray for the people, wonder who was left alive and where they had gone.

The next time it happened, it was closer to San Marcos, and then another village even closer. It was terrifying, like being stalked by a predator. The Beast.

"One day, at the end of a journey, we weren't far from home. We could have made it before darkness fell, but in the village, we had to keep our distance, try not to show how we felt about each other in front of other people. We decided to camp for one more night. Lie in one another's arms ..."

My voice has choked to a stop when the front door bangs open. Voices in the downstairs hall. Feet bounding up the steps two at a time. Robin at the study door. "Lucy." He sees I am sitting with the ashes, sobers. "Oh. Sorry." A pause, but sober can never hold Robin down for long. "Lucy, we need a lookout."

"Not now, Robin."

"But it's our memorial to Judith." That grin.

The telltale artist's portfolio and paint cans sit in the front hall, the boys gathered around them, mood jubilant. When Gord sees me, in a rare and generous explosion of verbiage, he says, "Hi, Lucy. Robin's back on the graffiti crew."

Even living in a house and taking baths, it's not a big effort to look like a bag lady, and the cane helps. The late-night car-people don't give me a second glance. The boys work their way around the government office buildings facing Province House. At one point we catch sight of the girls, dark shadows in an only slightly less dark night. We hear the creak of a pulley, one of the flagpoles on the Grand Parade.

It's very late when the boys snap off their plastic gloves, drop them into a public garbage can and melt like so many ghosts into the cold night air.

Robin and I make quick time back to the bus stop. Quick time for me, I mean. Slow for Robin, even carrying the artist's portfolio. In the streetlight at the bus stop we look at each other, I'm gasping for breath and, as if on some crazy cue, we break into laughter. Robin sobers, glances around. "When they see it, it won't take long to get the police out in this neighbourhood." Taking my sleeve, he pulls me back into the shadows, holds the portfolio behind him. It's really big, sticks out on both sides of his legs, smudged with red paint. It's a relief to see the lights of the bus approaching. "Come on," says Robin, then "Oh shit." He tries to pull me back into the shadows. "Wrong bus."

I feel laughter bubbling up again, swallow it. "No, let's take it. We can catch another one home from somewhere else."

I feel him glance at me in the darkness. "Okay."

I lead him into the pool of light at the bus stop. He helps me up the steps, the portfolio bumping in the narrow entry. "Can you make it up, Grandma?" he says, loudly. I have to hold my breath not to let the laughter go. There are a couple of other people on the bus, looking out the windows, tired faces doubled in the dark glass. We sit as far from them as we can, trying to be invisible. Yeah sure, tall, thin Robin, spattered with red paint, a huge artist's portfolio banging his knees and a bag lady with a cane, clinging to his arm. When we get ourselves into the back seat I kick him in the shin. "Ow!" He breaks into giggles.

"Here," Robin says and reaches for the cord.

"No." I grab at his sleeve. "Wait a couple more stops."

He looks puzzled, but his arm sinks back to his side.

Now he's waiting for my word, and four stops later, I give it to him.

We're deep in the South End. Robin looks around. Classy

suburb near the Northwest Arm. He frowns. "We can't get the number seven here."

"Doesn't matter. This way." I start walking down a residential sidewalk.

He stands in a pool of streetlight, watching me, his big portfolio obvious. A car turns the corner a couple of blocks away, comes in our direction. He hustles to join me under the trees. "But where are you going?"

I lead him up a leafy street, past big, expensive houses, until I find the one I want. At the end of the walkway a carved and painted plaque hangs on a fancy iron support. "Compton," it says.

"You devil," Robin turns toward me, probably grinning, but we're in the black shadow of one of the huge mature trees in the yard. "This is a mansion."

"Ill-gotten gains."

The portfolio brushes my skirt. "Maybe she'd like a Chicken Campaign logo on the front walk?"

"I was thinking just the words 'sell out' in big, red letters."

I hear the zipper, and in a moment, the cold metal of a spray can touches my hand. My fingers close around it, but I don't move.

I can feel Robin looking around. "Hurry, Lucy. It's the kind of street the police keep an eye on."

I pause another minute, then nudge his hand with the can. "I've changed my mind."

There is a brief silence, but he takes it and I hear the zipper again. I put my arm through his. "Let's go."

The buses have stopped for the night. "There'll be cabs on Quinpool," Robin says, and as if on cue, we look down at our clothes, decorated with lots of bright, red paint. We stand in the tree shadows on an empty upper-class street and laugh until we're gasping for breath.

CHAPTER FIFTY-SIX

———————

Our long trek takes us toward downtown before we can turn north toward home. I'm slowing, limping heavily. Robin stops in front of a coffee shop. "Treat?" He tilts his head in the direction of the glowing "open" sign. I look down again. "No one will care this time of night."

He buys me tea and a cinnamon bun, a coffee and muffin for himself. He sprawls in the little cafe chair, long legs poking out from under the table. "So, Lucy."

Oh dear. I've come to know what "So, Lucy" means.

"You said that huge house was 'ill-gotten gains.'"

"When continuing ed teamed up with the first private partner college, Dell told us we should all grab this opportunity to 'get in on the ground floor.' She bought a lot of shares. So did others in the university, which gave them even more motivation to get the accreditation through senate. That's why I asked if your dad bought shares. And when the private college went under, leaving the students high and dry, they kept all the money they had made, on top of their six-figure salaries." I put my cup down too hard, slosh a bit of tea on the table.

"Hey, Lucy, it's okay."

"No, it's not. We fought hard to get support for low-income students to go into those programs. They were desperate, left with debts they couldn't pay. One of the single moms ..." I choke up.

"You kept the obituary. It was with your papers in the Archives. It said her death was 'sudden.'"

I take a sip of my tea, which is going cold, but it gives me my voice back. "She jumped from the balcony of her apartment."

"Is that why you finally snapped?"

"Snapped. Sounds so dramatic."

"You don't think trying to push your dean through a window is dramatic?"

I take a moment to study his intent young face. He's not judging me. If anything, his look is admiring. "All right. You want to know?"

Obviously yes, judging by the way he pushes himself not only upward in the chair but forward over the table.

I imitate Dell's slimy "confide in me, I care about you" voice. "'The other program managers are unhappy that you refuse to pay your own way.'"

Switch to my own voice. "You know my students can't pay their own way."

Dell's voice, her "sympathetic therapist" nod: "I hear what you're saying, and by the way, as you know, we don't use the term students anymore; they're customers."

My voice again: "They're only 'customers' if they can pay."

Dell: "Of course, your programs are different. Everyone knows that, but can't you see how hard it is for the others when you refuse to pay your own way while they are working so hard to market their courses?"

Me: "I'm not refusing to support my programs. I've applied to every foundation in the country and some in the States. The demand for grants is huge, and they don't see any commitment from the College."

I reach over the table and pat Robin's hand in that patronizing way Dell had developed by then. "I understand, but you can see, can't you, how the other program managers feel resentful? We need you to pull your weight. After we've got a stable income stream established, we can afford to do some charity work." I let go, pull my hand back. "Charity work. As if the struggle for a just world is a hobby for rich people, like collecting stamps or something, after the real work of exploiting the poor is done for the day."

"It sounds like she was doing something reporters are taught to do in interviews," Robin says. "Repeat the same question or challenge over and over, ignoring what the person says, until they get flustered."

"Then they must teach it in MBA courses too. Dell never used underhanded tactics like that before she took a sabbatical to do a management degree. After that she started shmoozing with the big wigs, wouldn't talk to me except for calling me to her office to harangue me." I sip my tea, frown at it.

"Cold?" Robin says. He takes the pot back to the waitress, who looks annoyed. There's an odd light flickering on her face. I realize she has a small TV under the counter.

The tea is much improved. Robin stretches his long legs under the table, bumping the portfolio, its red streaks now dry, like the paint on his shoes and my skirt. I glance nervously at the waitress, but she's gone back to her TV.

"After a few more rounds of that … can't call it a conversation. Interview, you said? Anyway, as you also said, I snapped. I had had panic attacks before, usually when I got the summons to go to her office. I guess this was another form of it. You know the expression 'seeing red'?" Robin nods. "I actually did. That whole scene is tinted red in my memory, the front of her jacket when I grabbed it, her shocked face, the window behind her."

"She wasn't hurt though, was she?"

"It was one of those old houses, before the university turned into concrete. You know, thin, old glass, skinny, wooden strips between the panes. I tried to push her through it, but I wasn't strong enough. It was me that broke the window, with my shoulder. When the scene literally turned red, the blood was mine, but as soon as she saw it, she started screaming."

"But they thought you were dangerous enough to be put on probation."

"And medication. And you know the story from there. It's taken all these months to get back my self-control." He grins. "Well, most of my self-control." I smile back. "When does this place close, anyway?"

"It doesn't." He looks into my mug. "More?"

"No thanks. I'll be up peeing all night as it is."

"What all night, Lucy? It's five o'clock."

I check the clock on the wall as if he's made that up. "We should go home."

"Okay, in a minute. But I have one more question."

He's tireless.

"So Dell Compton, I heard she was a big cheese in social justice education before."

"When she was first hired at Walford College, it was to do economic development with low-income women. She was part of the team with me, Judith, Althea and the Community Council. Then when she got the job as Dean of Continuing Education, she expanded the community program and hired me, first on a series of contracts, then as faculty."

"And then she switched completely to a business model of education?"

"Yup."

"Ouch. But how can a person change like that? You know, their whole politics, their whole ideology?"

He's looks so serious, I begin to laugh. The waitress glances up. "You haven't been on earth long enough, Robin. I've changed at least that much in my life. If I could take you back to when I was your age, you wouldn't believe it. You'd absolutely hate me."

"Oh come on."

"People change for all kinds of reasons, love, money, survival, seeing more of the world, wanting to change it."

He is looking at his plate, picking up muffin crumbs on the end of his finger. "Too bad you lost your nerve back there. She could have used a Chicken Campaign logo on her front walk."

"I didn't lose my nerve."

He stops in the act of licking the crumbs from his finger, looks up.

"I've been so angry with her. I think I needed it to get through the months of probation, the thirty days in jail, but back there at her house, I couldn't find it anymore. It isn't her I'm angry with. She just fell in with new friends and something much bigger, the relentless march of the Beast, privatization, the 'extinguishment of the rights of common.'" I shoot him a look and he smiles.

The first bus of the day has just swooped to the curb outside. As Robin follows me down the aisle the artist's portfolio knocks against the seats he is passing. Several people glance. A woman dressed for office work notices the red paint. By the time we settle into a back seat, she is twisted right around, looking us over. I turn my face away, watch the lights of Gottingen Street passing the window, trying to be invisible. There is a police car travelling beside us in the other lane.

Robin is slumped down in the seat as far as his long frame will allow, the portfolio well tucked in between our knees and the back of the seat in front. "We should have walked," he mutters in my ear.

In a few minutes the bus approaches North Street. Below us the lights of the Angus L. MacDonald Bridge arch off into the sky. Someone has pulled the bell cord for the stop and I can't see the police car anymore. "Let's get off," I whisper to him.

Robin goes down the steps ahead of me and turns to help me, awkwardly juggling me, my cane and the portfolio, when the police car, or maybe another one, turns the corner. A tall wooden fence comes to an end right beside us. Robin pushes me toward it, around the post, behind the boards. The policeman has pulled up next to the curb and is coming around the cruiser. I flatten myself against the back of the fence as Robin turns to face him.

The cop eyes the red-stained artist's portfolio, the paint on Robin's pants. "I think you're coming with me."

He guides Robin toward the cruiser. I brace myself. He'll come back for me in a moment. But he drives away. He didn't see me.

CHAPTER FIFTY-SEVEN

The sky is greying just enough to see white-capped water. A light drizzle has started up. I need to sit for a while before I can even think of walking home. Leaning heavily on my cane, I make my way down the hill. The shelter of the ramp to the bridge is a relief. I lean against the concrete, propping myself with my cane, catching my breath. I'm worried about Robin but grateful for the luck that kept me out of that cruiser's back seat.

"Lucy?" It's Cindy, coming up behind me. My heart drops into my stomach when I see her. Low-cut black dress, dark stockings, heels. Her face is haggard under heavy makeup.

I look into her eyes. Oversize pupils. "What are you doing here?"

She drops her lids for a moment, then raises them again to face me. "What are *you* doing here?"

"It was just too much, Lucy." The sun has broken through and shines on us where we've settled ourselves on the log by the fire pit in the woods above the dockyard fence, a bit of warmth in it. "Those students, they treated me like some kind of star. I had to be gung-ho all the time. So what if I want to watch game shows in the middle of the afternoon instead of working on some petition or other?"

"And Patty?"

"It was too much pressure. We were fighting." She slumps further back against the log. "She and her boys moved into a smaller place."

"Are you still living in the apartment?"

"No. They took the boys again." She looks down at her hands, clenching and unclenching in her lap. "I'm not what those students think I am, you know? She addresses the dockyard in general. "I'm not a saint, Superwoman, whatever. I can't do it. I'm ... what Children's Aid thinks I am."

I reach over and untangle one of her nervous hands, hold it. "You are so much more than that, Cindy." My eyes wander up to the bridge deck. "Are you coming to help scatter Judith's ashes?"

"Oh God, I miss her. Who'll help me get my kids back now?"

"Bob Cumberland?"

She shrugs. "I guess."

"I miss her too. And there were some things I wanted to tell her."

Now Cindy's light laughter rings among the trees again. "Oh, Lucy, all that time you talked to her in hospital, not knowing if she could hear you or not. Now that she's free, isn't she *more* likely to be able to hear you?"

When Cindy leaves, she offers to help me up the hill and home, but there will be so much bustle there. I find myself studying the bridge as it curves up into the grey morning. We've got the wind Judith wanted all right, scudding the clouds through the November sky.

"Judith, can you hear me?"

I picture what will happen later, how it will look from here, the highest point of the sidewalk clinging to the side of the bridge, a wisp of ashes like smoke, dispersing into the wind.

For months I've been watching her curl up and dry out, a mummy in white sheets, a remnant, a husk. Now, suddenly, I see her as she was, straight, slender and elegant, dressed for court, with her fine skin and shiny ponytail, large and attentive brown eyes, warm smile. I will have a chance to say something about her when we gather up there on the bridge, but what? There are no words that can begin to say what I feel about Judith.

I collect myself for a moment, close my eyes. "We heard the village long before we got there, people wailing the names of the dead. The ruins of the houses were still smoking, survivors trickling in from the surrounding forest where they had run when the attack came. They were laying the bodies out along the edge of the graveyard. Some were covered with whatever people had — a partially burned blanket, a ragged coat — but most had nothing to hide them.

I pause for breath, realize I am squeezing the life out of a handful of grass.

"They are burned into my memory, Judith, carved on the inside of my eyelids, forever. Eyes torn out, hair ripped from scalps. Men, women, children. People I knew and loved. Emilia, just fourteen, hacked almost to pieces, her blood mingled with the dust like a giant scab. I only knew Marta's body by her long, shiny braid, the way she loved to weave it full of bright, cotton strips, soaked in blood now and crawling with flies. And then I found Adela ... Mía had already disappeared. Adela was pregnant too. She lay in the road. Judith, her intestines spilling out ... ."

My voice has squeaked to a halt. I guess if Judith can hear me at all, she can hear me tell the story in my mind, but no, I need to say this out loud. I breathe, swallow hard, until my voice comes back.

"I tried to tell myself she was already dead when they cut her open, but I knew ... . I ran into the bush and vomited until my stomach was empty and then vomited some more. My knees crumpled. I sat down, hard, on the ground, curled tight. I must have gone into shock; it was late afternoon before I remember anything again. A sound roused me, through the constant wailing, gravelly blows, scraping.

"The graveyard was only a few yards away. A few surviving men and boys were passing a pick and two shovels back and forth, taking turns digging graves. The women and girls sat in circles around their loved ones, weeping. Nicolás was there, dirty and stunned, but he had gone to work as a priest, praying and anointing the bodies, tears streaming down his face.

"I felt unbelievably useless. I was supposed to be the witness, the protection. I wandered out to where my class had their rabbit farm. The cages were knocked off of their legs and smashed into crooked remnants. Scattered all around them were the bodies of the rabbits, heads at odd angles, necks broken.

"A group of children were there with a big iron pot they had found somewhere. They were skinning and gutting the dead rabbits, cutting them up. Other children were searching for pieces of wood that were not yet burned. I began hunting for firewood too. It was something I could do.

"The villagers stayed in the graveyard until after dark. Everyone helped dig and fill in the graves. Nicolás said mass. Then the people came, drawn by the smell of rabbit stew, bringing what dishes and pots they could find, sitting in exhausted circles to eat.

"The survivors decided to scatter for the night, hide in the hills surrounding the village. It was unlikely the paramilitaries would come back so soon, but there was no shelter left in the village, and no one wanted to stay there anyway. In small groups, people gathered up any clothing and blankets they could find and melted into the bush.

"I found Nicolás in the graveyard, praying. His face was blank with pain and exhaustion. All I wanted was to comfort him. I put my hand on his arm. He slapped it away like he would a poisonous spider and looked at me. His eyes were cold. Filled with … disgust."

I am clutching my handful of grass so tightly my fingers are white. That look. It was the last expression I saw on Nicolás's face. For the first time, doubt tugs at me. If he is alive, if I can find him, will he want to see me again? My breath catches. I am full of tears, but I want to finish telling Judith first. I've never told anyone before. I might not ever be able to do it again.

"I ran into the jungle, huddled in a hollow for the rest of the night. When I crawled out, just before dawn, he was gone."

I pause, gulp down a sob that wants to escape, breathe in and out a couple of times.

"The next day we left the broken ruins of San Marcos behind. Quiet now, everyone trailed down the path together, carrying children and stretchers, supporting those hobbling along from age or injury. We reached San Piedro after dark and were met by a crowd of concerned relatives, friends and other people who had heard. By evening, the remnants of San Marcos were absorbed into the homes of San Piedro."

I fold my arms against my knees and sink my head into them. I've been holding back the tears. I give up. They clog into sobs at first, big, tight sobs that hurt my chest. Later they run freely, pouring out of me, on and on. My sleeves are soaked, my eyes gritty by the time I lift my head again. The motion lets the mucus from my nose run right down my chin. I grab a handful of my sweater and press the thick wool to my face.

I feel completely empty and so, so tired.

Just enough left to tell her one more thing. "Later it came to me … where was Adela's baby? The refugees here told me the government took them. If they survived, they sold them to wealthy Central Americans and adoptive parents all over the world."

CHAPTER FIFTY-EIGHT

The next thing I'm aware of is feet crunching through the dead leaves. "Lucy! Hey, Lucy." Next thing I know Robin's face is looking into mine, full of concern. "Cindy left a message at the house saying you were here. I came as soon as I could."

"Robin, the police, what happened?"

"I told them I did the graffiti, acting alone." He laughs. "They didn't believe me, of course, but I stuck to my story."

"The house. Will they search it?"

"Already have. Fortunately, they took their time getting there after they let me go. The girls were like a whirlwind. It helped that the machines and fabric were all packed up for the Shelter Society inspection. They took everything to Cat's grandmother's house. They'll have to work there for a while." Robin slips his hand under my arm. "Come on, old girl. Let's get you home and cleaned up for the ceremony on the bridge."

"Oh my God. What time is it?"

"Lots of time." He hauls me to my feet.

Feeling much better for a bath, nap and change of clothes, I descend to the kitchen. Bara is leaning against the kitchen counter. I glance around the room.

"She's not here," Bara's voice is cold.

Feeling heat in my face, I use the cane to ease myself into one of the chairs.

"I just wish I understood your thing about Cat."

"Did she ever find out where she comes from?"

"It's not your business but yeah, she did. Her grandmother finally coughed up a letter her father wrote to her years ago. He was a sailor and he, like, got this girl pregnant, in Peru. When Cat's grandmother found out, she made him go back for her. He paid her mother to give Cat up and brought her back here. Now she wants to go there and find her mother. But she wants to learn Spanish first."

"Oh."

"And Lucy? That house mother thing, it's, like, Robin's idea. Cat and I voted against it."

"'House mother thing'? What are you talking about?"

"Robin didn't tell you?"

"Tell me what?"

"While we were getting the flag stuff out of here, Robin went to see Bob. He'd thought of something while he was waiting around at the police station. He asked if Judith meant to give the house to the Shelter Society, like, specifically. Bob looked it up. The will just says, 'for use as a shelter.' Bob's the executor. He says if we want to incorporate the house as a youth shelter, there's no reason we can't. He'll help us. So Robin came home full of ideas, including he wants you to be official house mother."

I look up at her angry face and arms crossed tightly over her scant chest. "There's not a problem, Bara. As I said, I'm going away for a while."

A pause, and then she releases her arms. "Where?"

I straighten my back. "I'm going to accompany Mayan people in Mexican refugee camps back home to Guatemala."

"Oh. You mean, like, walk?"

I follow her eyes. She looks at the cane where I hooked it on the edge of the table, then at me, and I see what she sees: an old, crippled woman. I close my eyes against the tears waiting just below the surface. It doesn't help. They begin to trickle down my cheeks anyway.

"Oh, Lucy, I'm sorry." Bara hunkers down in front of me and

takes my hand. She has that little frown between her brows. Now her eyes widen. "Oh … . When you met Cat, she was wearing that scarf. You asked if it was Guatemalan. That's what this is about, isn't it? That's where you thought Cat came from.

"Lucy, whatever happened to you there, it's making you crazy. When I was keeping my sexual orientation a secret, I was such a mess inside. It's so different now that I'm open. The struggle is out there, in the world. Inside myself, I'm, like, all in one piece. I think you need to talk about what happened."

I find I can't speak.

"It's not just for you, you know. If we're all going to live here, you and Cat and I, I need to hear it."

I look into her earnest, attentive eyes. Oh my God, another Judith.

"No hurry," she says. "Whenever you're ready. And Lucy?"

I'm searching my pockets for a tissue.

"Will you teach us Spanish?"

Robin has come through the front door with such uncharacteristic quiet, we see him at the kitchen door before we know he's in the house. He takes in our odd position, as if Bara's proposing to me. "You guys okay?"

"Yeah." Bara rises. "Robin, you didn't even tell her about the will and everything."

"I was going to, after the ceremony.…"

Bara brings me a box of tissues from the top of the refrigerator. I blow my nose and fill my pockets.

"It's time," Robin says. "Are you ready?" He bounds upstairs two steps at a time, as always, and returns holding Judith's cardboard urn clutched under one arm.

Bara frowns at him. "Shouldn't you be carrying those more respectfully?"

He takes the urn in both hands, holds it out in ceremonial fashion. "Like this?"

I smile at him. Then a thought. "And will you get something else for me from upstairs?"

He sets the urn on the table. "Sure."

"In the drawer of my bedside table, leather cover, a Bible."

We walk toward the bridge with Robin on one side of me, clutching Judith's ashes tightly to the front of his jacket, Bara on my other side, her arm hooked through mine, carrying my cane in her other hand. My free hand is deep in my pocket, wrapped around Nicolás's Bible, looking for him, looking for comfort, but all I feel at the moment is old leather. Cat approaches from a side street. She gives me a wary glance. I smile at her. What was I thinking? She doesn't look Mayan.

At the corner of North and Gottingen, we meet a group of people coming up from the direction of St. Marks, the Community Clinic, the Friendship Centre, North Branch Library and Legal Aid. Familiar faces, Bob, John, Althea, Patty carrying her drum. I look for Cindy, but she's not there. Reverend Peter sticks up a couple of inches above everyone else. He's walking beside Althea, talking steadily. I catch Althea's eye.

We merge and move toward the bridge, falling in behind Robin. He matches my slow pace. The wind Judith wanted has risen since morning and changed direction, blowing North toward Needham Hill. Choppy grey clouds race past the green towers of the bridge, making that dizzying illusion that the bridge is falling over into the water. Below, the white-crested waves echo the sky.

Robin stops at the very top of the curve, the spot I was looking at this morning from the woods below, and turns to brace his back against the outer railing. We bunch together as tightly as we can, although the narrow pedestrian walkway forces us to spread out to either side. Bara goes to join Cat and I latch onto the handrail, hating the way the pavement swings and trembles under my feet as the trucks and buses go by.

Bob moves into the space beside Robin. He has to shout above the rumble of the traffic and the wind singing through the cables. "We have come here to remember Judith Maidstone, dear friend, colleague, teacher and mentor to many of us. She didn't want a formal service, so we'll just ask people to come forward ..." He pauses and looks around. "Well, coming forward might be difficult. Just speak up from wherever you are and tell us a little about what Judith meant to you."

There is muttering as those closer to Bob repeat what he said to those farther down, then a pause. We listen to the wind and water, waiting. Finally, a young woman in a leather jacket and thick makeup shouts out: "Judith defended me on a communicating charge. She didn't get me off, but I think the judge went a lot easier on me because of how hard she argued. I think some of those judges were actually scared of her."

There is a ripple of laughter, another voice says: "She made their lives difficult."

That opens the floodgates. Clients, former students, classmates from her days in law school, everyone has something to say. The wind snatches most of the words away, but the love and honour are there to be felt anyway.

John's bass rumble comes from right behind me: "I was a cop. I used to think in terms of good guys and bad guys. Working with Judith taught me that everyone does what they need to do to survive. And the system we live in, including the law, just doesn't deal the same hand to all of us. Justice can be pretty unjust." That wins a smattering of applause.

Reverend Peter raises his hands. "God our Father, receive the soul of our sister, Judith." His voice is big enough for all to hear and, as always, he's set to go on and on. If I were Judith, if I were even the old me, I'd come up with some gracious way to ask him to stop, so gentle he'd actually feel supported. I take a breath to say something in my new, less patient, way, but Robin grabs a pause between sentences, thanks him, asks if anyone else has something to say. People do.

Patty, looking shy, says something I can't hear, but then she raises her drum. She starts up a steady beat and, a moment later, her voice joins it, ringing out confidently now in an Honour Song.

When Patty says *"Wela'lin"* and lowers her drum, Althea casts me an apologetic look. "I can't help it," she says. She closes her eyes and raises her powerful voice to the sea and sky. *"Amazing grace, how sweet the sound …"* Many voices join in.

As the last notes float out over the water, I close my hand around Nicolas's Bible, begin to pull it from my pocket, clear my throat to read *"Bienaventurados los pobres,"* but it's caught in the thick fabric. I tug, trying to free it, but I can feel that something has changed. And then I know. I stop, take my hand out of my pocket. After a moment, I nod to Bob to continue. Nicolás is gone.

The sky is darkening. A few lights begin to show here and there along the shore of the Narrows. Bob looks out over the gathered people, leaves a space in case there are more tributes, then turns to Robin.

Robin holds the urn out to him. Bob hesitates, then takes it. He stands quietly, holding it for a few moments, then tries to slide off the lid. He can't do it with one hand. Robin reaches over to help. It comes away, exposing the top of a plastic bag flipping around in the wind. Robin untwists a wire tie. He and Bob steady both box and bag as they begin to tip it over the railing.

A swirl of grey ash curls out over the dark water, trembling in the air for a moment before dispersing. I think of all those bits of Judith dancing over the low-income neighbourhoods of North End Halifax and Dartmouth.

Suddenly the sky is an explosion of snowflakes, spinning out of the darkness, touching us and whirling away again, as if bits of Judith are dancing everywhere, blessing us all.

ACKNOWLEDGEMENTS

Like raising a child, a novel takes a village. I have many people to thank for their help and support:

Teacher Susan Haley and my classmates in the Acadia Lifelong Learning Creative Writing course;

The Humber College Creative Writing by Correspondence Program, where this novel began when my mentor, Susan Swan, invited me to ignore the usual page limit and submit as much as I could write in the time available, and where I have received continuing support from former director Antanas Sileika;

The Nova Scotia Humber students writing group — Marla Dominey, Marina Harris and Bosko Loncarevic;

My winter writing partner, Nina Newington, who has read more drafts of this book than anyone other than me. Sometimes I wonder if we are the only two people in the Maritimes who want to resist the arrival of spring;

The T.A.N. and Just Us Cafés and the Highwayman Restaurant, who have never complained about writers occupying their tables for hours;

The Writers' Federation of Nova Scotia for the H.R. (Bill) Percy Novel Prize and Wendi Stewart for her supportive comments;

My editor, Linda Little. Now I know why so many authors' acknowledgements say something like "this wouldn't be the book it is without you." I would add several exclamation marks to that if I didn't think you would suggest taking them out. Thank goodness I trust you and your writing skill as much as I do, or the process would have been more painful;

My copy editor, Fazeela Jiwa, for the corrected grammar, perfect spelling and helpful suggestions. Your eye for detail is a gift;

Bev Rach and the team at Roseway and Fernwood for your professionalism, belief in me and persistence in publishing progressive books;

My friends who read my drafts, giving me not only their response as readers but the benefit of their expertise in their fields: legal aid, poverty law, mental health nursing, social work, long-term coma nursing and anti-poverty organizing. I am sure there are still inaccuracies, but not for lack of your good advice. Thank you so much to Jane Cobden, Jeanne Fay, Malcolm Kempt, Susanne Litke, Liz McLaughlin, Donna Naugler, Dianne Pothier and Maureen Shebib. Also to Mary Burnet, who gave me important insights into Bara from the perspective of her generation.

As a work of fiction, this novel has grown out of my imagination, but many of the seeds came from my experiences in Guatemala and doing popular education and community development work in North End Halifax. For the former, I am deeply grateful to Lucien Royer and, for the framework to understand it, Bev Burke and Rick Arnold, Helene Moussa, Arturo and Florrie Chacon and my colleagues at Oxfam and CUSO. For the Halifax years, I can't even begin to list everyone. It would fill pages and people would still be left out. Many friends, colleagues and students will spot yourselves in this story — the work you did, community development models you created, demonstrations we took part in together or you recounted to me, your organizing and lobbying, class discussions, the personal stories and insights you shared with me, including direct quotes. I have been able to ask permission for some of these but not all. I truly hope that you will see your inclusion in the story as a tribute to your courage, insight and wisdom, and an expression of my gratitude for all you have taught me. Special thanks to Kim Covey, Valerie Carvery and Jeanne Fay. Also to my niece, Rosemary MacAdam, for the anti-globalization demonstration story.

Finally, endless gratitude to Jan for constant encouragement, critique of several drafts of this manuscript, research, generous sharing of your counselling and hospital social work expertise and requests to colleagues to share theirs. Not to mention the extra household and farm chores you take on so I can write.

A NOTE ABOUT POVERTY

This is a story about poverty, a condition that causes terrible suffering and stress. It grinds up too many lives and dreams, too many people's health, well-being and potential. We all pay its hefty price tag, but those payments are so "normal" to us that they are invisible. We are well taught that poverty is inevitable, something we can't do anything about or something we haven't quite eradicated yet in our best-possible country. This is not true. As Judith says from the steps of the provincial legislature, "Poverty in Canada is no accident, no aberration, not a case of a few people 'left behind.' It is a deliberate creation of legislation, indispensable to the political and economic system we live in. It is a choice." Eradicating poverty means confronting the wealthy and powerful. We are, with good reason, frightened of them and what they can do to us, but we must not let them stop us. We have to be wise, well organized and brave. There have been times and places where human and natural well-being took precedence over wealth accumulation and, even now, a number of countries have found ways to balance wealth with health. We need to follow their examples.

A NOTE ABOUT CULTURAL APPROPRIATION

My first creative writing teacher, Susan Haley, told us, "All novels are autobiographical, it just depends on how finely you grind it." This one contains some large chunks of my experience, but Lucy is not me. As she tells Bara, "There are people who break open and make a new, bigger self. But some of us are … brittle." Unlike Lucy, I was lucky enough to have been given the basic self-confidence and continuous love and support to come through each of my painful transitions with a new, bigger self. Lucy emerged from my asking, "what if?" What if I had been more brittle? What could have made me more brittle? Lucy has lost everything, to the point of being homeless. That has never been my experience. To create Lucy, I have taken the voice of someone less privileged than myself, which is cultural appropriation. I have done my best to do my homework and portray Lucy with accuracy, compassion and respect. Wherever my efforts have fallen short, I offer a humble apology. If you, reading this, are, or ever have been, homeless and you have a story you want to write, please reach out to me through my publisher. I will do whatever I can to move you forward in your dream of writing and publication. I am also open to discussing the difficult, complex, sometimes even contradictory issue of appropriation.

In writing this story, I have also taken many bits and pieces from others' experience, most less privileged than myself. This includes events, thoughts and even direct quotes. When I could, I have asked permission. Without exception, it was generously and cheerfully given. In other cases, what I have taken is, in my view, very small — less than a sentence — or I have fallen out of touch and have no idea how to contact the person. If there is a piece of your story or thinking here and I have not asked permission, I hope it gives you pleasure to see it. If not, I apologize.

REFERENCES

This novel names some specific books current in 1995–96, when the story takes place. Lucy's library includes:

Arnold, Rick, Bev Burke, Carl James, D'Arcy Martin, Barb Thomas. 1991. *Educating for a Change*. Toronto: Between the Lines and the Doris Marshall Institute for Education and Action.

Arnold, Rick, and Bev Burke. 1983. *A Popular Education Handbook: An Educational Experience Taken from Central America and Adapted to the Canadian Context*. Ottawa: CUSO and Toronto: Ontario Institute for Studies in Education.

Czerny, Michael, and Jamie Swift. 1984. *Getting Started on Social Analysis in Canada*. Toronto: Between the Lines.

Fanon, Frantz. 1963. *The Wretched of the Earth*. New York: Grove Press.

Freire, Paulo. 1970. *Pedagogy of the Oppressed*. New York: Seabury.

Gutiérrez, Gustavo. 1988. *The Theology of Liberation: History, Politics, Salvation*. Maryknoll, NY: Orbis.

The Holy Bible, authorized King James Version. The leather-covered edition Lucy grew up with was published in Cleveland and New York by The World Publishing Company, 1945.

Kingsolver, Barbara. 1988. *The Bean Trees*. New York: Harper.

Knockwood, Isabelle, with Gillian Thomas. 1992. *Out of the Depths: The Experience of Mi'kmaw Children at the Indian Residential School at Shubenacadie, Nova Scotia*. Lockport NS: Roseway.

Lee, Bill. 1986. *Pragmatics of Community Organization*. Mississauga, ON: Common Act Press.

Loewenstein, Andrea Freud. 1984. *This Place*. Boston: Pandora.

Marx, Karl. 1992. *Capital, Volume One: A Critical Analysis of Capitalist Production*. Harmondsworth: Penguin Classics.

Miranda, José. 1974. *Marx and the Bible: A Critique of the Philosophy of Oppression*. Maryknoll, NY: Orbis.

The New English Bible. 1970. Oxford and Cambridge: Oxford University Press and Cambridge University Press.

Those Judith was using in her research include:

Gonner, E.C.K. 1966. *Common Land and Enclosure in England 1450–1850*. London: Frank Cass.

Mingay, G.E. 1990. *A Social History of the English Countryside*. London: Routledge.

Richardson, Boyce (Ed.). 1989. *Drumbeat: Anger and Renewal in Indian Country*. Toronto: Summerhill.

Wright, Ronald. 1992. *Stolen Continents: The "New World" Through Indian Eyes*. Harmondsworth: Penguin.

Some of Lucy's theological concepts come from the work of José Miranda and Gustavo Gutiérrez, listed above, as well as:

Wink, Walter. 1984. *Engaging the Powers: Discernment and Resistance in a World of Domination*. Minneapolis: Fortress.

Her popular education approach to teaching is described in the work of Paulo Freire, Rick Arnold, Bev Burke, Carl James, Darcy Martin and Barb Thomas, above.

I freely used concepts properly credited in the endnotes and bibliographies of my own non-fiction work:

Bishop, Anne. 2015. *Becoming an Ally: Breaking the Cycle of Oppression in People, Third Edition*. Black Point, NS: Fernwood Publishing.
___. 2005. *Beyond Token Change: Breaking the Cycle of Oppression in Institutions*. Black Point, NS: Fernwood Publishing.

"The Diggers' Song" comes from:

Rosselson, Leon. 1975. "The World Turned Upside Down (The Diggers' Song)." Middlesex UK: Fuse Records. Recorded by Rosselson on *For the Good of the Nation* and *That's Not the Way It's Got to Be*. Also by Dick Gaughan on *A Handful of Earth*, Billy Bragg on *Between the Wars* and Aya on *Aya! A Benefit Tape for AIDS Vancouver*.

This story includes many references to the tragic history of Guatemala. For more background, read:

Menchú, Rigoberta. 2010. *I, Rigoberta Menchú: An Indian Woman in Guatemala. Second Edition*. New York: Verso.
Sanford, Victoria. 2003. *Buried Secrets: Truth and Human Rights in Guatemala*. New York: Palgrave Macmillan.
Schlesinger, Stephen, and Stephen Kinzer. 2005. *Bitter Fruit: The American Coup in Guatemala*. Cambridge, MA: David Rockefeller Centre for Latin American Studies.
Wilkinson, Daniel. 2004. *Silence on the Mountain: Terror, Betrayal and Forgetting in Guatemala*. Durham NC: Duke University Press.

The story of the Canadian volunteers who accompanied the exiled Mayan refugees on their return trek to their homelands is told in Anderson, Kathryn. 2003. *Weaving Relationships: Canada–Guatemala Solidarity.* Waterloo ON: Wilfred Laurier University Press.

Also see PBS Newshour's timeline of the Guatemalan Civil War: <https://www.pbs.org/newshour/health/latin_america-jan-june11-timeline_03-07>.

Stephen Schnoor's website about his libel suit against the Canadian Ambassador to Guatemala <http://www.schnoorversuscanada.ca/timeline.html>, which includes a timeline of Canada's history in Guatemala and Schnoor's ten-minute video on the evictions that paved the way for the Inco mine in El Estor.

And for those who prefer their history in the form of a novel, I highly recommend Kerney, Kelly. 2016. *Hard Red Spring*. New York: Penguin.

SPANISH, LATIN AND INDIGENOUS WORDS AND PHRASES:

Campesino: A peasant, sharecropper or landless labourer.
Educación popular: Popular education, a method of adult education and empowerment developed in Central America.
El Norte: Literally "The North," the phrase carries the connotation of the Global North and its exploitation of the Global South, especially Latin America.
Freeganism: An ideology and practice of minimal participation in consumerism, especially recovering waste food.
Huipil: Traditional blouse or tunic made and worn by the Indigenous women of Mexico and Central America.
Mi'kmaq/w: An Indigenous Nation whose territory spans the Maritime provinces and New England States.
Mano derecha, mano izquierda: Right hand, left hand.
Quiché: A Mayan people of the Central Highlands of Guatemala.
Terra firma: "Solid earth," came into English from Latin.
Wela'lin: Thank you in Mi'kmaq.

ACRONYMS:

CBC: Canadian Broadcasting Corporation
CIA: United States Central Intelligence Agency
GED: General Education Development Test, an internationally
        recognized test of high school equivalency.
ICU: Intensive Care Unit
LPN: Licensed Practical Nurse
MBA: Masters of Business Administration
MLA: Member of the Legislative Assembly
NATO: North Atlantic Treaty Organization
RN: Registered Nurse

PSYCHIATRIC MEDICATIONS REFERENCED:

Seroquel: An anti-psychotic drug used for conditions such as schizophrenia and bipolar disorder. Can also be used for depression, anxiety and difficulty sleeping. Weight gain is one possible side effect.
Trazodone: A medication used for depression, anxiety and difficulty sleeping.